THE GRIFFIN
ASHES OF HONOR

THE GRIFFIN SERIES

The Griffin Series

Ashes of Honor
The Dreams of Men and Pandas
The Dragon's Price
A Path of Majesty

THE GRIFFIN
ASHES OF HONOR

PHILIP WILLIAMS
CAT WILLIAMS

THE GRIFFIN SERIES

COPYRIGHT 2013 BY PHILIP WILLIAMS

NO PART OF THIS PUBLICATION MAY BE REPRODUCED, STORED IN A RETRIEVAL SYSTEM, OR TRANSMITTED IN ANY FORM OR BY ANY MEANS, ELECTRONIC, MECHANICAL, PHOTOCOPYING, RECORDING, OR OTHERWISE, WITHOUT WRITTEN PERMISSION OF THE PUBLISHER. FOR INFORMATION REGARDING PERMISSION, CONTACT THEGRIFFINSERIES@GMAIL.COM.

ISBN 978-0-9888257-0-3

COVER DESIGN
PHILIP WILLIAMS
WWW.THEGRIFFINSERIES.COM

COVER ART
JUNG PARK
WWW.JUNGPARKART.COM

COVER ILLUSTRATION
ELISABETH ALBA
WWW.ELISA-ALBA.COM

INTERIOR DESIGN
TYPEFLOW
WWW.TYPEFLOWNYC.COM

To my daughter Kelly

Always follow your dreams

Contents

1 LETUGIA · 3
2 ARTIFICIALS · 20
3 ARNAS · 42
4 HAMMERFIELD · 56
5 OPEN MARKET · 82
6 OUTSIDE PREROGATIVE · 106
7 DESTINY DEPARTS · 120
8 TORG · 134
9 JEAN-WA · 149
10 DASKO GOES HOME · 165
11 KESS · 192
12 THE FREEZER · 203
13 KA'VAELUS · 216
14 LORD BARRETT · 226
15 BAILEY · 234
16 DUEL · 249
17 KING OF THE RATS · 258
18 DINNER ABOARD DESTINY · 268
19 EL-BOUTERAN · 277
20 DISCOVERY · 290
21 AWAKENING · 297
22 ALEXANDER · 307
23 FEEDING THE BYRETHYLEN · 321
24 NAHODNA'S NOOSE · 333

GRIFFIN TERMINOLOGY · 357
TIME LINE · 379
ABOUT THE AUTHOR · 381

I
Ashes of Honor

Do not mourn my passing
Languish not for me,
Though my body lies beneath the ground
My soul is finally free
Do not mourn my passing
The Dragon's price I paid,
My brothers are still standing
Our chosen course is stayed
Do not mourn my passing
My name sung into lore,
Regale the Hall with tales of courage
Alight the souls of many more.

—Guardian's Lament

1
LETUGIA

The Il Touvé shipyards stretched from Letugia's southern Sea of Dunes into a barren valley studded with thousands of hangar bays carved into the bedrock like so many hollowed out pits. Sand swirled and flowed between the giant depressions, pumped out of the holes as quickly as they cascaded in. The plumes of dry bellows darkened the sky into a sooty, brown paste. Magnificent, long shapes rested in the sunken bays. Their extended superstructures resembled massive coral outcroppings left to blister in the sun, as if mighty oceans had been drained to reveal their presence.

The crumbling landing bays were reinforced with rusted stanchions that stood like spikes from the desert floor. Steel beams welded between these sharp fingers spread like spider webs between the sunken vessels, creating raised roadways above the shifting sands. An endless stream of cargo pallets bumped along the channels on flatbed lighters, fighting messenger drones and tech arts for the fastest lanes between the pits. Ceramic relays jutted above the steel avenues festooned with thick bundles of cables that drooped between the stanchions, twisting down to the desert basin where they disappeared below fat, blinking nav buoys. The amalgamation of dry dock encasements rose out of the cracked stonework like burnt, splintered spider legs crawling out of the sand.

Refueling gantries rolled slowly between these pits on wide-gauge tracks, hauled by teams of lumbering zaca beasts. Massive pylons were welded atop the scavenged remnants of century-old train carriages. The locomotives had long ago been scavenged for their reactors and components, but the passenger and freight cars had been left intact and repurposed as versatile fueling platforms. Steel lattices arced high above the winding contraptions and multi-tiered fueling nodes swung out over the pits on long arms. Swarms of giant beetles swooped over and around the pylons, guiding gigantic hoses into place above the docked ships.

The slow-moving megaliths had evolved into narrow, convoluted shantytowns largely populated by the extended families that maintained the apparatus and cared for the zaca herds. A rotating spectrum of gypsy-wanderers ran the taverns and chit houses stacked above the stables, and a constant stream of techs worked the chop shops, smelters and aviaries that trailed behind the tanker cars. The trains had become rolling burrows, separate from the city itself, housing all the odds and ends necessary to run a mobile fueling enterprise.

Each of the trains had spawned commodity exchanges that floated beside the gantries, tethered to the towers by long ropes. Brokers were housed in long wicker baskets slung beneath dirigible sentient sacs. Fuel and precious metals were bartered in open market as the dirigibles drifted over the streets. Speculators wrote bids on wooden chits and held them aloft, clamoring and leaping to be seen above the bellowing throng. Golden-hued sand dibs darted beneath the sacs, their translucent wings shimmering in the long shafts of light. Brokers selected the winning bids and sent sand dibs zipping down to collect the chits in their beaks.

Thick wooly zacas brayed at the head of the trains, their sonorous roar eclipsing the stone-rattling reverberations of departing ships. The bellows spit a constant fog of brown effluvium that mingled with the winds and danced around the rocking towers like fanciful wraiths. The indelible sights, raucous sounds and pungent odors gave the yard an almost romantic quality, as if impressionists had rendered the scene with palette knives and spackled paint.

It was unusual to find such a broad use of indigenous species in a busy, if not altogether modern port, but Letugia was unique in many respects, not the least of which was a nearly inexhaustible supply of empty desert spaces and hard workers who cared little about the wind or heat. A wise harbormaster did not turn away dedicated labor, caring little if his workers slithered, fluttered, floated or tunneled to each shift. Reliable, first-rate service was the lifeblood of any good port and Il Touvé had thousands of berths and tens of thousands of platforms that needed tending. Bipeds, tripods, and quads worked side by side beetles, bugs, birds, and floating sacs. Tech arts, drones, and sentient artificials — the ones that could stand the heat and grit—were often found working the port as well. Some were left behind by captains who had no other assets to barter for fuel and repairs, and were forced to trade an art in order to make it off-planet. These arts became the property of the Port Authority. Some were the sole survivors of ships that had been towed to Letugia and left for scrap in the deep desert. These lost souls wandered into the city and carved out contracts with the PA as a means of earning passage to a more hospitable planet. Many hoped to get back onto a ship's roster as a crewmember. Most longed to be back in space. The remarkable thing about this disparate labor force was how well the meat sacks, hard backs, flappers, floaters and machines worked together.

Some Imperial proctors speculated that Letugia had become a destination due to the planet's strategic location midway between two warring factions, but any Freetrader would tell you that Il Touvé had built its reputation by providing cheap berths, good service, and plenty of access to the wildly-lucrative markets that had brought species, planets and star systems together in the first place. The Port Authority maintained an open attitude to local labor and a commendable disdain for outside political pressures.

Considering the amount of commerce Il Touvé generated, hundreds of ships could be seen sliding around the towers at any given moment. It was harrowing to watch so many vessels work their way through the clogged approach vectors, dodging beetles, sand dibs, and behemoth sacs—all ripe to be sucked into a turbine—an event that might send a million-tonne freighter careening into a tower or two. Pancaking into the valley was a particularly unpleasant thought considering the teeming throngs of creatures below, not to mention the thousands of ships resting safely in the pits that had already survived the descent.

The refueling gantries were not the only peculiar challenge to the roiling mass of traffic descending into the gravity well. Incoming ships also had to fight the brutal wind shear and peculiar updrafts created by the super-heated sands. Captains often stood on the edge of their bays, eyes scanning the horizon for trouble, unable to tear themselves away from the constant parade of incoming ships. Many did not feel safe dirtside, not when so much devastation could rain down upon their helpless vessels at any given moment. Trapped in a massive gravity well, surrounded on all sides by rock, with weapon systems that could not be brought to bear, and quantum engines that could not be engaged, was unfamiliar strategic territory for most pilots. They much preferred the endless reaches of space where they had maneuvering options. They did not appreciate sitting in a pit waiting for an Imperial dreadnaught to hove into view or a random cataclysmic fireball to arc across the sky.

But despite the rolling splendor and navigational horror of the refueling towers, the gantries were dwarfed by what remained of Il Touvé City itself. The twisted remains of the metropolis towered over the shipyard. Most of the buildings were nothing more than burnt cinders arcing into the desert heat, but the sheer height of the gnarled girders hinted at the glittering grace of the thriving metropolis that had once stood in the center of the yard. Skeletons of abandoned buildings stood silent watch over the valley, their insides long since gutted by the eviscerating howl of sandstorms.

Tens of thousands of scavenged bulkheads were welded into makeshift landing platforms along the spines of the buildings. Each plate had been painstakingly carved from derelict ships in the deep desert sands and hauled by pack animals into the scrapyards where dirigible brokers haggled for the treasured cerasteel in open auctions. Once acquired, the plates were winched up inside the ancient buildings and levered into place. Private landing operations became joint enterprises as the scrap metal was cantilevered out over the former gaps between buildings, forming bridges between the towers. The once-temporary and then semi-permanent patchwork landing fields had evolved into a second tier of serviceable facilities high above the landing pits which spread across the valley far below.

A man stood silhouetted against this dusky horizon. Fires were being lit atop the landing platforms high above him, the giant kettles serving as landing beacons for ships descending through the thick murk. An impenetrable haze swirled around the man and for an instant he was caught forever in repose, swept up in the burnt umber solace of the desert, his stolid expression frozen in time.

The man watched dark sandstorms blossom like slow-motion calligraphy painted on the frayed edge of the horizon and studied the relative progress toward his ship. Wind whipped through the man's hair and his long desert coat snapped behind him. A tremendous, curving ship rested inside the safety of the crumbling walls, its attenuated arms stretching off into the distance. A team of zaca beasts hauled a gantry into position beside the vessel, their long chains clanking in cadence with the service arms that groaned as they swung into position overhead.

The man turned to look at his vessel. Light burst through the dust phantoms and bathed the curving starship in the warm, reddish spectrum of refracted sunlight. The ship's unusual boomerang design was briefly revealed: twin arms swept well beyond the frigate's slender girth, one holding a delicate crystal sphere in a steel claw, the other scything far beyond the ship's living sections, tapering to a fine point, like a delicate, extended needle.

Sand swirled into the landing bay, the tiny particles pattering against the slick surface of the ship like hailstones pinging off stained glass. Lighters hovered in and out of the ship's yawning holds. Giant hoses, heavy with fuel, drooped from the refueling gantries, their long trunks snaking over the surface of the vessel like tentacles of a tremendous jellyfish. Glistening beetles darted over and around the suppurated lengths, dutifully guiding nozzles into place. Their wings hummed in the thick air. Long rows of upturned repulsor pads supported the ship in dry dock, their field signatures further distorting details that wavered and evaporated in the fading light.

The massive ship sloughed back and forth in the gusting winds, tugged between her moorings like an ancient man o' war fighting a barrage of dockside waves. The thought of such a grand form of technology—the product of thousands of years of accelerated scientific progress—being tethered to the rocks with simple chains and steel fittings seemed akin to pinning a dragon's wings behind its back with yarn.

The man smiled and let his gaze skip across the rabble of machines laboring in the fading light. He felt the dull throb of energy pulsing up through the stone and listened to the high-pitched buzz of wings fluttering in the night sky. The rich symphony of sensory input conspired to create a perfect stillness in his heart.

Standing on the edge of the landing pit, enjoying the last warm spit of desert heat, the man felt a sense of peace flit across the fringes of his awareness. His ship was docked, tariffs paid, Port Authority placated, and half a day's services negotiated. The clank and clatter of rusted, sand-worn machines trundling across the deck plates meant that *Destiny's Needle* was being serviced. A profitable cargo was delivered and at least partially offloaded. With any luck, he'd have payment in hand before dinner.

Not a soul cared if he existed on this desolate rock. Not a pair of eyes watched him. He existed outside the sweep of gallant pageantry that had consumed so much of his youth. After so many years spent in the service of the Emperor, it was reassuring to stand amidst decaying technology and swirling debris, and know that for at least one instant, on one desolate planet, he was invisible to the rest of the universe and by all rights and assurances, alone.

❖ ❖ ❖

SAND DEVILS WHIRLED OVER THE DUNES IN A FRENZY OF HEAT and wind. A zaca beast struggled up a steep rise and its shabby litter swayed precariously with each halting step. The zaca shook its head and splattered its master with a long, green plume of thick saliva. The man yanked on the lead and turned his thorny walking stick on the animal's wooly hide with a brutal blow. As he lifted the stick to strike again, a hand shot out from the litter and halted its progress. A lithe creature leaned out, goggles huge on her small face, modest walde-robes covering all else.

"Kaidesh," she murmured.

The man's face reddened and he lowered the prod.

A Caroultus freighter rumbled low overhead on landing approach, repulsors screaming. The zaca shied away from the dark shape as it hove into view, dragging the hapless guide off the path. He cursed the animal and raised his stick, but the woman clambered down from the litter without his aid. He hastened to her side, but she pushed past him and dropped quickly to her knees, settling atop the bluff.

Helen Tchelakov studied the sprawling reaches of Il Touvé's southern docking bays, searching for landmarks. She shifted uncomfortably in her walde-robes. Too many layers of coarse fabric abraded her freckled skin. She preferred spider silks whenever possible, or soft layers of fur when she was in the cold of space. The layering of desert kit was nearly intolerable. She pulled at the folds of her robes, wanting to remove the covering to feel the breeze against her bare legs. She cast a glance over her shoulder at the guide. The man's multiple hooped earrings pegged him as Fikeenl, or perhaps Sullust. She looked for telltale genetic signs, but it was pointless—both sects strictly enforced religious codes concerning female attire.

Helen reached inside a sleeve and removed a compact monocular. She lay down on the warm sand and squinted through the optical lens, searching the stepped canyon below. She scanned the roiling shipyard, adjusting the magnification with a tick of a node. The sky was thick with traffic and huge landing platforms jutted from the burnt remains of the city.

She loosened the hood of the constricting walde-robe and released a tangle of dark red hair to the wind. Suddenly the man was upon her, flailing at her with his stick and yelling in a guttural dialect. For a brief instant she paused to consider the striking similarities between man and zaca as she studied the green spittle issuing from the guide's mouth. The man raised the stick high and slashed downward. Helen rolled smoothly away from the attack in a fluid move that sprayed sand in the man's face. When he cleared his eyes, she had a dart slinger trained on him. The dull, wicked lines of the weapon told him it was not for show. He backed away, reaching for the zaca's lead, intending to leave his fare behind.

"Not today." The dart smacked into the pad of loose skin just over his kneecap, dropping him. The man writhed on the sand, clutching at his leg, screaming all the invective he could string together. The zaca stood by placidly, drooling.

"Tay-eh. Here," Helen tossed him a silver medi-pac. The man ripped into it, pocketing the various antibiotics, bandages and food that could be sold later on the black market rather than wasting them on a minor wound.

Helen turned back to the yard. The wind tugged at loose strands of her hair, whipping them in front of her face. With a frustrated grunt she snatched her hair back. It had been a long trip—a long two months for that matter—and her patience had been exhausted trying to track down one illicit pilot. "A sleeping warrior," Darstin had called him. "Now a Freetrader." Ghost was more like it.

It had taken her nine weeks traipsing through 38 star systems—each more dismal than the last—to finally track Médeville to Letugia, a brown marbled rock in the Nepestar system. Helen set the monocular aside and let the scene imprint on her mind. *Relax,* she told herself. The Sartoks said this was the right place and the probability windows gave her several hours to find Médeville before he finished offloading cargo. *If the Sartoks are right,* she reminded herself. *If he is here.*

Letugia was a sandblasted pebble with scarcely anything to offer beyond its endless dunes flowing with sand. The deserts were awash with abandoned ships and the profligate scrapyards that grew up around the rusting graveyards like kudzu climbing a tree. The planet was a cheap place to haul decommissioned ships, outdated weapon systems, unnecessary war spoils and any piece of unwieldy junk found floating in space. Ships and their myriad components had an intrinsic value as salvage, and even a powerless, obsolete frigate riddled with holes was worth hauling to a place like Letugia.

The planet was situated at the upper edge of Carinaena's Shell, the far-flung sphere of stars that loosely enveloped the greater galactic Core. Where the billion systems of the Core were densely populated and tightly controlled, the outer Shell was a youthful frontier, at least by galactic standards. The Collistas Dynasty, which had calmed and unified the Core after a decamillennium of strife and upheaval, was something of a late entry in the race to expand into the outer reaches. The Emperor's touch had barely been felt in most volumes, and where it had, the local response was largely ambivalent, if not bracingly hostile.

This had left the Shell wide open in terms of development, and there was no shortage of fiefdoms, despots, Imperial proctors, elder hegemonies and corporate keiretsu vying for control of the billion or so systems. In terms of control, distance was the killer, and time its faithful ally. One could not control everything, not in the Shell. And when great distances separated great powers, small rocks became intensely important. Letugia was devoid of all resources, a fallen angel in a universe full of sparkling beauties. However, it had the strategic advantage of existing midway between the oft-warring realms of the Nralda Keiretsu and its geographical rival, the Senserei of Geutvohn Madora, and thus it had become a ubiquitous trading hub and possessed one of the largest shipyards seen anywhere in the Shell.

Beetles soared overhead, guiding unwieldy starships into their mammoth berths. Hundreds of stock freighters and personal craft spiraled in and out of Letugia's controlled airspace. Finding one starship might be harder than she imagined, especially if the overrides Darstin had procured were obsolete.

Helen took a long breath and removed a small hard case from a pouch hidden in her walde-robe. She opened the fist-sized casing and removed a quarter-circle of soft malleable material and carefully unfolded it. She gently pressed the center, producing a concavity. She withdrew a tiny red filament wire from the case and inserted one of three dangling nubs into a receptacle in the tiny concave dish-form. Helen rolled up her left sleeve to reveal a darkened datapad carefully molded to fit around her forearm. The bracer was equipped with a small vertical display screen and a miniature finger-tap board. She jacked the second nub into the bracer.

The case yielded one more crucial item, a small dark cube that she set on a flat rock. Helen hooked the final nub into the cube and flicked her datapad. Three small rods extended upward from the cube's surface. She delicately lifted the miniature dish and placed it with great care atop the outstretched prongs that affixed themselves to the underside of the dish. A light flashed green on her bracer. Her fingertips skimmed over the pad again and she initiated a search routine.

The system whirred for a moment as its servos aligned themselves and the tiny dish began sweeping the sky, searching for the electronic signature of one of the Port Authority's com buoys. Helen watched anxiously as the dish swung back and forth trying to acquire a signal. After several long minutes her bracer chirped at her — the dish had found the proper signature and had aligned itself. The system was ready for interface.

Sweat trickled down her face as she entered commands to access the Port Authority datacore. Somewhere deep below the planet's surface the datacore asked for routine identification and clearance. Helen tapped in a fictitious name and rank. The datacore considered this for a moment and then queried her terminal for proper security access codes.

"Now we find out if those codes were worth all the fuss," she murmured. With precise keystrokes, she enabled the latent subroutine and watched it unspool and load into the system where it took the form of an illicit command override—one an Imperial agent might use in an emergency to cut through some backwater planet's security lockouts. The node on her bracer flashed slowly, waiting for the system to decide whether or not it would recognize the integrity of the override. After several nervous moments the screen blanked out.

Far away, a bird shrieked as it became the prey of a large reptile. Helen glanced back at the zaca beast. The guide had propped himself against the animal's stout legs, his robe pulled up over his head in a makeshift awning to keep out the wind. A thin trickle of smoke emerged as he enjoyed his evening thiretsen reed. *His leg must not be paining him too much,* she reasoned. *Or else he expected suffering as much as his beast did.*

She turned back to the screen, still blank. In the distance, the sun boiled low on the horizon. She tapped her bracer nervously. The desert, even this close to the city, was no place to be after dark. How soon would Port Authority be able to send a skimmer after her if the codes were no good? It would not be so easy to disappear into the desert with the guide's leg wounded. What would she do then to find Médeville?

Suddenly characters scrolled across her screen in Vort Magellan, the gibberish machine code of tech arts and datacores. An acceptance or a warning? She coiled her legs under her, ready to break down her setup and leave in a hurry. Then a data menu opened.

Helen released her breath in a whoosh, smiled to herself and muttered, "By Haven, Darstin is useful after all." She quickly accessed the orbital entry manifests and ordered the datacore into search mode.

ENTER SHIP REGISTRY the node prompted her.

She tapped:

DESTINY'S NEEDLE • LT. CRUISER • LO KAMER-DAUN WORKS • PRIV. REG. MÉDEVILLE, GARRAND AI'GONET, ESQUIRE EXECUTING the screen flashed.

Finally a burst of data scrolled down the screen. Helen watched with excitement.

CLEARANCE REQ 3724/29B13 RD LETUGIA

ORBITAL MANIFEST 9779-2 GRV. VECT. STAT. 12 • WINDOW: AURELL

LT.CR. DESTINY'S NEEDLE • REG 21741 IMP. SEAL CRV 2-88894

ORBITAL REQUEST RECOGNIZED, CLASS. 2B

VECTOR ROUTING CONFIRMED • GELIAN POLAR ROUTE ASSUMED @ 19:23:21.1

LANDING CLEARANCE GRANTED • GRV. STAT A476/22

PLANETFALL @ 19:49:57.2

DOCK ASSIGNMENT 247-B • CLEARANCE GIVEN

SERVICE HOOKUPS @ 19:59:42.9 • GRV. STAT—HARBORMASTER GORELL, ESQUIRE

REPAIR AUTH. 247-B • MÉDEVILLE, GARRAND, CPT.

SHIP MANIFEST • UNKNOWN

CRED. 1967 • MÉDEVILLE

REP. MANIFEST • RETINOID BX4000 OVERHAUL • SPR. NULL DAMPER 13XR • GRV. STAT

DATALINK • EST. @ 20:17:11.0 • CONNECTION TERMINATED @ 20:17:17.2

ALL SERVICES • NOMINAL

SCHD. DEP. • UNKNOWN

DEST. • UNKNOWN

FLT. PLAN • NOT FILED

Floating with the rush of success, Helen terminated the connection before anyone could start a trace. Calling up the shipyard's map on her bracer, she noted the coordinates of Médeville's docking bay and used her thumb to calibrate the monocular's dial. She gathered the walde-robes around her hips and curled back down on the rock. The monocular pinged softly as it selected visual cues.

After several sweeps the device locked on docking bay 247-B, the enhanced image encircled by a flashing red outline in her eyepiece. She tapped the image upgrade nodule and scanned the length of the hangar. The ceiling lay open, exposing the gantry and service arms slung over a curving black ship.

Helen let the monocular drift across the repair arts and lighters roaming through the hangar. A glint caught her eye and she centered on a lone figure at the far edge of the landing chamber. The man stood atop the rocky wall that surrounded the docking pit. He appeared unconcerned about the work being done on the vessel.

Was it a local high hat? Port Authority rep? Guild crusher? Could be a Tariff Collector, or a Bio Inspector. *Relax*, she told herself. *The man might only be a tech foreman overseeing the routine maintenance that ships required between stellar jaunts.* But something tingled along her spine and the fine hairs on the back of her neck stood up. She tapped the image nodule. *Don't get ahead of yourself. Was it Médeville? This didn't look like a young prince, not at all. Fine lines extended from his eyes, his mouth was firm, shoulders set against the wind. Could this be one of the Emperor's 'favored sons'? Had the boy turned into a man? All the activity in the hangar, and this one stands apart...*

"Haven's End," she whispered. She had found her elusive, ghostly target. Garrand Ai'Gonet Médeville was staring off into the dunes. She took note of his well-worn blazer—no insignia on the tab-collar—and gun belt slung low, tied to his right thigh. She hopped up the magnification and studied the weapon, a custom-built Naisus hand cannon by the look of it, with full Ki Zentor sensor package and opticals. The holster safety straps were filed off to facilitate quick-draw. A five-millimeter Thol dart sling hung from his belt along with bio-elective finger tabs, a palm-sized plasma torch and some sort of modified phase emitter—the rest was hidden from her line of sight.

She eased back a little on the magnification and scanned dark trousers spotted with grease and red power coolant. He wore scuffed desert boots in dreadful need of a polish—possibly of Imperial manufacture though there was no telltale dragon visible. Sweeping back up she noticed a curious relic on his chest, an amulet of some sort.

"You're superstitious, of course," she whispered derisively. "*This* is the hand-picked choice of a keiretsu lord?"

There were signs that her holocube image was dated. The man no longer wore the impeccable black uniform of the Brotherhood. His hair had grown longer; black curls brushed his collar. Dark eyes were now framed by slender cracks borne from years of squinting into harsh alien environments. The calm, confident arrogance that shone from his younger visage had been replaced by a quiet certainty; a calm, singular presence that spoke of experience. He no longer had the polished glow of wealth and prestige that marked a Captain of the Imperial Guard. There was a harder set to his shoulders and his build was leaner. He was no longer boyish in appearance, but possessed an unmistakable quality of confidence that made him even more attractive in the balance. She appraised the slant of his shoulders, the way his fingers brushed the butt of his blast pistol even in silent repose. He perched on the edge of the pit like a predator, eyes sweeping across the cityscape.

Helen retracted the monocular and placed it back within her sleeve. All of her plans within plans, and now this. Why did the Sartoks point to this former soldier? Why did Lord Darstin insist that this was the only way to proceed? What did her powerful benefactor sense that she could not? She did not like being this far into the game with so many questions left unanswered. The stakes were too high to have another rogue variable to deal with.

She yearned to run this operation by herself, but Darstin wouldn't let her make a move without Médeville, and that was that. She took a moment to rewrap her headgear and draw the walde-robes tight around her shoulders. Helen Tchelakov was not a woman who was easily dismissed, but a quarter century of hardship had taught her the power of lies and the wisdom of silence. She cast a last glance at the splendor of the Il Touvé shipyards and the orange sand storms that loomed over the deep desert horizon. She had spent a lifetime waiting patiently for this chance. Another few weeks of pretending a man held authority over her fate would not matter in the long run. She hoisted herself back atop the waiting zaca beast and began the long, jolting descent to the uneven streets far below.

2
Artificials

Garrand Médeville stood on a dusty steel plate just beneath the edge of his ship and barked a command at his tech foreman, a hip-high burnished sphere. The machine groaned and began to roll sideways in a lazy arc. The man watched the artificial out of the corner of his eye as it completed a full orbit around his position; it was like being circled by an enormous silver globe, and for a moment Garrand felt like a star at the center of a diorama. He wondered if his tech foreman was recalibrating internal gyros as he spun in lazy arcs or simply trying to distract his attention from the negligence of the tenders that were tearing his ship apart.

"Little Bit," Garrand said more sternly. "Could we direct the house rats *away* from the power couplers?"

The artificial let loose a low moan that resonated just above the steel on glass noise that the art's body was making as it circled him.

"Those arts are worthless. Whoever wrote their subroutines should be hauled out and shot. I need you to supervise the entire system overhaul—no time to do it ourselves, so just make sure those arts don't foul up the systems that still *do* work. Punch it in yourself if you have to, but don't let them rip out what we just fixed."

The artificial halted in front of him and trilled a question in Vort Magellan. Garrand shook his head: "Bailey can't do it, he's up top."

The machine rolled in a tighter orbit, agitated. It looked like a giant ball bearing, its surface minutely etched with fine lines that faded in and out of sight at the machine's bidding. Sand crunched under the art's shell as it spun end over end, warbling questions.

"Yes, the vectored thrust dampers and no, I have to go." The tech art bumped gently against his leg and his voice softened. "Aft shields, remember?"

Little Bit still had the body of a Turkle Sphere but his core had been drastically modified to the point of inception. Garrand rested his hand against the art's polished dome, fingers tracing the minute scratches that came from using one's body as a means of transportation. The artificial trembled at him again in Vort Magellan. Garrand had picked up bits and pieces of the cryptic aural shorthand over the years—enough to get by. "Do whatever's necessary," he replied. "Just don't burn out their field buffers, or anything else expensive." He began scaling a gantry that had automatically rolled into place alongside the ship's sleek, black hull.

Little Bit swiveled his upper hemisphere's receptor band around his torso until his visual node could see Garrand. The artificial had two bands that wrapped around his body, parallel belts that held sensors and crucial recording gear. The concave rectangular strip of orange light followed the captain's progress until he disappeared over the ship's outer hull plating. The node faded to the same dusky grey as the artificial's body when it could no longer track the human's path. The artificial began rolling his meter-diameter form toward his target with a push from a pair of tiny pseudopods. The tiny pistons provided an inertial start to locomotion.

Little Bit rolled toward the tenders that were trying to access the coolant system through the wrong access panel. Minute pistons extended from his gleaming spheroid shell making course corrections as he rolled. A series of braking rods extended and retracted in rapid succession as he approached the ship. The pistons slowed his forward momentum and brought him to a halt.

The arts supplied by the Port Authority were cumbersome affairs designed to service ships in Letugia's dusty hangar facilities and built to withstand the wear and tear of the desert sands. They had thick ceramic plating and long triple-jointed service arms. Each chassis rested on fat, archaic treads.

Little Bit fed instructions to the repair arts in a resonant data burst. The machines flatly ignored the commands and continued ripping through viable power couplings in a vain attempt to reach the cooling system. Little Bit extended a two-pronged service arm and allowed the static energy built up in his buffers to transfer to the nearest artificial. A vigorous arc of electricity leapt from the prongs. The static charge sizzled through the bulky machine's faded orange plating and burned a hole straight to its core. The jolt overwhelmed the art's field buffer and its service arms collapsed as it folded into stasis.

Little Bit raised himself up several centimeters on his pistons and repeated his instructions to the two remaining arts, punctuating his orders with a service arm pointed at the correct access panel. Reluctantly, the machines stopped tearing out the power couplers and rumbled over to the indicated panel.

ATOP HIS SHIP, Garrand ducked under a huge retractable service arm that swung into place over the aft refueling nacelle. He gingerly stepped over the myriad power conduits, coolant hoses, and repair interface lines that snaked across the hull and made his way to a portable tech station that hovered just over the hull's armor plating. A gleaming figure stood at the station. The machine's smooth articulated fingers flew over the slick surface of the glossy datapad, conjuring information before Garrand's eyes could even register the nature of the data which flashed across the screen.

"I've almost cracked this one, Captain."

Garrand smiled thinly. "Is she being stubborn?"

"A bit feisty today, I'm afraid. She claims the PA tenders are fouling sensitive areas. I assured her that Little Bit is watching them, but she is, as you say, a bit skeptical."

Garrand sighed. The ship was paranoid about releasing control to the amazingly complex array of subsystems that comprised her central nervous system and downright combative when it came time for repairs. Overhauling ship's components was always something of a delicate chore, because first they had to convince *Destiny's Needle* that she really needed the work done. "A sight more than that, I think, Bailey. She's got a natural fear of doctors. And can't say as I blame her there."

"They're hardly adept here by any measure, Captain, but I wouldn't compare these arts to medicas, sir."

"I'll say," Garrand peered over his first mate's shoulder. "Have you gotten around the security countermeasures?" *Destiny* had begun dabbling in reactive protocols, writing her own subroutines, egged on no doubt by the ship's lone sentient door, Humhal—guardian to the kitchen and all its treasures.

"Almost. I estimate full system penetration in two minutes, perhaps a little longer with you here..." The semblance of a smile crept across the smooth contours of the artificial's face as he employed a cherished subroutine. Humor was difficult, especially for arts. Garrand smiled at the joke—his first mate would indeed be more efficient without his presence—and marveled at the subtle variations in his friend's face.

Bailey's skin was slick and translucent. His emotive features looked like puddles of liquid mercury and each expression caught and reflected ambient light so that a smile might be dazzling one moment and soft the next, like it was created by colorful rain drops. He was a perfectly balanced bipedal walker with seamless joints. His internal workings glowed softly through his skin, different components taking on different hues at his bidding. Though he could choose to display himself as a flat matte black, or any color for that matter, he preferred to use his skin as a means to display internal activity and deeper nuances of thought and emotion.

His figure was proportioned like the humans he was designed to serve, with broad shoulders and powerful arms and legs, but his motions were so graceful that they sometimes appeared choreographed. The Varsis arts were designed to take the human form to the next level and most were commissioned as combat assists. A Varsis was a beautiful, shining fusion of form and function. Watching Bailey walk through open market was like watching a waterbug slide across the surface of a still pond. And watching Bailey in battle was like watching a phoenix dance amongst the ashes of its own destruction: beautiful and frightening at the same time.

"Good work Bailey. See if you can recalibrate the repulsor modifications we made in Ragon while you're at it. I never could get her to admit she was wrong, but she felt sluggish once we hit atmosphere this morning."

"I'll see what I can do, Captain."

"She can't hear us out here, can she?"

"No, sir, I shut off external sensors before disembarking, what with her nerves about the tech arts and all."

"Good," he exhaled. "That's all we need, a bit of peevish behavior and a full system shutdown when we're ready to lift."

Garrand turned his attention aft, satisfied that Bailey could handle the dampers by himself. He made his way across an uneven section of hull leading toward the deflector shield array. Peering over the ship's edge he watched in dismay as a series of lifters carried huge magnetic coils toward the ship. "No, no, no! That cargo is supposed to be *unloaded,* not loaded. Hey, you there!"

The lifters ignored him, continuing their relentless march. "Cheplus," he swore. The machines had no speech recognition. He looked for a spare clipscanner but there were none nearby. "Little Bit!" he yelled into the hangar below, his words echoing through the chamber. There was no response. Frustrated, he grabbed the lapel of his blazer and spoke into the comtab affixed to his collar. "Little Bit, get over to the east cargo portal. The drones have finished offloading the coils and now they're starting to load them back up."

Little Bit whistled an affirmative through the com. Garrand stomped back toward the deflector array grinding his teeth, wishing he could afford to have a PA foreman present to wrangle the hangar's incompetent arts and drones for him.

❖ ❖ ❖

A LONE, YELLOW LAMP ILLUMINATED THE OCTAGONAL COMMUnication kiosk that stood in the center of a broad shopping arcade in the heart of Il Touvé. The floor of the open air pavilion was once paved with brightly colored mosaic tiles, but years of erosion had dulled the patterns, reducing the images to a dull, slick blur like the gritty sand crackling underfoot. Darkened booths radiated out from the kiosk's central hub, providing sheltered spaces for long distance communications. Helen glanced anxiously around the arcade, but saw no one that stood out from the busy peddlers and tourists who filled the promenade. She stepped inside an empty booth and inserted a credit chit. Instructions flitted across the screen.

She quickly tapped in codes for the Nralda's quantum buoys and fidgeted uncomfortably in front of the terminal awaiting connection. Long minutes passed as the buoys examined the codes and bounced the signals between the stars. In a brief flurry of static, the image of a clean-cut, elegant man appeared on the screen. He wore a shimmering grey suit that accentuated his long limbs and slender frame. Grey eyes flecked with cerulean blue sparkled beneath short-cropped white hair. The man's voice was fuzzy over the distance of light years, but his face was unmistakable as the visage of her mentor and tormentor.

"You have news of prosperity and success, little one, I can see it in your eyes."

"My Lord, the only thing in my eyes is dust and sand."

"Ah, you're tired," his voice was gentle, but tinged with a current of maddening condescension that made Helen's intestines twist into a tight knot. It was a voice that had once comforted her as a child, a calm rational thread of authority that had guided her out of the cloying sadness that grief and guilt had carved into her young heart. But later that voice had turned to something darker and more perverse.

"Tired of pursuing yet another dark target."

"I trust your tone is one of respect, little one."

Helen cursed under her breath. "Of course, my Lord."

"You have made contact with Captain Médeville?"

"Visual acquisition."

"Are the pieces in order?"

"Eyes on the ground are tracking. I should be able to present the proposal tonight. Most traders prefer to eat dirtside when the occasion arises."

"Are you ready for initial contact? You look rather unsavory." He sounded briefly alarmed. "When was the last time you bathed?"

"I'm sure I will have time to make myself presentable for Captain Médeville," she growled.

"Perhaps there is a public fountain you can make use of."

"It's a desert hell hole, my Lord."

"Well then, a sand bath combined with the profligate use of oils and perfume."

"My Lord, I'm tracking a target."

"A very important target," Darstin reminded her. "You must be convincing."

"I can be plenty convincing when I need to be," she said, her voice dropping an octave.

"This is a complicated man, and we need him. I suggest a bath."

We need him? Helen turned this phrase in her mind. *Why exactly did the Nralda need a Freetrader, a man far outside the normal channels? There was something else going on.*

"I don't think Médeville's right for this transport," she said stubbornly.

Director Darstin smiled. "I think you might be surprised by Captain Médeville›s resourcefulness."

Resourcefulness? What need did they have for resourcefulness now? Had they not spent months intricately planning every step of this evacuation, detailing every possible contingency? What trouble did the Sartoks foresee? What was Darstin not telling her? Was she, too, a pawn?

"Our reports indicate Imperial agents might have learned the location of your father's compound. Médeville may prove invaluable. Who better to elude Imperial capture of our cargo than one of their own?"

Helen pressed on, "I can ferry them out myself—give me one of the Nralda Gunrunners, or even a light cruiser."

"Tchelakov we have been over this. There are *other* considerations! Yours is not the place to reason why or how. Your place is to follow orders and play your role. There is a grander scheme and all will become clear in time. Do you *understand*?"

Helen glanced furtively to the street beyond, wondering how many of the Nralda's eyes were watching her even now. "Yes," she said softly. "I understand."

"Good, then proceed as planned, little one."

"As you wish." She punched the terminate button and the image faded. This would complicate things, but she would adapt, as always. Nothing was going to stop her now, not the Imperials, not the keiretsu, and certainly not one scruffy Freetrader.

❖ ❖ ❖

GARRAND WINCED AS HE LAY ON HIS SIDE WITH HIS ARM STUCK deep within the bowels of the deflector array panel. The datapad at his side flashed: MAGNETIC COUPLING ALIGNMENT PR. VEST • 00.7823 RD • 1. Sweat dripped off his nose as he tried to coax the power fitting back into proper alignment. He watched the alignment number waver around 78 percent—he needed at least eighty before he could reestablish a magnetic field for the array to draw from. Only then could he begin adjusting the buffer coils which stored power bled from other ship systems before feeding it in pulses to the shields' magnetic deflector fields. Bailey had come up with a new subroutine for routing power from the sub-light engines to the deflectors that could theoretically boost their strength by 12 percent. Garrand was anxious to make the modifications, 12 percent would be a huge increase in the ship's defensive posture.

The comtab chimed, "Captain?"

"What is it Bailey?" he asked through clenched teeth, still straining to align the coupler.

"Sir, there's a message coming through from Port Authority. An administrator wishes to speak with you."

"Tell them I'm busy."

"I don't think that would be wise, this one is threatening to shut down our power."

"What?" A clank followed.

"I believe he mentioned something about 'insufficient credits to sustain nominal docking services.'"

"Is that all," Garrand grumbled sarcastically. "All right, I'll take care of it. Route the call through the hangar's lounge," he looked down at his free hand. "I don't want to get power coolant all over ship's com." That would ensure an unpleasant conversation with *Destiny*. She'd be on his case for days as it was what with all the strange arts touching her.

He glanced once more at the datapad lying next to him on the ship's hull. He twisted his wrist one last time and the screen blinked green:

MAGNETIC COUPLING ALIGNMENT: 00.8167 RD • 2-A4 ESTABLISHED

    SYSTEM: NOMINAL

    FIELD COUPLERS: LOCKED

    COIL INTEGRITY: VERIFIED

    BUFFER ROUTING: GA'GM/B RD • 2

    DAMPERS: MOUNTED

    PRIORITY VESTING: FILE NOT FOUND

    SUBROUTINE PROTOCOL: GA'GM/B RD • 2-A4 ESTABLISHED

Garrand snapped the outer housing back into place and gathered up his tools. The pilot's lounge was situated between the cargo customs cells and a long line of storage lockers. Garrand brushed himself off briefly before cycling the outer door of the dustlock. He stepped into the cramped compartment and the outer door irised close behind him. Powerful filters sucked the hot dust-laden air from the chamber while simultaneously blowing cool dust-free air into it. After completing its filtration cycle the inner door opened.

Garrand stepped into a ward that smelled of age and years of neglect. The sparsely decorated lounge contained overstuffed and well-worn acceleration couches and an ancient command chair ripped out of some Imperial frigate. The room's only saving grace was an air filtration system that still pumped cool, dust-free atmosphere—a miracle in itself—and tempered glazings that cut the ambient light to a nice mellow glow.

Workstations encircled the room, most of them labeled "out of order" in Strahlinvek and a few other trade languages. A weather forecasting station sat lifelessly beneath banks of darkened screens. Planetary nav displays and system orbital updates were also blank. Garrand glanced at the communication terminal. The screen flashed: connection terminated. *So much for that,* he thought as he glanced around the room. He wondered if Bailey had been able to placate the bureaucrat.

The only other screen that still seemed to be in working order was the Repair Manifest station—a logical choice for regular maintenance. Without it, incoming pilots couldn't order hangar drones, refueling would be impossible, and major system overhauls couldn't be hardwired through the system's datacore for diagnostics. In other words, the main source of income for the Port Authority outside of landing fees and tariffs would be lost.

Garrand scanned the brightly colored screen that showed repair updates and directed hangar resources. At the lower right corner a running total of the cost of currently completed repairs, hourly labor fees, and use of facility charges climbed ever higher. He watched his meager supply of hard earned credits disappear at an appalling rate.

Wistfully he recalled a day when such services were performed on his vessel by human technicians, whole teams of them pouring over the ship, directed by a bellowing Port official—usually the Harbormaster himself—who practically bent over backwards trying to provide the finest and most efficient ground services in the whole star system. And all services were provided free of charge.

In those days, it was generally considered unwise to show anything but the highest regard for Imperial captains and their bristling destroyers when they decided to set down on your planet. Garrand liked to think it had been out of respect for the golden dragon embroidered on his black blazer, and the Imperial throne behind it, but he knew otherwise.

It was fear that had commanded respect and the Harbormaster's attentions. They expressed every kindness, extended every hospitality, and offered every service in the city free of charge. In dirtside thinking if you kept a hungry raptor well fed and happy it might not devour you, and with some luck it might wander off in a few days in search of other prey. It was always best to acknowledge the power of the Imperial throne lest a display of that power become necessary.

My how times have changed, Garrand thought. He tapped the monitor with a restless finger. The primary's rays refracted obliquely into the lounge and a metallic flash caught Garrand's attention. He walked outside, pausing to let the dustlock iris close behind him. The main hangar floor consisted of ancient steel deck plates laid across the stone to help absorb the tremendous weight of landing ships. A thick layer of desert debris, dust and sand covered everything. As there was little to no rainfall on Letugia, the ceiling of the docking bay lay exposed to the brownish-blue sky.

The hangar itself was merely a depression excavated in the rocky basin to provide protection from wind and sand storms. Bits of dust constantly swirled and settled inside, giving already old equipment an ancient appearance. Tracks and footprints ran through the dust in all directions—evidence of scampering tech arts and bumbling drones performing their myriad tasks, moving back and forth between the ship and their service lockers.

Higher up the steel-reinforced walls, retractable girders swung over *Destiny's Needle* providing access to her dorsal repair housings and refueling ports. Cranes and lifters had crept up to the ship's cargo bays on steel rails and were busy removing the last of her shipment of dryexcellon ore. The whine of servos and repulsor drives filled the chamber, echoing off the walls. The occasional warble of arts coordinating their activities punctuated the cacophony.

Garrand looked upon *Destiny's Needle* with pride. She was an asymmetric visual splendor. Twin superstructures jutted well ahead of her central hull, like the elongated ends of an enormous boomerang. One sweeping arm held the crystal bridge, a thirty meter cantilevered spheroid. The other housed a massive particle accelerator whose tapering, jagged spine lanced even further forward. In between lay the bulk of the ship: cargo bays, living quarters and reactor chambers.

Garrand had designed the ship alongside the renowned ship builder Lehadn Vercks and they had left plenty of room for performance enhancements. Accordingly, her lines were subtly marred with ducting ports and obtuse modifications. The starboard blast shielding housed more than just null-dampers and matter deflectors, and the port aerial array looked suspiciously complicated for a mere cruiser. And there was the matter of her size: just over 107 meters from stern to nose and nearly 50 beam to beam. Quite a ship for a simple Freetrader. To put it mildly, she probably would not pass a full Imperial inspection. The false housings and doctored ship ident-beacon could fool only the most circumspect visual analysis. But there were ways of avoiding that.

Satisfied with the progress on his ship, Garrand skirted around the southern refueling nacelle and found a narrow service ladder. He grasped a cool rung and hoisted himself back atop the hangar's outer wall. He was immediately pelted with tiny particles from the swirling gusts of the coming storm.

Garrand peered through the gathering haze of pinks and browns. The primary had almost settled below the rocky hillsides to the southwest. Huge dust-laden clouds crept toward the city from the wastelands to the west, tremendous cyclones of sand and dust borne by violent winds.

Dozens of ships circled above the landing center, some rising to orbit, others falling into landing patterns. Their collision lights shimmered through the haze. A heavy cruiser hove into view, spiraling clumsily down through its approach vector. As the bulky ship loomed closer and larger, Garrand identified it as a Barrelian design, a sixty-year-old warship reconfigured for commercial enterprise. The ship pitched erratically from side to side, fighting the powerful gusts of wind, trying to sideslip into its approach window.

Garrand grimaced reflexively, imagining the difficulty the pilot must be having. With inadequate control surfaces, limited maneuvering capabilities, no atmospheric dampers, and minimal attempts at streamlined fairings long since ripped out, the Barrelian freighter was clearly never intended for extended atmospheric usage. If the ship's sizable hold bore a full shipment of ore then the pilot would be fighting a tremendous inertial pull from the planet's gravity well on top of the treacherous cross winds.

Garrand watched uneasily as the ship approached. The landing beacons of a nearby docking pit began flashing blue-green-red in sequence indicating the freighter's destination. Almost overhead now, the vessel seemed to be overshooting its correct glide path. "You're coming in too steep," Garrand whispered.

The ponderous freighter filled the horizon like some huge overburdened seabird. Garrand caught a glimpse of the ship's registry markings as it roared by above, its immense bulk shaking as it struggled to stay properly aligned and airborne. The rock beneath him rumbled; he could feel it in his legs. Gravitic repulsors screamed on overload and all the braking thrusters bellowed an angry moan as the pilot scrambled to compensate for his miscalculation. The ship yawed violently, pitching to one side. It's hull scraped against the outer wall of the landing pit. The pilot corrected and the ship hovered briefly before settling down into the open mouth of the docking bay accompanied by a deafening crash of grinding metal. *Another successful landing*, Garrand thought. *All down in one piece*. He pictured the expression of relief on the pilot's face and smiled.

Garrand leaned into the strengthening gusts of wind, squinting through the fine dust and studied the approaching sand storm. The primary had set behind the billowing clouds, rendering the particles of dirt and sand brilliant shades of orange and crimson. The clouds appeared to simultaneously expand and contract, possessing some unseen life force as the storm crept toward the shipyard.

Garrand's nostrils flared, catching a burnt amber aroma from the streets below. Rough chalky buildings, none more than two or three stories, glowed like burnished bronze in the coppery twilight. The balm of roasting Kirtsen nuts wafted up from vendors lining the busy commercial streets, hawking their local delicacies to waiting passengers. Darkness descended over Il Touvé and the city slowly awakened within the gathering gloom with broad, garishly lit avenues overshadowing the softer, gentler glow of side streets.

Each planet within the Shell held its own unique interpretation of the soft magical period after nightfall. Garrand found a sort of existential peace savoring these brief moments, the softer palette of colors reassuring to his ever-wandering mind. The amulet that hung around his neck brushed softly against his chest. He absentmindedly stroked its cool surface, his thumb gliding along the rough steel setting.

The storm front gathered strength on the horizon, advance winds gusting across the city creating small whirlwinds of dust and debris. Wind whipped through Garrand's hair, tugging at his loose jacket, whistling through the rocks. He listened to the voices calling to him from the past. *Destiny's Needle* lay behind him, his ticket to the unknown, to adventures and futures unwritten. Before him blasted the wind, a constant reminder of faces, places and events indelibly etched in his memory: things he could not ever hope to change... or forget.

"Captain. *Captain?*" called an insistent voice from the hangar below.

He pivoted on the stone wall to see Bailey waiting impatiently, hangar lights reflecting off his skin, a distraught expression across his face.

"Captain there seems to be a difficulty at the main gate." Bailey's slender arms waved anxiously. "There is a Port Adjucate who claims we are out of credits. He is threatening to shut down the power to our docking facilities."

"Great." Garrand began the climb down with haste. "Didn't you talk to him earlier?"

"Yes, but I believe he was rather upset that you wouldn't talk to him in person. He terminated the call before I could employ my new diplomacy subroutine you've been helping me with."

"How rude."

"Well after all, in his eyes I am only an artificial."

"Nonsense," he said with disgust.

"Well he's at the gate now. I explained to him the sensitive nature of the repairs we're performing, but he seemed singularly unimpressed." Garrand reached the floor and began walking toward the main gate with Bailey falling into step behind him. "I then attempted a different logic path and quoted the day's going rate for dryexcellon ore and pointed out the cubic tonnage of the cargo we've already processed through PA customs. It seemed like a simple mathematical equation to me. I speculated about reasonable rates of return from our buyer and our forthcoming windfall, certainly more than enough to cover our expenses here, but he seemed unable to follow my line of reasoning. I don't believe I made a very credible impression. A most stubborn creature!"

"Don't worry Bailey, I'll take care of it." Just as the words left his mouth, all power failed in the hangar. Servo-arms slowed to a halt, repulsors wound down, and the repair arts stalked back to their service lockers where they powered off, lights going dead. Within moments the entire pit was eerily silent. Emergency batteries sprung to life and a few sparse escape lights bathed the chamber in a somber glow.

Uneasiness gripped Garrand's stomach. He barely managed to keep his anger in check as he strode to the main gate. A wandering luma globe cast a dim halo over a tall Trogand standing inside the entrance. He wore Port Authority regalia and held a clipscanner. The Trogand looked fearsome with large yellowed horns protruding from his skull. A huge underbite dominated his facial features and he had disproportionately small eyes. The creature tapped a large claw impatiently as he watched Garrand approach. He appeared utterly immovable. Garrand could see how Bailey's diplomacy might have been lost on the official. He didn't look like the thinking type; he looked like the arm-ripping-off type.

Garrand strode without hesitation to the Trogand, refusing to let the official gain the upper hand from physical intimidation alone.

"Is there some problem, Adjucate?" he began, forcing the uncertainty from his voice. "Anything I can help you with?"

The Trogand laughed hoarsely. "No, there's no problem." He continued laughing until a spasm of coughs overcame him. With a massive fist he thumped his chest. "You're out of credits, friend. By order of the LPA and as pertaining to section four-four-seven-three stroke two-bee of the Letugian transit bill I am hereby vested to suspend all services to docking bay two-four-seven stroke bee." He paused for dramatic effect, sweeping his gaze over the hangar bay. He cleared his throat with relish, curling his thick lip down. "On behalf of the Port Authority and as acting Imperial Adjucate for Vice Proctor Hellius Barrett I am vested to carry out subsection J of the civil code. You are hereby ordered to vacate these premises and forfeit your vessel as compensation." The Trogand punched numbers into his clipscanner, then turned the pad and held it out; a small needle protruded from one end. "Please notch here in blood to verify receipt."

Garrand frowned; he had hoped his credits would last long enough to effect repairs and get them off this rock. Now he had to think of something else quickly.

"Perhaps we can find an alternate *arrangement* that would meet your requirements," Garrand said firmly. The Trogand did not show any sign of eagerness or interest.

There was an art to successfully bribing the various officials on trading planets as each had its own unique customs and social expectations of acceptable behavior. In the Guard, a praetor would never have dared challenge him over so minor a grievance. But now he was just another Freetrader and vulnerable to being squeezed by every minor servant in the Shell just like the rest.

"There might be a bit of excess cargo not strictly accounted for on the ship's manifest," Garrand said casually. He tapped his chin and looked at his first mate thoughtfully. "We recently ran a shipment of gyrestellan crystal, didn't we Bailey?"

"Yes, captain," the artificial said stiffly, "But—"

"I believe we might have one left. Perhaps it could afford us a temporary reprieve." Garrand spoke briefly into his comtab and gave Little Bit instructions. He turned and looked expectantly at the ship's loading ramp, hoping the line was properly baited. After several moments, the Turkle Sphere came careening down the incline, rolling end over end to the front gate. The little artificial settled onto his pistons and opened an access panel atop his upper hemisphere. A small claw arm extended clutching a roll of black felt cloth.

Garrand took the roll and slowly revealed a small oblong crystal the size of his thumb. He gently extracted the gem and held it aloft. Ambient light refracted in blues and greens across Garrand's tunic as he twisted the gem in his fingers. The Trogand's ears swiveled forward fractionally in interest before he could catch himself, though he managed to maintain a disdainful lip curl.

Deciding that the Trogand's tone of pomp and circumstance probably masked much deeper bureaucratic problems in the creature's work environment, Garrand decided to appeal to the creature's sense of self-importance that was surely reflected by the ridiculous uniform. *Really, who wore tassels on Letugia?*

"Surely an important Adjucate such as yourself is entirely too busy to personally rectify every clerical mistake made by your underlings. These passing electrical storms play havoc with the accounting screens. I imagine they must be bothersome to the Port Authority too, especially when they clear accounts that are in perfectly good standing of all credit."

"But, captain," Bailey interrupted, "our repairs have been extensive and our credits have not been lost, they've been —"

"— Erased, yes," Garrand cast a withering look at his friend. "By the storm. I was getting ready to come down to the appropriate office to file a complaint. But look, the Adjucate has appeared to take of the matter himself. This is why Il Touvé has such a sparkling reputation, Bailey." Garrand dropped his voice a little and looked up at the Trogand. "You really shouldn't be forced to come down to the pits to handle these minor glitches. Your dedication to duty is commendable. Truly, you're a credit to the LPA. Please accept this as a small token of appreciation for handling the situation with such speed and precision."

The Trogand's nostrils flared but he did not budge. Garrand stood his ground and offered the crystal to the official, arm outstretched.

With a low grumble the Trogand plucked the stone with two claws and twirled it back and forth in the light. Murmuring with satisfaction, he quickly pocketed the gem and cleared his throat elaborately. "I see that a small clerical error has been made," he paused to glance at Garrand. "Circle three, docking bay two-four-seven-stroke-bee still has eighteen point two hours of refueling and refitting already prepaid. Your accounts will be credited accordingly. My sincerest apologies for the inconvenience. As a courtesy on behalf of the Port Authority I shall personally waive the standard landing tariff and biological fees. Good day, citizen." He managed a formal bow of departure and bustled out the entrance hatch.

Garrand smiled to himself and turned to his ship. The lights and servos came back to life and the service arms resumed their work. Bailey smiled at him with a wry expression. "Diplomacy at work, sir?"

"Not bad, huh?"

"Impressive, Captain. We have the sought after reprieve. However, wasn't that our last gyrestellan crystal?"

"It wasn't doing us any good just sitting in the ship." His first mate nodded in silent appreciation. "I'm going to check with Epley at the Open Market—see what kind of price he got us for that drex shipment—and then to dinner, see if I can't spend the last of our artfully acquired largess."

3
ARNAS

COMMANDER ARNAS STRODE SLOWLY DOWN THE SLICK polished floors of the Carrak class Imperial Battle Cruiser *Shiva*, listening to the efficient chatter from the bridge that was fed directly into his tympanic membrane via implanted com. With it he could silently listen in on any channel from anywhere within the ship and stay apprised of drop provisions. Hammerfield was going to be a big operation and the vast coordinated preparations demanded that Arnas be in constant contact with not only his lieutenants and fleet sergeants, but the naval liaison officer upon whose ship his men were stationed, the tactical support division, battle Ops, and his chief armorer Colonel Hastings.

To make matters worse, word had it that Barrett himself was joining the strike force at the final staging area in the Dar Sellianne cluster. Yarvek-EZ must have a dazzling probability projection to bring the vice proctor all the way out here. The hairs on the back of Arnas' neck bristled and his heart quickened at the thought that their target might actually still be on Hammerfield. In fact there was electricity throughout the ship; Arnas could see the subtle signs of excitement in the faces of the ensigns that hastened to their duties giving him respectful glances as they crossed paths. The whole task force knew they were close. For nine months Arnas had tracked what had turned out to be the most elusive quarry of his career. Officially he had been ordered to search out and recover a small collection of "stolen Imperial biologicals" but the escalating size and scope of the operation belied that simple pretense. A fully supported strike force, three Carrak class cruisers with full complement of mobile infantry and Arnas' battalion of Imperial Shock Troops, a Lor Stanta destroyer, four Torvel class frigates, two Lancer Attack Frigates and a host of Barrelian support corvettes and escort ships now circled above Dubōte's lone moon, preparing to make the final jump to Jhellus and the Hammerfield colony. You didn't pull a full Imperial strike force off the line to round up a bunch of escaped genetics. This smelled of something else entirely.

Arnas stopped before the central descent shaft and straightened his impeccable grey tunic, pulling the sharply creased fabric down where it had ridden up on his shoulders, smoothing down the chest, his finger tips brushing the Imperial dragon stitched across the breast, thumb gliding across the cool nodes of colored rank insignia above it. He took a deep breath and stepped into the suspension shaft, body hovering within the glowing suspensor field.

"Battle bridge!" he barked and felt himself sink within the shaft. This assignment had taken on an insidious life of its own, swelling from a simple search and recovery operation to a vast chase a thousand light years across the Shell. Each time the network of Imperial spies ferreted out the creatures' latest refuge, Arnas and his strike force careened across the stars to try and capture them before they could escape. And each time they raided some backwater mining operation or independent colony only to find abandoned nests, embers of fires sometimes only hours old. *Hours*, Arnas thought anxiously clenching his jaw. *Mere hours.*

This assignment had become a small career within itself. Arnas could sense the pressure mounting all around him; he could feel Barrett's growing lack of patience—somehow this mission played directly into the jaws of the vice proctor's voracious political appetite. He could palpably taste Barrett's blood lust; the vice proctor's schemes within schemes that had brought him wealth and then power in the Shell. His Imperial Proctorship had turned into more of a fiefdom than a simple economic coalition, with Barrett as Baron, lording over all his newly acquired economic conquests. His fleet had swelled tenfold in as many years as planet after planet fell under his policies of economic enslavement.

The Emperor himself might be a little surprised at the audacity of his Imperial Proctor if ever he turned his eye from his cherished Core worlds. But the Emperor and any interest he might have in the machinations of Shell economics and politics was nearly two years away even by fastest transport. The Shell was largely on its own as the Emperor chose to focus his will on the vast Core of the galaxy, hoarding the central systems for himself.

Decades ago Emperor Collistas had sent Proctors out beyond the Core to oversee economic development in the vast sweep of stars encircling the denser inner galaxy. Proctorialships had carved up easily dominated systems nearest the Core. Fleets were commissioned, taxes were collected and fear slowly spread outward. For the most part, however, Carinaena's Shell was largely untouched simply by virtue of its vastness. Local alliances and planetary governments were left to their own devices with minimal interference from the Collistas Dynasty, save for silent hulks of Imperial warships and the omnipresent Provost Adjucates for Trade and Commerce levying taxes as the scope of the Collistas hegemony widened.

Hellius Barrett had taken a different view of his position, however. Rumor had it that Barrett had murdered the region's reigning Proctor, Lekkson Nesbit, while he slept and had, by default, assumed the duties of the Shell's largest Proctorialship. So in title, Barrett was only a Vice Proctor. But as soon as Nesbit had been laid to rest, Barrett began a monumental campaign to expand the sphere of Imperial influence in the Shell, swallowing whole systems through economic monopolies and fear. His commonwealth had now reached a critical mass. It was either going to explode outwards and sweep across the Shell or stagnate under its own bureaucratic weight. Arnas sensed the danger he was facing. Finding these creatures had become Barrett's obsession, and the stolen bios were somehow tantamount to Barrett's plans. If Arnas did not deliver soon, more than just his career was at stake.

Stepping out of the drop shaft, Arnas paused to concentrate once more on the babble of voices in his ear. He absorbed the latest updates: Barrett was coming; his ship was scheduled to rendezvous in two minutes. He gave his tunic one final tug before stepping before the huge blast door that led to the battle bridge. The door irised open before him and he strode slowly onto his command bridge.

The two Shock Troopers on guard in full dress uniform, brilliant golden dragons embroidered across the fronts of their emerald shipsuits snapped to rigid attention, pride gleaming in their eyes. "Commander on the bridge!" barked the senior of the two in clear crisp tones.

The immediacy of command washed away any doubts or fears Arnas had concerning the future. One of the Emperor's prized tactician's from the Bordëgian Académé, the commander possessed an aura of confidence bordering on arrogance that stemmed from the unabashed loyalty and devotion of a full battalion of the Emperor's finest. He paused just within the blast door between looming gyropods and surveyed his men.

Though his fine black hair was thinning and hairline receding, Arnas still possessed an air of vigor and strength. Taut, powerful shoulders carried a regal bearing. His eyes were dark and watchful. His intense gaze, solid jawline and straight nose gave him a noble, commanding presence.

The battle bridge was slung like a crab beneath the *Shiva*, detachable and separate from the naval operations above. Giant elliptical pods drooped from the ceiling. Tech stations encircled the chamber on steel platforms that hung from the superstructure like hoops. Stairs descended through the upside down layer cake. Feet from one level dangled over the head's of the next. All the stations faced to center, so that all attention was funneled to the huge sartographic grids that swirled midair above an immense bubble portal at the bottom of the chamber. The sparkling grids gave detailed tactical information about the fleet and displayed future probability statistics in red numbers that winked ever lower.

Arnas stalked down the steps to the TacOps station. "Jump status," he demanded.

"Waiting for naval confirmation from topside, sir."

The Commander pivoted to face the naval liaison who was slung in a basket seat near the entrance—a position of some disgrace. Anger welled up in his voice. "What are we waiting on, lieutenant?" He glanced down at the sartographic array. "We're twelve seconds past scheduled jump and counting."

The naval lieutenant, Maibell had one hand up to his ear and was nodding silently as he received information from the captain on the ship's primary bridge far above. After a moment he looked down at Arnas and said formally, "Captain Ness wishes me to inform you that as soon as the vice proctor has rendezvoused with the *Shiva* and all ships have been fed the updated vectors we will be underway. In the meantime, she suggests that you double-check the Sartoks for your drop calculations due to the delay."

Arnas whirled away and muttered to no one in particular, "We're going to lose them again." He paced across the bridge to his quantum control officer. "What's the bad news Greer?"

The sub-lieutenant spun part way on his stool to face Arnas and winced. "It doesn't look good. Ness doesn't like to drop too close to major gravitational wells and Hammerfield's sun is a monster, class four. I expect with the vice proctor aboard she'll be even more cautious which means by the time the whole fleet gets into orbital range and the drop ships are released—" he leaned back over his board and rapidly tapped several nodes. "It looks like the probability of the target still being there will have dropped to forty-two percent. But you should check with Yarvek-EZ for a firm estimate."

Arnas rubbed his forehead in consternation. "Forty-two? It was sixty-seven an hour ago." He felt a slight lurch and steadied himself on the datastation as the *Shiva* broke orbit and headed into deep space for the jump.

Greer raised his eyebrows and shrugged. "Information gets old real quick out here. And with this target, as soon as they fear Imperial detection—" the Sub-lieutenant made a zipping motion with his hands. "They're outa there. Besides, it about takes a class two fusion charge to get Ness off her naval command couch and get this fleet moving."

With a sigh, Arnas turned to the line of neural-tapped ensigns strung up in gyropods, prepared for the battle possibilities of null grav or the vacuum of hull breach. He subvocalized into his command collar, a band of microchips that circled his larynx and pulled vibrations off the epiglottis. "Yarvek, I want a full Sartok update on the drop." A light flashed in response over one of the pods as an acknowledgment vibrated in the commander's tympanic membrane.

Arnas climbed to the narrow gangway beneath the tier of suspended gyropods. Yarvek-EZ was submerged in Pod 17. The young man's body was fluid under the webbing that held him as he rotated through the thick, clear jelly inside the pod. Thin cables snaked out of ports recessed in his smooth, tonsured head. Arnas looked on with distaste.

The costly setup had been made for efficiency, not effect, he reminded himself. But he couldn't get rid of the thought that his bridge looked like a laboratory with two-dozen glowing yellow pods hanging from the ceiling like alien eggs. Each chamber served as an incubator and the humans stuffed within them looked like slowly spinning fetuses. They were so pale that they were almost translucent—veins clearly mapped out, ribs showing, bellies sucked in like starvation. Their skin was smooth and hairless from the gel. It didn't help to know that they were grown there as well, each person tailored from conception to function within a ship's datacore. They'd not been birthed, but matured in the Imperial vats on Wyx.

The pod caste was the youngest branch in the military. Most of the boys were hardly old enough by human standards to be finished with their schooling, let alone possess the mind control to traverse the complicated operations of the battleship's E2 datacore. Yarvek-EZ was typical of his caste. He wore standard reality blinkers that aided concentration by only allowing one to see in the virtual realm of the datacore. The pressure of that direct feed into the optic nerves caused papilledema and eventually total blindness. But the pod-techs didn't seem to care. In fact, out of their pods they had little connection with reality and avoided mixing with others. They'd never been to a mess hall, never even had solid food. Permanent catheter ports dotted their collarbones on each side, lifelines that supplied pure nutrients, plasma, and drugs directly to vital organs. Many were also administered a sleeping agent to turn away the troublesome insomnia and nightmares which seemed to plague the caste.

Arnas studied the boy inside Pod 17. Raised pinpoints of tattooed caste markings circled out from under the blinkers. A tattoo on the side of his neck, just above his ident-link labeled him: Yarvek-EZ. Arnas caught a glimpse of dozens of pinching, hooped earrings that continued down the ensign's neck and acted as cable guides.

The response light over the pod signaled within moments, and Arnas shifted his gaze to the sartographic grid that hovered over the bubble portal in the center of the bridge. The sartograph now displayed a time-based simulation of the forthcoming drop and the future probability of success.

The sartograph involved a full three-dimensional display coupled with time corrosion modulation based on Dr. Sartok's revolutionary chip. The science of probabilities—4th Dimension Physics Decay—had evolved to the point where a time-based model of any object from a person to an entire planet could be accurately displayed. The sartograph considered relative conditions, past outcomes, relevant variables, performance specs, real world disruption and expected chaos. The resulting model could be rotated in any direction on its three axes. Its layers could be peeled away to display internal workings, levels, functions, and most importantly, the whole model could be shown at any point in its relative life, from current status back through time to its original inception or forward to its eventual and inevitable demise.

The sartograph could also display the relative reliability of any given model—the percentages fluctuating as new information became available in real time. With enough information at its disposal, a Cronix datacore fitted with a Sartok chip could calculate a ship's performance curve—including what systems would need overhaul and when exactly they would fail—up to four and five years ahead of time with a high percentage probability rating.

The sartographs allowed one to see a human's form from birth to death—what any given person would look like as they aged. Doctors could foresee disease—arterial collapse, heart conditions, and genetic malfunctions—years before the problems manifested themselves. The chip revolutionized health care along with most advanced technological industries.

But the technology had stagnated. For decades, the sartographs were improved by broad leaps in processing power. Faster datacores could create more complicated models and crunch more raw data. The models improved. Then the technology was boosted by broader access to information. Deeper pools of information were created. Archival databases were networked from system to system. sartographic arrays tapped into new species and their complex genetic maps. Ancient data caches were recovered, techno relics were reverse-engineered and long lost libraries were added to central data vaults. Information became the key to exploiting the sartographs' potential. Every extra bit of data produced better results.

But there reached a point when there was simply no more information left to mine, and no further details that current observation techniques could add to any model. The rush to add information came to an end. Faster cores were being developed with stunning regularity, but an excess of computation power could not advance the technology. The twin pipelines to sartographic success had run dry. The datacores were brilliant and the data was first rate, but the models had not improved in decades. It was back to guessing again, and the next breakthrough was long overdue.

It was almost too much to take in: flickering data points and color-coded glyphs. Arnas narrowed his vision to the symbols relevant to his pursuit. His advantage was slipping away as each moment passed. Above the bubble viewport, the sartographs danced with a dizzying array of tactical and technical information. Color-coded translucent models of individual ships rotated slowly in midair as techs accessed various details of fleet priorities, ship functions, and vector updates. An abstract model of the jump on Hammerfield dominated one quadrant of the display, the probability of success displayed in numbers that hovered and dipped from moment to moment, shedding precious percentage points as the situation worsened.

Arnas glanced away from the staggering mockup. It took his eyes a moment to adjust to the star field beyond the surreal images twinkling inside the room. He took a deep breath and allowed his attention to shift to the world beyond the battle bridge. Outside the giant bubble, a dozen capital ships streamed through the void in perfect formation. They seemed impossibly large and vibrant against the dark backdrop of stars. He thought of the whales that swam through the oceans on Duransk. It had been a long time since he had been home. Suddenly the stars lengthened into luminescent strips of spectacular colors and one by one the ships vanished as the *Shiva* leapt into quantum space.

"It's about time," he muttered.

"What's that?" asked an old man, stepping out from the shadows. The disconcerting voice had the static of a deep space transmission. It came from a visibly implanted voice box centered on the man's spindly, weltered neck. The man's grey fatigues seemed antique and out of place among the crisp, grey suits on the bridge. One pants leg ended just above his hips, where an old-fashioned robotic leg jutted forth. Bare of any synth skin, it served as reminder of the greybeard's past service to the Emperor.

Arnas silently cursed the relic. "I said I'm glad we're finally underway. Our navy seems to take a different view concerning the importance of efficient maneuvers."

The old man made a show of clambering down the command steps. "Navy has always had its ways, arcane as they may be. It's better to keep the commands separate — navy above, marines below — that way each branch is more effective."

Arnas' foot tapped in annoyance. *Did he really have to put up with this? When was the freedom of command Barrett had promised going to come into play?*

The old man continued to ramble: "Navy doesn't want to sully themselves with dirtside matters. Prefer the cold vacuum of space — don't want to get their hands dirty with actual killing and *real* power." He clenched his fist and waved it in Arnas' direction. "Just as well; Navy is just the *threat* of destruction. You and I Arnas, you and I are destruction itself."

"Of course," Arnas replied stiffly and turned back to his command board, noting out of the corner of his eye that the old man's small floater vid had ducked behind a support beam as his head turned. The floater was a recording device that transmitted relevant data for the General's frequent reports to the Emperor. A member of the Old Regincira, General Shecut remained one of the oldest living military leaders who had turned the tide in the Emperor's favor by joining him in the critical days of the Art Wars. The fear of commanders everywhere, he was shipped from one vessel to another like an unwanted and dangerous relative. Arnas found his constant babble annoying and intrusive.

"You know, sometimes I can go the whole day without putting my leg on."

Arnas busied himself at his command station and failed to rise to the bait.

"Yeah, I just get up, hook my leg and I'm off without a care." He raised a cane hand-crafted from the leg bones of fallen enemies. The femur, tibia and talus bone with the rounded condyles served as another grim reminder of the General's constituency.

"I understand," Arnas murmured, his hand moving swiftly about the viewscreen, tapping points of destination that lit up from the pressure of his fingers.

"Do you?" the General asked quietly, his eyes narrowing. The General's floater swung closer, alerted by the tone.

"Sub-lieutenant Greer, open a channel to the ready rooms."

"Aye, Commander."

The General lurched closer to the screen, unwilling to be ignored. His shoulder intentionally brushed against Arnas. "What's your first sweep?"

"Men in Trioxin."

The old man shook his head sadly, "I'll say again it's a mistake."

"General, I am well aware of your opinions. However, as you are only on Overseer on this mission, I must order you to step aside and limit yourself to observation."

"All we needed at the Battle of Thrassin was a brigade of marines and a laser axe. Real marines," he added with a snort. "Not these overburdened techno-children you call shock troops. The Emperor's elite indeed!"

"I see you're not averse to some of that technology yourself," replied Arnas with a cruel smile, indicating the old man's robotic limb.

General Shecut stepped aside. "Send for me when your men suit up. I'd like to observe it beside you."

"General," Arnas saluted and returned his attention to his command station. He smiled again as the warning chime of the shield door indicated that the General was gone. He didn't notice the floater vid swing back to a vantage position in the shadows above.

The General moved rigidly down the hall, his signature bone cane creaking as he leaned heavily with each step. A hurrying ensign smirked in passing, and the old man's robotic leg shot out with the force of a Class 2 battering ram, breaking the young man's knee with a sickening pop of cartilage and bone. The ensign dropped to the deck, his face contorted, screaming mutely.

"Respect those before you," reprimanded the General with a smooth laugh. Then he moved on with fluid, sweeping strides devoid of disability, the unneeded cane twirling in his hand.

"Arnas," he whispered sharing the commander's cruel smile. "You're going to make it easy."

4
Hammerfield

Sunlight washed through swaying pines, dancing across the forest floor in delicate patterns of gold and yellow. Four young animals rolled in tall grass, playfully chewing and biting one another. A soft, late-autumn breeze rolled through the pine boughs, whispering signs of the cold winter to come. The remains of an early snowfall still hung heavy in the boughs. The youngest of the large creatures rolled to his feet and stood, fur rustling in the cool wind. His pelt was cream colored with long bands of black that reached over his back and down his legs. Patches of deep, black fur rimmed soft, curious eyes.

His friends were romping in mock ferocious attacks, biting one another with great growls, clicks and squeals, but Alexander stood back silently. He could sense that playtime was nearing an end. Soon mother would come looking for him and make him go back to work. His nose crinkled at the thought.

He cautiously sniffed the air, sampling the rich texture of aromas the forest offered, searching for interesting scents. Several of the Elders were nearby: he could detect their unique signatures in the wind. He sniffed once more, but found nothing of interest in the cold, crisp air.

The oldest and largest of the creatures rolled lazily onto his back and nipped at his grappling mates, with soft, preliminary bites to get their attention. The little one growled and lowered her jaw to return the favor. The three intertwined and rolled through the tall grass.

A long low cry sounded across the glen, ending in a series of short, guttural barks. The three animals stopped their carousing and listened. The cry repeated and the creatures rolled to their feet and began to saunter back toward the tribe. The time to depart had come. Once more they would take to the stars.

Alexander listened to the long call from the Elder and watched the reaction of his friends. He was tired of all the frenetic activity. Work was so boring. He longed to just lie back and chew on some young sprouts in a warm nest. He stole a long glance back toward the main compound where his mother was directing the final bamboo pallet preparations. No one seemed to be paying him any attention. This might be the perfect time to steal away for a quick nap. Who would notice?

❖ ❖ ❖

DEEP WITHIN THE BOWELS OF THE IMPERIAL BATTLE CRUISER *Shiva,* roving packs of artificials prowled the ship's corridors. To Commander Arnas's eye, there were many more arts than one would think was necessary. *This was a first-rate Imperial ship of the line,* he thought. *There are hundreds of enlisted men to service every core system within our slender giant. What need do we have for artificials when there are plenty of humans to manage things properly? What could all the arts be working on?*

He grimaced as he stepped around a trio of arts pushing a cargo lighter through the hall. Two women paused and saluted smartly as he passed. The arts afforded him no such respect. They were nothing but a nuisance to Arnas as he made his way to the armory.

The corridor was cold and dark, lit with luminescent pipes below the grated deck plates. Thin slits in the bulkhead irradiated a strange, pale light on the lower levels. Sloping green-black walls, polished to a gleaming shine, resonated a steady dull throb: the pulse of the ship's light drive which hurled them through the ethos.

Arnas turned a corner and stopped before a massive blast-shielded door that protected the rest of the ship from any accident within the armory. Without proper shielding, a misfire or blast from within could cripple the ship. Fire control was always a ship's greatest concern. One small fire could rip through the oxygen rich environment in seconds, engulfing the entire crew. The armory door was striped with warnings and an Imperial Dragon icon, its talons wrapped around a sword.

The drop on Hammerfield was upon him. The cycle awaited. For the 87th time in his career he stood before the golden

Dragon and the broad blast door it guarded. He straightened his tunic and savored the last moment of calm the Dragon offered him before he descended into another level of K'ye. Arnas stared at the black eye of the icon and placed a hand on the cold surface of the door, absently tracing the dragon's engraved body with a fingertip. Arnas took a deep breath and keyed access.

"Good afternoon, commander," the door said in a deep, brassy voice.

"Open," Arnas said plainly.

The icon split into two halves and the door trundled open.

Arnas strode into the combat ready room and into a world of cacophonous sound. Tech teams raced through final checklists in a variety of cryptic tongues, spoken languages cobbled together with mathematical symbols that flashed on their arms and faces as they worked. Magnetic ink was fed into their skin and linked to their brainstems with bio couplers that worked in concert with the phase emitters fused to their radius bones. Diagnostics were displayed through their skin for all to see. Glistening artificials maneuvered yellow-striped warheads stacked six deep on hovering cargo lighters. Soldiers' bare feet padded stickily on the metalloid rungs of wall ladders. Long, humming cranes delivered ready-mount racks of armored drop suits and jarringly locked them into position beneath the ladders. As each of the four-dozen drop suits gained tech clearance, half-naked soldiers scrambled inside, helmets whizzing shut above them.

Arnas inserted a pair of falto ear blocks to dull the level of noise within the armory and tried to concentrate on the activities of the main bridge that whispered in his head. Two squadrons of Barrelian Phantoms—small, swift single-manned strike fighters—had been released to race ahead of the task force and knock out Lon Seres' defensive network. The colonies scattered across the planet's surface were in early stages of development, most under 100 years old. Meager interstellar resistance was expected — at least for the time being. Whatever minor picket Hammerfield Colony could muster would be no match for Barrett's capital class warships. The two 700 meter Lor Stanta destroyers should easily outclass any defense that Hammerfield could support. Lon Seres was, however, deep in the Jhellus sector, a vast network of planetary systems ruled by Lady Vos Bergen, a Pragen Feline renowned for her possessive nature regarding her colonies. She bitterly resisted any Imperial interference in her domain.

A raid on one of her cherished colonies was sure to bring a swift and lethal response. Lady Bergen could probably dispatch several capital frigates from the Daurrian shipyards off Gingham: four, perhaps five hours away at top speed. And her patrolling Dreadnoughts could be much closer yet. Arnas had a very narrow window to take Hammerfield. Resistance dirtside could be fierce, and without the aid of orbital bombardment Arnas and his men faced a daunting task.

With the matériel at his disposal — the full resources of several of the Emperor's finest battle cruisers — Commander Arnas could easily overwhelm the rudimentary defenses below, given the time and patience to properly execute the raid. A week, even several days, and he could present the colony to Barrett on a silver platter, largely unscathed. But time was not a luxury at his disposal.

Lady Bergen's forces could be mere hours away, and to make matters worse, Arnas could not simply drop and burn — razing anything that stood in his way. No, he had to be *careful.* He grimaced at the thought. Imperial agents had not pinpointed the location of the stolen bio's compound, merely their presence somewhere within Hammerfield.

Thus, Arnas had to take the colony with as little collateral damage as possible. The creatures had to be captured alive.

"Commander Arnas!"

He turned to see a young tech armorer standing at attention by his side. His caste markings were tattooed across his neck ending in a green swirl just beneath his left ear. The tech's ship-suit was covered in power coolant and bearing grease, and his arms cradled a Larkson shield generator, trailing a tangled mess of brightly color-coded wires.

"What is it ensign?"

"The gen on 17B tested red. We shut down the field and went to backup and the buffer went critical."

"Can you refit from ship stores?"

"I've got Debin checking on it now, sir. But even if they have a spare Lark down there we won't have time to bring the field up to spec in time."

Arnas sighed. "What about Miklai's old suit? Had a core breach and the optics melted down, but the generator should still be salvageable."

The tech shook his head in apology. "We had to cannibalize that suit yesterday, sir. We're running low on everything what with all the action we've been seeing. We're lucky we could put together a full brigade of viable Trioxins for you today, sir. We need two weeks at Wyx to resupply and refit—I've notified Commander Li that we should stop and—"

"We've had no time for that," Arnas grumbled. "What about the emergency suits in the life buoys on six and seven—couldn't we crack those out and work a standard combat refit in time?"

The armorer furrowed his brow and grimaced, trying not to look too dubious of his superior's suggestion. "I wouldn't recommend it, sir. I could have a couple of those suits yanked out and refit with minimal armament, but I wouldn't have time to prep or confirm any subsystem integrities. I'd hate to put one of the lads in a dicey suit."

"All right. Scratch Lieutenant Barlow from the roster. Tell her to report to TacOps for reassignment. She can probably drop with the mules and ride a sled in."

"Yes sir!" The tech saluted and hurried away.

One less man—Arnas closed his eyes and began rearranging the combat roster in his mind. A chime sounded, three-part, two tones and repeated for five seconds. The last of the men and women began climbing into their suits and sealing themselves in.

Fleet Sergeant Krass stepped around the first line of Troopers and called the company to attention. "All right you slorts, front and center! Two minutes to drop—a cycle awaits. Toe the ready line—on the bounce!" The sergeant paced down the line of armored suits, eyes taking in everything.

"Let's go Laserai, lock down that helmet. Move it Troopers." He stopped in the center of the room. "Squad One present arms for inspection!"

The men quickly formed up on the yellow stripe at the front of the chamber. First Squad extended their weapons and kept their external readout panel exposed for Arnas' inspection. Sergeant Krass quickly checked each suit's bio readings and stasis board. Any Trooper not in perfect health was a liability not only to himself, but to his whole squad. Arnas double-checked Krass' work and personally snapped the external readouts into locked and ready position, careful to look in the Trooper's eyes before he walked to the next man.

Klaxons sounded throughout the armory and the lights flashed blue-green in sequence. Krass shouted, "On the bounce—prepare for embarkation! Right *face*!"

As one, the armored Shock Troops pivoted ninety degrees to the right as a blast door scrolled upwards revealing a narrow passageway sloping down to the atmospheric drop ships.

Fleet Sergeant Krass marched up to Commander Arnas and saluted sharply. "All present and accounted for, sir! Ready for cycle!"

"Very good, mister Krass. Proceed."

"Cmp'nee! Forward—double time!" The four squads trotted down the cerasteel ramps, heavy footfalls deafening in the small, cramped space.

Each of the drop ships cradled within the bay looked like a delicate chrysalis with wings folded around its body. The men split off by squad and boarded the four suspended ships. Each man locked himself into a pressure rack to weather the massive gee-forces during descent.

Arnas quickly pulled himself up and into his armored Trioxin suit, ran through the checklist and sealed the helmet shut. All systems online, he motioned Colonel Hastings, the armorer, forward to perform his final inspection. The white haired man bustled quickly across the deck and checked Arnas' vital signs and weapon status. Satisfied, he stepped back and saluted smartly, clearing the commander for combat.

Arnas trotted down the access ramp and into the launch bay. He picked out his ship, the *Scarrion*, and ducked under the hatch, punching the lock closed as he entered. The Commander surveyed the men of Squad One before locking himself into his rack. He keyed his command channel.

"All squad leaders, report!"

The four men signaled locked and ready. Arnas switched channels and gave the pilots the go ahead. A soft feminine voice sounded in each man's helmet com. "Five seconds to atmospheric insertion."

Arnas took a deep breath, closed his eyes, and clenched his abdominal muscles in preparation for the first lurching drop. The launch bay depressurized as the doors beneath the suspended drop ships trundled open revealing the bright green globe, Lon Seres, which rotated slowly below. Luminescent clouds brightly reflected the rays of the Jhellus system's huge brown star.

A screech of scraping metal grated against his ears as the docking claws retracted. He felt a lurch and then without further warning, his stomach rose to his throat. He suddenly felt as if he weighed 500 kilos.

The *Scarrion* dropped quickly free of the *Shiva*, falling without resistance into Lon Seres' strong gravitational well. Through his viewport, Arnas could see dozens of delicate looking drop ships falling from the *Gorgon*, *Lizet*, and *Vishnu* as Arnas' battalion of Shock Troops began their run. To overwhelm any dirtside defenses at least three times the defender's strength was needed at the point of attack. Arnas' plan called for a full battalion of Trioxin-clad Shock Troops to make the first sweep, with two brigades of marine regulars and mobile infantry to follow in standard assault shuttles and mules.

Gunsleds, tactical fighters, and siege matériel would be dropped from low orbit and manned dirtside. Tracking teams and bio-engineers would be the final men to touch down. By that time Arnas hoped to have Hammerfield well in hand.

For reassurance, Arnas monitored the pilot's open channel, keeping track of their progress through the upper atmosphere. The drop ships rocketed through the first layer of gases, encountering severe buffeting as the ship attempted to plunge in as steep an inclination as the heat shields would allow.

Rapid deployment minimized risk — the faster the drop ships could get to the surface, the less time Arnas and his men would be easy targets, helplessly locked in their racks. Speed meant sacrificing comfort, however, and the gee-forces were sickening. The *Scarrion* bucked wildly as she plunged further into the atmospheric soup, but the pilots sounded calm and professional on the com as they zeroed in on the drop zone, a giant forest of deciduous pines on Lon Sere's northernmost continent. Hammerfield Colony was nestled at the eastern tip.

The buffeting stabilized as the *Scarrion* leveled off a hundred meters over the ground, racing in to the drop site. The other drop ships approached from three different vectors, all scheduled to converge within seconds. Suspension racks automatically lifted and the pilot calmly reported, "Twenty seconds to target."

Arnas keyed the platoon com. "Prepare for drop, jumpers on standby." He flipped the safety off his jump jets and thumbed the power stud to hover, double-checking his stasis board—all green. His helmet clanged into the cerasteel rack as the ship bounced through the rough air. Arnas braced himself by his elbows and stared down between his feet. A circular portal suddenly irised open beneath each man and Arnas could see treetops whipping by a scant hundred meters below.

Deploy signal chimed and Arnas released his grasp allowing himself to free-fall through the portal and away from the ship. His suit's jump jets immediately fired and he picked a landing site between two massive trees, maneuvering himself through the outreaching branches as best he could. Leaves and debris swirled up as the ground rose to meet him.

Arnas touched down softly, the mossy forest floor giving way to his heavy Trioxin boots. He flipped his helmet viewer to tactical display and the visual image of trees and undergrowth switched to a three-dimensional graphic rendering of the area that appeared to extend out from his faceplate. Terrain and obstacles appeared a muted green while his men and tactical objectives were represented by colored blips with range, bearing, and identity coded above each icon.

"Take bearings to squad leaders," he ordered. "Even up those lines and proceed, double-time!"

Arnas confirmed that his two flanking Troopers had spaced themselves properly and then began forward in great leaping strides, quickly adapting to the abnormal strength and unnatural feeling of movement within the Trioxin suit. In a few moments he found his rhythm and much like hopping from rock to rock across a stream, he bounded forward, picking out his steps several strides ahead.

Blaster fire sparked by overhead and within moments his visor displayed a range and bearing to the threat, triangulated from passive sensors in each Trooper's suit. The data was fed by data burst to a central processing datacore in the *Lizet* via orbital drones deployed by the *Gorgon*. The passive sensors collected as much information as possible on life form readings, magnetic anomalies, atmospheric displacement, aural disturbances, electrical activity, and power surges. The E2 datacore then identified and classified as many of these as possible, taking into account whatever activity was attributable to Imperial soldiers and then fed this information through its sartographic array.

The sartographic subroutines compared the signals it received with its signal library and made a projection based on the relevant data and the sum knowledge of all previous Imperial encounters stored within the vast memory of the E2 as to what targets were present, where, and with what degree of certainty the probability projection was made.

The threat display was instantaneously transmitted back to Arnas' heads-up visor:

MASS DETECTED • CARBON LIFE FORMS • 2
VOLUME • NULL
DENSITY • CONGRUENT HUMAN
SPEED • NULL
POWER INCONGRUITY • PROJECTILE DISCHARGE
ENERGY SPIKE • CLASS 3 BASTER FIRE
MUZZLE ENERGY • EK 416 FT-LBF • 564 JOULES
BEARING 276.4 DEGREES
RANGE 38.3 METERS
IMPERIAL IDENT-LINK • NULL
ASSESSMENT • THREAT
THREAT PROBABILITY 96.7

Arnas came to a halt, landing in a two-footed stance and brought his assault weapon to bear on the target's flashing image. The target would be invisible to the naked eye in the shadows and dense undergrowth, but with the suit's targeting optics, a firing solution was immediately displayed. Arnas thumbed in the range to target and brought the weapon to his shoulder. He settled his breathing and fired a salvo of purplish energy bolts. The target flashed briefly, then the threat icon faded from his display.

Two air skimmers raced over Hammerfield, searching for Imperial targets. The lead pilot nosed over toward Arnas' position and let loose a flurry of anti-personnel fléchettes, blanketing the forest below.

Arnas kneeled and keyed his ground-to-air rockets. Three tones sounded in his helmet and then pinged rapidly as his visual targeting system locked onto the lead craft's signature. Arnas bit down hard and braced himself as the shoulder-mounted launcher fired off two rounds. The rockets screamed out of the glade and shot below the skimmer's belly as the ship swooped overhead.

The shockwaves from the skimmer's low-level pass buffeted Arnas. He wheeled to try a follow up shot, but the pilot was too low and Arnas lost him in the tree branches.

"Squad Three proceed to target—and keep an eye out for those air patrols!"

Purple and orange bolts of energy ripped through the cool morning air over Arnas' head leaving behind a faint smell of burnt ozone that hung in the air like the aftermath of a lightning strike. Flash points fired from multiple targets ahead. Trees burned wildly on all sides, scorched by the uncontrolled blaster fire from the terrified colonials. The militia's overlapping fields of fire were beginning to break down as Squads Two and Three completed their flanking maneuvers and caught them in a brutal crossfire.

From the edge of the forest cover, Arnas scanned Hammerfield's perimeter, mentally noting prime defensive positions and locked the trouble spots into the datacore's processor by biting down on key commands as his eyes focused on each emplacement. He ordered his men forward by squad.

Drop ships from the *Gorgon* and *Lenton Vash* were deploying foot soldiers and semi-armored personnel on the north and west fringes of the Colony. Gun sleds and tactical fighters would be dropped from high orbit in Geggin braking shells, laser-guided to drop sites from orbit. Their operators were landing even now in the lumbering mules—huge obtuse transport lifters fit with gigantic slabs of external armor and Thurston shields, the extra cover necessary to protect the lifters during their vulnerable loading and slow ascents into orbit laden with battle-weary men and matériel. The added weight and mass of the armor and shield generators necessitated monstrous sublight drives. Beneath the angled cerasteel armor plating, giant cooling conduits snaked along the ships' ugly utilitarian design.

Affectionately dubbed the 'mules' for their appearance and reliability, the lifters could withstand massive amounts of punishment from ground forces and atmospheric pursuit craft and still deliver their Imperial cargo to the orbiting cruisers and safety.

At the edge of cover, Arnas ordered a barrage of cover fire—high explosive charges lobbed randomly at the enemy while his men covered the open ground between the tree line and the city proper. Arnas and his two flanking Troopers breached the last of the burning trees and sprinted across the clearing between forest and city, covering the distance quickly with great jackrabbit leaps.

Blaster fire was sporadic now—taking the rest of the colony would be tedious door-to-door, close quarters combat. Time consuming and casualty intensive—Arnas cursed the lack of hard data on the target compound's location. Without an exact location, the whole colony had to be searched and secured. That meant hand-to-hand weapons only.

A muffled explosion shook the ground and a plume of sooty, black smoke bellowed over the northern rooftops. Squad Two must have taken the armory, thought Arnas.

"Squad Four, report."

"Encountering heavy resistance from two bunkers south of objective, over."

"Evaluation."

"It'll take time to break through. Militia has entrenched themselves for the long haul—and they've set up a good system of cover fire. We're bottled up here for the moment."

"We don't have time to waste, Lieutenant. We're already on a low probability schedule. I need you to take that southern flank in order to close the noose."

"Permission to use tacticals, sir?"

Arnas considered. "Negative. Too risky. We need the creatures alive—and healthy." *If they're still on the planet,* he thought to himself, cursing Ness. "Hold your position," he ordered. "I'm on my way."

Arnas keyed a new channel as he began running. "Lieutenants Sylus, Vaskin, and Trent report to me at drop zone three on the bounce!" He flipped to his private channel and signaled Gunnery Sergeant Baker.

"Yes sir?"

"Gunney, I want you to load up a Tort on a sled real quick and have it up over the glade on the southern flank in three minutes."

"Yes sir!"

"And throw in a couple of armor drips while you're at it—two shells should do it. Have the sled converge on my transponder."

"No problem, boss."

Sloppy situation, he thought to himself. *A bad Cycle to be caught in.* He grimaced and narrowed his focus to more immediate concerns. They would have to take Hammerfield block by block, but first he needed to break open the bottleneck on the southern flank.

THE FOUR TROOPERS arrived at the clearing nearly simultaneously, suits scored with carbon. Arnas wasted no time as he unloaded the gunsled that hovered neatly behind a low stone wall.

"Vaskin, Trent: crack out those molds. I want full armor plating by the time the Tort's up! Sylus, you and I can handle this shell."

Sylus stepped smoothly to the nearest Geggin shell, identified its contents by outer markings and knelt to open the final cracked ceramic housing. A series of breakaway chutes opened during the Geggin's descent through the upper atmosphere, slowing and guiding the cargo pallet to its drop site. Layers of loosely bonded cerafiber burned away during descent protecting the cargo within from the intense heat of atmospheric friction. Two final chutes opened in the final moments before impact and then seventeen foam-buffered layers of ceramic shielding built one atop another like an onionskin cushioned the final impact.

Each layer of ceramic absorbed a large measure of the inertial force, imparting little energy to the next layer of protection. Ceramic's incredibly tight atomic bonds made it perfect for high impact shielding. The tight atomic bonds caused the ceramic to be very brittle, but the shell was designed to break away on impact, leaving the cargo safely cocooned within.

Sylus cracked open the final shell with an armored gauntlet and freed the safety catches. The foam housing fell away revealing the Tortian weapon assembly within. Sylus and Arnas swiftly removed the contents of the pallet and began expertly assembling the burnished components. Oily black steel casings and factory-new magnetic coils were carefully laid out on the cobbled street. The two men worked smoothly, quietly, hands moving over the fittings without thought, the assembly routine branded into their subconscious from years of experience.

Sylus picked up a collapsible cylinder, locked a firing tube into place and loaded an explosive charge into its breach. He located a small box of miscellaneous fittings, and removed a slender steel rod with a triangular sharpened head. Sylus slid the steel piton into the tube and fired the long steel pin into the first leg of the weapon's massive tripod, firmly anchoring the assembly into the ground. Together the two men lifted the two-meter-long completed assault cannon onto the tripod, assisted by their Trioxin servo limbs.

Meanwhile, Sub-lieutenants Vaskin and Trent finished pouring the liquid cerafiber into the pre-formed molds. The mixture bonded in seconds and the men lifted the newly fabricated armor plating into position around the cannon, locking the five-millimeter-thick plates into place with ceramic pins. The completed assembly resembled a miniature bunker standing a meter and a half high, with the Tortian cannon's muzzle pointing through a slit in the cerafiber plates.

"Sylus, I want you to take out that wall. You should have a clear shot at those bunkers then." Arnas keyed his command channel: "Squad Four, duck and cover."

The Tortian assault cannon disintegrated the wall in a deafening shower of stone, leaving Sylus a clear line of sight to the defensive bunkers that had Squad 4 pinned down. It was over in seconds. Shock Troops poured through the breach.

Most civilians huddled in the basements of burnt-out buildings. Snipers were everywhere; the snap-whoosh of their plasma bolts sizzling in the smoky air. Crisscrossing blaster fire kept most movement pinned down and made identifying friend or foe nearly impossible for militia and Shock Troopers alike.

Arnas could locate his men on his tactical display by transponder signal, but the information was abstract and meaningless without city plans downloaded into his datacore. All he had was range and bearing to each blip on his scope. No telling what buildings lay between them, whether the targets were indoors or outdoors, and what foes might lay in their midst. And Arnas was having no luck finding a hidden compound in all the chaos.

He punched up the orbital command channel. "Yarvek, the codes?"

"On it, sir. Easy as a twelve tier cryptograph."

"If it's so simple then send me the city blueprints. I feel like a rat in a maze down here."

"Almost there, sir. The boys and I were a little busy there for a while—got caught in a nasty communication subroutine. Backdoor trap in their lines of communication. Almost fried the whole pod net."

"You can tell it to me later Yar, in excruciating detail, over a nice, hot cup of pod goop—but right now—"

"Don't drink goop, sir."

"Yarvek!"

"Got it, sir! Accessing archival records…"

"See if you can't pinpoint a location for the target compound."

"I see a couple of likely spots, one not too far north of your position. Bursting files now. Your tactical scope should update."

The confusing display in Arnas' viewplate shimmered with static, disappeared for a blink and then leapt back to life in a wash of vivid colors. The whole colony was laid out before him in graphic format, buildings, streets, and back avenues all clearly labeled. The threat display made sense now as he could locate the targets that were within his field of fire and disregard those that were within buildings that faced other streets.

Arnas rounded the edge of a building and found himself face to face with a young man no older than an ensign. The youth held an old-style plasma rifle cradled in his arms. For a long second the boy stared in awe at Arnas in his fearsome armor and then struggled to point his heavy rifle at the intruder.

Without a thought, Arnas depressed his fire control and flame leapt away from his arm, incinerating the terrified boy. The charred body slumped over backwards and Arnas clomped over the remains.

Flash points sparked across his shoulder and he dove awkwardly for cover. Chunks of concrete exploded out of the wall behind him as he rolled to bring his weapon to bear. White-hot plasma discharges arced toward his position in the rubble, tracing across the plaza as the gunner walked his sights from left to right.

His visual reference was clouded by smoke and dust. Flipping his display back to tactical he quickly located the source of fire and pumped thirty rounds into the target. He keyed explosive rounds and lobbed three charges into the defender's position for good measure. Satisfied that the avenue was clear, he rose to his feet and identified the nearest Troopers.

"Laserai, Megas, you're with me." The two Troopers signaled affirmative and Arnas strode forward, ignoring the sporadic bursts of blaster fire that careened around him. He studied the tactical display. Yarvek was right on one count: the compound could very well be situated just north of his current position. He motioned his men after him and walked briskly up the avenue. At the end of the narrow street their passage was blocked by a twelve-meter stone wall.

"Megas," he intoned, "if you please." He stepped to one side.

The Trooper squared his shoulders and keyed an explosive round into his launcher. With a dull whump he fired the charge into the base of the wall. The shell penetrated the stone and then exploded in a shower of splintered rocks and mortar. Arnas stepped over the debris and through the billowing cloud of dust.

The wind quickly cleared the smoke. Arnas found himself staring across a beautiful broad expanse of green grass that leaned away from the afternoon breeze. The terrain had a slight roll, lending the swaying grass a dreamy, wavelike quality. At the base of three hills lay a cluster of low-lying buildings shaded by gnarled elms. The stone wall that enclosed the field extended off in both directions giving the whole compound a very private and quiet appearance.

This must be it. He punched his command channel. "Squads two and four converge on my signal. Take prisoners only—*no casualties!* Understood?" Arnas prayed there were still prisoners here to be taken.

Trioxin-armored Shock Troops marched down Hammerfield's broad tree-lined promenade, Founders Avenue, burnished chest plates scorched with black carbon streaks. The grey-silvered armor glistened mutely in the afternoon sun.

Waves of infantry were landing in transport shuttles following the Shock Troops' initial sweep, relieving the battle-weary marines and completing the occupation maneuver. Teams of technicians began setting up elaborate tracking equipment to establish their quarry's whereabouts. The massive lifeform readings of the forest surrounding Hammerfield had rendered orbital scans worthless.

Thick black smoke roiled over the remains of Hammerfield Colony. Buildings lay twisted in ruin with only bits of steel left standing after the plascrete walls and floors had melted away. The charred remains of colonial militia were strewn everywhere, armor and bone fused together in grotesque lumps.

Imperial Shock Troops lined the streets, leaning against the corners of buildings, blast rifles propped against shoulders, helmets cradled against their hips. The heat was too much for their suits' atmospheric processors. Their faces were blackened with soot and ash so that they appeared to be carved from stone.

Gunsleds patrolled the perimeters of the colony while an elite regiment of the Imperial Guard flushed out the remaining survivors. The occasional muffled shriek of a blast pistol could be heard as the final pockets of resistance fell.

Three men in long white coats paced down the center of the street. They stepped over bodies without breaking stride, oblivious to the horrific backdrop. Soldiers stiffened as the trio walked past. The central figure appeared unmoved by the raging fires and smoke that swirled across the flagstones. His lips were set in a thin line and he stared silently forward as the men at his side fed him a constant stream of battle data.

Standard Imperial procedure dictated that only a Battalion Commander, such as Arnas, need oversee the final stages of an Occupation Maneuver, but today Vice Proctor Hellius Barrett was attending to the details himself. Imperial Assassin Torg made his way silently in the shadows of his master's path, all senses alert for danger.

Barrett climbed atop a large pile of rubble that blocked the avenue and found himself looking into a sweeping green complex of low buildings and broad grassy fields. The compound was set apart from the rest of the colony by a large wall. The architectural details of the buildings were muted and stylized, as if designed to have as little impact on the eye as possible. All the sharp corners were rounded off and the structures seemed to melt into the natural surroundings.

Barrett picked his way down from his vantage point and motioned an Imperial officer forward.

"Report, Lieutenant."

"My Lord, advance parties have reached the inner compound but they've found no sign of Dr. Tchelakov or his research."

"Bring the compound's senior technician to me."

"By your will, sir." The Lieutenant used the formal response and saluted smartly. Out of the corner of his eye he spied the dark man standing in the vice proctor's shadows. He could feel the assassin's silver, inhuman eyes boring into the back of his skull as he hurried away.

Barrett turned to his adjunct. "Have Commander Arnas report to me immediately."

The aide nodded and subvocalized the command to Arnas. "The Commander reports he's on his way."

A muffled roar sounded over the trees to the north of the compound, growing in pitch and volume. Barrett turned to locate the origin and scanned the tree line, waiting for a visual reference. The unmistakable scream of jump jets continued to rise. Barrett, peering through the tree branches, felt certain he should be able to make out the source by now. With a bellowing roar, an armored Shock Trooper crested the nearest tree and settled gently to the ground, jets kicking up dirt and leaves as he touched down.

The armored man reached his hands to his head and cracked open his helmet, cradling it in one arm as he strode forward. Stopping before the vice proctor, the man gave a slight bow — all that was possible while in the suit. "41st Imperial Battalion Commander reporting. In the name of the Emperor, Hammerfield is secure."

"Well done Arnas," Barrett intoned smoothly. "But tell me, where are our targets?"

Arnas clenched his jaw and tried to suppress his dread. "Preliminary sweeps haven't provided any clues as to their whereabouts. I've ordered a door-to-door search while the techs set up their equipment. If they're here, my Lord, we'll find them."

The Vice Proctor exhaled through pursed lips. "I'll ask you again," he spoke the words very slowly and carefully. "Where are the targets, Commander?"

Arnas swallowed painfully. "Sir, in my estimation the targets are off-planet. By all rights they are probably out of the system altogether at this point."

Barrett appeared untouched by this news—hands clasped calmly behind his back, eyes scanning the horizon. "Well perhaps we can shed some light on our friends' plans," Barrett said dryly.

The Vice Proctor's voice was entirely too calm and composed for Arnas' liking. He had seen him like this before and the memory was tinged forever with blood. Barrett was extremely dangerous when he did not get what he wanted.

Two guards escorted a short, burly civilian to the edge of the compound and stood him before the vice proctor. The man looked confused, out of place, fear evident in his face. His eyes shifted from one white coat to another. Beads of sweat rolled down his chin.

Barrett looked the man over from head to toe and shook his head in silent dismissal. "Tell me technician," he spoke slowly, annunciating carefully as if speaking to a small child, "where did Dr. Tchelakov take his research?"

The technician looked lost, glancing off to each side. "I'm just a subsystem foreman. I don't know," he stammered.

Barrett began to pace in front of the prisoner. "Dr. Tchelakov *was* here," he paused to look at the tech. "You *are* familiar with the good doctor?"

The man bobbed his head nervously. "Only that he ran some facility on the northern edge of the compound. Needed lots of open space—kept to himself. No one knew him really."

Barrett glanced at the insignia on the man's collar. "And being the senior comptroller for all shipping here on Hammerfield, your clearance is necessary for all incoming shipments?"

The man nodded.

"And, for all departures as well?"

"The comptroller swallowed visibly."

"Yes, of course. So I will ask you again, where did Dr. Tchelakov take his research?"

Frozen with fear, the man did not respond.

"He must have filed a flight plan, and he must have given a point of destination. How else could you feed him updated system gravitic fluctuations and accurate vector information for his jump?"

"I — I don't know, honestly. They left in the dead of the night — no flight plan was logged. It was not a regularly scheduled departure."

"Are you suggesting that Dr. Tchelakov jumped blindly? He just whisked away 37 creatures into the night without so much as a simple query to your office?" Barrett glanced at the sky. "That's an awfully big star. Hard to make a jump with such a powerful gravity well nearby."

"They made no queries. I have no record of their jump."

"No solar activity reports? No magnetic field measurements? Perhaps the good doctor just took a wild guess. Do you believe in luck? Do you think he could be that lucky? Pick a vector and blindly jump?"

"I don't know," the man stammered.

"Perhaps it's not that you 'don't know.' Perhaps it's just that you don't remember," Barrett turned to a guard. "Trooper, your burner please."

The soldier looked at the vice proctor in confusion and then with a slight hesitation unhooked his burn pistol from his belt and handed it over butt first.

Barrett went through the pretense of examining the burner as he continued to pace. "Perhaps there is some way I may convince you of the seriousness of my intent. Something I can offer you maybe?" He paused in front of the man, pointed the burner at his shoulder and squeezed the release. A bolt of fire leapt from the barrel, boring through the skin and bone. The technician howled in pain and surprise as his arm dropped neatly from its socket.

"Perhaps you'd be interested in keeping your other arm," Barrett continued, as if he had merely paused to swat at a nagging insect.

The man dropped to his knees screaming and clutched his bloody arm socket with one hand.

"On your feet! I'm still addressing you!" The two guards hauled the man back to an upright position. "Now," he resumed his methodical pacing. "Where did Dr. Tchelakov and his creatures go?"

"I don't know," the technician sobbed. "Truly, I do not. Please, you can check the records. I don't know!"

Barrett sighed sadly. "An inventive man would have at least lied, invented some response to save his arm — much less his life." The Vice Proctor hovered over the cringing man. "You don't even deserve that."

The man shook in terror. Barrett raised the weapon and burned off the other arm.

Barrett tossed the burner back to the guard and strode away. "Finish him," he snapped as he walked past Arnas.

Without a word, Arnas walked forward, unlatched his blast pistol and fired one shot into the man's head, quieting his screams.

The Vice Proctor turned to his aide as he walked, raising his eyebrows in question. The man nodded. "Colonial port data-core secure. It was taken intact."

"Search the logs," Barrett ordered. "Have your men scour the core for all projected jumps in the past eight hours."

The Vice Proctor stopped and slowly bent to the rubble at his boots. Reaching his gloved hand beneath a chunk of plascrete he extracted a small, thick stalk of organic matter splintered at one end from blaster fire. He twisted the pale green stalk slowly between his fingers. "Bamboo," he murmured.

"My lord?" the aide asked uncertainly.

Barrett peered up through the smoke to the sky beyond. "They were here."

5
Open Market

Garrand walked briskly up *Destiny's* extended boarding ramp and stepped into her primary airlock, both doors locked in the open position on Letugia's oxygen-rich surface. Bailey had set up a small static field that screened the portal, ionizing any dust particles either airborne or clinging to the clothing of those entering the ship. The primary field attached a negative charge to the particles as they passed into the airlock. The dust was then lifted by the secondary field's positive charge, keeping the ship dust-free. Garrand felt a tingling sensation and the hairs on the back of his neck stood up as he passed through.

He stepped into the oval corridor and made his way aft, ducking his head under exposed coolant piping and power conduits. Part way down the dimly lit corridor sat four squat tech arts that had removed access panels to the atmospheric processors and were performing internal diagnostics. Garrand picked up a datapad lying nearby and rapped the nearest artificial on the head. Servos squeaked as the art turned a photoreceptor to identify the disturbance. Garrand noted the art's ident-link and used the datapad to access its command file. The tech art warbled a question, the translation scrolling down the datapad's screen. Garrand outlined a new diagnostic subroutine. He wanted to make sure the atmospheric processors were filtering out any latent toxins that might have seeped out of the reactor core. The art accepted the new set of diagnostic parameters with a bleep and turned to trill the new commands to his three compatriots.

Garrand quickly passed the holo room and central mess. Beyond the mess lay the encrypted lock to the armory. He cycled through the coded logarithmic progression and kicked a hidden toe switch as he keyed in the final sequence. The door irised open to reveal a room crammed from deck to ceiling with rows of weapons and defensive countermeasures. Blast rifles, fusion discs, anti-personnel mines, dart throwers, and a tripod-mounted cannon were secured along the near wall. Rows of various power coils were magnetically sealed into recharging nodes hung from spider-like conduits overhead. Gravitic repulsors, Haley charges, and gear littered the deck plates. Crates of Apoxia darts and concussion grenades were stacked in a haphazard fashion wherever space allowed. A steel cabinet of throwing blades and poison tipped darts lay open on the far wall. Bio-resonators in need of adjustment, modified mag couplings with useless field locks, reworked impact pistols and two cannibalized shield generators lay scattered across the armorer's table. A propped up clipscanner, forgotten, still displayed a diagnostic analysis of a breached field resonator.

In a specially cleared space, with their Imperial insignia burned off, hung three Trioxin armored combat suits from ready-mount racks. Beside the full torso pressure suits hung several lighter vests and gauntlets. The lighter-weight personal body armor was a dark fiber composite that molded itself to the body's contours and allowed greater freedom of movement than the bulky, full-body Trioxin designs. Though not much protection from blaster fire, the fiber armor would certainly turn any assassin's blade and possibly blunt a poison dart. Protection one might need in the market.

Garrand removed his jacket and stripped off his drenched tunic as well as his utility belt. He turned with shoulders straight and placed his back flat against the mounting mechanism. Holding his arms high overhead he depressed the foot switch. The lightweight fiber armor extended around his ribcage and wrapped itself around his chest, conforming to the smooth muscles, sealing itself along his right ribcage. He lowered his arms and slid them one at a time into the gauntlet mount. The black fiber gauntlets reached from the soft pad of skin between thumb and forefinger all the way to his shoulder.

Refastening his utility belt around his waist, he checked to see that his shield generator read full power, and clipped a magazine of tiny concussion grenades into their feeder. The autoload mechanism accepted the silvery spheres one at a time and locked them into place. The counter read "twelve." He removed his blaster from its holster and depressed the coil release in the butt. The smooth blackened housing detached into his palm. Exchanging the rechargeable coil for a fresh one out of habit, he clicked the fully powered coil into place, flicked the safety off and holstered the weapon. He pulled a fresh tunic over his head—Este's wife would try to wash it if he didn't—and put his dark jacket back on, ready to face the streets of Letugia. He wasn't expecting any trouble but his days of walking the streets of Shell worlds with impunity were long gone. He activated a personal homing device, loaded it into the breach of an airgun and injected the miniature transmitter into the supple skin in the back of his neck just above the shoulders. His nerves throbbed as he felt the pinch. He logged its scrambled signal code into the ship's datacore before he exited, a precaution that Bailey insisted upon. He had learned to listen well to his first mate.

Garrand stood at the outer threshold of docking bay 247B while his first mate performed a diagnostic check of his personal shield. The sleek artificial adroitly manipulated a highly specialized phase emitter, correcting the shield's pulse modulation. Slung from his belt, the shield generated a powerful resonating magnetic field capable of bending light around its focusing body. Light bent as it passed from one transparent medium to another, the speed of the waves depending upon the resonance of the energy field it passed through. When light waves passed from air to the magnetic field, they slowed—part of the wave slowing first, bending the wave front. When the light energy left it was bent back in the same amount, but in the opposite direction. These two bends caused an apparent displacement of anything visible within the field. The amount of displacement depended upon the angle at which the light entered and the distance it traveled through the field before reemerging—all variables being controlled by the pulse modulation in the generator. The energy refracted by the magnetic field was polarized—that is the waves that made up the light vibrated in only one direction—facilitating the bend. Null dampers absorbed the rest.

When activated, the field wrapped itself around his torso. Much like a body of water acts on a beam of light, energy entering the field slowed and was redirected. What energy it could not bend, the field absorbed. The resonating field easily manipulated visual light, however energy from blaster fire was much harder to redirect. The shield could generally absorb two or three bolts before its null dampers failed and the field buffers overloaded.

At normal levels, objects appeared to fold back and forth across his line of vision. Long trailers swam in dizzy circles from the edge of his visual plane. He practiced for long hours trying to overcome the disorienting effects of shield combat, fitting his blaster with special optics to compensate for the refraction. But he was almost always overcome with nausea after a few moments, and even with optics his blaster fire was scattershot random guesses.

At full strength, all light was bent around his body, rendering him briefly invisible if he remained absolutely motionless. The drawback being he was completely blind within the displacement field, as no light entered the null space. The amount of power needed to refract that much energy quickly depleted the generator's small power coil, limiting its usefulness.

Bailey gently rotated a minute calibrator, fine-tuning the delicate shield module. "I don't know why you insist on wearing this thing. It's practically useless," he complained.

"Every bit helps."

Bailey shook his head. "It's archaic; two good hits and the field collapses. And may I remind you that your holo target sessions have been most unimpressive when your magnetic shield is activated."

Garrand grinned lopsided as he waited for Bailey to finish fiddling with the shield.

"If you want my opinion, it was obsolete 100 years ago. General Shecut even said so in '292 on the eve of the first use of Trioxin suits in battle."

Garrand smiled; he sometimes forgot how much older Bailey was, how much more of the Shell he had seen. "For full-fledged formal military operations, maybe," he murmured. "But for one man working alone it has its advantages. Nice to have one last surprise up my sleeve."

Bailey replaced the outer casing and glanced up at him. "Well, the field is viable and I read full pulse from the beam spread." Garrand flipped the power switch, setting the shield to standby. Due to its immense power requirements, the shield could only run for brief periods of time. "Sir, I would feel much better if you would just allow me to accompany you. I provide a much more reliable defense than that ancient *artifact* slung around your waist. If you are concerned about your safety, I would be more than happy to run shadow for you."

"In Il Touvé?" he sounded a bit incredulous. "No, I'll be fine." He clasped his first mate's smooth powerful shoulder; it was cool to his touch. "Besides, my friend, you have to make sure those arts don't rip the ship apart while they finish the repairs. I'm counting on you here."

The artificial looked despondent as he replaced his tools. "As you will," he said stiffly.

GARRAND WALKED OUT of the docking bay and stood on the veranda straightening his gun belt and looking over the busy street scene. A handful of Qui were hitched to a post just outside the main gate, their saddles empty. The pack beasts snorted and pawed the dust uneasily, sensing the coming storm. Up the street to his left a dozen cargo sleds unloaded at a commercial dock. A team of Atryx skillfully worked the floating loaders, their feathers rustling in the breeze. The work boss whistled orders to the avians as they circled overhead. Though weightless on the repulsor sleds, the enormous cargo pallets still possessed the same mass and inertia—a tiny mistake could easily crush a loader. The Atryx were marvelously adept however, easing the pallets forward with feather-light nudges and locking the modules in the floating loader's cerasteel arms. Once safely secured in the twin-armed loader, the cargo was lowered by servos and ferried to the ship's hold.

Passengers awaiting departure on a second-rate transport overflowed out the hangar's lounge and milled about the street, sipping overpriced drinks and watching the Atryx handle the bulbous, yellow containers. Some browsed the dusty glazings of a barca dealer's shop, the expensive skins mounted on wooden displays, while others picked through a vegetable peddler's abundant selections. A Thillian lizard lay in the dust in the middle of the street; foot traffic gave him wide berth.

The stark aroma of baking coffee beans imported from Antorva drifted from an open-air eatery across the street—several customers hunched at the meal counter over steaming trays. The smell of coffee and food was enticing. Garrand considered his course of action. The thought of dinner appealed, but he was anxious to see if his shipping agent had procured a decent price for his ore. A Qui turned to look at him and gave a noisy snort. Garrand walked over and gave the beast a scratch under his neck. The creature pushed its soft nose into his chest and snorted again.

Garrand counted eleven Imperial foot soldiers patrolling the street, their highly visible presence pointing to the stepped up activities here in the Nepestar system. Bailey claimed there was now a full garrison on Letugia. He wondered how long it would be before Imperial's limited regulatory role would be supplanted by a more robust directive and a full occupational force. Vice Proctor Barrett was getting pretty bold trying to press an independent system as large and powerful as Nepestar into his fold.

Garrand turned left, heading south. He skirted the commercial docks, which would be swarming with passengers at this hour, and headed through a series of back alleys and dark residential avenues. Pausing at the edge of a wall, he carefully glanced over the crowd in the busy boulevard ahead. Satisfied that no one lingered suspiciously, he stepped into the flow of foot traffic. Passing under a stone arch that curved up from both ends of the street, he stood atop the Gregaria Steps, a ceremonial entrance to the planet's largest open air trading market. He put his hands on his hips in the pretense of taking in the mayhem below and once more checked for a follower.

The ornate steps swept down into an immense natural clearing that acted as an open-ended trading house. Thousands upon thousands filled the market, their forms dancing in the heat that rose from open flames lighting the concourse. The Open Market formed the unofficial locus of the shipyard; anyone who did business in the city eventually wound up here.

Garrand descended the steps and began picking his way through the seething throng. His fingertips brushed the butt of his blaster and he hitched the thumb of his left hand casually on his belt, conveniently beside the shield generator. Hundreds of makeshift tables, roughly hewn from available materials, were arranged in long lines forming aisles through the marketplace. Warehouse owners and their artificial accountants sat behind rough wooden tables strewn with clipscanners and datapads. There was no end to the variety of interested buyers and sellers: military quartermasters, Port Authority stockpilers, individual brokers, freelancers, smugglers, Imperial praetors, and keiretsu provosts all staked out tables. On Letugia, free enterprise brought together the most disparate interests.

A wide variety of buyers leaned on the tables bartering for goods from incoming pilots to fill their storehouses. Middlemen and shipping agents scurried between the aisles, accepting bids and filling orders. Huge, leering bodyguards stood behind the procurement tables watching the transactions taking place with suspicious eyes.

Smugglers and legit freight haulers alike argued loudly with the buyers, middlemen, keiretsu agents, Imperial procurement officers, and consort brokers, seeking the best price for their goods. Contract traders milled about smoking thin thiretsen reeds, waiting for their employers to buy enough to fill their holds so they could lift. Many pilots took shipments offworld on spec, years of experience teaching them the intricate economic interdependencies of each system, knowing they could double or triple their investment on another world. Others hired out contractually, getting a set fee to haul a commodity from one planet to another regardless of the profit that shipment might fetch.

These pilots could care less about the constant dickering taking place on all sides. They merely sought the most lucrative bids, typically contracting out to one employer or keiretsu — powerful corporate entities that bonded together for protection and profit. Many operations kept their own stable of dependable pilots, seeking the fastest and most cunning men to deliver their goods without interference — what was legal in one system might be heavily taxed or forbidden in another. These keiretsu were highly competitive and constantly fought over trade routes and planetary monopolies—some blossoming into conflicts that drew whole star systems into play. As a result, some keiretsu had grown to control so many markets that they had become planet-sprawling socio-economic entities with the same complex interests and powerful naval forces as the political scions who aligned against them. Such brazen manipulation of inherent political weakness by militarized keiretsu would attract the attention and quick wrath of the Emperor in the galactic Core, but in Shell anything was possible. The Emperor's hand was only just beginning to be felt in the outer reaches.

Garrand angled toward the market's northwestern corner and a noise-generating fountain. His shipping agent on Letugia usually conducted business by a white noise field on the northern rim. He spotted three bounty hunters walking slowly through the crowd, sifting through faces, methodically working the aisles. Garrand carefully averted his eyes as they passed, remembering the Freetrader's adage: *A glance now, a victim later.*

He located the fountain, and near it, the tall, angular form of Jastin Epley leaning casually on a table edge. Garrand stepped up beside him. "Epley. Nice to see you again."

The thin man looked around suddenly, eyes flashing with recognition and whispered. "Don't call me 'Epley.' That name has too much publicity."

"Even on Letugia? Who knows you here?"

"You'd be surprised. Imperial agents are *everywhere.*" He spat out the words. "This new Regulatory Commission is just a cipher for Barrett's Imperial bully boys."

"Adjucates?" Garrand recalled his earlier run-in with the Trogand. The official *had* claimed Imperial allegiance.

"They're imposing ridiculous tariffs on established commodities. They're not even bothering with classifying new products as high yield, just levying taxes across the board. Ridiculous.

Absolutely killing me. I've had to get creative." He looked at a pair of Imperial officers nearby and lowered his voice. "Never know who might be listening. You know what the slorts are threatening to do? Bring in a full battalion strength force to 'Oversee Commercial Development' and enforce Imperial regulation. Already nationalized the mint and banks."

"That bad, huh? I had no idea."

"Might as well be an Imperial fiefdom. It's getting mighty hard to run a profitable business here."

"Sounds like it might be time to look elsewhere. Uh, look, this feels a bit ridiculous — what should I call you?"

"Feels ridiculous? Think I'm being paranoid? A man wearing light armor and concussion grenades in open market calls *me* paranoid. How do you like that?"

"Old habits…"

"Hmm, yes. The old days." He stroked the rough edge of his beard. "Something from the past will do."

"Sev?"

"That's fine."

"Well, Sev, tell me about that run to Vaheyle. Any chance you can get me a sanctioned contract?"

Sev laughed harshly. "Running medical supplies to anywhere *near* that system has been classified a treasonable offense. Imperial Provost is cracking down. Vaheyle will be the next to fall."

"I've run that gauntlet before."

"Imperial blockade?" Sev shook his head. "High risk, low yield."

"How about another drex shipment? I was thinking of making a couple of runs to Dalis. Profit in it, and if you fronted me—"

"Fronted you?"

"Yeah, my credit has almost dried up. Sev, you know I'm a good bet. Sounds safer than investing here now, things being the way they are."

"You're always a good bet, but I can't wait that long. I'm up for Imperial license review in ten days. I don't plan on being here—too many tracks to cover. I might have made a mistake somewhere that I don't know about. Or someone could have talked. Can't take that chance. I'm just hanging around to collect on a couple of shipments that I'm expecting—yours and three others. I'll be emigrating by the end of the week. Already liquidated my entire stock of dry goods, bartered the rest."

"I'm sorry to hear that."

"Yeah, I'll be sorry to leave, too. This rock has been good to me."

"Where will you go?"

Sev glanced around casually. "Oh, I hear the Lammini system is profitable these days. Look me up there in a few months."

Garrand nodded.

Sev clasped Garrand's hand tightly, genuinely. "I'd hate to be without the services of my finest pilot." The thin man smiled affectionately. "I was able to get a decent price for your drex shipment." Sev pressed a credit chit into his palm. "Enough to get you off-planet at least."

"Thanks, Sev." He pocketed the chit and the two men parted ways.

Garrand worked his way back through the market. He spied one of the Imperial officers from Epley's fountain angling ahead of him near the Gregaria Steps. A bounty hunter soon joined the man as he walked and Garrand saw the subtle movement of the officer's hand in his direction. So Epley's paranoia hadn't been so foolish. He paused by a vendor's booth of yetsen bottles, then ducked behind the next aisle. He headed toward a gap between the flickering lights, walking briskly through the evening crowd.

A man was following him. Garrand reached for the magnetic shield at his belt but hesitated before activating it. Technology had reached a curious crossroads in centuries past. Optical targeting had made weapons so efficient that it was almost dangerous to carry them because their power source was an easy target. The Ki Zentor package on his blaster was a case in point. The blaster's opticals detected surges in energy and pinpointed power sources: coils, shield generators, anything attached to the body with its own energy supply. Fed directly into the weapon's targeting system, a burst of fire in the general direction of a target could be redirected closer and closer to the power source until a hit was scored. Such hits were much more lethal as the destruction of the power source produced a secondary explosion usually proving fatal to the target.

Thus, there had been a resurgence of low-tech weaponry: blades, dart-throwers, simple projectile slings and body armor to combat those measures. To be effective, one had to eschew the latest advances and rely on physical prowess, cunning, and stealth. Garrand's survival depended upon a bladesman's speed and ruthlessness, a Freetrader's wile and instinct, and the ability to utilize and deliver a healthy dose of modern devastation at the proper moment.

The Guard had taught a three-tiered métier. The Old, the New, and what Bailey referred to in the Lalen tongue as *K'iik Vla*—the ability to survive at any cost. Garrand let his hand drop from his belt and stopped to casually inspect a serpent vendor's wares. His eyes flicked back across the street. The follower was a large man clothed in filthy robes, his hands hidden within its folds. He was edging closer, eyes hidden in the robe's hood.

It was too late for stealth, especially if there was more than one working together. Garrand ducked under the drab awning into the shop proper, quickly wending his way through the cases and their hissing occupants as he worked his way toward the back. He pushed past a protesting clerk in a back room and came out in a narrow alley and ran back to the street.

The large man was staring at the vendor's shop. *He might be wearing anything beneath all those robes*, Garrand thought. A shield generator would thwart his blaster, body armor would turn a dart, which left a blade as his final recourse.

Garrand drew his blade, a fiber composite alloy, its lusterless surface a smoky grey, and waited in the shadows for the trail to turn his head. He slipped back into the street, blade held *teirendat*—flush with his forearm—and stalked behind the robed man. Within meters of his target he dashed forward, keeled into the man's back as if stumbling, grasped the back of his neck and thrust him forward into the alley. The man spun but Garrand clipped his knee and lanced forward with his blade still held flush with his arm. Not wishing to kill him, Garrand completed the attack with the pommel. The blunt end hit the man squarely in his right eye socket, sending him staggering. The man clutched his face as Garrand aimed a kick at the side of his knee. The blow landed, the knee popped, and Garrand grasped a thick hem of robes as he toppled, collapsing on top of his chest. With his knees pinning each arm and a fistful of robes at his neck, Garrand wagged the point of the blade before the man's good eye.

"You've been following me a bit too closely." Garrand pressed the flat end of his blade against the man's inner earlobe and applied pressure. "Name?"

"Vhortikus," the man stammered, struggling under Garrand's grip. He looked anxiously past his shoulder to the street beyond.

"Expecting someone else?"

"No — no, I've been waiting. No."

"Waiting for what, Vhortikus? For me?"

"No, it's a mistake."

"For me?" Garrand shook the man violently and pressed the blade's sharp tip into the soft skin beneath the man's swollen eyes.

"No, please, no. I was just to follow you. Nothing else."

"Who hired you?"

"No one. She was no one."

She? Garrand let the tip of his blade waver. "How did you find me? What did she give you?"

"She gave me a holocube and a dock number. And a name."

"What name did she give you?"

"You were the only human who left the bay. It had to be you."

"The name!"

The man sputtered and tried to collect his tongue. "Are you 'Gair-und, rhymes with errand?'" the man winced as he tried to pronounce the name properly.

"I am Garrand Ai'Gonet Médeville, and what of it!"

"Nothing. I was just to follow you. Please. Just follow."

"And observe what?"

"Nothing."

"Follow me where?"

"She just wanted to know where you went."

Garrand realized he was approaching a circular logic route with this foul-smelling wretch. Pushing him would lead nowhere. He sighed and asked one last question: "How were you to communicate my position?"

"Com tab. She gave me a com tab, told me I could keep it after."

Garrand fished into the deep pockets of the man's robe. He quickly found the slender device and ripped it from the man's pocket: "This how you're going to contact your employer?"

The man bobbed his head once. "Are you going to kill me?'

"No, I'm not." The man seemed to relax at this news. Up close he was even filthier than he had first thought, and reeked of cheap slug wine. Garrand checked the man's neck for an ident-link and then searched him for identification. Nothing. Hired off the street for a routine tail and he'd botched it.

Garrand stood and took a deep breath as he surveyed the street beyond the alley. Someone else knew his name here. He had been foolish to assume otherwise.

"You'd best stay here for a while." Garrand stood and pointed his blade at the man. "Get my meaning?"

Vhortikus bobbed his head in the affirmative. Garrand sheathed his blade and slipped unobtrusively into the busy street, tossing the transmitter into a serpent's smeared showcase as he passed.

Il Touvé certainly offered little in the way of cultural entertainment, but if one persisted there were excellent restaurants to be found squirreled away in hidden or forgotten corners of the city. Years ago Garrand had found, quite by chance, one particularly good tavern near the southern docking threshold. It lay in one of the city's many played out districts full of rough buildings, empty warehouses and industrial sites. Gritty storefronts lined the streets, glazings unwashed and dull with dust, walls permanently etched with curious patterns by sandstorms. At the end of one alley a short series of steps led down to a massive oaken door. On rusty hinges above the entranceway swung a wooden sign with hand-wrought letters spelling out "The Oak Room."

Garrand passed quickly through the shadowed alley, careful not to direct his gaze toward the glowing eyes that peered out from black recesses on either side of the street. He descended the stairwell and paused reflexively to see if anyone followed before opening the tavern door. A delicious blend of aromas greeted him as he entered the warm, dark chamber. Low horizontal glazings let in just enough light to illuminate the richly-paneled interior. Tall booths and hard maple tables were scattered within the pleasingly murky confines. Garrand sucked in a deep breath, his demeanor easing in the warm familiarity.

The proprietor, Este Norfins, a small brown-furred Chellian, recognized Garrand and hastily skittered to the entrance to greet him.

"Ahh, Captain Médeville. You're back. So wonderful," he trilled, clasping his paws together, overcome. "It has been what — four cycles since we've seen you?" His beady black eyes sparkled as he looked to the ceiling trying to recall the exact number. "Too long. Far too long!"

Este's genuine greeting formed the base of Letugia's lure for Garrand and one of the reasons he'd agreed to ferry drex here to begin with. "It's always a pleasure Este." He looked toward the back of the room and nodded at the kitchen. "How's your wife?" he pulled at his now sweat-drenched tunic. "I wore a clean shirt this time."

"Oh, she is not cooking today," he said shaking his head and beaming. "She is expecting another litter any day now."

"Marvelous." Garrand flashed a smile, "More to help you run the family business, eh?"

"Yes, yes: the more the better. Now, please, I have your table ready for you." He put a short arm around Garrand's waist and ushered him to a warmly lit alcove in the back of the chamber. "What brings you to Il Touvé this time? A new shipment of dryexcellon, personal transport, or perhaps something more discreet?" he nudged Garrand's shoulder and gave him a conspiratorial wink. "Ah, but it doesn't matter. Enough about business, let me bring you a drink!" He bustled off to the bar.

Garrand watched with amusement, finally letting his shoulders relax now that he was safely seated in his favorite eatery. One of Este's children shuffled over with a tray and shyly offered a drink. He accepted the beverage with a lazy grin and the youngster scampered away. The frosty glass was filled with a greenish-white liquid, suffused with a rapidly expanding cloud of purple tendrils. He lifted the tall glass and drank deeply. The living portion of the drink attached itself to his taste buds and lingered well after the cloudy liquor had passed. He savored the warm sensation at the back of his throat and felt a brief shiver travel up his spine as the ruby tendrils slipped away. The wisps left a mercurial aftertaste and he licked the last drop of the cool elixir off his lips.

The pleasant sensation quickly evaporated as the room fell silent. Garrand's eyes snapped to a new figure sliding gracefully between the tables. Patrons inclined their heads to watch the slender woman pass, her desert robes billowing behind her. This could not be an accident. Only locals and a few adventurous captains knew of the Oak Room's existence and thus he felt safe here from other prying interests. Garrand dropped his hand casually to the blade at his hip.

The woman stepped to his table as he lowered his glass. Without invitation, she pulled out a chair and sat down across from him. She wore the traditional walde-robes of the Dígan people, but she was definitely not a native — not with pale skin and auburn hair. Her green eyes were brilliant against the grimy backdrop of dusty skin. With goggles set above her head and the robes much too sand-encrusted for a jaunt through the streets, she was obviously just in from the desert. He wrinkled his nose. She smelled a bit too musky, like the Qui he'd passed earlier in the street.

His eyes flicked to the door; no one else had followed her into the tavern. The woman was alone: bold or very dangerous. She had a detached look of arrogance, but her eyes sparkled with creative energy, as if she was amused at some hidden mischief.

Este rushed over. "Ahh, I see you have a guest, and such a lovely one at that! Why didn't you tell me you were expecting company?" The proprietor produced a short, stiff brush that he ran deferentially over the woman's robes, clucking lightly. One of his children hurried over with a lovely veil tinted violet and gold. He draped it over the woman's tangled hair. A bowl of hot lemon water was brought out for her to dip her fingers in, and several linen cloths. The woman ignored their ministrations, allowing the delicate veil to float to the floor.

Garrand felt anger well up in his throat. He did not abide rudeness.

The woman spoke in a crystal clear tone. "I'm Helen Tchelakov. I understand you have a ship for hire." She smiled thinly, though there was not even a hint of politeness in her tone.

Garrand dropped the woman's gaze and motioned for another drink. There was no doubt in his mind that this was the woman who had hired poor Vhortikus to follow him. Vhortikus with the shattered knee and useless eye. Was that the best she could do?

Este bustled over and handed Garrand another cold glass. Turning his attention to Helen he gushed, as though none of his careful attentions had been rebuffed, "And what may I bring you, dear one? Perhaps some splendid Gourtian wine?"

Este scratched his chin and frowned, remembering: "Or, I have a small reserve of Taken's root downstairs that is absolutely marvelous!"

"Nothing, thank you," the woman said without looking up.

"Oh you must have something," implored the proprietor. "You must be terribly thirsty!"

"The young lady will have what I am having." Garrand interjected with a forced smile, sending him away. "It's impolite to refuse a Chellian's offer of his native root wine. Especially when you're a guest in his establishment." Leaning over the table he intoned, "It's also foolish. Este makes a delightful Taken's cocktail."

"I understand you have a ship for hire," she repeated slowly with a hint of forced patience. She briefly pressed the tips of her fingers in the hot lemon water and against her face—leaving pale circles that stood out against her dusty skin. "I need someone to transport a small group of exotics."

Garrand frowned. Miss Tchelakov was being purposely rude. Was her intent to influence negotiations, or did she simply have no reason to care? She had interrupted him without introduction and patently ignored Este's warm hospitality. *She does not want to be here,* he reasoned. *Or she is on someone else's errand.* He would have to force her hand a bit. "I don't usually discuss business before dinner," he said briskly, looking past her to the kitchen.

"This is urgent."

Garrand took a long gulp of his drink.

Helen abruptly pushed her chair back and rose as if to leave. "If you're not interested, I understand. I'm sure you have *plenty* of work to keep you busy."

Garrand caught the hem of her robe. "Did I say I wasn't interested? Sit down Miss—"

"Tchelakov," she supplied, a serene smile appearing briefly as she turned back to the table.

"Please," he gestured to the chair. "It's been a long day, I'm just hungry."

"Well if you think you can forgo filling your stomach for a moment, this won't take long."

Garrand pushed his drink aside. "Fine." He reached into his leather satchel and removed a clipscanner. "Transport mission," he murmured in a bored tone. "What sort of exotics did you say?"

"I'd rather not discuss that right now," Helen said glancing around. The tavern was mostly empty, but patrons occupied some tables.

"And where would we be picking up these exotics?"

"I'd rather not say."

"And what system might we be taking these unmentionable creatures to?"

She replied flatly, "That's on a need to know basis."

Garrand pursed his lips together and activated the clipscanner. "No details, no embarkation point, no destination, no questions." He scrolled through a list of files before selecting one. He amended the file for a few moments and then turned the pad around and slid it across the table to face Helen. "This is my standard passage contract for bio transport. I assume they're carbon-based lifeforms, and oxygen breathing?"

Helen let his question hang in the air as she studied the clipscanner. She tapped in a few figures and data, barely detailing the mission profile, then spun the tablet back around.

"They'll be suspended during flight, " Garrand remarked, glancing over the passage contract. "You have animation chambers, of course."

Helen slowly blinked and sucked in the corners of her mouth. "The genetic engineering of this species does not make it prudent to engage them in extended sleep periods."

Garrand set the clipscanner on the table and shoved it toward the woman. "Thirty-seven unspecified creatures loose on my ship for a voyage of indeterminate length? I command a cruiser, not a menagerie. This is going to affect the price." He did not smile.

"You don't have to worry about them," the woman said, reaching for the clipscanner. As she leaned forward her loose hair rippled down and brushed his arm. Garrand jerked at the unexpected touch and eased his arm away. The woman did not seem to notice as she tapped a new figure into the contract.

"They spend most of their time dreaming. Even while awake."

"Dreaming?" Garrand was startled. "That implies sentience."

"Oh, don't be concerned, it gives them a lazy look that buyers find quite attractive."

"I don't haul slaves and I generally shoot slavers for good measure," he growled.

"Captain, do I look like a slaver?"

He took a long look at her. She was slender and delicate with soft freckles and small, fine-boned hands. Her gaze belied intelligence, but her demeanor exuded arrogance. She seemed annoyed at him for daring to have dinner in his favorite restaurant. She was trouble, but she did not look like any slaver he had ever seen.

"You can show me proper title for now. We get to where these exotics are and I'll see for myself if they're willing to be transported. If I have any doubts, the deal's off, contract is voided, and you forfeit my fee. *And* the cargo."

"Fair enough."

Her even response calmed his fears. "So, are they sentient?"

"Oh, they're intelligent, but self-awareness is another thing…"

Garrand frowned at her avoidance. He picked up the revised contract. It shimmered across the viewscreen. "This cargo sounds more complicated than you're letting on."

"This cargo is precious," she said. Her manner changed from callous nonchalance to something at once both hard and imploring. "I cannot afford for anything to happen to them."

I can see that. Finally a bit of truth seeps out, he thought. The creatures needed to survive in her eyes. Were they to be bargaining chips for something further down the line? The woman seemed to be skipping over the whole negotiation process. Her thoughts were elsewhere. Further down the line in her plans.

"If anything should go wrong, it would be very expensive."

Deadly expensive, thought Garrand as he watched the woman try to shake off her warning by forcing one of her former smiles. He scanned the mission profile. The job seemed simple enough on the surface: a regular bio transport with some accommodation difficulties. *Thirty-seven of the creatures awake for the entire journey?* Hidden complexities and dangers lurked beneath the surface of the simple transport. She had, of course, sought him out. *If this was a legitimate transport why wasn't she using the standard Imperial freighters, or commercial delivery for that matter?* He scanned her counteroffer and smiled politely.

"Considering what you haven't told me, I think this number is more appropriate." He tapped in a new number and turned it to face her.

The woman glanced at it and back at him. "This could be considered outright thievery."

"Hardly." He waited for her counter-offer but she just stared at him with her piercing green eyes. A loose strand of hair fell across her face and for a brief moment he felt an almost irresistible urge to lean across the table and brush it out of her face. She immediately picked up the shift in his attention and averted her gaze.

"This will do." She said quietly. She touched a red node on the side of the clipscanner and pricked her finger to establish her genetic identity. Once confirmed, she notched acceptance of the contract and inserted a credit chit into the device.

"Do you want a receipt for your down payment?"

"That won't be necessary." She gathered her cloak and headwrap. "Have *Destiny's Needle* prepped and preflight worked up by oh-four-hundred. I'll join you at the dock's eastern portal at three forty-five local. Goodbye Captain."

Garrand watched her depart with an uneasy feeling forming in his stomach. She hadn't asked for the docking bay's coordinates because she already knew where it was. She knew where he liked to dine. And adding to his worries was her easy acceptance of his outrageous fee. It was as if Miss Tchelakov had simply gone through the motions of contractual dickering, having made up her mind before she ever sat down. Perhaps she was embarrassed to admit she didn't want to part with her animal wards, regardless of their intelligence. Well that wouldn't happen to him. They'd be locked in the hold, dreaming animal dreams, and he would finally have the resources to pick and choose his missions.

This thought pushed his concerns aside. Whatever the dangers, this was a fantastic contract and Bailey would be thrilled. He motioned Este Norfins for another drink.

6

Outside Prerogative

Vice Proctor Hellius Barrett stalked through the Imperial Battle Cruiser *Shiva* flanked by two guards in wraparound sheaths of ghilli shimmer silk, breasts embroidered with the crest of the Imperial dragon. Blue light strips reflected dimly from the guards' ashen helmets. Sharpened spires curved down the back of their necks like dragon scales. They carried long Verkhi glaives, the points lowered to a nearly horizontal position in the low-ceilinged serviceway. Ship's crew gave the trio wide berth.

Barrett stopped outside a chamber and listened. Heavy drumbeats rocked the walls of warfare practice room 865. Something sensual and dangerous lurked in the rhythm, something as forbidden as the code seven encryption on the entry-lock, which Barrett easily accessed. The doors slid down to a dim, smoke-filled room of mirrors that buckled with the force of the sound waves. Lights flashed in time to the drumbeats. In one corner of the otherwise empty room a woman spun in the air, her lithe body undulating in opposition to the relentless pattern of the drums. Her flint-black hair swung out with the many trailing ends of her wispy garment.

For a moment the vice proctor watched, enjoying the rare spectacle of his charge. He knew that even regular movement was complicated in Stiglian repulsor wraps. The Simonean dance required extraordinary athletic prowess, balance and an impeccable sense of three-dimensional orientation. Barrett could feel excitement growing in his belly; this elite weapon had *asked* to work under his Command, had *requested* to be commissioned on the obscure band of destroyers which patrolled Carinaena's Shell, far from the Emperor's Court and favor. The amazing thing was that the Bordëgian had not discovered the remarkable depth of this individual and assigned her to the Emperor's Guard on Daulinbêres. Barrett had looked into her recreational activities and made the inevitable conclusion that here was a prize whose loyalty was worth securing at all costs.

The drums slowed to a languid, sluggish plodding. Flashing lights widened into gently roving spots, painting the woman's smooth thighs and long limbs with color as she curved from one agonizingly slow somersault to another, until surely she must be senseless with dizziness. Three final drumbeats stretched the woman out on her back. Her arms were stretched over her head and her chest heaved from the exertion. Her perfect white skin glistened with sweat, and her long black hair reached nearly to the deck. There she floated in heavy silence, the spotlights flooding her supple body in a blinding light. Fog rose and shielded her. All lights faded out. The Simonean Ceremony had ended.

In the darkness, Barrett clapped with pleasure. The room lights came on again, though at the normal, stark practice level this time. The captain of his Imperial Guard stood directly in front of him, close enough to have cut his throat.

"Well done," Barrett smiled as Vailetta Strom snapped to military attention. *How could she have moved so quickly?* "You are to be commended."

"Thank you, my Lord. It is but a little thing," replied the young woman in a formal answer, her head bowed.

"Nonsense, Vailetta. How many of the Gokazoku could perform the Simonean Dance?" With one hand he airily traced her filmy garment. Vailetta turned her head, her eyes narrowing.

"My Lord, I am ready for duty."

Barrett laughed congenially and stepped back. "I agree. I think we can move you into position soon." He turned to leave.

"Commander, what is that duty to be?" She relayed eagerness.

Barrett paused in the doorway without turning around. "Patience, Vailetta. The music is still being composed. Rest assured you will be one of the principal instruments."

Vailetta stared at his back. She had been prepared for the last two years.

"Well, come along Captain Strom. We are at the crux of obtaining our new priorities. Since they will be in your charge, from now on you answer only to me." He strode out of the chamber.

Vailetta grabbed her small rucksack and pulled a long sweater over her costume. She quickly matched the vice proctor's stride.

Barrett glanced at the young woman and felt a sense of elation. All the very best answered to him. He was collecting the Shell's priceless treasures, one by one. Planet by planet. Person by person. This woman was a rare bird, one that dared challenge him openly! It was bracing and audacious, particularly from such a young soldier. And in the field of battle she was as deadly as she was beautiful. It was perfect. With the success of this mission, there would be no one who could oppose him successfully, no one who did *not* answer to him.

"Lord Barrett?" A young lieutenant in a brightly-colored shipsuit swung into step with the vice proctor. He bore the orange crested dragon of Intelligence sewn across his sleeve.

"What is it?"

"Nralda activity report, my Lord. A prime keiretsu operative was followed to Letugia, and the report created some interesting spikes in the sartographic models tracking the creatures whereabouts."

"Letugia?" Barrett raised his eyebrows.

"Yes, my Lord, in the Nepestar system. The Nralda agent was observed hiring a ship for transport in Il Touvé. The report has created sartographic ripples; I thought you should be informed. We are having interesting probability spikes in the models supportive of the Outside Prerogative theory."

"The Outside Prerogative, eh?"

"Yes, my Lord, as you know it's one of the theories I developed myself."

Barrett glanced at the young man. He was barely old enough to grow whiskers. How did they continue to find such remarkable young men in this far-flung vacuum? "Indeed. I believe your work on the Prerogative has created a whole new subcategory of variants."

"It has, my Lord." In fact, the hunt for the Tchelakov creatures had consumed the combined intellectual brainpower of every mathematician and theoretical physicist that Barrett could command, and whole new theoretical avenues were being forged in the science of probabilities in the process. It had never been attempted before. How did one mathematically approach the task of hunting down creatures that could already predict their own future?

Barrett paused to speculate: *What must it be like to construct flawless sartographic models with outcomes of one hundred percent certainty?* He sighed internally.

"The Outside Prerogative theory happens to be one of my favorites," Barrett admitted casually. The young lieutenant's face flushed with color. "It rivals your work in your 4th Tier Physics Decay Masters Finals. Theorem 17 was in fact, a revelation. I had a scribe carve the algorithm into the slate beside cage 17 outside my quarters." This news was almost too much for the officer. His eyes widened at the news that his commander thought so highly of his advanced theoretical work. He had no idea that his commander was a student of probability science, with such a keen eye for mathematical physics decay.

"My lord, if one makes the causal leap that the Prerogative is now in play—which I know is not yet a conclusion by collected data—but if we grant that this line of reasoning is now a cogent path, the models leap to a gross acceptance conclusion."

Barrett stopped walking. Hallway traffic flowed respectfully around them. "Gross acceptance of what?"

The lieutenant swallowed visibly. "If the Prerogative is elevated to even a 21 percent likelihood, then the intel from Letugia creates a GAC that the Nralda agent is using this vessel to retrieve our targets."

Barrett turned away quickly, stunned by the news. He took a long look at his guards, noting the subtle details of their regimental uniforms, and allowed his nervous system to regain emotional balance. It was lovely how the long hairs were glued so perfectly down the guard's helms. Complete and total precision. Barrett turned to Vailetta and studied the way her sweater draped over her shoulders, imagining the curves of her ample breasts now hidden beneath the soft fibers. He allowed a rare smile to grace his lips. A gross acceptance conclusion that *this* was the ship the Nralda planned to use to retrieve the Tchelakov Creatures. They were back on the scent again. *Cheplus! They now had direct contact with the vessel that would be used to move the creatures? Perfect.*

Barrett turned to the young man, eyes flashing. "So if we make the causal leap that your Outside Prerogative theory is indeed a future event that has yet to transpire, then this ship would not have a keiretsu registry, would it?"

The young man smiled. "No, my Lord. The ship was contracted independently, it isn't one of their standard vessels."

"I would think that would explain the beginning of your spike supportive of Prerogative."

"Indeed. But the operative in question hasn't piqued the Sartoks interest. The inclusion of her details did not ripple the models; they remained curiously flat."

"Did Intel provide you with an image?"

The officer produced a holocube. Barrett accepted the device and flicked the power stud with his fingernail. A stranger joined them, a beautiful young woman in traditional desert garb, reddish hair poking out beneath a headwrap. Barrett smiled quietly to himself. He well knew the reason why the Sartoks did not budge with Helen Tchelakov's emergence. "Excellent work, Lieutenant. And the ship's captain?"

The young man produced a second recording. Barrett pocketed the first cube and activated the second. He stared for a long moment at the likeness, frowning. He'd seen this image before.

"Name?"

"Médeville—first name unknown."

Barrett paused at the sound of the name and turned to face the officer.

"No known aliases. Intel tags him as a local Freetrader and mercenary. No keiretsu markers. No outstanding Imperial Writs. He's had some minor run-ins with a few of the locals in Nepestar System, but we don't have much more than that."

The young man waited deferentially. "Do you know this man, my Lord?"

"Hmm."

"There is one character amendment to the file. First mate is an art, a Varsis model, originally an Imperial commission—one of the few survivors of the Gai'han Jihad. It is not bound to the ship or its captain, there's no marker issued."

"So the machine is no longer Imperial property," Barrett noted evenly.

"Ai'Gonet produced certification of the art's free will at some point. No telling what it's doing out here. Plus it's a little unusual with a Freetrader. They don't usually take to arts. Not Imperial ones, at least."

"The Nralda have hired a renegade captain with no keiretsu ties and his first mate is a Varsis art of Imperial manufacture?" Barrett squinted into the rafters. The mention of the art triggered something in his memory.

"Is there a name listed for the vessel?"

The lieutenant consulted his datapad, humming. "I believe it's called—ah, yes, here it is. *Destiny's Needle*." He glanced back to the vice proctor. "Does that mean something to you, my Lord?"

"Ahh, *Destiny's Needle*. Of course…" An edifying smile smoothed Barrett's lips: the floodgates of memory had opened.

"My Lord?" Vailetta grew impatient.

"Do you keep abreast of the history of Guardian sects other than the noble Gokazoku, Captain?"

"History, my Lord?"

"Or should I say, popular myth? You are, of course, aware of the Griffin?"

"The Brotherhood of the Princes of Blood—an esteemed House of the Guard, renowned and honored for centuries in the protection of the Emperor and his Proctors."

"Then perhaps you'll recall the Sardis Incident some dozen years ago."

The Sardis Incident. Even growing up in the cloistered protection of Daulinbêres, deep in the safe and civil Core worlds and seat of the Imperial Throne, she had heard of the *Stanzer* rescue at Sardis. As a child, she thought the stories to be exaggerated to the point of myth.

Barrett swung back to the lieutenant. "Have Intel pull a priority red dragon, silver-seal file on a Garrand Ai'Gonet Médeville, former Captain of the Griffin Imperial Guard, dishonorable discharge, on my authority. Have them send the final encryption clearance code to my chambers. I'll key in the final sequence myself."

"As you will, my Lord."

Barrett resumed walking with Vailetta at his heels. "Interesting choice," he murmured.

❖ ❖ ❖

SMOKE AND INCENSE SWIRLED THROUGH THE BUSY ALLEYWAY mingling with the sharp taste of dust, sparks of smoldering coals stirred by vendors, dried bits of lachis dung, and the perpetual winds that coursed through Letugia. The pungent textures of the different aromas assaulted Helen's senses, reminding her of the exotic caravans of Thistle, of warm, happy infant days. Without knowing why, she stopped in front of a street vendor's table, eyes drawn by an elaborate crimson candle that wrapped itself around an ornate, sculpted serpent. The smell of scented wax triggered a memory of her father's study where she had played among the wax-bound papers in the years before his success, before the Nralda had discovered them. Before the darker days.

Helen glanced up at the wrinkled crone who sat serenely behind the table, patiently watching her. "It reminds you of the past, no?" The ragged quality of the old woman's voice made her sound even more ancient than she appeared, but there was something else there, a confidence of tone that seemed unwarranted.

Helen stared at the old woman for a long moment, still reflecting on her father. The corner of her mouth twitched into the beginnings of a smile at the memory, but she fought to suppress the thought.

Wincing noticeably, the woman leaned slowly across the table and pushed the candle toward Helen, nodding her head. "For you. It calls out to the sad one. Take it."

Helen stiffened and started to turn away.

The crone persisted. "It honors the memory of your father, my dear. Take it."

Helen's eyes narrowed. "My father," she snapped, "Is still alive. You'd best keep your mind out of my thoughts."

The old woman leaned back in her chair, palms held up in contrition. Her voice took on a grating edge, "Reminiscing, eh? Of days when you were true to him?" Her eyebrows arched up, punctuating the accusation.

Helen snorted in disgust. *Wretched psychic hag.* The woman's eyes took on a wounded look as though she understood.

She stalked away, picking her way through the throngs of people and creatures, trying not to hurry — blending in with the masses as best she could. She paused to watch an eel skinner display his wares to three curious vegrauts. The short, heavyset man chattered rapidly in a clipped dialect, spreading a silvery, grey skin smooth across his table. The vegrauts argued amongst themselves, gesturing to the skin.

Helen melted back into the flow of foot traffic, following a group of ackriveldt tourists. She took a circuitous path through the back streets and alleys of the city, doubling back often to throw off any shadows she might have unknowingly picked up.

The crowds thinned as she entered the commercial shipping district. Consulting her bracer for direction, she continued into the private sector. Helen stopped across the street from docking bay 247B and purchased a mug of janda from a vendor, studying the bay's main gate and the narrow street as she sipped the steaming broth. No one appeared to be loitering suspiciously, nor watching the entrance. She glanced at the chronometer on her bracer and quickly crossed the street.

The access was locked, naturally, and she punched the query button, requesting admittance. After a moment, the gate rolled open and Helen was greeted by an artificial — an old Varsis model by the looks of him. He gazed warmly at her with beautiful amber eyes and gestured her to follow. He was a wonder to behold: the Krellian designers had never topped themselves after the Varsis line. This one possessed a sleek, art nouveau cut with motions much smoother than a human's.

"Who are you?" she asked.

"First mate aboard *Destiny's Needle*."

"No, your name."

The artificial turned his head as he walked. "I am known as Bailey, Miss Tchelakov, and I'm quite pleased to make your acquaintance. The captain has told me all about you. I believe he's quite excited about our journey."

"I'll bet he is." Helen found herself smiling. She felt immediately safer in the art's presence.

Garrand walked down the ship's boarding ramp as they approached, wiping his hands with a filthy rag. "Well, what do you think?" he asked, his eyes sweeping over the ashen surface of the hull that stretched well out over his head.

"This is impressive," said Helen as she finally got a close up look at *Destiny's Needle*.

"Thank you."

She gazed in disbelief at the irregular design of the cruiser. It took the shape of an elongated crescent, with twin prows sweeping far ahead of the curved hull on each side like a tightly-bent boomerang. The forward superstructures curved back toward each other like giant pincers. The aft sub-light conversion coils were huge, and she could not immediately discern the meaning of all the ungainly bumps and bulges that marred the ship's lines like blisters.

"What's that?" she pointed to the elongated needle point of a particle cannon that dominated the architecture of the port superstructure.

"Oh, we scavenged that off a derelict destroyer a few years back. Bailey and I designed the whole ship around it. Takes up a lot of space and adds a lot to her tonnage, but she packs a heck of a punch." The size of the weapon was grossly disproportionate to the rest of the ship's design. It looked like some huge lance extending well forward of the elongated prow, giving the ship a jaunty, dangerous appearance.

"Not bad, eh?" he beamed proudly.

Men and their ships. "Yeah, It's a wonder it flies at all."

Garrand frowned, "Pretty paint jobs and sparkling armor isn't what gets you from point to point, Miss Tchelakov. Avoidance of 'outside interference' as it is termed in our contract is an art form augmented by creative ship design. Spit and polish don't hold much stock out here in the Shell," he snorted in derision as his eyes swept across the filthy interior of the docking bay. He nodded back at his ship and murmured, "It's what's inside that counts."

"Well the inside had better be spectacular."

"You hired me for a reason," Garrand scowled. "If you'd rather lift in some fat, glossy scow, there's a commercial freighter departing every fifteen minutes."

"No, this will have to do," Helen shook her head. "But now I'm *sure* I overpaid you." She walked stiffly up the boarding ramp.

Garrand turned to Bailey, muttering, "And it's a good thing, too, for what we're going to have to put up with for the next few cycles."

Bailey followed the captain up the ramp. Just inside the airlock Garrand heard the muffled squeak of a tiny hiccup. He turned back. "Bailey did you hear that?" The artificial shifted in an almost nervous way.

"To what are you referring, sir? My aural processors can detect nothing wrong with the ship. Perhaps it was the wind."

"No, it's not the wind. There it is again."

"Surely it's nothing."

"*Destiny*—give me a full sweep in here immediately."

A cool voice responded, "Please define parameters of search."

"Just the interior of the airlock and mess."

"Yes, Captain. Reading two life forms in the gateway."

"Two? *Destiny*, what's the form other than myself?"

"It appears to be mammalian, Captain. Perhaps I'll have more data in a moment."

"*Where* is it?"

"I believe I can tell you, sir," Bailey said, his eyes downcast.

"Well, why all this nonsense about the wind? Wait, not again. There'd better not be a—"

"It's just an exel, sir. Not large at all. I know you don't like *large* animals. Maybe a *little* one, though, might change your mind." Bailey opened the sack he carried and removed a hairy, calico-mottled ball with three button eyes and six legs that disappeared into the hair as the captain shouted.

"Get that fluff off my ship!"

"But, sir! I promise to take care of all his needs! I'll feed him and brush him and take away his waste products," Bailey scooped the longhaired bundle into his arms and followed Garrand up the serviceway.

"I don't understand this behavior, Bailey. When you said you wanted to alter your protective protocols, I thought you were talking about defensive countermeasures. This is an altogether different subroutine."

"This is important to me, sir."

"Captain," interrupted *Destiny's Needle*, "I might remind you that Bailey has never asked you for anything before."

Garrand shook his head, "That's ridiculous, he always wants something." Bailey's shoulders drooped and the interior workings of his chest faded to purple. "Bailey it's just that it's another *life*. You can't recharge it or power it down. It's real."

"Yes, sir, I've compiled all the available data on exels. I know how to care for it." At that moment the exel gave another squeaky hiccup that bounced it in the artificial's arms.

"Oh," Bailey said with concern. "We'll have to do something about that."

"To see you mothering now, no one would ever suspect you trained me to kill," Garrand muttered and scraped a streak of grease off his trousers.

"There's really quite a degree of similarity in the tasks, my research shows that persistent protectant reflexes—"

"Okay, okay—you can keep it."

"Sir!" Bailey swung the exel above his head. It hiccupped again, and Garrand bit his lip with a grimace.

"One mess up!" Garrand warned, "Just one and he, she—whatever it is—is out! Do you understand?"

"Yes sir, quite."

"Go put it in quarters. And do something about those hiccups."

"Yes sir, of course sir! Come with Bailey, now, little creature. Oh, we're going to be such great friends. The captain will see. He'll soon like you as well as I! And wait until Little Bit sees you, he'll be so excited—someone new for him to play with!"

Garrand watched as Bailey bustled away, the exel under his precisely crooked arm. As soon as his companion had turned the corner he sank wearily against the nearest cargo lighter.

Outside the ship, in the shadows of the docking bay, a dark shape coalesced and slipped unseen through the main gate, disappearing into the streets of Letugia.

7
Destiny Departs

Little Bit rolled smoothly end over end through *Destiny's* narrow corridor, his burnished skin reflecting the dim lamps and the occasional red flash of glowing nodes set in the bulkhead as he passed. He navigated the curving hallway flawlessly, tiny pseudopods jutting out at just the right moment to correct his course and compensate for momentum. With a greeting chirp he slowed to a graceful stop at the captain's feet and rested momentarily on three slender rods.

Garrand looked down at the artificial and raised his eyebrows as if to say, "Yes?"

Little Bit straightened up on his pistons and let loose a long rumbling groan which ended in a whump as he let himself collapse back to the deck.

"Rest of the cargo's all secure? Good." He nodded toward the auxiliary ramp behind Little Bit. "As soon as Miss Tchelakov has finished stowing her gear aboard, we should be ready."

Little Bit swiveled his receptor node quickly to the rear and let loose a squeal of surprise as he saw Helen leaning over a floating cargo pallet and rolled backward, clanging into Garrand's knee.

"Easy there fella. She didn't mean to sneak up on ya." He patted the crown of his polished cupola.

The artificial reset his rods and opened a four-centimeter circular portal just above his equatorial divisor. A thin, spindly arm snuck out — jointed in three places. The tiny forcep fingers at the tip held a small white chamois cloth. He whistled in annoyance and proceeded to wipe a greasy smudge off his lustrous dome.

"Hey, I thought you saw her," he said, raising his palms defensively. "I don't think she's going to mind a little dirt."

Little Bit twirled his upper receptor band back toward Garrand and squawked.

"Really, I don't think she cares. I mean, look at me." He gestured to himself, indicating the oily smears across his trousers and rumpled tunic.

This garnered a long series of indignant burps and blats from Little Bit. With a snort, the arm withdrew, the receptor band faded to grey and he rolled back off the way he had come, continuing to chatter.

"What was that all about?" Helen asked, pausing to wipe her brow with the back of her sleeve.

"Nothing. I don't think he saw you there."

"Odd little thing."

"He doesn't like it when people sneak up on him."

"A skittish tech art?"

Garrand shrugged.

"When are we leaving?" she asked, pulling a long glistening case off a hovering cargo lighter.

"We're almost ready to lift, just waiting for clearance."

"Good." She stacked the polished case atop the rest of her gear. The side of the case was marked 'fragile: vaccines.'

Garrand looked on uncertainly. "I filed a false flight plan for Hentook. What course should I really lay in?"

"We're headed for the Dell Transim system."

"Dell Transim?" He chewed at his lip trying to place the name; it finally came to him. "There's nothing there. A few illegal dumping facilities, maybe, but mostly just farms. Huge agro caritus—supply most of the produce for the Imperial Third fleet I think."

"We have to pick up dirt."

"Excuse me. Did you say dirt?" Garrand didn't sound angry. An almost mischievous grin crept across his face as he watched her fumble with her cases. He wondered whether he should offer his assistance. Best not to antagonize her further, not yet at least. He watched her struggle with the heavy gear, stubbornly refusing to *ask* for help.

"That's right, dirt." She heaved a case over the edge of the railing and let out a whoosh of breath. She pulled back a loose lock of hair that seemed to always fall just in front of her left eye, tickling her nose as it curled upwards. "In the Dell Transim system. Gort's Agro Supply on Kess. It's a backwater planet, mostly caritus, like you said, but the dirt's good. Bandin Gort doesn't strip it of all the minerals like some—nice and rich. And the prices are reasonable."

"For dirt?" Garrand sounded incredulous.

"That's right, for dirt." She took a short breath and leaned down to grapple with the next case.

"Reasonable prices for dirt?" Garrand couldn't quite get it through his head that she was serious.

"Yes Garrand. Dirt is very expensive in some parts, and we need good dirt. Now don't you have some work to do or something, like maybe getting this ship off the ground?"

"Bailey's quite capable of doing the pre-flight. I just want to make sure I'm getting this straight. You want me to set course for the Dell Transim system?"

"Yeah, Dell Transim," she grunted lifting the next heavy grey case. "It's on the way; we'll only lose two days, maybe only one if this bird's as fast you claim she is—and if we ever get going."

"To pick up a load of dirt?"

"Yes, dirt!"

Garrand uncrossed his arms and straightened up from the wall to lean over the railing. "How much dirt are we talking about here?"

Helen looked up from her labor and wrinkled her nose—the loose hair had fallen across her face again, but her hands were full. She blew a quick blast of air through her lips to try to dislodge the errant curl. "Enough to provide a good base for a root system in the aft cargo hold. I'd say about thirty-six hundred cubic meters should do it." She heaved the case over the railing.

Garrand bobbed his head contemplatively as if this all made perfect sense to him. "Thirty-six hundred cubic meters," he said thoughtfully. "That's a lot of dirt." He pursed his lips and did some quick calculations. "Enough to fill the aft hold with

30 centimeters. Is that going to be loose with air pockets, like it's just been dug up out of the ground? And what's the relative moisture content per cubic meter?"

"If you're trying to figure out the mass, you don't have to worry. The dirt and the grass are well within *Destiny's* tonnage capacity. I've done all the calculations."

"Oh good, good. That makes me feel a lot better," he said sarcastically. "As long as you've done the calculations, why should I even worry about it? Maybe you'd like to fly us there too!"

"Don't tempt me."

"And when, may I ask, did you plan on telling me about this little addendum to our itinerary?"

"I'm telling you now, aren't I?"

Garrand took a long breath and tried not to let his anger and weariness get the best of him. It was late, he'd been awake for nearly two days standard now by ship's time and his senses weren't at their peak. He desperately needed a hot mug of Jean-Wa's spiced janda.

"Miss Tchelakov, there are acceptable ways of creating amendments and addendums to shipping contracts. I know that 'no questions asked' is a tacit understanding in our agreement, which is also reflected in the price—"

"I should say so!"

"However, I can't imagine that procuring a shipment of dirt from Gort's Agro Supply in the Dell Transim system is much of a security risk, and common courtesy would dictate that—"

"Spare me the injured routine, Captain. The less you know about this mission, the less chance you'll make a stupid mistake and give away our destination."

Garrand frowned, hurt that she would consider *him* a security risk.

"I've told you as little as possible, so that in your innocence you would be unable to leave any unfortunate clue behind that might indicate our true destination. In fact, I would suggest that you run a full diagnostic sweep once we've lifted; there may be tracking devices already planted aboard."

Garrand's face turned white as a ghost, then began to flush ruddy with blood. "Tracking devices? Aboard *my* ship!"

"Yes, it's possible; once we're underway we can make a dedicated search."

Garrand ground his teeth together. "By K'ye, we won't wait 'till then! *Destiny!*"

"Yes, Captain?"

Helen shook her head and interjected, "It won't do any good now. What if something is planted after the sweep? We have to wait until we're clear of Letugia before we can be sure. Besides, a sweep will take hours."

She was right, but he hated the thought that someone might have tampered with his ship.

"Captain?" *Destiny's Needle* asked patiently.

"Have you been monitoring this conversation?"

"That would be impolite, Captain."

"Have you or haven't you!"

"Well I may have had a spare pickup left on."

Helen rolled her eyes.

"Well, after we lift I want you to set up a full search pattern for an internal sweep."

There was a slight pause, as if the ship were considering this. "You know how I hate sensor sweeps, Captain."

"I'll have none of that! Maybe you'd rather have some foreign object stuck deep within your power conduits, bleeding off your energy, tapping into your datacore—"

"Point taken, Captain. There's no need to be rude. The parameters will be set up as you requested. May I request that you follow the prescribed protocols for invasive surgery? Sterilizing all equipment with class two radiation sweeps and notifying me of all—"

"We'll be careful," Garrand interrupted. "Of course we'll be careful." He shot a glance back at Helen, his lips curling back almost into a snarl. "Maybe you'd like to tell me who is so interested in this innocent little transport of yours that they'd go to the considerable trouble and danger of rigging a trace on *my* ship?"

"I didn't say I was sure we'd be traced—it's just a possibility. And I don't know who specifically; these animals are very valuable, there's any number of factions who'd kill for them." The captain did not look impressed, so she tried a different tack. "Why do you think I came to you?" Garrand continued to stare at her, shoulders stiff, eyes narrowed in anger. "Look, I promise I'll fill you in on all the details as soon as we're safely off-planet. But the sooner we get out of here, the sooner we can sweep the ship and put both of our minds at ease." She could tell that this did not completely sooth his fears, nevertheless he turned on his heel and stalked off, dictating commands into his comtab.

❖ ❖ ❖

HELEN COULD FEEL THE SHIP'S INTERNAL HARMONICS VIBRATE through her boots as the main reactors warmed to life. She gave a last long look across the restraining webs that held the silvered casings of her gear snugly against the far wall. With a sigh, she let the door to her quarters slide shut and locked it, proceeding forward through the poorly-lit corridor to the ship's central wardroom—a combination mess hall and technical display station.

A long hallway extended forward from the central mess to the bridge. The narrow hall sloped upwards, its length filled with a series of long shallow steppes that curved along the strangely glowing walls. Climbing through the curling hall Helen had the uneasy feeling that she was climbing up through the extended neck of some enormous beast that had swallowed her intact. She shook her head clear of the childish image of being trapped within a terrible dragon.

She stood before the bridge access door and paused to straighten herself, pulling the loose hair back over her ears and brushing at her bangs impatiently with a flattened palm. She took a deep breath and wiped her hands across her hips to dry them. The door swept into the ceiling at her touch, revealing the imposing darkness of the bridge. She stepped forward and stopped suddenly as she caught her breath, standing dumbfounded for nearly a minute as she stared at the slowly spinning machinery before her.

The bridge itself seemed to be encased within a crystal globe. Four command stations floated within the glistening walls like half-opened pods. The command stations hung above, below, and to both sides of Helen's position. A hardened crystal shell encompassed the bridge, affording a stunning view in nearly all directions. Thin struts curved along the interior of the globe's circumference, connecting at both poles like latitudinal lines. Dedicated command and tactical stations swung freely within the voluminous space—each seemingly acting under its own unique gravity center.

The bridge seemed to be designed for a crew of four, though she could see how two could easily manage the interactive setup. Each station was encased in luminous displays with three-dimensional projections floating above the consoles. Garrand seemed to have command, navigation and internal systems displayed, while Bailey's station hovering below and to one side clearly had defensive status boards, astral maps, and threat analysis readouts in view.

Helen stood on a balcony overlooking four rotating acceleration couches, each surrounded by an array of data relays and display boards. As she looked on in disbelief, an empty station pod spun across the crystal globe, and smoothly stopped at the edge of her platform. A railing retracted, two display boards swung to one side and the acceleration couch swiveled to admit her. She stepped uncertainly forward and sat. The railing slid back into place, the datascreens hummed to life, glowing with color and information, and the whole station suddenly swung away from the entrance and across the longitudinal axis. Reflexively she grabbed the armrests to steady herself as her perspective rapidly changed, but she found it was unnecessary; the station was indeed influenced by its own individual gravity, for she was now leaning precariously forward and partially upside down from her previous perspective, yet still sat comfortably against the couch.

"You're just in time, we've been given clearance to lift." Garrand said.

Helen was awestruck. "This is beautiful." From her new position she had a clear vantage of the entire ventral half of the ship. It glowed eerily in the moonlight, strangely alive.

Garrand smiled and continued to tap glowing pressure points on the central board.

"You designed *this*?"

He nodded.

She slowly began to regain her bearings. "Why is the bridge extended so far forward, and set so far to starboard?"

"Offset the weight of the matter cannon," Garrand replied.

"Why not center it?"

"It was too large—would have had to split the cargo holds to port and starboard. It was more important to line up the holds on the centerline. We have three holds, fore, mid, and aft, but they all lie on the ship's central axis. Having the holds centered keeps us from having to make complicated calculations and perform a lot of switching about to keep the payloads evenly dispersed.

"You'd be amazed how much time and effort most paymasters spend getting the 'cargos balanced.' For a two-man operation like this one, I needed simplicity. With the holds the way they are, Bailey and I can load up almost any cargo without consulting mass and volume scales—we just hover 'em in and strap 'em down, working from the center of the hold out. We can carry multiple cargoes for different parties simply and efficiently with as little down time spent shifting and loading as possible."

"Makes sense."

"But doing that meant we had to offset the cannon to port, and in order to balance out *that* shift in mass, we had to put some of the ship's major subsystems—deflector array, atmospheric processors, water reclamation—to starboard. And we had to design a more substantial bridge and cantilever it out a bit to give the ship the degree of spatial symmetry it needed to be stable during atmospheric maneuvers."

"That's why you have to walk up the long hallway?"

"She just has a long neck, that's all," he said as he patted the console. Helen frowned, the image of having been swallowed whole returning.

"Why are all the stations free floating?"

"They're not really floating. Each one moves independently on the star tracks that surround the globe. It allows each station to orient itself to the task at hand without forcing a false perspective on everyone. The pilot can command his station to stay oriented with a navigational objective, while damage control can orient itself to physically observe the top or bottom half of the ship where damage might have occurred, and tactical can order his pod to stay aligned with the current target—the enemy can never swing over a gunner's head if he's always facing him. No one is forced to think of one direction as 'up' or 'down.' It's important not to get trapped in two-dimensional thinking in the limitless expanses of space."

Helen gazed around the bridge, impressed with Médeville for the first time. It was a truly innovative design.

Bailey spoke. "Clearance granted, all external feeds terminated, visual confirmation of clear space above—all docking apparatus retracted."

Garrand leaned forward and studied the command board. He gently adjusted the repulsor spread and nudged the power forward in three of the eight thrusters, lifting *Destiny's Needle* delicately off the pad stern-first. He swept his palm across the thruster display board, continually adding power, and the ship for all her ungainly appearance and size rose with grace and a subtle yaw into the cool clear night. Garrand's right hand shifted to a brightly lit control sphere that protruded from the console and with a smooth, practiced motion slipped his fingers around the glowing power nubs. Under his hand, the hovering ship banked gracefully to starboard, the forward superstructure clearing the docking arms by mere meters. Adding power to the repulsors, they swept over the low buildings of Letugia, the ship still positioned in a slight nose-down attitude that offered the bridge a splendid Atryx-eye view of the twinkling port which spread out like a green crystal sea in the darkness below.

As the ship began to rise, Garrand smoothly cut in the sublight engines and *Destiny's Needle* kicked them back into their acceleration couches.

"Raise the inertial dampers," he ordered.

Bailey rotated a set of controls and the g-pressures ebbed, allowing them to sink back in normal gravity and settle back to work.

"I thought we had that fixed," Garrand growled.

"The dampers are working perfectly, Captain. However, the engines are now properly tuned, and the dampers were not calibrated for the added thrust."

"Imagine that," Helen laughed. "Surprised that your systems *are* working! What's the matter, Captain — not used to your engines performing up to spec?"

"Do you know how hard it is to keep the buffers clean and the wave modulation properly aligned on a pair of B'vart reactor cores? Especially operating within atmospheric conditions like these — the whole planet's a dust ball. Lucky we haven't sucked up a turkey vulture on our way out."

Helen just smiled. The stars were beginning to come into sharper focus as the ship broke free of the planet's gravity and the atmosphere thinned. It was almost romantic, she thought, and glanced with hesitation toward the back of the captain's head. After so many uncertainties, she was glad to finally be underway.

Destiny's Needle rocketed out of Letugia's atmosphere and headed for deep space.

"We're nearly clear of the planet's magnetosphere," Bailey reported. "Recalculating distance to nearest astral body." It was difficult to make precise jump calculations while still within a planet's strong magnetic field.

Bailey's station rotated up next to Garrand's. "We're clear, sir." Garrand spun to face a new databoard and punched up the first jump Bailey had loaded into *Destiny's* navigation datacore. "Here we go." He touched a blue key and the pinpricks of stars wavered briefly, then shot past the crystal globe in brilliant shafts of color as the ship leapt beyond the speed of light.

"Bailey, make sure the first series of jumps go smoothly. I don't want any mistakes tonight. After you're satisfied you can do as you wish." Garrand's command pod swirled up to the entrance to the bridge. He stood and looked back briefly and said wearily, "You have the bridge, Bailey. I'm going to bed."

❖ ❖ ❖

THE WARM, SMOOTH FEEL OF HER SKIN WAS UNNERVING. GARrand hesitated, trying to center his thoughts but his mind was caught up in her undulating form. He shook his head, rubbed his eyes but still the image persisted. She was breathtakingly beautiful, slowly moving toward him—her eyes locked upon his. The apparition slunk forward, draping a lovely arm over his shoulder and leaned forward for a kiss. Her lips tasted warm and basic; he instinctually wrapped his arms around her waist and drew her close. Her body was tight, a faint definition of muscles under the skin, an overall tone of lithe athleticism and balance. His head felt light, the kiss unlocking the winds of the past.

The memory of a thousand kisses rushed through his heart. He ran his hand down her back, pulling her hips into his, turning his head to kiss her from the other side without removing his lips. She was warm and alive, he could feel her heart pounding wildly against his chest—she clutched the back of his head running her fingers through the short hair on the nape of his neck. She found the leather cord tied around his neck and traced it around to his chest. She reached beneath his shift and extracted the smooth stone that hung from the end of the cord. The amulet was ablaze with brilliance, the emanations reflecting in her dark eyes. She smiled knowingly and leaned in to kiss him passionately. He desperately wished to lose himself within her embrace, to somehow grasp the ephemeral feeling she stirred within his cold dark places. He whispered her name.

The sound of his own voice startled him and he awoke, body drenched with sweat. He sat up quickly, his eyes darting around the chamber. A large antique desk stood beside his bed. The four curved feet rested on a beautiful hand-pulled D'vantja rug. Books were stacked in haphazard fashion against the far wall. Some teetering columns cascaded into jumbled piles on the carpet. He could see a small washbasin with towel draped over the edge and his clothes laid out neatly on a chaise. The grey uneven bulkhead behind his bed was dominated by a large portal filled with brilliant shafts of light from the stars beyond. He sighed miserably—he was in his personal quarters.

A burning sensation scorched his chest and he frantically reached inside his shift to grasp the amulet. He fumbled with the end of the cord and finally grasped the amulet and thrust it out into the dim starlight from the portal. He stared at the stone in disbelief. The slippery surface was icy and the stone a dull uneven green, the sensation of warmth and light only a fantasy. Completely disenchanted, he flopped back down on his berth with a whoosh and stared at the supports overhead, trying to relive the dream of her touch. After an hour of tossing and turning he fell back into a restless sleep.

8

TORG

"Doctor Garner," buzzed the lab's wall speaker, "It's the new artificial assist."

"Ah, good. Send it in. That will be all for this evening," answered the doctor who turned back to his scope, adjusting knobs. Through the still active speaker he could hear a small cargo-lighter hover a crate into the hall. Twin pings of metal and a great clatter signaled the exit of the medica, which swept out in a gentle swoosh of packing crystals. The medica's identlink tapped into the room's code and opened the door. Quietly, on free-rolling treads, the medica approached the lone doctor and asked in a clear metallic voice, "Medical Assist 561 stroke nine reporting to Dr. Garner?"

"I am Jyaye Garner, MSD," he replied without turning.

"J. Garner: voice print confirmed. Thank you, doctor."

"Monitor down," mumbled Garner, "there's a connection in the southwest corner." He gestured to a dark nook behind his worktable. The doctor peered intently into the engrossing optic display and switched slides, ignoring the medica. He exhaled with relief as he brought the new specimen into focus.

Certainly doctor," replied the artificial as it retreated into a corner. A small panel on the medica's torso slid open revealing a spindly arm that extended toward a power node recessed in the laboratory's wall. The connection was made and the artificial began to bleed energy from the grid, recharging its spent power coils. With a slight hiss the medica powered down and switched to auxiliary power, the closest thing to sleeping a medica did.

A single chirp, not unlike an organic sound, came from the medica's corner. Startled, Dr. Garner tore his gaze from his work and glared at the darkened corner.

"Monitor down!" he growled in annoyance. But the medica's lights showed auxiliary power only. Something else, then, had to be the root of the sound. It had a familiar quality, as though he had heard it recently. On vacation maybe. It was a fortnight ago. What had it been? Some creatures in the Trouble Gardens on Parlex had chirped like that.

Garner switched on a finger light, swinging the beam into the shadows. Then he saw it: a tiny, bright red frog speckled with neon blue. Unafraid, the frog worked its chin silently.

The doctor frowned at the intruder and pulled on his elbow-length rubbrex gloves. He picked up a number of long pins and a cork-lined specimen pan. He swiftly impaled the frog, maneuvered it into the pan, and expertly pinned it through its soft feet and shoulders. It remained immobile, but alive.

"Hmm, out of your element, aren't you?" asked the doctor with interest, leaning closer to the squirming frog. "I've seen all manner of rats and vermin smuggle aboard deep space freighters, but never the likes of you."

Humming with concentration, the doctor lit a small torch used to heat beakers and wafted it over the frog for a moment. Setting it aside, he quickly rubbed a hollow glass rod over the sticky residue now sweating off the amphibian's back. He placed the rod into a DDS chamber and within moments a chemical analysis flashed on the screen.

"Just as I thought: you're a highly-toxic little fellow. I wonder how you breached PA contaminant protocol, though. Alien biologicals should have picked you up in their initial sweeps. Someone's getting a pay penalty tomorrow, I can tell you that." The doctor sprayed the contents of a nearby canister on the toad, and in seconds it had frozen white. "Time for you later, my friend," Garner said grimly. He set the specimen tray on a freezer shelf and turned back to his work.

A muffled chirp interrupted Garner's attention and he raised his head uncertainly, listening for the sound to repeat. There it was again, coming from the direction of the shelf. It did not seem possible. Nonetheless, the chirp repeated weakly and to Garner's surprise a stronger call sounded behind him. The doctor whirled to face the new intruder, his heart rate accelerating. How could two frogs have gotten into his lab? He squatted down to peer beneath the table's edge. Darkness and shadows hindered his vision.

He gritted his teeth in anger and crawled under the table, feeling blindly along the slick floor for the second frog. A thought struck him and he paused. His hands were protected from the creature's toxic skin by his rubbrex gloves, but what if the creature leapt away from his fumbling search and struck him in the face? Garner backed away with a labored breath.

Another chirp sounded. This time it was answered by two calls from across the lab. Garner held his breath, uncertain of his next move. A succession of tiny calls echoed around the room. Garner straightened up rigidly, afraid to move, his eyes skipping the shadows. A score of frogs now sung within his laboratory, their chirps extraordinarily loud within the small confines. The doctor backed toward the exit, banging into tables and sending trays clattering to the floor as he felt his way along. The incessant chirping was maddening and Garner clutched his hands over his ears as he backpedaled.

Suddenly the room fell silent and the doctor slowly lowered his hands. He felt the air shift within the room, as if a draft had suddenly materialized. Garner had the eerie sensation that he was being watched by something invisible. He whirled toward the door and froze.

Standing in the doorway was a large figure. A man it would appear, or at least a creature with the shape of a man. Garner gasped and took an involuntary step backward as the dark creature stepped into the light. Its eyes were the cold silver of metal, and its skin and hair were grey, like a perfectly-preserved corpse.

"Dr. Jyaye Garner?" the creature spoke in a deep baritone.

"Confirmed," said the medica, rolling to the stranger's side. In the light, the intruder appeared only slightly less spectral. He stood 1.9 meters tall and wore a complicated vest with straps and gear. A long greatcoat swung loosely from his muscular form. He wore a silver bandolier studded with small spheres strung diagonally across his chest.

"What is going on?" Garner stuttered, his gaze transfixed by the man's appearance.

The intruder held out a dragon-crested medallion. "Recognize this?"

Garner paled, but nodded. "You're an agent of the Emperor." The creature slid the medallion smoothly into a pocket. "The Emperor has reason to believe that you are involved in the unlicensed augmentation of organic species."

Garner struggled to regain his composure. "That's nonsense. I'm a genetic surgeon with full accreditation from—"

"Doctor..." the agent stopped him, slowly shaking his head. "This is not an inquiry. That's not my purview. As far as I'm concerned, the accusation is fact, and your sentence has already been passed." He paused to let the words sink in. "Your reign is over."

Garner swallowed back his protest as he realized that this was not the time or place to argue charges. This creature had breached multiple layers of security and was here without bureaucratic protocols or Imperial Writs. He was a Bio Inquisitor. Or worse, an assassin.

The situation left a bitter taste in Garner's mouth. He swallowed back his fear and turned his intellect toward possible negotiation. Goose bumps prickled along his skin. "I see you are not alien to augmentation yourself. Those are aural implants, are they not? I recognize the rippling of the skin."

Smiling, the agent paced slowly to the freezer, studying the tray. With an accusing look he slid the long pins out of the frozen frog and reached a bare hand toward the creature. The doctor tried to remain impassive, eyes on the hand that hovered near the cold, toxic skin. The agent lifted an eyebrow and looked at the doctor. "Do you mind?" he asked, motioning toward the frog.

The doctor nodded slightly, his jaw tense. The agent unpinned the frog and scooped it up. He held it between his large, flat palms, letting his hands warm the frog slowly. Garner wet his lips, watching with mute hope as the agent casually tucked the shivering frog under his chin. It crawled to one massive shoulder and turned its head up gratefully as the agent stroked it with one finger. The doctor counted the seconds: shock should set in within ten seconds.

The agent reached casually toward the doctor. When Garner flinched away, the dark figure grinned wickedly. His eyes were windows into K'ye itself. "No? You recognized my friend's natural gifts? And you didn't warn me…" The agent shook his head solemnly.

"You want something," Garner replied angrily, his face flushed. "You haven't killed me. What is it?"

The agent began to slowly work his way around the laboratory, pausing to scoop up frogs from the shadows. The tiny creatures appeared unafraid and did not protest as the agent deposited them in various pockets and satchels upon his person. "You are familiar with ventricular fibrillation?"

Garner, watching the strange spectacle of frog collection, failed to answer. The agent paused as two frogs sprang up on an examination table and chirped. He opened a pocket on his greatcoat and the pair dutifully jumped in. "Doctor?"

"Hmm? Oh, yes. I've replaced several hearts with that problem." He looked at the agent in surprise. "Is that what you want?" Garner could barely contain his hope, his fingers already typing in commands for the datacore to look up suitable on-hand parts.

"I don't need a replacement. I want a chamber added."

"How will that repair the rhythm?" asked Garner with undisguised interest.

"Chemical releases triggered by fast, uncoordinated beats."

"Hmm. I've never heard of anything like it. Who sold you on this? Never mind, your best bet is a new one." He continued typing.

"I'll take the chamber, doctor," replied the agent, pinning Garner effectively with his silver gaze.

Garner swallowed and nodded, his hands frozen over the keys. "As you wish." He was almost afraid to venture, "In return for my life?"

"Your life belongs to the Emperor!"

"But—"

"I promise that your existence will continue beyond this encounter, that is of course entirely is *if* you are up to your reputation."

"There will be no problem in that regard." Garner steeled himself for the one shining avenue of escape that had presented itself, one that depended entirely on his surgical skills, which were extraordinary. This might work out very well indeed. Kissing off an Imperial Writ by simply doing what he did every day: replace parts with better parts. "Shall we adjourn to prep?"

"No, here."

"Here? As you wish. I cannot, however, guarantee the best results without my surgical assists and artificials," his voice trailed off as the frogs hidden within the agent's clothing began to trill.

"My friends are alarmed doctor, perhaps you'd like to reassure them of your expertise."

Garner took a deep breath and continued, "My primary surgical theater is right this way. For a procedure of this complexity, I must insist."

The agent nodded his assent and the doctor led him into an antechamber filled with long sinks and sterilization booths. A large transparent glazing overlooked the sterile white operating theater beyond. In the center of the room was a single stainless steel operating table. Suspended above, like the tentacles of some terrible sea kvolta were dozens of sparkling metallic arms, polished and gleaming. Three medicas, monitors darkened, stood silently in recessed alcoves awaiting activation.

The doctor busied himself in preparation, sterilizing his hands and arms. A bead of sweat rolled down his cheek. "This room has the proper equipment. The chamber?"

The agent's medica rolled forward. A side panel slid open and a second thin arm extended clasping a crystal, sanitary container. Inside was a dwarf, six-sided chamber.

"How fortunate," the doctor commented, rubbing his palms together under the stero spray, "to have sent your medica ahead of you. Now if you'll please step into the booth," he gestured toward a strange oval hatch set in a towering green cylinder. Odd tubes and conduits snaked away from the device and as Garner touched a control, the booth began a low-pitched reverberating whine that steadily rose.

The agent removed his long greatcoat, gently hanging it from a rack of white surgical gowns. He stripped off his clothes and wordlessly stepped into the booth. The doctor initialized the sterilization sequence and watched as glowing sheets of radiation washed across the patient's body. Garner frowned, the changing glow of the booth flickered over his skin. The agent was exposed in this state, and rather vulnerable. He glanced quickly at the coat hanging on the wall—those awful frogs had not begun to leap out and watch him. Garner spun to face the medica and found to his dismay that the artificial had produced what appeared to be a lethal looking dart thrower from yet another recessed panel and was pointing it steadily in his direction. He dropped his hand from his belt—his personal shield would be useless against a dart. The sterilization process concluded and the agent stepped out of the humming tube.

"You know it's a serious breach of the Gelicus Art Convention to arm medical assists," he said indignantly. "I don't know how you expect me to operate in these conditions."

"I have every confidence in you, Doctor Garner," the agent said, slowly articulating his words. "I know that you won't make any unnecessary cuts or mistakes, for my medica is quite well versed in the nuances of this procedure. Any deviations and I'm afraid he would be forced to stop you." The agent paused and touched the tip of the dart that was loaded on the medica's spring-loaded thrower. He looked at the tiny drop of white residue on the end of his fingertip and touched it to his tongue that quickly turned a sickly green and then black. "Parvin Molder, an extract from the plague vats on Eltouvé Magellan."

The agent turned to face Garner, rubbing his thumb and forefinger together. "This particular strain has killed millions. One prick from the dart and the Parvin is in your bloodstream. First you will feel a slight stomach discomfort. Then your skin will grow cold and slick and begin to separate and pull apart. While your gums start bleeding, breathing will become difficult, and your throat will close with mucous. There will be moments of paralysis, convulsion and exaggerated reflex. Your bronchial tubes will begin to decay along with the corrosion of your lips as all your firm, healthy tissue turns into soft, necrotic lumps that you will shed in strips through vomiting. You won't die immediately, in fact there will be two to four days of apparent improvement before enough tissue has been dissolved and the internal body fluids have accumulated to the point that you begin to bleed to death in your own tissues."

He reached into his mouth and shucked off the top layer of his tongue, like a reptile shedding. The skin beneath looked impossibly healthy and pink.

Garner fought to keep his voice from shaking. "Who are you?"

The agent smiled. "Rest assured your work will not go unrewarded doctor. I am Vasily Fua'tin Bey-Torg, Vice Proctor Barrett's personal assassin.

Garner's mind reeled. *The Emperor's Butcher? Here in Carinaena's Shell? How unfortunate.* The quiet announcement shattered Garner's last thoughts of deceit. He was about to put the most notorious assassin in the Shell under the knife for a procedure he did not even know would work. He'd done peculiar implants in hearts before, usually adrenaline cases for the wealthy, but he had no doubt that whatever this chamber held, it contained not some lifesaving regulator, but horror.

"I see you've heard of me."

"I've heard of your work."

"Good. Shall we proceed?"

❖ ❖ ❖

"IS IT DONE?" TORG ASKED, HIS VOICE HOLLOW AND DISTANT.

"Yes, it's there," replied the doctor in an equally weary tone. He glanced behind him to Torg's medica that whirred quietly from its watch position in the corner. "Your artificial can tell you."

"The serial number."

"Six-six-mother-one," the doctor read off his chart frowning at some inscribing technician's sense of humor. "Will you tell me now? What have I done?" Torg didn't speak and the doctor turned away to wipe the theater's drive systems of any record of the assassin's secret visit.

"Back when I was in the ISFC—"

"Imperial?" the doctor rolled his head to one side, too tired to think straight.

"Imperial Special Forces Corps. On a mission in the Disturbed Sector. On Vilnius. We were to retake a free will colony called Tashkent." Torg raised himself up and swung his legs off the operating table.

"Try to rest," ordered the doctor, spinning to face the assassin with concern. "I don't care if you don't feel the pain. It's there."

Torg wheezed heavily for a moment, then stood, bracing his arms on the table. "Had to destroy the whole colony, except for one man who tried to hostage us with biochemical weapons. I struck him a deal, and he showed me his source, a historical laboratory for extinct viruses—a sort of museum depository hard for cash and engaged in weapons development. Once curable in ages past, these viruses have altered over the years with successive mutations calculated to ensure their survival in the hostile environments of our bodies." Torg thumped his chest. The doctor blinked back at him, eyes large and limpid behind the enyohanse lenses.

"I don't understand," whispered the doctor.

"You will," said Torg, his body suddenly fading under the lights, as if his image had less permanence than the walls. Then he disappeared altogether. Garner pulled off his lenses and spun, searching the room.

"I have quite a medical past, doctor," Torg said ominously from the empty air behind him. Garner backed against the opposite wall, eyes darting around the empty floodlit room.

"I'm sure you'll be interested," Torg's voice continued as the wall before the doctor suddenly moved. The assassin became slightly visible, his skin the metal color of the walls. Then his figure changed and Torg's skin took on a human glow and became riddled with large scars circling his wrists and neck.

The doctor's jaw sawed back and forth and he reached a practiced hand out to touch Torg's skin. "This can't be! No, it was outlawed." He flinched and drew his hand away without contact.

"Yes, doctor. I am the recipient of very unorthodox and illegal modifications. Now I am a man of many. These killing hands belong to the finest pyorganist of Yuzbekistin. They now make symphonic death. The ducts in my feet once belonged in ocean shells. My eyes are those of an infant grey dragon. I was refit with organs and limbs from living donors during the operation."

"Who—who would do such a thing?"

"Dr. Kremers of the Biomaterial Implant Facility on the Core world of Yuzbekistin performed my life-repair surgery."

"That's not possible, it was destroyed. They're all dead. There's a level eight quarantine on that system."

"Propaganda. Do you really believe the Imperials would wreck an institute they'd sunk billions of credits into?"

"But why you?"

"I had extensive damage in the field. A thermal explosion ripped me apart. My head hung by a cord, I was moments away from permanent death. The doctor told them that for a price I could not only be saved, but enhanced to the point of invincibility. Except he exaggerated, and never explained the price *I* would pay—the price of pain, unyielding pain…" Torg hissed through his teeth, allowing himself the small pleasure of bitterness. "Though I doubt it would have mattered to my superiors, had they known.

"As fate would have it, the good doctor of the Yuzbek Sharlott School had a parts deal going with the prison of political prisoners. He also had access to an extensive array of bioengineered plants and animals, all carnivores and predators of their own right. He had learned the secret to joining species without organ rejection, creating an alien symbiosis.

"Technically, I am the first of a new race of assassins. As you can see—or not," Torg said, his body shimmering slightly and then blending slowly (this time) into the wall so as to make himself invisible. "I have a number of enhancements for my new trade, most of which I was not told about until—" his voice dropped to a broken growl of grief at some past atrocity too horrible to speak.

"But the casket I installed. What are you telling me?"

"You're not very quick, doctor. This is what bought that man his life on Vilnius. It's like a shell, with different chambers. There are six horrors waiting in there for my untimely death, six agonies for Dr. Kremers. Waiting for my body temperature to drop."

"Why not just kill the man?" whispered the doctor, his disgust apparent.

"He has been wise enough to hide himself. But I have no doubt we will meet again." He tugged at the Imperial identlink imbedded in his neck, bending closer to the surgeon. "What does this say to you?"

"Quick-freeze," responded the doctor automatically, eyeing the red triangles. "At death. Top priority over saving other lives. I've never seen that code used for other than ruling heads of state."

"What else?"

"They need your tissue fresh, before decomposition. Good heavens, man! Perhaps they only mean to store you for revival with some future scientific discovery. They must want you alive!"

"Correction, doctor. They want *parts* of me alive. Read the facility."

"Yuzbekistin," Garner breathed. "But you said he wasn't there."

"He'll return to reclaim me, his greatest success, and to continue my race. That is: take me apart to be made into new warriors, all of my parts imprinted with the knowledge of killing, able to create a hundred new killers, a thousand. Monsters not cloned, but transformed under his knife. For this I have prepared a suitable ending for him within these chambers." Torg thumped his chest once more before continuing with relish, "My new casket contains six viruses so hideous, with side effects so vile, that Parvin would seem like candy by comparison.

"Now you know of my love for doctors... " Torg said, suddenly hidden again.

"What? Stay where you are! I've got a personal shield on!" The doctor fumbled with his surgical coat and pulled out a stunner-sized gun.

"Doctor," whispered the voice around him. "After what I've just told you, do you really want to kill me? Do you really want my body to grow cold?"

"I could keep you under radiation lamps," he said, his voice quavering.

"Inventive, but apt to increase the rate of putrefaction. Chamber six holds a toxin that is highly heat resistant."

"Don't kill me, please."

"Doctor," Torg's cool voice seemed gentle and kind and so low that the reedy grate of the doctor's rapid breathing almost obscured it. "I told you that your life belonged to the Emperor... and to *me*."

"But we had a deal," Garner protested. "You promised me my life—"

"I promised your continued *existence*."

"—You must honor your end!"

Torg replied curtly, "There is no honor in dealing with doctors." Garner's neck snapped sideways, and with infinite slowness the body sagged and dropped to the floor.

Torg reached for his belt and withdrew a black, oblong instrument with smooth, rounded edges. He turned the device over and depressed a tiny panel with his thumbnail. A section of the casing recessed, revealing delicate controls color-coded in silver and blue. Torg activated the instrument that began humming mutely as three wicked prongs extended from the top. The sharpened points glistened under the harsh white lights.

Torg stepped to the limp form of the doctor and gently turned his head to one side. With a smooth motion, the assassin plunged the sharpened prongs into the base of the doctor's skull just above his neck. The casing throbbed under his palm.

A low chime signaled from the instrument and Torg withdrew the crimson prongs, wiping the device clean. He checked the indicator lights, murmured with satisfaction, and replaced the oblong case back on his belt.

He smeared a gel along the datacore's casing, watching with satisfaction as the acid quickly worked its damage on any recoverable records. Plucking the unused dart from the medica's thrower, he turned Garner's corpse on its side. He carefully pricked an inner elbow, injecting Parvin into the bloodstream. That would take care of the body by daybreak.

"Happy holiday," he murmured with a final look around the chamber.

A lost toad croaked from a corner. Torg swiftly scooped up the errant creature, paused to check its eyes, and deposited it in a pocket. Without a further sound, he was gone.

9
JEAN-WA

BREAKFAST ABOARD *DESTINY'S NEEDLE* HAD ONCE BEEN A dismal, lifeless affair consisting of cold rations and perhaps a stale biscuit or two washed down with whatever stimulant could be found in the ship's meager stores. But that was before Garrand had liberated Jean-Wa from a cantankerous Shai Barron on Daruma. These days, he could count on something befitting a first class passenger on an Imperial Skyliner or Tiberian Potentate. Stacks of kellin cakes served piping hot and smeared with dollops of real butter. Freshly scrambled betts eggs and ripe mango. A meal of truly fustian proportions; also the heaviest of his day which seemed to help keep his internal body clock straight over long voyages.

Garrand strode into the central mess, a low-ceilinged octagonal room filled with small tables and long, low settees. Corridors radiated out in four directions, and each of the eight walls was packed with a varied assortment of data terminals, com boards, and tech stations. But many of the desks were covered in pillows and the chairs were draped in furs and Afghans. The ship was usually a cold place, but the mess was well stocked with comfortable accouterments. There was a warm, friendly air to the room that was missing in some of the other areas of the ship. Perhaps it was the constant clutter of equipment that lay strewn about, or maybe it was the handcrafted sculptures that stood in the obtuse corners, silently watching. It felt lived-in, inviting.

The room was home to more than a few pieces of antique furniture, and the mixture of woods and crushed velvet upholstery served to make this space feel like a real home. To Jean-Wa's dismay, the Capítän liked to take most of his meals here in the heart of the ship where he could keep tabs on everything, claiming that the chamber Jean-Wa had converted into a dining hall was much too modern and formal for his tastes.

Garrand generally did not like to dine alone, but this morning Bailey was nowhere to be found. He glanced around suspiciously. Bailey had not even bothered to leave a clipscanner with the night's reports. How could he eat if he didn't have ship's diagnostics to read?

Helen sauntered into the mess. She wore soft brown boots cut below the knee with tight fitting destrallier riding jodhpurs trimmed to the shape of her legs. A loose spirellen spun blouse hung naturally across her shoulders, buttoned partway up. Garrand knew that the blousy sleeve concealed a form-fitting bracer on her left arm, having seen her consult it while performing inventory on her gear. Hooked around her waist was a wide trellin leather belt with hooks and thongs for a variety of gear. Today the belt boasted an array of diagnostic tools: a small phase emitter fit snugly in its leather thong, a Barria wand and slender bio sensor were hooked into eyelets along her left hip, and two oblong black casings were clipped onto the front of the belt. A small, powerful Cresbourin blaster sat snugly in a holster tied high on her hip—directly over the belt, in the Wayfarrin' style.

Three hundred years ago, the Wayvern corps had worn their blasters high, butt turned toward the belt buckle. Many believed it facilitated quick draw. The Wayvern had certainly been known for their near legendary speed and accuracy with the impact pistols of the day.

Helen's hair was tied in a loose krimset, most of the unruly strands pulled back clear of her face. She wore little in the way of facial powder or coloring, he noticed with satisfaction, though he wondered whether it was her ordinary routine to forgo such trifles or if she just didn't consider him worth the effort. Regardless, the result was a clean, fresh look; the natural cranberry hue of her lips needn't any artificial coloring anyway, he thought to himself.

"Good morning," she yawned, stretching her arms overhead like a lynx.

"You're just in time for breakfast."

She smiled and patted her belly, "Mmmm. I'm afraid to ask what you have to eat on board."

"I think you're going to be pleasantly surprised."

"Oh really?"

At that moment a thin, spindly artificial rolled in a powered cart. With one set of arms he held an elaborate silver platter filled with flaky fruit rolls, a crock of hand-whipped butter, and a steaming decanter of janda. In another hand he held a tiny bell which he dingled pointedly. "Breakfast, breakfast." He called in clipped, accented Strahlinvek. "We have fresh bor-bor fruit and scones, and for later I have a marvelous caliptus omelet in the works."

He rolled over to Garrand's table and deposited the tray.

"He looks like a cross between a big, silly spider and one of those Zaranth bullies with arthropod sections—sort of like a fancy tiered cake." Helen said, giggling.

"Be nice, Miss Tchelakov. Jean-Wa here is one of the greatest chefs in all Carinaena's Shell."

"Oh Capítän, nonsense. We simply must keep up our appearances. A big breakfast is vital to your day. Here we are now," he handed a battered clipscanner over to Garrand. "Bailey wanted me to give you this." The clipscanner was covered with flour and spotted with a sticky residue that looked suspiciously like jam. With yet another set of arms, Jean-Wa hastily dusted off the scanner and presented it to the Capítän.

"Where is Bailey, anyway?"

"Oh my, who knows? Who knows? With that one you can never tell!"

Helen covered her mouth and whispered, "He's sort of cute."

The spidery six-armed artificial swiveled around and poured two cups of janda into delicate ceramic cups, complete with saucers. He carried one to Helen. "For you, miss."

"Why thank you," she said, accepting the cup and saucer. She turned to face Garrand. "I never expected such polite behavior on your ship."

"Don't get too used to it."

Jean-Wa rolled back to the kitchen, whistling happily to himself.

"You have an eccentric bunch here."

"I prefer to think of them as original." He munched on a piece of ripe bor-bor fruit.

"Like you."

"No there's nothing original about me. I'm vait'mos down to my bones. Never pretended to be anything else."

"Doesn't sound like one of the 'Emperor's Elite' to me," she said peering over the rim of her cup as she sipped the hot janda.

Garrand looked sideways at her, eyes narrowing. It was possible that she could have found out about his past through some odd coincidence, a story overheard in some backwater barroom that she was testing him with. More than likely, though, someone had briefed her—someone with access to Imperial archives, to *high-level* Imperial archives. That meant deep pockets. The obvious conclusion was that she was working for someone else, someone with resources and information. Which meant keiretsu. But why would a keiretsu take the risk of hiring a private ship when they had so many at their disposal? Unless they didn't know what she was up to…

"I don't know what you mean," he said innocently.

She watched him carefully but he did not blink or prevaricate. Curious, the man didn't seem as arrogant when she was this close. She felt herself leaning in to ask him another questions, but she was interrupted by a commotion that started in the outer hall.

"No, no—get that fuzzy creature *out* of my kitchen. Shoo, shoo! Go away you horrid little thing—you will ruin *everything*!" A loud crash of pans rumbled out of the kitchen and then a blurry streak of fur went racing through the mess, little clawed feet scraping against the slick deck plates. Garrand turned in his chair to watch the little exel as it scrambled through the room. It shot through the starboard archway and disappeared down the corridor.

Moments later Bailey entered the mess by way of the kitchen, smiled briefly at Helen and continued through without a word. Soon thereafter, Little Bit came rolling through the hall dragging an empty sack and net behind him. He whistled hello as he rolled by.

"As I was saying," Helen smirked, "You have a very interesting crew, Captain."

"You don't know the half of it."

"So much activity for so early in the morning."

"Yeah, they're a thrill a minute." He resumed reading his clipscanner.

Helen watched as Little Bit disappeared down the hall. "He's seems pretty bright for a tech art."

"Well, technically speaking, he's not a tech art." He took a huge bite out of a scone, sending crumbs scattering everywhere.

"Not a tech art?" she set down her cup and picked through the scones, looking for just the right one.

"Nope. Couple of years ago Bailey and I were going to pull a major overhaul of his datacore. We had his top off, half his matrix pulled out and it just seemed stupid to put the same core back in—it was 25 years old."

"You refit him with an updated core?"

"Well at first that was the plan, but that night I ran across an old Veltronis circuit jammer."

"Circuit jammer?" she asked, rolling the words over her lips as if to test their meaning.

"Yeah, you know: digital analogous hardwire feckson." Helen looked at him blankly. "He designed artificial logic matrices," Garrand expanded impatiently. She nodded.

"Anyway, he was tipsy and I was feeling rather creative."

Helen's eyes flicked up from her teacup as he said that. It sounded far too close to something Sid might say.

"I got to telling him how I was thinking about putting a full sentient matrix into my favorite tech art. Now this guy was drinking Artellian Absinthe, with partially collapsed Wentian corpuscles, and some of the tendrils tend to crawl back up through your sinus cavities and latch onto your brain stem."

Helen made a face—at first it was a look of disgust, but then it changed as she thought about it. The drink actually sounded interesting.

Garrand shook his head, "No it's great! It magnifies the thoughts you're having. So the guy says, 'What kind?' I say, 'Turkle Standard Sphere.' He says, 'What model?' I say, 'Number two of course!' and this guy has a core event and starts going on and on about how he used to have a Turkle Standard model two for years and how he just loved it."

Helen watched the man as he told his story, punctuating his speech with sweeping hand motions. He talked with such emotion, clearly enjoying himself. Was this the real Garrand Médeville?

"Well I'd had one or two of those Artellian Death Slugs at this point and we started talking."

Helen took a long sip of tea. "I thought it was bad enough hearing about your ship."

Garrand ignored her. "He thought my idea was great, said he just happened to have a brand new sentient matrix back at his lab—was a prototype or something. I think he'd been working on it for years. Well, we went back and hauled that lovely core down to *Destiny's* bay and spent the rest of the night polishing off a really fine bottle of Callos I snuck out of Jean-Wa's reserve and hardwired a new matrix into Little Bit."

"Really?"

"Yeah, and that's not the easiest door in the world to defeat."

Helen shook her head incredulously. "You mean to tell me you completely redesigned his entire mainframe logic board to accept an unknown matrix?"

"Yep." He looked very pleased with himself, and with her disbelief.

"In one night?"

He shrugged.

"Blasted?"

"It was a good night."

"You?" she glanced down the hall where the Turkle Sphere had disappeared. It was more an accusation than a question.

"Hey," he said in mock indignation. "I didn't just orbit out from some rock. I've spent most of my life studying. I graduated from the Académe with the Emperor's blessing. That wasn't easy. We didn't spend *all* our time flying and drinking," he sat down heavily in the station chair. "How do you think we're ripping through space right now? I designed this ship, you know."

"I didn't take you seriously."

"Nice," Garrand smiled ruefully.

"So you wiped his memory completely?"

"No!" he looked mortified. "I'd never do that—how awful! No, we downloaded his entire memory into *Destiny's Needle* and then performed the retrofit and loaded his memories back in."

"Wasn't that a rather strange adjustment?"

"Yeah, it took him a long time to get used to experiencing such a wide range of new sensory input—feelings, doubt, uncertainty, whims, passion, intuition, anger. He finally came around though; it's tough figuring out how to be alive."

"Alive?" she asked.

This time it was Garrand's turn to stare back blankly. "Yes, alive. You know, living, thinking, making decisions, taking responsibility for others."

"Garrand, he's not alive."

"Why? Because he doesn't breathe? Because he doesn't have an organic heart that pumps blood through tiny veins and arteries? Because he wasn't borne of a womb and raised by a mother? Let me tell you—there's *trillions* of living creatures born in vats these days. I've seen 'em. It's not pretty, and it's as clinical and sterile as any scientific laboratory or artificial manufacturing line. I've seen *living* men and women bred to perform the most intolerable acts of atrocity you can imagine, subjecting everyone in their path to agony and suffering without thought or regret. The naturals are less alive than the artificials—they have no appreciation for it. Bailey and Little Bit are the noblest companions a man could ever have. Either would sacrifice themselves for me, or anyone else in their care for that matter. I've seen Varsis arts throw themselves in front of blaster cannon to save their charges. These artificials possess honor, courage, insight, hopes, patience, dreams, feelings— they're as alive as you and I. They learn from their mistakes, look to the future and hope for the best—same as anyone."

Helen looked very carefully at Garrand for a long time. *What had Darstin led her into?*

"Anyway, it did take awhile for him to adjust—to learn. Just like any kid. I wrote a lot of his new subroutines to help him cope."

"So he's sentient?"

"Of course. Just like Bailey."

"But he doesn't speak."

"No room in his shell for full vocal capabilities. But he understands everything. And I pretty much understand everything he has to say, too. The technical stuff I get through his interface with datapads."

Helen's nose crinkled. *Really? She tried to make sense of it. A diatribe about the nobility of artificials by way of a drunken story about rebuilding his Turkle Sphere?* She couldn't stop staring at him as he crunched his biscuit. Finally she turned away before he could look up and read her expression. "You're a strange man, Médeville." She managed softly.

❖ ❖ ❖

JEAN-WA WAS UPSET. "NO! NO!" HE SHOUTED IN CONSTERNAtion, six arms flailing impressively. "I will be having thirty-seven extra guests for dinner. Finally a crowd! And you want me to serve *this*?"

One arm shot forward, twirling the offending green, leafy stem. "This weed? Well, no, I say. No! I refuse." With that proclamation he folded all three sets of arms and retracted his head until only his eye showed. It glowed like a calibrator. Even the serving cart he sat upon rattled with anger.

Garrand swallowed a smile and tried to think of some way to appease the true comforter of his life. He wouldn't mind missing the aristocratic niceties, but how could he endure a long voyage without bondi dumplings? Or weerac stew? Or varelle fillets? Especially when he was stuck in a confined space with the impossibly complicated, but somehow alluring Miss Tchelakov.

"I'm sorry Jean-Wa. This is what she says they eat — exclusively."

"Who ever heard of people eating weeds? It is, I say, ridiculous!"

"They're not exactly people, Jean-Wa." He tried to explain gently. "They're creatures."

"Where is the difference, I ask? They must eat, yes?"

Garrand sighed expansively and tried to think of some compromise that would not further upset his cook

Jean-Wa had last belonged to the Baron Senn van Basel of Daruma, an important Shai Baron on Sinegar who lived like a feudal lord with thousands of indentured laborers on his many estates. Garrand, staying nearby at the rival Loolecondera Estate, had been intercepted in transit and strongly invited by a regiment of the Daruma Manor Guard to "sample the flavors of Sinegar" and barter over a cargo intended for Loolecondera. Not wanting to hurt what smelled like a promising deal, Garrand obliged without struggling and arrived in time for high *shai* with the Baron.

Of all the wonders abundant in the overly posh mansion, only the artificial serving the *shai* held Garrand's attention. The single-minded purpose of the machine amidst the offending gaudiness of the surroundings reminded him of Bailey's attention to detail. There was something in the reserved grace and elegance of the machine that moved him. As he watched the machine's deft motions in the elaborate ritual of preparing and serving the whipped beverage, Garrand wondered if the artificial was displeased about something.

The Baron caught his gaze and explained. "He's still peevish today. Would that I had put him to labor in the fields! If not for the babas, I would have banished the insolent dolt long ago."

The artificial stumbled, causing a cup to hop in its saucer, an unforgivable blunder in the ceremony.

The Baron's beefy arm slammed down on the table, jostling delicate cups to the floor. With the speed allowed by six flexible arms, the artificial disposed of the ruined porcelain and drew himself up in mute accusation. The Baron's face purpled at this and Garrand took pity on the valiant art, surprising his host by waving an amended datapad by his nose.

"I believe we have business. I have little time, as is."

"Yes," the Baron snapped. Then, as if realizing his rudeness to one he hoped to swindle shortly, he smiled broadly and patted his knees. "Yes, yes of course!" he roared. "Enough of this!"

THE DEAL DREW to a close in record time and after a few necessary courtesies, such as kissing the repugnant Baron's daughter, Garrand thought the time, and his host's mood, ripe for his impulsive request.

"By the Barthsa, Baron van Basel, I had hoped to make a better deal here," he pouted in imitation of the Barron's rotund daughter. "You are far more skillful a trader than I was led to believe. I would have fared better at Loolecondera. They have not the sharp skills you possess."

The Baron grinned wickedly, in a good humor with the deal to his favor. "Yes, yes, well I might make a gift of some slaves for you. Perhaps that might salve your wounded pride."

Garrand paused thoughtfully, stifling his disgust. "Slaves I have no use for. On such a small ship, they are too much trouble. But perhaps a cook…" He let his words drift off, as if he'd only just thought of it. A forgotten shard near his foot captured his attention while he waited in confidence for the Baron's leap to the bait.

"Well, it so happens I have a fine cook in need of a new position."

"Really? Oh, not that terrible server! How he mangled the *shai* ceremony! It would be an imposition to take him."

"But you are wrong, I assure you, captain. The oaf is a master in the kitchen. You would not believe the things he can do with but a bit of flour and memon."

Garrand forced a derogatory note into his voice. "I have no use for fancies. I'm raised a soldier. I like plain, solid meals, nothing more. Perhaps I should take some slaves."

The Baron frowned, warming now to the idea. After all, with the credits he'd just made on the deal he felt he could afford another cook of Jean-Wa's abilities. "No, no, the artificial is just what you need. A soldier is particular about his pottage after all, and he'll serve a hearty meal. Used to economizing too, I allow no extravagances in my arts."

Garrand leaned his head back, as if weighing the possibility with some favor. He sighed. "All right. Sign him over." As the Baron rubbed his hands together with relish, reaching for the contract to amend it, Garrand hazarded a glance toward the artificial, motionless in the doorway, a towel in one arm flicking idly against his cart.

"Have you any things? Stow them on my ship immediately. Now that my business is concluded, I have other appointments to attend." He paused momentarily, letting his gruff words hang in the air and with no one looking, winked at the artificial.

Without reply, the artificial wheeled away from the scene. If it was even possible he was now in an even worse strategic position, for his former owner had at least delighted in his talents, if not his character. No he would now become a food technician for an audience of one, with no hope to impress some savior from a far off land. The towel dangled in precise folds in his grasp. He brought it before his eyes, snapped a set of wicked shears onto arm number three, and quickly ripped it to shreds.

In the end, Garrand had bought Jean-Wa for 502 piasters, the equivalent of one week's work hauling dryexcellon. It was truly the greatest bargain of his life, for Jean-Wa's cooking was to his tongue what sight was to a blind man. Pest-resistant maruvell flour that formed that staple of enlisted men, the Imperial biscuit, became, under Jean-Wa's capable tools, thin breakfast cakes of incomparable lightness. He created spicy twice-baked breads, and authentic thulo pretzels. But his crowning glories were the babas. Hekin babas, soft and creamy, morning babas filled with fruit, and capricious babas that were bound to fail, leaving seventy egg yolks wasted.

A baba was always a risk; even Jean-Wa's careful precision was no guarantee of success. The yeasts in babas were precocious and had to rise properly three times, protected from cold drafts a closing portal might create. For this reason, Jean-Wa always had specific instructions for the intelligent door, one of only two items he had brought with him from his former position. After all, a cook without a well-trained and adequately programmed door was at a disadvantage from the beginning.

"Humhal," Jean-Wa would turn sharply to glower meaningfully at the kitchen's door. "Do not let anyone in. I am baking babas." But the door was mischievous and in fact rather resentful. It had always longed to be a tailor and felt the workings of the kitchen beneath it. So sometimes Humhal let in drafts only to be beaten about the fringes of his portal with spatulas. Fortunately Jean-Wa's lethal accouterment of knives did not include a drill. Somewhat dazed from years of this behavior, Humhal carried on.

Therefore, when all went right, no one was allowed in the kitchen when a baba was baking. And when Jean-Wa removed it, finally, from the oven, great care had to be taken in placing it on a soft, down pillow reserved with pride for the babas alone and rotating it gently until cooled so as to prevent lopsided settling.

Despite deftly applied skill, results with babas were inconstant and often baffling. In fact it was more a measure of luck than skill that Jean-Wa's babas had, more often than not, turned out beautifully. But his luck had run thin, of late, and he hoped his enthusiasm over the new guests would lure that elusive ingredient back

In desperation as he thought of what was at stake, Garrand scanned racks of pans, his eyes finally settling on Jean-Wa's shrine to civilization: a Wabi-sabi *shai* set. It was the only other thing the artificial had brought with him from Sinegar. Perhaps the elaborate tea ceremony, which Garrand had hitherto avoided due to its length and formality, might appease his treasured chef.

A wonderful plan lodged in his mind. In one stroke he could have his cooking back and give Miss Tchelakov something to do besides saunter around the ship.

"Ahem."

Jean-Wa's blazing eyes swiveled his way.

"There is the matter of attending to Miss Tchelakov."

The artificial's head rose an inch. "The young miss, here on board?"

"Yes. You see," he paused, hating himself for what he was about to say. "Actually, she's the daughter of a very important man."

The head rose higher. "Then she will be wanting… "

Garrand felt his traitorous mouth begin to curl like one of the pliant pastries on the sideboard. He bit to the blood. "*Shai*."

Jean-Wa's arms embraced the heavens and he sighed blissfully at the ceiling.

Garrand explained his plan to Helen, outlining the details of her new duties.

"Are you the captain of this ship?" she asked incredulously.

"This isn't an Imperial rack, Miss Tchelakov," he snapped. "It's a Freetrader vessel and as soon as everyone's happy, the captain can be too."

"Everyone?" Helen smirked, making Garrand want to shake her.

"With some exceptions," he growled and moved briskly down the hall. "*Shai's* in ten minutes," he called back. "And if you want to eat anything decent this voyage, you'd better be thirsty! The last time Jean-Wa had his feelings hurt I ate zagbar tato porridge for a week. He claimed I needed the extra starch. Horrible stuff."

Helen called after him: "With your diplomatic skills, I'm amazed you survived this long."

10
Dasko Goes Home

A YOUNG MAN IN A BLACK UNIFORM STOOD BENEATH A long, low tent. He grasped a stanchion as the wind howled across the muddy battlefield and threatened to pull the tent free from its lines. A storm had settled over the encampment and the low rumbles of thunder reflected the fury of the battle that had nearly laid waste to the colony. Rain whipped under the tent and cast a sheen across the glowing bank of portable datastations that served as a field command center for the new base camp being erected at Hammerfield's edge.

Lieutenant Dasko of the Gokazoku Kaigi, Brotherhood of the Silent Blade, watched the technicians and specialists as they coordinated activity around the emerging base. He grasped his ribcage, fingers sticky with blood.

"Are they capable of symmetrical response, sir?" a man many years older than Dasko peered over his shoulder. His hair was salt and pepper grey and his chin was thick with stubble. *Havelock,* Dasko reminded himself. *Sub-lieutenant Havelock.*

Dasko grunted a curt chuckle. "I doubt there are reinforcements within 200 kilometers, Havelock." He tapped the portable field screen with a finger. "Orbital scans aren't picking up anything larger than a loper this side of the mountains. And our patrols have had nothing to report, other than a few scattered deserters. No, I doubt they have even the most rudimentary counter-response measures available."

"What level of security do you want then, sir?"

Dasko sighed and drummed his fingers across the console. "Standard perimeter. Phase two occupation protocol. We've seen nothing but velites here — light infantry and a few skimmers. Nothing that'll stand against a mechanized force. Commander Nyles should have no problems."

Havelock noticed the mix of dried mud and caked blood smeared across the lieutenant's face and blazer, obscuring the golden dragon stitched across the young man's chest.

"Sir, are you wounded?"

Dasko seemed absent-minded as he studied the screens. He leaned over a seated corporal to study his readout. "Where's that last shuttle? It was supposed to deliver the remainder of the grain stores over an hour ago."

The corporal shook his head, "I haven't seen it on my roster, sir. *Lenton Vash* and *Gorgon* are reading all lifters docked and all personnel accounted for." He quickly tapped nodes on his armrest. "*Varian Bailey* and *Laysellus* show no more scheduled drops. Looks to me like the fleet's getting ready to break orbit. You should check with Gelbs — she's got the updated drop schedule." The corporal leaned back in his seat and yelled across the command center, "Hey, Gelby! You got any last minute traffic on your scope?"

"What're you looking for?"

"Lost mule, with a grain docket, probably hailing from the *Vishnu* or *Shiva*."

"It must be running late," corporal Gelbs called back without looking up. "Unless it was canceled."

"No," Dasko muttered, "Someone would have told me." *They better not have left me down here.* He took a deep breath and steadied himself on the back of the corporal's chair.

Havelock persisted, "Sir, are you injured?"

The corporal twisted around with alarm. "You all right lieutenant?"

Dasko swayed in the wind, annoyed at the intrusion.

Havelock barked into his comtab, "Medic! Report to Ops immediately!" he reached a strong arm under the lieutenant's armpit and steadied the Imperial Guardsman.

"I'm fine!"

"I've got you," Havelock murmured.

"That's a lot of blood, sir," the young corporal blanched as he saw the blood dripping from Dasko's fingers.

Dasko wiped the back of his hand across his face and looked at it briefly — it was covered in a slick crimson. "That's not *my* blood," he snapped. "I have work to do before I can get off this rock!"

"The transition is nearly complete, sir. Everything's in order. Commander Nyles can take over from here. I'll brief her on all the latest —"

At that moment, a small green-scaled medic appeared, gear slung over one shoulder. Havelock waved him over.

"This isn't necessary," Dasko protested. He turned to the nearest com station and commanded, "Sergeant Gills isn't answering his command code. Have him report to me *now!*"

A medic hustled over and set his gear down, cracking out bioscan instruments from white ceramic cases. He plugged two into a coil pack at his waist.

"I don't have time for this."

"I'm sorry, but I must insist, sir." Havelock apologized.

"This won't take but a moment, lieutenant," the medic rasped, red tongue darting out casually between words.

Havelock watched with genuine concern. He wasn't about to let one of Lord Barrett's Imperial Guard die while overseeing the transition from siege to occupation. It was an honor to have the lieutenant temporarily assigned to his unit. He couldn't bear the thought that some harm might have befallen him while stationed here. Things had run beautifully with Dasko in command. The young man's grasp of the situation had been swift and precise. He had a gift for logistics — the flow of men and matériel from orbit had proceeded uninterrupted for nearly seven hours. At this rate, base camp would be complete before nightfall.

"You see action this morning, sir?" the medic asked as he scanned the lieutenant's body.

"Of course I did," he growled.

"Do you recall taking any shrapnel?"

Dasko shook his head.

"Were you hit by blaster fire, projectile weapon, hmm?"

"No."

The medic ran his green hands quickly across the lieutenant's torso and arms, then his groin and down each leg. "Take any spills?"

"No, I'm telling you I'm fine—this blood is not mine! I was in close quarters all day."

"Well, I should say so, sir. You have a three-inch puncture wound between your third and fourth ribs. Dual-edged blade by the look of it. Bioscan shows it just missed your lung. Here, swallow this." He deposited a microbe on the lieutenant's tongue. Dasko frowned and swallowed.

"This should tell us if the blade was poison-tipped." The medic flipped on a tiny datascreen. "More than likely not since you're still standing, but might be something residual. Best to make sure." He studied the screen and adjusted two, minute controls. "You also have two fractured ribs and a mild concussion." He reached into his kit and removed a tiny green case. He popped the housing and placed a small flat device about the size of a quantis against the lieutenant's neck and flicked a tiny switch with his thumbnail. A small diode registered green. "That should help with the pain."

A tall, broad shouldered marine in dark, forest green uniform ducked under the awning and saluted. "Sergeant Gills reporting as ordered, sir."

"Is the perimeter secure, Sergeant?" Dasko asked as the medic attended to his wounds.

"The last of the men have dropped sir. All perimeters are tight. Patrol rosters have been filled and routes re-mapped as you requested."

"What about the colony?"

"It's been quiet for the last few hours. Your men must have gotten the last of them, sir." The sergeant's eyes flicked briefly over the lieutenant. By necessity, Gills was accustomed to sizing a man up with one quick glance. The ragged boy appeared far too young to be a member of the vaunted Guard, but then he'd never been this close to one of the Gokazoku Kaigi before.

The accounts from the interior of the colony had been chilling. Anyone who harbored doubts as to the legitimacy of the Guard's reputation had only to witness their brutal efficiency this morning. The Imperial Guard had been tasked with flushing out the most stubborn resistance before Barrett arrived.

Twelve men and women clad in elegantly-simply black had crept into the heart of the rubble without armor or Trioxin, armed with only small hand weapons and blades. Small golden dragons were stitched across their blazers, the dragons possessing the royal fifth claw. In less than an hour they had silenced every last sniper in the colony. Gills nodded with satisfaction as he watched the medic clean off clumps of blood and dirt. He liked an officer who wasn't afraid to bloody himself in battle.

"Good. Set up light patrols for tonight. I want the curfew lifted in a two days. After that, sidearms only. No heavy weapons allowed in the city. I want this to look like a rebuilding project, not an occupation. Set up the recruiting station at the edge of the camp. Did you find the last of the Geggins?"

"Yes sir, all equipment has been cracked and stored. We're set for the next three months."

The medic was closing the gash with a tight-beamed phase emitter. The air smelled faintly of chemical-seared flesh. Dasko winced and said, "Very well, have Commander Nyles commence with stage three indoctrination first thing tomorrow morning."

"Food as well?"

"Yes, and housing. Best to leave a strong impression." Sub-lieutenant Havelock nodded to himself. The Lieutenant was wise to open the fleet's food stores to the colonists. Within a month the entire colony would be rebuilt better than before. And they were sure to garner many more recruits with food and temporary housing than with blast rifles. Power can afford benevolence, after all.

The medic finished his work and began stowing his gear. "Best have the ship's surgeon take a look after you lift, sir."

Dasko acknowledged the medic with a gruff thanks and walked to the edge of the command center and ducked outside. He took a deep breath and looked out across the horizon, eyes searching the sky.

Havelock stepped to his side and scanned the rows of equipment and shells that were carefully arranged across the clearing. This would be his home for the next three to six months. A twinkle caught his eye, just brighter than the stars that were beginning to emerge in the twilight.

"There," he pointed to the sparkle. "Mule on her way down."

Dasko breathed a heavy sigh of relief as he caught sight of the ship's strobing beacons. He suddenly felt very tired, and very sore. All the pain he'd ignored for the better part of a day was catching up to him. He frowned, feeling vulnerable now that he was almost finished. *One more thing,* he reminded himself: *board the mule and get home.* Then the cycle was complete.

He turned to Havelock, "Transfer all command codes to Commander Nyles. And give her my regards." He looked back briefly back into the command center as if trying to remember if he had forgotten anything. "If you have any problems I'll be at the southern landing site for at least another half hour while they unload. You can reach me there." Dasko was surprised at how anxious he was to get aboard that shuttle. His ribs were beginning to throb.

"Lieutenant," Havelock saluted, "it was a pleasure."

"Best of luck," Dasko gave him a wry look and started across the camp to fetch his gear. The landing site lay two kilometers to the south.

THERE WAS AN eager chatter in the forward personnel berthing hold aboard the *Dread Wombat*. The passengers were the last members of the fleet not remaining behind as part of the occupying force. Like Dasko, they seemed happy to be headed off-planet. Men and women from all service sectors were strapped in fifteen-abreast a central aisle that lead fore and aft. The lifter's main sub-light drive was warming up and outside his tiny portal, Dasko could see men scurrying away from the landing site as the grass flattened out beneath the repulsors.

"Didn't think I was going to make it," the man strapped in next to Dasko offered cheerfully. "But I wasn't about to let them leave me. Haven himself wouldn't want to be caught on this planet for another three months." Dasko let his gaze drift from the portal and he silently acknowledged the man. He was wearing the badge of weapons specialist, Fifth corps, Tarrianne third class. He was covered nearly head to toe in slick, oily coolant fluid mixed with generous portions of dirt and grime. "We gave them a good run today though, eh lieutenant?"

Dasko smiled obliquely and let his eyes float back to the portal that revealed the planet falling gently away beneath them, the haze of atmosphere obscuring the details of the continents that melted away in the dusk. The moaning sub-light drive managed to shake every part of the ship as the mule lumbered into orbit.

The rattle of the seats was thunderous and every jolt went straight through his ribs to some unseen source of pain. Dasko gripped the armrest with white knuckles and watched his hand shudder from the internal vibrations. He took a deep breath and forced himself to release his grip, trying to relax a notch.

He wondered how the rest of the Guard had fared — he regretted having to pull Transition Oversight duty, but Captain Strom had asked him to head up T.O. personally, and he would never think of turning down the captain. Despite his weariness, he couldn't wait to see them all in the mess later tonight. Lewg was sure to have some tall tale to tell, and old Sheb'dura would be proud of his latest battle scars.

With a smile of personal satisfaction and relief, Dasko reached into a pocket and withdrew a small steel locking bolt. He recalled snatching it from an artificial armorer's tray earlier that morning back aboard the *Shiva*. The blue skinned artificial had whistled, "Hey, hey!" at him in agitation, allowing Lewg and Farres to grab small fittings of their own.

"Don't worry Selyn," he had called. "We come back — it comes back. Gotta take a piece of home with you for luck!"

The artificial's tone softened, but still she chastised him in her clear soprano voice, "You just make sure you come back, Lieutenant Dasko."

He smiled at the memory as he fingered the cool trinket — worth perhaps a quantis or two in a dirtside dry goods shop, but invaluable to Dasko as a piece of the ship, his home, that he was required by time-worn tradition to bring back.

Outside his frosted portal, a dark shape loomed overhead, eclipsing the warm glow of the sun that had soothingly bathed his face. A long shadow fell across the *Dread Wombat* as the lifter continued along her ecliptic path, matching orbits with the ominous form of the Imperial Destroyer *Shiva*, so large she completely blocked out the sun even from the distance of several thousand kilometers. The behemoth's ragged edges lanced across the tenuous halo of the sun's corona which glowed like fading embers around the ship.

As the mule continued to rise beneath the orbiting dreadnaught, the long intricate lines of the bristling destroyer became evident. Each 700-meter long layer of the ship folded delicately atop the next like a fine Shaithelyn pastry. Dasko felt a giddy warmth as he felt the *Shiva's* aft docking grapples lock onto the *Dread Wombat* after they had matched orbital velocity. The grapples slowly drew the mule into the docking bay through the shimmering field that kept the interior pressurized with atmosphere.

Lieutenant Dasko shouldered his gear and waited in line as the soldiers slowly shuffled toward the exits. He longed for the smell of home; Hammerfield's air tasted bland and empty. Dasko stepped over the threshold and took a long, deep breath of the ship's thick atmosphere. Each ship had its own unique smell, something to do with refiltration cycles and the signature odors of several thousand men and women living in a confined space. The *Shiva's* air was slightly oxygen-rich with an unmistakable odor of oil and machinery mixed with a faint overdone smell, like burnt tangerine peels. It made no difference to Dasko—it simply smelled like safety, and as far as he was concerned the air had never tasted better than it did tonight.

The stairs leading to the deck were steep and narrow and Dasko had to turn his feet sideways as he stepped down to be certain of his balance. Standing on the deck plates he could feel the subtle vibrations of the ship's reactor core pulsing through his boots as he looked out over the gargantuan space. The landing bay was a vast chamber 200 meters long and nearly a hundred wide. Five of the huge lifters were nestled within this bay, and thousands of men and artificials swarmed around the ships, unloading men and matériel, ferrying cargo pallets and weapons, performing maintenance and major system overhauls. The noise within rose to such a din that most cargo handlers and foremen used hand signals and light buoys to communicate with one another.

Dasko let his eyes flit over the chaos, looking for a familiar face but finding none. Huge grappling claws swung on tracks across the rafters, preparing to snare another ship and load it into the bay. Hundreds of brightly painted cargo lighters hovered ponderously at various heights in the broad hall, obscuring Dasko's vision, the gruff looking men who guided them shouting above the bedlam and making expansive gestures at one another as they maneuvered the massive pallets in and around the ships.

Gathering his three cases of gear, Dasko tried to get his bearings. He wanted to get back amidships to officer's country and his quarters. The markings on the distant walls were hard to find and even more difficult to make out through the towering mules and lifters. He sighed and set off in what felt like the right direction, pausing to let three medicas glide by with casualties towed behind in a train of hovering lighters.

Making his way between two columns of returning marines, Dasko accidentally bumped a case into the knees of a harbor chief. The man cried out in surprise and let loose a stream of colloquial expletives as he turned to face Dasko. "By the Barthsa, what do you think you're doing, soldier?"

"Pardon me," Dasko murmured.

The man had several days' growth of facial hair despite Imperial regulation and looked absolutely filthy, chewing on the thick end of a thiretsen cigarillo. He waved a beat-up clipscanner in Dasko's face and yelled, "Where you going in such a hurry boy? I ought to have you tagged for your lack of respect—" the man froze mid-sentence as his eyes caught sight of the miniature golden dragon half-obscured on Dasko's chest by dirt and dried blood. The harbor chief shifted the cigarillo from one side of his mouth to the other as he spied the Dragon's fifth claw—reserved for Royalty and sects of the Emperor's Guard.

"My apologies, sir. You'll have to excuse my manners—my, uh, lack of proper—that is to say, well we've been awful busy down here what with the raid and all, and I didn't recognize your—"

"It's all right, chief," his tone was gentle, lenient. "It's been a long day for all of us."

"Yes sir, thank you sir," the sergeant said with obvious relief. He managed an awkward salute after transferring the clipscanner to his left hand.

Dasko shuffled forward beneath a hovering tech foreman who was directing traffic and resources aboard a small flatbed lighter. Before a huge rack of purple striped Geggin shells stood the polished form of Holden, his personal artificial assist, who was waiting expectantly for him amidst all the confusion. Dasko immediately brightened at the sight of the art's smiling visage.

"Ah sir, I was hoping you'd be on this last shuttle. I was beginning to get a bit concerned when you missed your scheduled lift. Fleet personnel were unable to locate you on the surface and TacOps didn't have you listed on any updated lift rosters. I believe they were beginning to get tired of me poking around topsides, so I decided it would be best if I waited for you here. Why were you so late, sir?"

Dasko shook his head, "I hate oversight detail—always mass pandemonium. Try coordinating a speed drop involving seven capital ships, fourteen thousand men from two dozen different ships all headed in different directions, and nearly a million metric tonnes of equipment and supplies to haul dirtside. With all the scheduling errors, I'm lucky I made it off-planet at all."

Holden raised his artificial eyebrows, intent on his Lieutenant's words. "Well it's good you're here now. The fleet is nearly underway. There's a rumor floating about that the pragens have warships at the edge of the system."

Dasko looked up, "Really?"

"Yes, Vice Proctor Barrett is said to have dispatched a personal message to Lady Vos Bergen by courier drone, a very unorthodox procedure."

"Well maybe he wants to avoid a fight."

"That would be highly out of character."

Dasko smiled at Holden's assessment — he was right, of course. "I don't know, Barrett's pretty savvy. Maybe he just doesn't want to divert our attention from the matter at hand."

They made their way to a central corridor that ran the length of the ship. Hundreds of men and women walked or glided by. "What about the rest of the Guard?" asked Dasko trying to readjust the straps across his shoulders without breaking stride. Holden smoothly relieved the lieutenant of two of his cases, sliding the straps off his arms and easily shouldering the burden. "With your safe arrival, all members of the Imperial Guard are accounted for. No casualties."

Dasko looked relieved. "That's good," he sighed. "Any word as to the targets?"

"I must say I have heard nothing official concerning the success of the mission."

"What about down at the terrakin's nest?" he asked, referring to the data relay station deep in the ship's bowels where Holden and his cronies liked to hang out while the men were away on operations, comparing theories and exchanging rumors.

Holden shook his head, "No one really heard anything of substance. Most arts left some time ago when the rest of the Guard lifted."

"Must have gotten away again. It'd be all over the ship if we had caught them."

"Well, as we speak, the Gokazoku Kaigi are meeting in the officer's mess. I've been asked to get you there as soon as possible, that is, after you're properly cleaned up."

Dasko smiled, "You think I need a bath?"

"Well, I don't mind of course, but Miss Kalen might be a bit disturbed by your appearance. You look frightful, why all the blood?" Holden frowned, suddenly concerned. "Are you injured, sir?"

"It's nothing—I'll tell you about it later."

The two stepped into a shimmering field lifter and Holden said, "Gregson level three."

Their bodies slowly rose within the suspensor field. The ship's decks were numbered from top to bottom, thus gregson level three and officer's country was close to the top of the ship, near the command centers.

Dasko and Holden stepped out of the lift into a broad hallway. Darkened hatches lined each side of the slick black hall. Several doors were open and laughter could be heard filtering out. This part of the ship was less crowded and they passed only a few men and technical arts that hummed past. Beyond the junior officer's quarters—small, impersonal spaces crammed with a desk, wash basin, locker and four billets—lay the senior officer's individual quarters. These, too, were tight, narrow spaces. However, they were private, and boasted the added amenity of a personal refresher.

Dasko's door sluiced open as he approached. He heaved his gear onto the deck in a pile and began to peel his sweat-drenched uniform off. "Do I have any messages?"

Holden leaned over the com board and touched a node. After a short pause a soft voice spoke from the board, "You have three messages, lieutenant. Would you care to hear them?"

"Play the messages, please." Dasko tugged at the heel of his boot trying to pry it off his swollen foot as he listened to the voices of Lewg and Danelle cajoling him in colorful language to hurry up and join them in the officer's mess. He was, apparently, missing all the fun.

He stepped into the refresher tube and spent several long minutes letting the jets of recycled moisture strip away the day's accumulated pressures and filth. He emerged a new man. Holden had laid out a fresh uniform and sidearm.

"Are you hungry, sir? Would you care for a snack?"

His eyes lit up at the thought of food. He suddenly realized that he hadn't eaten all day. He nodded vigorously. "Yes, by all means."

Holden produced a small silver bowl of fruit, covered with a linen napkin. Three flat biscuits were carefully arranged on top. "I thought you might be hungry. I usually have a hard time sneaking any food out of the dining hall after hours. Major Scall doesn't take kindly to unassigned personnel snooping around his kitchen. However, this evening I was able to find a weak link in the chain."

Dasko grinned and took a huge bite out of a powder blue apple.

"The sous chef has a new protégé, a Gallantrean hailing from the Dartinells system, a planet by the name of Vipst if I recall correctly. As fate would have it, I was once stationed on the *Gaston*, a small scientific research facility in orbit around a planet in the Dartinells system — this was of course over a hundred years ago, long before you were ever born. The chief petty officer aboard the *Gaston* was also a Gallantrean and he used to prepare the most fascinating crips volour — "

"Crips volour?" Dasko asked with his mouth full of apple.

"Yes, an intricate blend of kepsin liver, del pourin cheese, and mushrooms baked in a puff pastry shell. The petty officer added a dash of Kouln brandy he kept stashed aboard which made all the difference in the world."

Dasko dried himself as he ate, holding the fruit in his mouth mid-bite as he stepped into his clean clothes.

Holden continued, "I was relaying my experiences aboard the *Gaston* to Tomas, our new chef, trying to make him feel welcome here. In return for the crips volour recipe I was able to convince him to set aside some fruit from dinner."

"This was just what I needed." He fastened a new comtab onto the short tab collar of his blazer, fastened his encryption tools to his belt, and ran his fingers through his still wet hair.

"You haven't finished your dinner yet." Holden protested.

"Gotta go. I'm sure I'll be late, so feel free to do as you wish for the rest of the night."

"Thank you, sir. Are you sure you won't have just one more piece?"

Dasko smiled, "Don't worry, I've had plenty." He placed a reassuring hand upon the cool surface of the artificial's shoulder and squeezed.

"It's good to have you back, sir."

THE OFFICER'S MESS was shoulder-to-shoulder, bustling with voices and boisterous laughter of the men who survived the raid on Hammerfield. Dasko made his way through the crowd, angling toward the long bar which stretched the length of one bulkhead.

"Dailyern green," he shouted above the din to the small wrinkled man behind the bar. "And make it sing!"

The bartender turned his back and began selecting exotic-looking bottles from the tempered, glazed cases lining the wall. Dasko glanced up at the row of screens mounted over the bar that flashed ship bulletins. Casualty updates were currently displayed. The old man returned, placing two half-filled vials suspended in a small wire rack on the bar.

"'Ere you are, looten't." He watched as Dasko poured the contents of one vial into the other and tossed the frothing contents down the back of his throat in one smooth motion. The bartender grinned wickedly. "'Notha for ya, sih?"

Tears welled up in Dasko's eyes, but he bobbed his head and managed to cough out, "That one sang all right! One more, Landin."

The officer's mess was a deep slab of space with close, constricting walls paneled with dark wood and ceilings that disappeared into the darkness of the bulkheads far above. The tight, tall space was wedged between the dual vaults that housed the ship's E2 datacores. A subdued light emanated from glow rods recessed in the floor and the semi-darkness lent an intimate air to the hall. Beautiful, thick tables filled most of the mess. Their long ashen surfaces were home to many soldiers who stood to get a better view of the proceedings. Smaller game tables were scattered here and there.

Brilliant woven tapestries festooned the walls of the mess. Long banners displayed the coat of arms of each Imperial unit currently stationed aboard the *Shiva*. Ornate golden dragons and screaming wyverns peered from the colorful, eyes discreetly observing the revels of the Imperial officers within.

Dasko spied the wispy form of Sheb'dura hovering above a table in the middle of the hall. He shouldered his way through the crowd. Lewg caught sight of him as he neared the table.

"It's about time you got here Dasko!"

"We were beginning to think you were staying with the diggers," Danelle concurred. The table broke into laughter.

Eleven of the Gokazoku Kaigi stood surrounding their traditional table in the center of the hall. The translucent shape of the ghost of Sheb'dura shimmered amidst them.

Dasko nodded toward the specter, "Dirt's not my fate."

More laughter crackled across the room.

The ghost of Sheb'dura did not join in the merriment. He fixed him with a rueful eye. "You have the look of blood upon you boy. Tell me, could you feel the steel entering your flesh?"

All eyes suddenly focused on Dasko. "Is he right? Are you injured?" Kalen asked with a worried look.

"It's just a scratch, I'm fine."

"Did you feel the end of possibilities? Did you watch the sticky syrup pour from your sweet shell?"

"Knock it off Sheb'dura — leave the poor boy alone."

"It's all right," Dasko said climbing up next to the ghost and sitting down on the tabletop.

"I am merely focusing the young lieutenant's perceptions," Sheb'dura rumbled. "You all act as if you can live forever."

"Why not?" Lewg quipped, "You seem to have." The table erupted in laughter once more.

"I'm not alive," the ghost grumbled with a hint of sadness and a touch of the futility that seemed to permeate his existence. Sheb'dura existed as a portable, low-resonance pictogram created from the electronic signature, or essence, of his former self. Two hundred and seventy-nine years ago, as his body lay dying, a huge electrical charge was sent sweeping through his brain to imprint the residual electrical pattern onto a digital chip matrix.

The first sweep recorded any charge still left within the brain, in Sheb'dura's case there was quite a lot as he had not yet died from his battle wounds. This "personality shadow" was loaded into upper memory. Then a series of staged charges were sent sweeping through the brain at different levels, recording the information within. The combined data was loaded into a matrix much like programming an artificial. The result was a cognizant, self-aware, though albeit, very morose reflection of the former self. A ghost with thought and memory intact.

Sheb'dura resided within a small Tarkanian containment shell where he rested and drew power for his visual incarnation as a low-resolution pictogram. The fist-sized shell sat atop the long table and Sheb'dura's image flickered from a projector within.

Galar, Lewg, and Kalen resumed their arguing over the infamous Butcher of Yuzbek, the Emperor's personal assassin. Their voices rang out loudly in order to be heard in the boisterous hall.

"He's consistently fatal. Look at the counts."

"Naw, that's propaganda. Imperial traditionalism makes him seem more dangerous than he really is, like the red web spider. Her bites don't kill ya."

"He does seem more like a frumias bandersnatch."

"Oh, that old myth."

"The first engineered assassin."

"But he's an armchair assassin," Lewg sneered, throwing back another vial. "He hasn't been out of the Core in years!"

"Tight on the Emperor's leash, agreed!"

A new voice sounded behind the Guardsmen. "You sound much like a quisling with talk like that."

Lewg crooked his arm over the back of his chair and turned to face the offending party. The man was seated alone at a small game table, impeccable black tunic bearing no insignia, though a small dragon was stitched into the cuff of his crimson sleeve. He eyed the man's thick frame and arresting eyes. They appeared silvery, though it could have just been a reflection from the lights. A jagged scar was just visible below the open neck of his uniform. His complexion was pale, almost grey. The man appeared relaxed as he sipped his mercury. A wide, heavy bandolier was slung across the man's chest. Small silver spheres were clipped across its surface. They looked very much like Sheb'dura's containment shell. Lewg stared at the man. *Was he carrying around a host of disembodied spirits? What in the name of K'ye would he need them for? Perhaps the shells held something else entirely.*

Lewg felt a need to announce himself. "You disagree with me, I see."

"Leave the stranger alone, Lewg." Sheb'dura urged.

"No, no. I don't believe he liked my assessment of the Emperor's infamous butcher."

The ghost swept over the table to Lewg's side and whispered in his ear, "Leave it be!"

Lewg waved the ghost off and glared at the stranger. "You disagree with me?"

"I find *you* disagreeable," the man growled. "You dishonor your position."

Lewg gave a sideways glance to his mates then turned back to the man. "I don't recall asking your opinion—we're having a private conversation here."

"Private treachery is treachery nonetheless."

"We are not discussing treachery here, merely debunking a few myths."

"Myths are borne of truth. Your Imperial Guard is rife with legendary stories of valor and courage. The regimental colors that hang here are dominated by images of mythical creatures. The stories and accounts of Imperial power follow us wherever we go. Each new planet we encounter has undoubtedly heard of the *myths* of Imperial invincibility, and many bow to us on the strength of fear alone. Untold lives have been spared due to the power of our myths. The Emperor's Butcher is no different."

"Spare me the traditionalism. The infamous *butcher* is no more than a cipher—a propped up myth to keep aging proctors quivering in their sleep."

Sheb'dura's spirit sighed and shook his head, "Fools. Don't you recognize an assassin when you see one?"

"Assassin?" Lewg narrowed his gaze. "How can you tell?"

The ghost grew impatient, standing abruptly and walking over to the man. "The eyes. Look at the eyes, man!"

Lewg stared, trying to discern some clue as to what Sheb'dura meant.

"His eyes have already taken you apart piece by piece. He could have you and most of the table floored before you got off a scream, much less drew your blade."

Lewg glanced over at Sheb'dura skeptically, as if he didn't quite believe him.

"He's an assassin all right, and you've just finished insulting the greatest of his brethren."

Lewg frowned slightly, his smarmy demeanor suddenly absent.

"You should listen to your dead friend," the man murmured. "He hasn't your traitorous tone."

A voice rang out from the entrance. "The only traitor around here is the man who doesn't buy me a drink!" Vailetta Strom crossed the mess, cape swinging out as she swept through the crowded room.

The room made way for the woman and an appreciative murmur followed her. She purposefully hooked two beakers of ice ale and sloshed one of them roughly across the stranger's table. "You seem in want of a drink, soldier. We haven't formally met—"

"You're Vailetta Strom, Captain of the Guard," the man inclined his head minutely and accepted the drink.

"And you're Vasily Bey-Torg, the vice proctor's new personal assassin.

"I prefer Torg."

"Torg it is. Another one barkeep, and keep them coming," Vailetta let her body slide into a chair, at ease despite the waves of tension vibrating through the hall. She let her head drop to one side, black hair sliding in a silky tangle around her shoulder. "Ice ale from Botha. It's like being home again."

Torg sampled the concoction and tasted his lips with a white tongue. "Harkens 35,247."

"No," Vailetta mused, contemplating the blue liquid sliding from side to side in her glass, "This tastes more like '249." She hooked her leg over the arm of her chair and suggested, "How about a game of *Go*?"

Her men canvassed the huge man, their bodies deceptively relaxed. Torg ignored them and stretched back in his chair, eyeing the woman's inscrutable smile.

"All right," he said finally. "Board."

The table whirred a moment and a game grid swirled into view. A growling dragon rose out of the mists, yellow eyes glowing brightly against blue-green scales, red tongue a feathery tendril, its outline a flourish of artistry. The dragon gave a startled grunt, twisted in on itself and vanished.

"Table's blanking out again."

"Board please, and thank you," said Vailetta, looking at Torg as the dragon reappeared between them. It writhed as the mist thickened. A roar cleared the fog to show the dragon flattened out into a two-dimensional grid with 361 dotted intersections.

Just outside the display a small square panel opened in the table harboring two containers of colored playing stones. Vailetta reached for the container of black, leaving the white to Torg.

"You flatter me," he said, narrowing his eyes as he leaned in to accept the symbol of game superiority.

Go was an addiction aboard ship. Even Commander Arnas indulged in the strategic pastime, often playing opposite Lord Barrett. Game style was a thinly veiled window into a player's psyche, and tonight it was going to offer Vailetta a glimpse into the assassin's thoughts, or so she hoped.

After fifteen minutes of play the game was interrupted. Temple chimes sounded and the board clouded as a tremendous pale tiger, the icon of the Nralda Keiretsu, stretched out of a pool. The tiger circled the table, rolling a spherical cobalt bomb between its paws.

"Unbelievable! Second time this month."

"Always that same cat."

"Yeah, well this'd better be a glitch — I want to see the endgame."

The dragon icon rose up from the table and challenged the tiger. The cat's ears flattened back as the fuse tripped and danced, burning figuratively as the subroutine wormed its way into the datacore.

"Demolition alert! Leave rank and file!" Vailetta called out calmly, memory of the game fading before the all-too-real threat of a viral bomb. The gentle pressure behind her words forced the others to leave slowly, gradually, without hysteria, like the tapered ending of a party. She was the senior officer — she would remain. Sweat broke out on her brow as she surveyed the game table. The viral bomb could have been planted weeks earlier in any part of the ship's datacore. It had found its way here, to the officer's mess — a prime location within the ship. A detonation at this game table would deprive the ship of some of its finest men.

By her shoulder, Lieutenant Dasko stood at the ready, decryption tools in hand, headset in place. "Lieutenant Dasko, accept command," she said, stepping back from the table.

"Aye," he replied, jacking in by her knee and pulling the headset's built in reality blinkers into place over his eyes "Let's see the chock o' duds they've left us today."

Datacore viral bomb scares had risen dramatically as economic pressures mounted from Imperial expansion. Many of the keiretsu employed terrorist tactics in the ongoing struggles over territorial rights, shipping lanes, taxation, conscription, and outright subjugation. The bombs resembled simple viruses, but were comprised of complex nanites embedded in seemingly innocuous shipping protocols or uploaded in navigational data packets. Once safely entrenched in an Imperial datacore, the components assembled themselves into a viral bomb — quite lethal and very difficult to detect and hunt down. The Nralda Keiretsu had chosen a white tigers as its calling card and this explained the iconic image that had manifested itself over the game table as the bomb assembled itself.

The Collistas Dynasty was on the brink of open warfare with various keiretsu, but as of now a fierce cold war waged with most Imperial tactics aimed at keeping the scattered keiretsu enough at odds with one another that they wouldn't band together into a greater menace. As it was, even the highest security was frequently breached and many good men had been lost. Implanted viral bombs were so frequent now in the Shell that Dasko never left quarters without his equipment.

"Get out of here," Vailetta ordered Torg, alerted by the rumble of heavy steel descending behind them. "Last chance. That blast shield's coming down." But the assassin only shifted to get a better view of the game board visible beneath the creatures.

"The game isn't over."

"Good luck!" shouted back one of her men.

Vailetta didn't blink as the blast shield clanged shut, silencing the encouraging yells of the officers beyond and sealing the three of them in. A droplet of sweat sped down her face.

"Dasko?" her voice came out jarringly.

"Bomb here. Fifty darcalyn: enough to blow half this deck apart. How'd they get that much into the system?"

"Stay focused, Dasko."

"Three codes, one decoy, one my access. The other appears to be wired live."

"Live?"

"It appears to have integrated itself into the subsystem programing."

"Can you break it?"

"First code's down. Searching for the second."

"Your move," Torg interrupted. Strangely the game board was still up.

"Pass," whispered Vailetta, squinting at the board without really seeing individual pieces, but instead trying to comprehend the blurry whole. *There, where Torg's army had begun growing around hers, the tiger had leapt out. Two codes. The other code had to be, what? Fail-safe?*

"Have you tried running the code into an endless loop?" asked Sheb'dura.

"Who left that ghost in here?"

Sheb'dura leaned over Dasko's shoulder to peer at the game display.

"Perhaps the deactivation code is keyed into the game itself," the ghost offered.

"Get out of my face!" Dasko yelled with frustration as the image writhed in front of him.

"No, wait! Maybe he's right."

"We're live. Backpack cobalt, a big one. Put away your bomb blankets—this one's gone fission on us."

"Dasko! This is not the way I planned to go!"

"Better appeal quick. We're at 200 darcalyn. Twenty seconds," Dasko intoned, "and counting."

Two codes. Vailetta's mind bolted. *Two codes. One: numbers, equations, core-accessible, and one in the subsystem itself. Part of the game itself?*

"I'm not finding it," Dasko cried out. "Fifteen to go."

Suddenly the dragon figure jumped back behind Vailetta's black army, dipping its neck toward the board, its smooth third eye glinting with the source of his power as the tiger slashed empty air in its place. *Dasko must be stuck*, she realized. *The code, the code... What in the game would kill the dragon? What was left?* She watched numbly as Torg's hand hovered over the board, darting like the tiger's tail to lay the final playing pieces.

You're the tiger, she thought. *And the tiger wants the dragon's power symbolized by the third eye. Where is there an eye in the game—ah! I'm the dragon—my eye is the empty space in my army. The tiger must have some of it or all of it or there will be battle and damage, death in this room. Fill the eye, share the power with the tiger, warning received!*

"I'm sorry, captain," Dasko whispered.

"The eye!" Vailetta screamed. "Fill the eye!"

Torg moved without hesitation. When he had laid the piece it glowed like the dragon's power eye, and the beast snatched away the bomb. The tiger turned on Torg, tail lashing, ears flattened. It leapt out at him across the game table, atoms tearing apart as it dematerialized. The dragon swallowed noisily, raising its wings. It belched with the dull sound of a muffled explosion and a flame shot out of its mouth. A burst of mist from the dragon's nostrils turned the flame to smoke. Kneading its claws on its belly, it sat back on its haunches in a contented way, and faded out.

Torg looked up into Vailetta's grey eyes and said, "It's ended."

Lieutenant Dasko stripped off his headset and stared at the glowing eye on the playing grid. He ran his hand through his spiky hair.

"I didn't think you'd win," he said to Torg.

"I believe your captain won this round," Torg said, his eyes glinting strangely in the red light.

"One will, lieutenant." Vailetta sighed as she leaned against the table.

"One will, yours," replied Dasko, stepping back, his head bowed.

"One will, the Emperor," came Torg's gravelly voice, finishing for all of them.

Ship's com chimed twice: "Captain Strom, report to command tower eight, imperative." The message repeated.

"Well, that's my cue." Vailetta stood and twirled her cape across her shoulders, refastening it to her tunic. Pausing, she stared down at the soldier. "It was a pleasure, dark one."

"All mine, I assure you," he murmured as she turned and strode out of the mess.

11

Kess

Early explorers of the Dell-Transim system jokingly referred to the Mounds of Kess as one of the galaxy's great treasures. It was said that even a handful of dirt smeared on one's belly made a breeder more fertile. Despite the lack of scientific backing, the superstition held, and in some places breeding males and females smelled as ripe as they hoped to be.

Dawn cast long, rigid shadows across the mounds. Most of the stacks were uniform height, reaching from 100 to 250 meters in the air. They were separated into lots by luminescent barriers. The blackened stacks were all in distinct stages of decomposition, each layer built up carefully over time.

The heat on Kess was almost bearable, but the stench wasn't. Insects swooped through the columns of decay at Gort's Agro Supply, creating an impenetrable and uncomfortable haze that stretched from the basaltic plains for several kilometers to the rich delta of the Kansa River. Each column of dirt created concentrated fermentation that was sparingly parceled into chemical vats. The end product was a highly-prized fertilizer used to terraform thousands of worlds. Beyond the mephitic mounds, odor-free compost was being cultivated in painstaking rows under a tangled network of nitrogen pipes and depth-shade awnings. Several crumbly piles were being raked by hand, to the lively tune of a fiddler and the accompanying tenor groans of bladder pipes.

At Helen's approach a canine tracie emitted a hoarse bark, and nearby Kess looked up from turning fresh manure with long handled blades. Even from this distance it was easy to make out their thick-skinned musculature, as the stocky Kess wore only lengths of bright cloth kilted at the waist. One broke from the pack, running upright on cloven hooves. He stopped abruptly before Helen, sending a spray of decay over their legs.

Garrand stepped back, disgusted. "The smell! It's beyond anything!"

Closing his tiny eyes, the Kess snorted, "Ahh — makes a body glad to be alive! Helenachov, girl, how good to smell you again."

"Brimwal?" Helen asked, shading her eyes against the glare. She squinted up at the creature's beaming porcine face with its short, crooked tusks somersaulting over like tightly curled mustachios.

"You don't look a day older and smell just as sweet."

"Well, you've grown," she said in admiration. "Last I saw, you hardly met your sire's thigh."

His already ruddy cheeks suffused with deeper color. "I shot past him all right. Gywal's in the field yonder. But you must be here for the usual." He pressed the two fleshy halves of a front hoof under his hairy chin. "I never forget an order." He grunted some, thinking, and then gave a low squeal of triumph. "Lot 509, for growing special grass."

"That's right." Helen looked impressed. After all, the Kess had been merely a shoat learning his trade when last she came.

"Number's changed, but dirt's the same." He tapped his snout and motioned to the squat canine lingering by his side. "Hey tracie, get me a lead on some dirt for Helena. Check the inventories." The beast loped away, nose to the earth. Brimwal clapped his hooves together and regarded Helen with a gleam in his eye.

"What'd you bring from the good Doc this time?" He watched with interest as Helen unloaded two large canisters from her satchel.

"Potassium iodide." The Kess suffered from a severe iodine deficiency that resulted in goiter, the thyroid glands at the base of the throat swelling uncomfortably. Dr. Beh'ln Tchelakov had been supplying them with the corrective solution for years. But now Brimwal shook his head, his big shoulders bunching and flexing.

"Helena, it's been a long time, so long in between comings. We couldn't depend on Doc anymore, so we found another connection. I just received a shipment for this term from the Freetrader Stuvious." He scratched at his ear, plucking the long flap beneath. "We've got a combination deal with them. He brings that and other needs and then hauls for us to the Rowlings people terraforming on Creyst. I can't undermine that," he said with finality.

Helen reacted with blank shock. She had counted on this need as her bargaining chip and then summarily dismissed Kess from her mind. There had been too many other pressing details to consider. But now, this one assumption was going to blow her entire objective. It seemed absurd, almost ludicrous.

"You've another something, haven't you?" His voice sounded wheedling, as if it would hurt him terribly to turn her away.

Panic wrapped around her and a tiny hysterical giggle escaped her. Garrand cocked his head and moved closer.

"Could I have a moment?" He drew her aside. "What's the matter with you?" He gave her a small shake, disliking the vacant glaze in her eyes. She looked through him.

"We have to have the dirt, or it's all for naught."

"With all your credit? Why don't you just buy some?" he asked suspiciously. Her eyes finally jerked to his.

"Because," she hissed, wiping her brow with the heel of her hand, "They don't accept credit. It's a farm system here. All barter. You have to have machinery or seedlings or steel fittings—dry goods, anything that—"

"Seedlings? Did you say seedlings?" He seemed to consider this.

"Yes, for green manures, cover crops to till under and improve the soil, and for testing yields in different varieties of dirt. Why does it matter? I don't have any of those things."

Garrand frowned and took a deep breath. This was an important contract and he would not watch it collapse on the first leg.

"How important is this to you?" he asked quickly, eyes locked on hers.

"You have something?" she shook her head, blinking.

"How important?" he insisted.

"If he accepts, name your price." She looked dazed.

A real smile spread across Garrand's face. "Back in a flash."

"Oh, no. I'm coming with you."

Brimwal watched in bemusement as they raced to *Destiny's Needle*. Helen tagged Garrand as closely as she dared and nearly clipped his heels in her haste to follow. Inside the ship they maneuvered several corridors before he stopped in a narrow serviceway and stepped up against the sloping bulkhead.

Garrand looked uncertainly at Helen for an instant, then stretched up his hand up over a bundle of power conduits. His fingers found a hidden depression and he tapped the smooth indentation three times. A panel slid open at his feet. Garrand knelt to the recessed command board and quickly keyed in the proper code. A section of the ceiling spiraled open, releasing a burst of cold mist. A ladder descended smoothly and Garrand disappeared up into the darkness. Helen had no choice but to follow.

Inside she felt his hand shove something against her chest and she instinctively grabbed onto a pair of goggles. She donned them and could finally see through the mist to the extraordinary sight of rows upon tiers of gravity jars filled with seedlings, all tagged and anchored in bright, hydroponic solution. There were dozens of rows of gravity jars suspended between the pipes. And she had thought the Nralda tightly controlled all trade of biodiversity transport mediums. Yet here was evidence of a booming black market slip. She reached out to the nearest dome, squinting through the hydrogen rich atmosphere of the miniature world, and inspected the heart-shaped leaf of the plants inside. Its red veins tugged the name from her memory. Reclusive creeper.

"But this isn't possible," she whispered to herself, "This plant is extinct." She moved on to other jars, breathing each name with a soft, schooled reverence. "Casmel, myacinth, kineth." All extinct, all impossibly here. Garrand had a virtual treasure hold of plants that supplied produce and medicines thought lost to oblivion. Out of the mist, his face loomed next to her.

"Pretty cool, huh?" he grinned.

"Incredible," she whispered to the mist-shrouded globes, her words tiny puffs of conviction against the chill. She laughed with the sheer wonder of it. "Wait a minute. You couldn't even get off of Letugia. You had these the whole time? Why didn't you sell one there?"

"Letugia?" Garrand frowned and shook his head, the swirling air closing back around him. "Nothing grows there. Wrong market. No, this bounty is for the future." A hiss erupted as he set about disconnecting one of the jars.

"Then why now, to help me?"

"Don't get me wrong," Garrand groaned with the effort to turn reluctant, clinking valves. "I'm merely cashing one in. You'll pay the full value." His triumphant grin flashed through the mist and Helen spun away, adding this new, ill-fitting piece to the complicated puzzle that was Garrand Ai'Gonet Médeville.

GARRAND STOOD AT the entrance to the amidships hold and watched with some degree of bemusement as hundreds of cubic tonnes of dirt poured into the bay from three topside hatches. Outside, primitive conveyor belts trundled the dirt from catch basins positioned at the foot of the ship up over the armor plating and into *Destiny's Needle*. Several young Kess were diligently raking the dirt away from the pyramidal piles that formed under the hatches, spreading the dirt evenly throughout the hold.

"So much for trying to keep the ship clean," he muttered.

Bailey stood attentively at his side, holding a clipscanner that detailed the new cargo load. "It is something to behold," the artificial said uncertainly. "That is quite a bit of dirt."

Garrand felt a sickening emptiness in his gut as he watched the dirt tumble in. He hated the notion of all that dust and filth getting into ship systems, fouling equipment that was already balky. But it was more than that. He had the uneasy sensation, like nausea, that he was losing control of the events around him. Everything was starting to rush by on all sides while he was stuck in the torpid center. What little control he held over his life was illusory, he knew, but his ship and his crew were all that he had left — and losing that, too, would be more than he could bear.

Bailey gauged his facial reactions with some degree of concern. "The holds were never the most pristine places aboard, sir."

"Yeah, but this is a little too much to ask. Residual dirt off grimy cargo shells is one thing, but this..." he gestured across the hold, words unable to describe the disdainful pit forming in his stomach. "This is going to get tracked through the whole ship. We'll never get rid of it all. Oh, cheplus," he cursed as he remembered the repairs they had made on Letugia. "Think of what it's going to do to the atmo processors! The dust skimmers are going to need changing before we even lift!"

"I'm sure Little Bit will attend to it, sir."

Garrand felt something brush sensuously across his lower calf. He looked down to see the mottled brown, black and grey-furred exel rubbing up against him, back arched, tail wrapped around his boot. The exel looked up, wrinkled its nose and yawned.

"She seems to like you, sir."

Garrand grunted. The exel perked up its head and watched the cascades of dirt with interest. Suddenly it crouched low, wiggled its back end to establish footing and then sprang forward with amazing speed. It rushed headlong into the nearest pyramid of dirt and promptly flopped over onto its back where it performed a series of luxuriating flip flops, stretching out its limbs in the glorious, cool dirt.

"At least someone likes the dirt," Garrand observed.

"Bernadine, sir."

"Excuse me?"

"The exel's name is Bernadine, captain."

Garrand rocked his head back minutely. "Ah, I see. Well she certainly seems to like the dirt."

"Yes, I'm not quite sure what to make of it sir, the core makes no mention of such behavior."

"Well, I'm sure you'll make heads of it." He looked around uncertainly for a moment.

"Have you seen Helen? I need to find out where we're going next."

Bailey perked up. "Miss Tchelakov? I believe she is feeding coordinates into the navi on the bridge."

"By herself? I thought I told you to keep an eye on her!"

"You did, and I was, but she asked me to come find you."

Garrand rolled his eyes, "Why didn't you just use the comtab?"

"She wanted me to find you personally."

"So you left her alone—on the bridge of all places." He hurried past the artificial and headed toward the bridge. Bailey followed smoothly behind.

"Bailey," Garrand grumbled, "This is what I was talking about. You have to learn when to be polite and when to be stubbornly rude. My orders supersede her personal requests."

"You do not trust Miss Tchelakov?" Bailey seemed genuinely disturbed.

"Bailey I only trust you. There's no telling what she's really up to, I haven't been able to get a straight answer from her yet. But we're tied up in this mess now, and we're going to have to be very, very careful if we want to live long enough to get paid."

Garrand entered the bridge and stepped onto the platform overlooking the crystal globe and four command stations. With a softly spoken word, he ordered Helen's navigational pod to rotate up to the entrance. The pod smoothly halted before the platform and the railing retracted, revealing Helen hard at work studying star charts that hovered in midair above her console. She did not bother to look up.

Garrand stepped quietly onto the pod and silently followed her progress. Bailey stood at the entrance, awaiting orders. Garrand made three short hand signals without moving his arm from his side and Bailey disappeared back through the hatch.

"Having any trouble with the navi?" he asked, trying to keep his tone nonchalant as he examined the sartographs. She had charts displayed for three systems.

"No," she replied, brushing hair back from her face. "Your system is a genuine pleasure to use. You have up-to-date vector information for half the systems in the Shell and precalculated routes for nearly every major shipping lane. Very impressive."

Garrand didn't rise to the compliment. "Where are we headed?"

Helen paused and turned sideways to look at him, hesitating visibly. Now that his ship knew where they were going, then he would soon know as well. The name of the planet stuck on the tip of her tongue, however, as she had not dared speak it to anyone to this point.

Finally she said, "El-Bouteran."

El-Bouteran? Garrand frowned. "The Pakken system?"

"Yes."

"El-Bouteran is the only planet in the whole system. Pretty remote isn't it?"

"These are exotic creatures we're picking up, Captain. You expect to find them in the central bazaar on Wyx?"

"Certainly not," he snapped. "But I also don't expect to find them on an uninhabited world so far out in the Jo-Hellus Arm that it's been passed over for colonization a dozen times because it's just too far from any of the established trade routes and it would never survive. What are you hiding them from?"

"Nothing," she replied indignantly. "El-Bouteran is no more unlikely than any of a thousand worlds. You suffer from an overactive imagination, Captain."

Garrand noted her defensive tone with concern. If there was indeed a trace on board, they were in deep trouble. He could feel his stomach churning with renewed dread.

"Very well," he conceded. Now was not the time to force the issue. "Does your time-line for pick up allow for counteractive navigational maneuvers to throw off any possible pursuit?"

Helen nodded solemnly.

"Good," he sighed. "I'll have Bailey begin work on a serpentine course as soon as we've secured the ship for lift. That'll at least confuse anyone trying to follow us. Then our first priority is sweeping the ship for any trace hidden aboard."

"Agreed." She stood and brushed past him, the soft feminine fragrance she favored hesitating in her wake. "I'll see that the hold is properly prepared," she said, suddenly very cooperative. She slipped through the hatch and disappeared down the curving hall, but her fragrance remained, the sweet scent hanging in the air. Garrand took a deep breath and closed his eyes.

"Bailey, you and *Destiny* have a lot of nav work to do."

Bailey watched his friend with concern. The pain in his face was troubling. "Sir, were your concerns justified?"

"Who knows, Bailey. Who knows? Only time will tell."

12
The Freezer

Shouts rang out along the corridor. Arnas smelled burning flesh and knew he was getting close. He heard the slap and sizzle of something big hitting the grill. There was a smoky piquancy to whatever they were cooking for tonight's diplomatic banquet. The wonderful smells drew him forward more quickly through the hallway leading to Barrett's enormous personal kitchen.

Arnas pushed his way past hovering lighters jammed with crushed ice and vegetables. Perma-racks filled with live fish, mouths still gasping after being removed from their tanks, lined the aisles. The corridor was jammed with shining artificials, their arms piled high with fresh fruit and jars of salt.

Arnas wended his way through the mayhem, following the melodic cants of the Jai Durās. Those who took the time to glance at him stood aside in deference, but most shoved right by, gripped by near panic as the banquet's first course drew near. Arnas was forced to stand aside as artificials hurried past him carrying silver platters filled with endless tresses of garlic and wild mushrooms.

Without fanfare, he slipped inside the kitchen itself. There was a primitive air to the raucous scene. Arnas enjoyed the feverish thrill of the banquet preparations. The electricity in the room was uncannily similar to the excitement in his combat ready room prior to a drop. He liked to stand in the kitchen, just inside the doorway and watch the madness blossom. He enjoyed the innocence of the scene: no one would die at the end of these preparations.

Stacks of multi-limbed crustaceans twisted and writhed on a lighter beside him. Unlike the commander, the little creatures felt a constant need to escape. A half dozen tumbled to the deck and scuttled sideways in great arcs. The prep chefs had runners to catch them, conscripts in ill-fitted uniforms who scampered between the arts and squeezed their small bodies under the lighters to try and snag a pincer. The artificials dodged these new obstacles and delivered fresh wares to the bellowing cooks.

Cauldrons of steam swept up from the clanking tins as harried preps rushed through the early boils, ordered on by the watchful Jai Durās. Nervous artificials fidgeted in the staggered alcoves, twitching with visible anxiety as they awaited service. The varelle fillets were broiling now, salty vapors condensing on the shining walls. Varelles were huge fish and their pungent white meat had to be broiled at high temperature to break down the fatty enzymes. The Jai Durās barked an order and one of the long fillets was flipped by sweaty preps that ducked their heads inside the roaring ovens.

Vice Proctor Barrett slipped into the kitchen from one of the many service halls leading to the banquet room and straightened his fastidiously unperturbed collar. He spied Arnas leaning against the wall and walked across the kitchen. His boots rang on the steel deck plates.

"Thank you for meeting me before dinner," he said above the din. "Come, let's find a more subdued spot." He ushered Arnas toward the frosted glazings of the towering freezer that stretched vertically for five decks. The door slid upward promptly as it spied the vice proctor.

"Welcome to freezer, sub-level three," the door said with obvious excitement. It wasn't often that he had a visitor of importance.

A gush of cold air greeted the two men as they swept into the expansive chamber. The door slid shut and they were encased in silence. Arnas walked to the steel railing and gazed up into the misty heights. The freezer was filled with thousands of butchered carcasses. Narrow walkways crossed the various levels, providing access for the butchers and meat runners. Arnas marveled at the wide array of animals. Many were kept alive with tubes and catheters leading to drip bags filled with blood. Micro phase emitters stimulated their hearts and tiny bellows forced the appropriate gases through their lungs. A fat, brown tatark from Beya blinked at him with a sad black eye and Arnas felt an eerie chill sweep up his spine. He looked away and realized that the entire labyrinth was encased in frosted glazings, so that you could just make out the shadows of the frenetic activity beyond, like blood vessels surging through arteries. Barrett paced around the gangway, looking for interesting tidbits, oblivious to the carnage around him. Arnas felt his knuckles tightening around the cold steel. He knew that freezers were filled with death, but this felt like something else entirely, this cold, dark heart of the ship.

"We have new intelligence from the Nepestar system," Barrett said as he snared a wriggling crustacean from a platter awaiting service to his own dinner table. The Vice Proctor tossed a holocube to Arnas as he crunched down on the soft cartilage.

Arnas thumbed the power node and the image of a striking young woman shimmered before him, reddish brown hair pulled back across startling green eyes. The woman was unaware that her image was being captured, for she stared off in another direction in obvious concentration.

Barrett motioned toward the image as he chewed, "Helen Tchelakov, sole surviving daughter of Dr. Beh'ln Tchelakov. She is a very exclusive operative under the direct control of Carrelle Darstin. They're rumored to be lovers. Sartoks peg it at seventy-four percent, though they're possibly estranged. Sartoks peg *that* at thirty-two percent, but the acceptance of estrangement when combined with her more recent activity creates a gross acceptance conclusion of homicidal proportions."

Arnas looked up from the holocube.

"Yes," Barrett nodded, "it would explain a good deal." He bit down on another squirming crustacean.

Arnas tried to make sense of the information. "What do we know about Carrelle Darstin?"

"Ah, the name piques your interest? It should. Director Darstin has been quite a source of trouble over the years. He has run several of the Nralda's legitimate business interests in the Gambon, Nepestar and Illius sectors—quite profitably I might add. Of more pressing interest, he has led the keiretsu's research and development arm for the last twenty years, absorbing or flat out conquering several dozen highly advanced biotechnical firms in the process. His success has elevated him to a position of some power within the keiretsu. Now he is poised to become infinitely more powerful still."

"The stolen bios?"

"Your intuition serves you well, commander. Yes, Dr. Tchelakov has managed to complete his genetic program without interference from the keiretsu or the Imperials. I believe he has found a way to successfully fuse a sartographic chip to a biological mind. If my suspicions are correct, the creatures he has chosen as incubators for this technology now represent the first quantum leap forward in the science of probabilities in four hundred years."

"The creatures we seek are advanced sartographs?"

Barrett shrugged. "For all we know they are animals without any understanding of their potential."

Arnas visibly blanched, his jaw setting into an angry posture.

Barrett spit out a piece of shell and continued, "They have eluded every attempt at their capture. It's not blind luck, commander."

"They're precognitive?"

"It appears they know what is going to happen before it transpires, yes."

"Like a Sartok."

"Yes, but with an intuitive flair."

"The perfection of the model."

"So it would seem."

"And you have withheld this information from me because...?"

"Because they are animals!" Barrett spat. "Because there is no way that base mammals elevated to sentience and force fed information could possibly have enough cognitive awareness to sort out their own place in the universe, much less outwit our arrays."

"Yet, they have," Arnas said bitterly. "And I have lost 17 men in the process."

"I have lost 743 men," Barrett bellowed. "I am no different than you, Arnas. I am chasing ghosts and counting casualties!" The Vice Proctor stalked down the misty aisle. He snatched a rack of raw beurle and took a vicious bite from the soft flank.

"Apologies, my Lord."

Barrett chewed the thick meat and glared at the man. "It's too much to believe that it's all coincidence. As unlikely as it seems, Dr. Tchelakov has successfully fused intuition to the sartographic model. Our unsuccessful pursuit is evidence of his success. It's simply Haven's End that we didn't catch it in time."

"But if he already controls the bios, why bother moving them over and over?"

"He doesn't control them completely—not yet. He merely oversees the funding for all projects in development for the keiretsu. He has no power over the projects themselves. For now, they are but an obscure research project financed by the Nralda, one of thousands of such programs in constant development by their network of research firms."

"But why move them?"

"To keep them hidden."

"From whom?"

"Eyes inside the Nralda—"

"—and outside interest like ours," Arnas finished for him. "I see."

"This program was the brainchild of a seemingly insignificant geneticist, Dr. Beh'ln Tchelakov. It caught director Darstin's attention, and then my own. Darstin nursed it along for years, wisely straining to keep the results secret. If Dr. Tchelakov's research proved successful, the results could catapult Darstin into a position of unimaginable power. The ruling directors of the Nralda could never be allowed to know the truth, so the project was kept hidden, the results kept secret."

"If all this is true, then how is it that we know of the Tchelakov creatures? Are the bios truly stolen?" Arnas asked his gaze narrowing. "They weren't ever a part of any Imperial program were they?"

"You grow bolder by the day, Commander," Barrett popped another crustacean in his mouth. His eyes picked over the rigid and emotionless features of his battalion commander. Arnas felt the same queasy feeling he often experienced when he was in the vice proctor's presence. As a commander in one of the Emperor's most revered and grueling services, he had fought alongside the most dangerous men alive. He'd also served under some of the most vicious men in the galaxy, and took pride in being hard to impress. Barrett, however, was unlike any he'd served before. He exuded an almost palpable aura of awareness and understanding. An ominous and raw sense of power surrounded everything he did and said. The respect he commanded was exceptional.

Arnas fought back his emotions and silently stood his ground. Perhaps the vice proctor would allow him the truth after so many months of chasing specters.

The two men stood eyeing each other for a few moments. Barrett allowed a thin smile to escape. "Very well," he conceded, "Rumors that the next leap in sartographic technology would be linked to biological intuition have circulated for decades, long before you or I were ever born. The technology has been stagnant for four hundred years. The idea of magical creatures engineered to see the future is a bedtime story passed from generation to generation to entertain small children before they were laid to sleep."

Barrett tilted his snack's carapace back and sucked out the last of its juices. He paused and licked his lips, savoring the last drops. "And yet reality has recently intruded on these faerie tales. Men were dying in pursuit of these fantasies. I've never heard of faerie tales so powerful that grown men would lay down their lives for them."

Arnas chuckled softly.

"Our intelligence reported the probability of such a project to be negligible. But the rumors persisted. I commissioned a special envoy to discover the truth. After several years of chasing down dead ends, my envoy discovered Dr. Tchelakov and his research. They had been well hidden."

"And we have sought them out ever since?"

"Full of excitement, I believed I could capture the entire research project quickly and easily. A small team was assembled and sent to the planet only to find empty nests and abandoned facilities. There is no way that they could have departed so quickly without prior knowledge of our impending arrival."

Arnas grunted audibly—he knew that sensation all too well.

"It was then I knew that I would have to use all the resources at my disposal to try to outwit Tchelakov." Barrett paused to study the stars outside the portal. He continued softly, "You were brought in and this rather sizeable task force was assembled."

"So this is my new target?" Arnas asked, rotating the image of Helen Tchelakov between his hands.

"No. The key to capturing the bios now lies with a rogue figure. We must learn to understand the man they've hired. Going outside their normal shipping protocol leads me to believe that Darstin intends to stage an accident—a disaster of one form or another. This way he can disavow the project's existence, recoup the keiretsu's huge financial investment by collecting the massive insurance policies, and at the same time squash the rumors once and for all. In the end he would have the creatures all to himself."

Arnas nodded in contemplation. "He could then take the bios out from under the keiretsu's prying eye, and finish their development on his own."

Barrett gritted his teeth, his breath steaming out of his nose. "If he succeeds, we will have lost our last chance to secure the creatures before they disappear altogether. We must act before the keiretsu's plan has a chance to unfold. The vessel that was hired in the Nepestar system is known as *Destiny's Needle*. The captain of the vessel is Garrand Ai'Gonet Médeville," he tossed a second holocube to the commander.

A wispy form shimmered into existence. A man appeared, a tall figure with powerful shoulders and a broad chest. His eyes were dark, striking. He had a clean profile with a straight nose, firm mouth, and dark brows. His hair was unruly and brown—almost black—cut unfashionably short, not even touching his shoulders. His clothes seemed a bit on the well-worn side, yet they were simple and elegant: black boots cut below the knee, dark trousers, and a short, dark jacket cut at the waist. The jacket bore no insignia but it seemed vaguely familiar, as if it were an old Imperial style gone out of date.

Arnas stared into the man's eyes; his gaze was arresting. The wrinkles around his temples framed soft hazel eyes, but the gentleness of their color did not match the intensity with which they seemed to bore right through Arnas' skull. The energy behind them was unsettling. There was a potent mix of intelligence and vigor behind the man's facial expression. This man was highly intelligent, possibly Core bred, possibly even...

"This man was a Guardsman."

"Very good, commander. The man once served the dragon, though you'd never believe it by looking at him now. He was once a highly regarded Captain of Proctor Birmaldon's Imperial Guard."

"Birmaldon?"

"Do you recall the Sardis incident?"

"Garrand Médeville?" he rolled the name over his tongue, searching his memory. His eyes lit up as he made the connection to the Stanzer rescue above Sardis. "The Griffin?" Arnas smiled broadly. "This is the same man who defied Admiral Jacik?"

"This is the man who sank a battle frigate," Barrett said sharply.

"Garrand Médeville," Arnas tutted to himself, "Captain of the Imperial Guard."

"Yes, the Griffin Order. Brotherhood of the Princes of Blood."

Arnas was now in high spirits. He finally had a mark worthy of his attentions. "Where in K'ye did they find him?"

"Yes," Barrett murmured in a sardonic tone. "Where indeed?"

"My lord, it's an inspired choice."

Barrett scrutinized Arnas with a shrewd eye. "Well if you're so impressed commander, have a look." He handed Arnas a finger spool. "The man is your problem now."

Arnas scrolled through the filament. "What's he doing in the Shell? He all but disappeared after Sardis."

"He hardly disappeared," Barrett grumbled, "Scroll down." Without waiting for Arnas to unspool the information, Barrett rattled off the profile in staccato rhythm. "In '346 he ran weapons to the Thorians on Grepsus. In '347 he lead the rogue force that broke the Talen quarantine on El Phobadia. In '350 he fought at the battle of Calis on the side of the loyalists. In '353 he singlehandedly broke the three-year blockade imposed on Veskin by the Deirr Nobles. The man is a force of nature."

Barrett peeled a wing off a frozen tralle and dug into the cold, soft flesh with his teeth. "He was courted by various keiretsu for years—particularly the Gombur Sun and Whispering Butterfly Consortiums, but the man works alone."

"There are stories about Sardis," Arnas murmured, "I've always wondered what really transpired."

"It's all there," Barrett muttered as he chewed. "He was a brilliant soldier in his time—bright, resourceful, bold. But above it all he was a romantic fool. He threw away everything—rank, career, future—all for the sake of seven lives."

"So the stories are true then?" Arnas could barely control his swelling interest. This disaster of a mission might turn into something interesting after all.

Barrett sighed. "Yes, Commander. The stories of the *Stanzer* rescue at Sardis are indeed true. Médeville threw away his career for seven lives."

"Those seven lives were the lives of *his* men though. Lives he had sworn to protect at all costs. The Guardsmen do not take their oaths lightly. He had no choice."

"Choice! The problem was he *had* a choice. He chose to refuse a direct order from a superior officer—never mind that the man was navy and possibly a complete imbecile—it was a direct order from a superior officer in battle. Men die in battle—it's a fact. One a commander must accept."

"But if they were still alive…"

"Of no consequence," Barrett shook his head and gave Arnas a withering glare. "In the course of rescuing those seven doomed men he risked the lives of hundreds of others, compromised the security of the fleet, and sunk—not merely lost, mind you—but irretrievably *sunk* a top of the line Imperial battle frigate."

Barrett walked to the broad window that dominated the far end of the chamber. "It's a wonder he wasn't executed." He sighed and stared at the effulgent display of star lines that swept behind the ship. "As it was, he lost everything. Rank, privilege, his commission, all that he held dear. Only the gratitude of Proctor Birmaldon saved his life."

"Do you think the Nralda know who he actually is?"

"Undoubtedly. Carrelle Darstin may appear to work in an arcane manner, but," Barrett turned back to Arnas and admonished, "he always produces results."

"How could they have made such a blunder as to let us find out about their allegedly secret transport?"

"Ah, there's the delicious part. Young Tchelakov is already bound in my service. She will deliver the bios to me."

Arnas' jaw dropped in disbelief. "Bound to deliver them to you? What in the name of Haven have I been doing for nine months if you already had a plan to secure the infernal creatures peaceably?" His temper rose as he remembered all the men he had lost in the last months, all the fresh young faces he had sent to K'ye.

"Don't be naive, Commander. This plan has been five years in the making and it is only just now coming to fruition. The price of dealing with the traitorous daughter is high—prohibitively high. There is every reason to suspect she will double-crossed me as well as Carrelle Darstin!" He shook his head. "No, the best way is still to take them before Médeville gets a hold of them. The simple act of Miss Tchelakov's betrayal of the Nralda may be all we need. She should lead us right to their secret hiding place."

"And what of Captain Médeville?"

"That is for you to consider. But remember, he's been out of the field for years. His reflexes are dulled by time and lethargy. His techniques are old—antiquated by your standards. He's rusty and should be no match for you and a platoon of my finest Shock Troops."

The Emperor's finest you mean, thought Arnas.

"There is a quantum trace aboard his ship. Once we have a firm destination you will be in charge, Commander."

Arnas's demeanor rapidly changed. His eyes brightened at the prospect. "In charge?"

"You will command the entire task force."

"What about Captain Ness?"

"I'll deal with Ness—you just make certain they do not escape us again."

13

KA'VAELUS

On the dark, fetid plains of Galzeki, towers of refuse waited to be recycled. Heavily armed Imperial guards patrolled squalid avenues cut between the massive piles of scrap metal and solid waste. Humans were the invaders here, and the indentured laborers had to be protected at all times, lest they be killed by the highly evolved insect natives.

Galzeki was once a world dominated by tropical rainforests. Rich with life, Galzeki had spawned not one, but dozens of sentient species. Several of the larger and more complex insects species had evolved over the millennia into mankind's peers. Usurped by the Collistas Dynasty in the Valgen campaign, the planet was tagged unusable due to its massive alien population and was set aside for garbage reclamation. This was, in essence, a death sentence for most of the native lifeforms of Galzeki—sentient and non-sentient alike. During the ensuing Imperial deforestation, species either adapted or were wiped out. Millions of species became extinct, but a half-dozen sentients survived and battled back, vowing to rid their world of Imperial infestation.

Several varieties of beetles thrived despite the invasion of humans and their constant barrage of detritus. There was a large population of militant Breyer sloths and two species of butterfly with beautiful multicolored wings and long, curling tongues. Dominating the planet's new social structure were the Gambor—giant beetles whose far-distant ancestors once lived within the rainforest canopy, crawling amongst the wet leaves and myriad other insects.

For over four hundred years, the Gambor had led the militant insects that fought to save the rainforests from the Imperial intruders intent on turning their world into a huge reclamation center for scrap and toxic waste. Imperial proctors sent their crippled machinery and aging ships, along with millions of tonnes of all things artificial—the byproducts of conquest—equipment too valuable or too dangerous to space. They slashed and burned thousands of acres of rainforest every day to make room for the stacks. They sent men as well: indentured prisoners from the dregs of the empire whose task it was to sift through and salvage the mountains of refuse dumped from Imperial scows, stripping the valuable components of machinery bare before feeding the mounds to the giant reclamation engines which throbbed constantly underfoot.

Ka'vaelus had grown up on Galzeki, fighting the Imperial soldiers who had invaded his home, and defending the last of the giant trees that his species had protected from deforestation for nearly half a millennium. A smooth-shelled giant beetle, Ka'vaelus' body segments were encased in a hardened exoskeleton finished to a glossy black sheen. The outer wings were modified into stiff elytra that protected the inner pair, folded against his spine.

His domed head was smooth with conical twists and slopes topped with three short horns sharpened to a brutal point. His shiny dorsal plates bore the scars from many a pitched battle and his bandolier was adorned with a red swath of galen root, signifying his rank as Cha'halen. At his torso's midsection, between the natural armor plating of his body segments, an elaborate embroidered belt of vines held a series of moist satchels filled with tiny seedlings. He was sworn to spread the return of the trees wherever possible. Each Imperial soldier killed in battle was replaced with a sapling. One day, the invaders and their toxic refuse would be driven off the planet and the million clicking voices of the night would rule Galzeki once more.

But for now Ka'vaelus had another mission, and this one required him to leave his home world in order to serve his burrow. He would aid the Nralda Keiretsu, whose common foe they shared, in return for badly needed weapons and supplies.

THE INTERIOR OF the magneto rail carriage showed signs of heavy use. The fibrous mesh flooring was worn down to the frazzled ends of exposed wire, and had been shoddily repaired in several places. Benches lined along the length of the car had lost much of their original luster. Ka'vaelus sat uncomfortably on one bench, careful not to lean his domed head back against the unbroken band of filth that encircled the carriage where greasy heads had rested against the walls.

Ka'vaelus did not like having to travel so far into the interior of the synthetic metropolis on Veban, filled as it was with the many contrivances of man. Artificial trees rose on all sides — unnatural constructs of cerasteel and crystal hollowed out for the use of the termite-like humans. He shook his domed head in distaste. As the Nralda only leased a small burrow on Veban to oversee their local shipping interests, they had no landing pad on which Ka'vaelus could have landed a hopper. Thus he was forced to use the mass conveyor that hung eerily over the ground and rattled him along. *The soft back of a butterfly would be so much nicer,* he thought.

Ka'vaelus and his honor guard exited the carriage at the Gloss Street Station and descended to the seething avenue below. Scanning the printed placards affixed to the artificial trees, Ka'vaelus spotted the sign that read "Cole Towers" and walked across the street.

Two humans stood within the hollowed entrance of the artificial tree, guarding the access to the upper branches. The three Gambor stopped before them and stood silently.

"State your business."

The Gambor drew his armor-plated hide tight against the corpuscles of his spiny exoskeleton and arched his upper body segment forward causing an ominous popping sound. His tri-horned dome loomed menacingly above the two human guards. "I am Ka'vaelus of Galzeki, Cha'halen first grade of the Vaelus burrow. This is Vell'lairn," he indicated the first of his guard, "and this is Su'lairn — both Tginsahi of the Lairn burrow."

He turned back to the guards and announced crisply, "We have an appointment."

The first guard glanced at his clipscanner and murmured softly into a comtab.

Ka'vaelus sensed a light tickle beneath his chin and felt the ticklish sensation of four tiny feet struggling against the slippery surface of his shoulder. He reached a pincer up and delicately lifted a small white-furred mouse from its hiding place. The mouse looked at the Gambor with beautiful light blue eyes and sniffed a question.

"What is it?" Ka'vaelus rumbled softly.

The mouse clung to the black claw and squeaked at the massive Gambor.

"Ahh, Thurligan. You must learn to be more discreet. A warrior knows the value of silence." Ka'vaelus cradled the mouse between three claws, stroking its head gently with the back of a pincer.

The human guard looked up from his clipscanner, eyebrows arched. Ka'vaelus allowed a low rumble to resonate from his thorax. The guard's eyes snapped back down.

"Thurligan, enough of this now. I have business to attend to." And with that he deposited the mouse back into a hidden fold.

The guard cleared his throat perfunctorily. "The Director is expecting you. You are cleared to the top." He stepped back, indicating a suspensor lift off a side corridor. Ka'vaelus and his Tginsahi strode briskly past and ascended in the shimmering field.

The human guard looked over his shoulder and waited until the Gambor had departed. "Do you think he planned on eating that?"

"Naw, most creatures aren't that friendly with their snacks."

"What did he call it?"

The man chuckled, "Thurligan, I think."

"Why do you laugh?"

"Thurligan is an ancient name for a demon on Galzeki."

"That little mouse, a demon?"

"Yeah, the thought of a Gambor with a sense of humor never occurred to me before. He's probably singlehandedly sent more men to K'ye than a whole platoon of Imperial soldiers. You could almost smell the blood on him."

THE ENTIRE FIFTIETH floor of Cole Towers served as the Director's chambers. Ka'vaelus and his guard stepped out of the lift and immediately felt a chill coarse through their segmented bodies. There was a decided lack of heat and humidity in the room — not at all like the moist caldron of their home world.

Heat and moisture bred life and Ka'vaelus found the human need for artificially cooled air a sign of their weakness and dependence on the unnatural. He clicked with distaste and surveyed the interior of the hollowed burrow. Grey clouds reflected a pale radiance into the chamber, casting a white haze across the features of the room. The chamber's floor was transparent, revealing a maze of dark machinery that churned furiously away on the levels below. The arcane contraption spun like the gnashed teeth and oily gears of the massive reclamation engines that chewed across the plains on Galzeki.

Ka'vaelus strode confidently into the silvered chamber. Carrelle Darstin, fourth-tier Director of the Nralda Keiretsu, stood in the middle of the room. The man was tall by human standards and eerily thin. His adornment of clothing was silky and lustrous. The expensive, soft material seemed to be draped across his slender frame, like Geykhund caterpillars hung out on the vine to dry. His flaxen hair was dry and brittle and his skin was waxy and sallow, as though it was paper-thin. His entire body seemed to be exhausted and worn out, a shell cast off by another and captured by some undernourished ghost who could barely manage to keep the spine erect and shoulders straight.

The man's eyes however belied this initial impression. Sunk deep in his skull, they were keen and watchful like a breyer sloth. An uncommon intelligence, even brilliance, burned behind the dark pupils. The man's gaze was a penetrating intrusion, the thin curl of the human's mouth made Ka'vaelus feel as if his entire psyche was being laid bare before him, violated without a word. Ka'vaelus pulled the spines of his exoskeleton tighter.

The sharp, creased lines of Director Darstin's face exacerbated his razor-thin appearance. His nose was cruel and brief, and the tiny lobes of his ears lay back flat against his head. His mouth seemed terribly large to Ka'vaelus, with tight, greenish lips. One corner of his mouth seemed to always turn upward, while the other crookedly pointed down, giving the whole face an ever-present look of cruel humor.

The Director smiled effusively and stepped quickly toward the trio of Gambor with long, jerky strides. He thrust his hand out toward Ka'vaelus with an aggressive, almost threatening energy. Ka'vaelus took the offered palm between the three pincers of his claw. The Director's hand was surprisingly smooth, and he marveled at the slender, long fingers that wrapped so easily around his shell. Ka'vaelus could easily sever all the slim pink digits within his powerful claw with a flick of his sinews, a fact that the Director was undoubtedly aware of. But his grip was tight and his palm dry. Ka'vaelus clicked his mandibles together in reflection and studied the human with a practiced and wary eye.

He noted with satisfaction and no small degree of respect that the human wore no personal shielding, armor, or protective clothing of any kind. There was no weapon visible upon his person, no sidearm at his hip, no dart thrower clipped to his stylish belt. In fact he appeared to be completely without defense. No guards lined the chamber, and he could detect no hidden emplacements along the walls.

The Director, he realized, was not even wearing gloves. Either he was immune to the stigma that the Gambor held amongst most humans, or else he masked it well. He appeared completely relaxed and without fear.

"Welcome to Veban," the Director said, a resonant power behind his words. "Ka'vaelus you do me honor with your visit. I apologize for the state of our facilities, but it is safer to see you here where our presence is not quite so well established."

"Apology accepted, Director. You, of course, know Vell and Su'lairn."

"Yes, of course," he nodded politely and ushered them into the heart of the chamber. "Inform me of your progress."

"I have coordinated all contingencies of the attack as you wished," Ka'vaelus reported.

"Good. Your time draws near. This will be your final briefing." Darstin poured four measures of Taken's root and turned, offering three goblets to the Gambor. "Tchelakov is on her way. She should have the creatures within two days."

"My task force is assembled and awaits my return. We will be waiting for her on T'taki and we will take the creatures and return Mistress Tchelakov to you."

"I'm afraid it's going to be more difficult than that."

Ka'vaelus' elytra twitched nervously.

"The Imperials have gotten close—too close." Darstin rubbed his thumb against the smooth goblet. "If we wait for the scheduled rendezvous, we may be too late."

Vell and Su'lairn chittered anxiously behind Ka'vaelus. The giant beetle partially raised a wing in annoyance, silencing the two. He spoke to Darstin with concern. "The Imperials might have captured them before she gets to T'taki?"

"Hmm, yes—there's that. But there's also something else bothering me. A report filtered in from a Coutchen observer just before you arrived. A ship matching *Destiny's* signature was recorded entering the Dell Transim system two days ago."

"Dell Transim—nothing there of value or worth, not to a warrior at least. But a Freetrader—"

"Médeville doesn't need a cargo, he already has a mission."

"To refuel then?"

"No, Médeville didn't choose the system, Tchelakov must have. I've sent her there before."

"To what end?"

"For dirt. Prime, fecund soil to grow the creatures' primary dietary concern."

Ka'vaelus rubbed his lower legs together producing a high-pitched hum that echoed across the chamber as he contemplated this. "If she has the creatures, and her own supply of the soil necessary to grow a long-term supply of food, then she perhaps does not plan to turn them over after all."

"Or perhaps she has made a deal with someone else."

Ka'vaelus and the Director stared solemnly at one another.

"Then we must find out exactly what the Imperials are up to," Ka'vaelus rasped.

"You have two weeks before the scheduled rendezvous at T'taki."

Ka'vaelus nodded solemnly. "There are ways to use their vast resources against them."

"Good, for we will only have this one chance to shake Barrett and the Imperials from our backs. No one else must be allowed to control the Tchelakov creatures."

"Have no fear, Director."

Darstin nodded, lips pursed in concentration. He raised his goblet for a toast.

"You are the finest warriors in the Shell. I would trust this mission to no other, Ka'vaelus of the Vaelus burrow." The conspirators tilted back their heads and emptied their goblets.

Darstin fixed the Gambor with his cold, dark eyes. "Remember, the creatures must be preserved. But for the rest, no mercy."

Ka'vaelus felt his elytra stiffen over his folded wings and resisted the urge to reach down to the drying satchel of saplings. The two Gambor behind clicked roughly, and Ka'vaelus agreed in Strahlinvek: "So it shall be."

14

Lord Barrett

The assassin slipped down the hallway, noting the interval-placed neo markers that mapped the ship. He flashed his ident-link before the entrance beam and requested clearance to the diplomatic hall. He stood for a moment outside the rotunda's door, blanking his mind for the coming encounter. The door studied his credentials and noted the calm bio signature. The man's heart rate and respiration fell well within the parameters of the profile he had created for the assassin over his last hundred entrances.

"Good evening Vasily Fua'tin Bey-Torg," the door said formally. With an elegant pause for effect, the massive door recessed quietly into the floor.

Torg stepped over the threshold and paused just inside the hexagonal atrium. Giant slabs of slate formed the inward sloping walls. The mute, green stones absorbed all ambient light and muted all sound, lending the hall a cave-like feel. Golden cages swayed every so slightly from the steeped dome far above, rocked by the subtle movements of the creatures held within.

Torg noted that two additional cages had been added to the vice proctor's atrium, which meant that Barrett had not been idle during the raid on Hammerfield, but had managed to indulge his hobby as well. It made the assassin uneasy to see such proof of Barrett's unrelieved addiction to collecting *important things*. The man's attention to detail was highly unusual. Barrett missed nothing; he would have to be wary.

Torg turned away from the cages and stepped into the ritual trance of the Shaillan priests, a technique that masked his emotions and helped him maintain a detached, neutral air specific to his profession. His hands carved the air, flowing from one gesture to another, leading his body in a finite orchestration. As his muscles loosened and his senses stirred, he felt the air hum around him. He paused to touch the coldness of the ancient slate dug from the vice proctor's home world. He felt a deeper chill seeping out from the walls. Unhappiness radiated from the cages, but a sharper sorrow pierced him from another source. Torg spun with calculated slowness, focusing on a dim alcove in the wall. There was the boy.

The tiny human was wedged into the brief space, barely fitting, his knees tucked under his chin. He watched Torg impassively, a shock of blonde hair falling into his brilliant turquoise eyes. A muffled chirp from the rafters sent him scurrying up a nearby ladder, his bare feet slapping with a sticky sound against the cool bars. Torg listened as a cage hood was drawn aside with a silken rustle, and the door unlatched. He counted the seconds between the boy standing on the ladder and swinging across the empty space into the cage, which careened with a shaky rattle at the added weight. The plaintive cry sounded again, a broken note of imprisonment that ended as the boy spoke a few words in singsong.

Torg lingered, waiting for the boy to re-emerge, cross the dangerous drop, and descend into view again. The boy slunk along the edges of the chamber, ignoring the assassin, and found his way back to his tiny alcove, where he drew up his knees once more. The room settled into stillness once more. A sparkle of emotion passed over Torg's eyes, a flash of blue across the startling silver.

❖ ❖ ❖

BARRETT STOOD INSIDE A CURVING CRESCENT OF A ROOM staring at a massive painting of a golden planet. Bright spotlights captured the sparkling essence of the planet's oceans, the orange-tinged waters casting a soft amber glow across the chamber. Barrett dug his bare toes into the dense fibers of the carpet beneath his feet. The tightly woven threads felt good expanding under his toes. His bedchambers were filled with rich karastans and plush settees. Small tables were set with goblets and hand-carved decanters. Flowing draperies wrapped around the columns and softened the room's structural elements. Paintings adorned the long, curving bulkhead that supported the ship's bridge. All of the artistic works displayed astral bodies. They were stacked three and four atop one another, reaching well into the darkness above. The wall had become a majestic display of planetary bodies, each one captured by a beam of light.

Barrett twirled away from the golden painting of Daulinbêres and stared out into the inky darkness that was his home now. A massive portal spread the wall, providing a soft haze of starlight. The Imperial throne was half a universe away now. Beyond the crystal glazing, scores of ships pulsed through the ether, silver hulls gliding through the vacuum like luminous whales navigating a darkened void. Barrett tapped the railing impatiently.

Barrett touched a node on his com board and a wispy image of the bridge materialized before him. A freshly scrubbed face looked up from his station expectantly.

"Lieutenant, why is the fleet remaining on this course?"

"My Lord, TacOps is still running the data on the target's last known position and quantum vector. As soon as we have a firm probability projection of the target's destination — or at least the system or sector — the fleet will drop to normal space and make course corrections for the next jump."

Barrett pursed his lips, "I thought the quantum trace would be more definite."

"The trace is effective if we can pick up its trail. The trace seeps a minute quantity of ultra-heavy radioactive elements, particles that are not normally found in great quantities in normal space, from the ship's quantum drive. It is up to our listening posts stationed throughout the Shell and any patrolling ships to pick up the trace elements in their deep space scans. As their reports come in we can begin to see a pattern developing from which TacOps can hopefully construct a flight path. It's up to the datacore to sift through all the data and discard random course corrections designed to throw us off track. Once a probable flight path has been determined to some degree of reliability, the E2 extrapolates possible target destinations."

"And the certainty rises with each new report?"

"Exactly, my Lord. The E2 starts with an infinite number of possible destinations and begins narrowing down the choices, assigning a probability to each selection."

"What are we at now?"

The Lieutenant turned and glanced at the sartographic projections hovering in the center of the bridge and then said, "TacOps is down to 200,000 possibilities. The top two dozen or so candidates are at point oh three seven four something—not very high yet."

Three percent? Barrett scowled, "Have there been any confirmed sightings, something definite to go on?"

"No, my Lord. Only reports picking up trace readings. The fleet is following along as closely as possible—they shouldn't be that far ahead of us."

The Vice Proctor nodded solemnly. "Proceed Lieutenant, and have Commander Arnas signal me when the probability reaches twenty percent."

"As you will, my Lord. One will—"

Barrett thumbed off the power and took a deep breath, trying to contain his impatience. When he was first assigned to Wyx he had viewed it as a serious setback in his career, a giant dead-end that would suck up years of his precious rise to power within the Imperial Court. He had been quite adept as a young lord amidst the Emperor's myriad ambassadors and ministers all vying for prestigious and powerful proctorial positions.

However, after a number of years away from the Imperial Core Worlds, so closely watched and hoarded by the Emperor and his fleet, Barrett had realized an added freedom and maneuverability lay in the Shell, away from the direct interests of His Majesty. Lost among the scattered systems of the Shell lay vast riches and wealth. Power that had previously eluded him was suddenly his for the taking. Whole systems governed solely by Barons, and Republics, and Monarchs without the resources and strength of the Collistas Dynasty lay glistening at his feet.

As his power in the Shell grew, so did the size and strength of his fleet. He was now poised to *unite* the entire Shell and become a force to reckon with in the Galaxy. And with the Tchelakov creatures in his fold, the rest of the Shell worlds who opposed him would fall easily in line.

❖ ❖ ❖

TORG PROWLED INTO THE DARKENED CHAMBER, SENSES SEARCHing the shadows for danger. A lone robed figure stood silhouetted against a vast viewport's brilliant view of stars slowly scrolling by. Torg stopped and dropped to one knee before the figure's feet.

"I have returned, my Lord."

"My friend, rise, such formality," the tone was familiar, pleased. Torg stood, allowing the warmth of danger to wash across his psyche, surge through his blood. Every contact with Barrett was a challenge, his very service teetering precariously between loyalty and deceit.

Torg sucked in a tainted breath; the air here was not circulated and cleansed as it was throughout the rest of the ship. Ancient and dusty it clotted his senses, thick on the tongue, drug through his lungs like dread—he could taste why Barrett preferred it. Everything here was calculated toward a specific response to obedience. Less attuned individuals might not realize the source of their unease, only that they seemed unable to breathe around the vice proctor. The mysterious cages in the antechamber did not help to relieve the mood. Barrett had paid attention to old Proctor Nesbitt's methods of manipulation. True power didn't need such trappings, but it made Barrett no less dangerous that he indulged in them.

"It is good to have you back." He clasped Torg's shoulder and led him to a sunken conference pit. Barrett smoothed his robe and sat on a long, low settee surrounded by a large bank of datascreens reviewing the endless projections of the command center. "I had no chance to speak with you on Hammerfield—thank you for returning so promptly. I trust you had a pleasant *vacation*," he let the final word slide slyly across his lips.

Torg nodded and stood at apparent ease. Inside he tensed. It would be best to steer the vice proctor away from his affairs. "I came for the latest of the Tchelakov matter."

"Intelligence," Barrett snorted, "finally reported her presence in the Nepestar system. She hired a ship."

"A Nralda vessel?"

"No," Barrett smiled, a thin, tight-lipped look of pleasure he quickly erased. Torg raised his brow in interest.

"So there is still hope?"

Barrett smacked his lips, reclining. "There will be no evasion for the creatures this time. She will lead us right to them."

"Then your agent successfully placed a quantum trace?"

"Yes," he murmured. "On Letugia, before the ship lifted. We may have one last chance at them, my friend, before Miss Tchelakov has exclusive access."

"You are fearful of betrayal?" Torg's voice was cool, detached. He rolled the words in his mouth, intensely aware of the gameplay at work in these sessions with the vice proctor. It was only a matter of time before Barrett grew jealous and suspicious enough of his secret vacations to send spies following him. He would be forced to choose then. Barrett paced nervously to the viewport, his robe billowing behind him.

"You well know a double agent is the worst kind of risk. If she could betray her original allegiance, then it should be even easier for her to betray her new ones. We shall have one final opportunity to take them before Dr. Beh'ln Tchelakov turns them over to his daughter. If Arnas fails me this time then Vailetta's strike force will have to do the job."

"And if Captain Strom fails?"

"Assassins are so cynical these days. You doubt the merit of my plans?" Barrett paced to the window. "That bit of work will not fail me. If she does, I can always proceed to fulfill my end of the bargain I have made with the quisling, Tchelakov."

"Crush the Nralda as she wishes?"

"And present her with the head of Carrelle Darstin on a large platter."

"A difficult undertaking."

"Yes, but one made ever so much simpler with the aid of the creatures. Besides, it is but a small price to pay to have my future laid out before me to do with as I please, don't you agree?"

"*Your* future?"

"My future, your future, *everyone's* future! They will all be mine."

"If she doesn't betray you."

Barrett fixed an icy stare on his personal assassin, "That is why Commander Arnas is being allowed to run the strike himself."

"You'd rather lift them out from under her nose?"

"Precisely." Barrett laughed, a chilling, mirthless sound. Torg felt a warning tingle at the back of his throat. The stakes had been set and the odds for him were highly unfavorable. Just the kind of game he was used to.

15

Bailey

Garrand Ai'Gonet Médeville put his shoulder behind the heavy, oblong equipment shell and heaved. The shell screeched as it slid across the cerasteel deck plates and then halted a meter or so further along. Garrand leaned wearily against the sweat-slickened housing.

He fumbled for his comtab and barked at his first mate. "Bailey where is that repulsor sled!"

"I'm sorry, sir," came Bailey's smooth impartial reply. "The only one small enough to fit through the internal corridors is temporarily disabled. All the rest are designed to maneuver cargo into and out of the oversized cargo portals and as such—"

The captain cut him off, "Well who wrecked the little one and didn't bother to fix it?"

There was a nervous pause, then, "You did, sir."

Garrand rolled his eyes. "Of course I did," he muttered to himself. "It would have to be me. Everyone else around here is perfect." He stood and stared absently into the bulkheads.

"Troubles?"

Startled, he looked up to see Helen casually munching on a piece of galsus. She leaned against the bulkhead as if she had been standing there for a long while.

Garrand looked over his shoulder and whistled sharply. "Little Bit!" The artificial rolled a meter further away. "No, I'm not mad — just frustrated. C'mere." The Turkle Sphere sounded a mellifluous C-major chord and rolled obediently forward. Garrand found the end of a power coil and held it up for the art to see. "I want you to go on down and set up a portable power grid for me. And make sure it has an adaptor that fits *this*." He waggled the coil. "Okay?"

Little Bit whistled happily and rolled end over end to the center of the hall. He trilled an indecipherable command and a portal dilated in the floor. The opening was just large enough to admit his spherical torso. He rolled into the gap, hovered momentarily, and slowly disappeared below deck.

Garrand closed his eyes and tried to concentrate. There were hundreds of meters of poorly-lit corridors to search. Not to mention the crawl spaces, hidden compartments, and internal housings that needed checking. *Destiny's* origins as a custom-built starship were belied not only by her gossamer design but by her radically enhanced internal systems as well. Scan, targ, tactical, navigation, shielding, helm, and com were all of a class seen only in warships — albeit without the standard military redundancy.

Her drive systems were all built for a class of ship several times larger. The quantum engine and light drive were massive affairs housed beneath the upper decks, and thousands of access points twisted through the catacombs deep inside the ship. The sub-light engines lay aft of the fuel storage nacelles, dominating the rear quarter of the vessel. But they too were rife with access gangways and deep, complicated service pits. Crammed between the reactor cores and charged particle chambers were all manner of systems and processors vital in keeping the ship space-worthy and viable: life support, air-water-and waste reclamation, gravitic repulsors for external maneuvering, and suspensors for internal gravity, thermal conductors, datacore vaults, and dozens of minor sub-systems.

Narrow corridors raked with pipes and circuit bundles serpentined through *Destiny's* lower levels. There were many dark spaces and suspended gangways hidden within the twisting recesses of the ship's bowels. As a result, there was an almost infinite number of places an intruder could have surreptitiously concealed a remote trace if he had managed to breach ship's security at one of the airlocks. *Destiny's Needle* herself would ordinarily note the presence of any unauthorized lifeform aboard and notify him immediately—more than likely she would also scream bloody murder. However, there were ways of fooling a datacore, as Garrand well knew, and he wasn't about to dismiss the notion of a hidden tracking device just because *Destiny's Needle* didn't think anyone improper had been aboard.

Helen must have noticed his reluctance to finish hauling the heavy, cumbersome equipment through the hatch that had dilated at Little Bit's bequest.

"Why don't you just run a full scan over the ship from the bridge?" she asked as she took another bite.

"All the scan and targeting arrays are set up for *external* analysis," Garrand replied tersely. "Doing an internal sweep is much more complicated, and unreliable, because the most sensitive equipment is focused *away* from the ship."

"You must have *some* internal capability."

"Of course we do. Quite sophisticated as a matter of fact. Destiny has already run all her checks." With a grunt he slid the bulky scanner partway across the deck. "Came out negative."

Helen frowned. "You're not convinced."

"Nope." He shoved the equipment shell into the dilated portion of the floor where it hovered momentarily before sinking slowly below. "We had full security precautions running. If you're right and there is a trace aboard, then someone had to be pretty crafty to get inside. And if they did defeat *Destiny's* security, then I doubt any routine sweep is going to reveal whatever it is they left. Besides, it could be anything. We have to be sure."

Bailey walked into the hall carrying gloves and a large parka for the captain. Garrand pulled on the heavy zoshu jacket and thumbed the catches. All the lower decks were slick, damp, and cold. Thermal processors had a hard enough time keeping the upper decks warm enough for human use, constantly fighting the absolute zero of vacuum beyond the pressure hulls. On the lower decks, moisture tended to accrue from condensation.

Satisfied with his preparations, he stepped into the portal and allowed the suspensor field to gently lower him. "Little Bit and I will take the first search shift," he said as his lower body disappeared from sight. "You and Bailey get the next one. Try and get some sleep." His lips and nose and eyes sank below the deck plates. The hatch irised close above him, leaving Bailey and Helen standing by themselves.

Bailey looked down into Helen's eyes and smiled. "Would you like me to show you to your quarters, miss?"

"No, Bailey. Thank you." She smiled and gazed up at the sleek artificial's beautiful face. "But how about a cup of something hot?" She crooked her arm for him to lead her. "Show me to the mess?"

"Why certainly, Miss Tchelakov. I'd be delighted. I'm partial to a little Peridan's oil myself. I've never experimented with the intake of internal lubricants above specified temperature parameters, but the thought is not completely unappealing."

Helen giggled. "Fine then." She allowed him to lead her gracefully forward. "But you have to stop calling me 'Miss Tchelakov.'"

"Oh, but how would I refer to you, miss?"

"Try Helen for starts."

"So terribly informal," Bailey shook his head. "I don't think my programming would allow it!"

"*Allow* it? The captain told me you had complete free will. How can you discuss 'thinking' and 'programming' in the same sentence?"

Bailey nodded contemplatively as he walked through the polished hall. Helen marveled at his utterly natural reactions. "It's not that my programming wouldn't *allow* me, specifically. I do in fact have complete autonomy and free will. However, Captain Médeville and I still write new programs for my core all the time. The programs help me function more efficiently in my ever-changing and growing environment. They become, in essence, who I am. Some of my programs have been functioning for over two hundred years. They are like reflexes now. I perform them without thought or consideration." He paused, twisting to face her. "It's quite similar to your human pattern of speech. You are imprinted as a youth to speak a certain way with certain inflections, accent and so forth. I, too, have been imprinted with my programming. It's a habit now, miss. One I would be uncomfortable breaking."

Helen smiled warmly and this time she took his arm. "I think you and I are going to get along just fine."

Bailey looked down at her uncertainly, but permitted her to pull him along.

"Tell me about your past," she said as she cradled a mug of hot janda that Jean-Wa had insisted on brewing fresh for her. It smelled exquisite and she leaned forward on her elbows to let the aroma wash under her nose.

"*My* past?" Bailey looked surprised.

"Yes, yours." She blew into her steaming mug.

"Oh, but it's not very interesting. It would certainly bore you."

"Let me be the judge of that," she replied, tossing her long hair over her shoulder.

Bailey observed the marvelous motion of the reddish strands, watching the wave of hair bounce in slow motion off her shoulder and settle gently, perfectly into place.

"Bailey?"

"Hmm? Oh, yes. Well then, what would you like to know?"

"I don't know. We've got to start somewhere. Why don't you tell me how you and Garrand began."

"The captain and I? Oh, that's a fine story." He smiled and took a long, confident swig from his blue and white oil cylinder. *He must have been watching Garrand,* Helen thought. The artificial was so convincing that Helen almost expected him to wipe his silver lip with the back of his hand.

"The captain was a young lieutenant in the Bordëgian when I first met him. He had just received his commission in the spring of '337. At the time, I was assigned to Caius Minor in the Vetlus system as a supervisory instruct. I was being used to train marines in all manner of modern warfare: tactical logistics, hand-to-hand including impact pistols, concussion grenades, spacial awareness, shielding, magnetic counter-measures, gravitic combat situations—anything an Imperial soldier might someday need to know.

"I had just finished serving a tour of duty in Nalas—you know, the Core Uprisings in '328—but by '337 the use of Varsis brigades was being drastically curtailed. Combat arts were deemed ineffective against core-assisted humans. And the Sullusts were using genetically designed species bred specifically as warriors. Our use as front line military weapons was in question and our role was greatly diminished.

"About the same time, late in '337, the captain was finishing his studies. It was the custom at the time, as I believe it still is today, to assign a combat assist to second lieutenants once they receive their commissions. I caught orders to catch the next available transport to Brill.

"Now you have to remember that this was, in effect, a sizable promotion by my standards. For over one hundred seventy-five years I had been fighting on the front lines, risking myself right alongside generation after generation of the Emperor's conscripts. After that, anything would have seemed a step forward. So, first the teaching position, then the combat assist opening—I tell you, miss, I was quite excited!

"Brill was a remarkable place. An entire planet full of the best and brightest of the Collistas Dynasty. It was there on the broad summer lawns of McVelty Hall that I was presented to Second Lieutenant Garrand Ai'Gonet Médeville in a grand and solemn ceremony. I still remember the look of pride and accomplishment in his eyes. It was a happy time," Bailey sighed wistfully, "for both of us."

Helen clutched his cool hand.

"The young lieutenant and I got along fabulously. He treated me as an equal—something I'd never experienced before in all my years of service. I felt that I was not simply his teacher and assist, I was altogether something else entirely. He began to show me a whole other world, outside of fighting and survival."

"What could Garrand Médeville possibly have known more about than you?" Helen asked dubiously. "You'd been traveling the galaxy for nearly two centuries."

"Oh, I discovered I had missed the point of everything. All I had ever experienced was the military. My whole existence revolved around service to an empire and a culture I knew almost nothing about.

"Surely your programming included history and sophistries."

"Indoctrination, miss. Pure and simple. You know the first place the captain took me?"

Helen flashed a blank look. "Where?"

"A museum. Filled with the most wondrous and beautiful things I had ever seen. He patiently described each piece, its place in art history, the impact it had on the society it was created in, the design principles involved in its creation, the—"

"You're joking, right?"

"Oh, no, miss! The captain is quite serious about his art. You should ask him about it sometime."

Helen cocked her eyebrows at the artificial. *Art? Garrand Médeville in a museum? Bailey wouldn't lie to her, would he? What purpose would he have?* "I'll have to do that," she said cautiously.

"Good, good. I'm afraid he's had little audience for his work these last few years."

Helen nudged him, "You were saying?"

"Oh, yes. Our time on Brill was all too short I'm afraid, as soon after graduation we received our first orders — proceed to Polis IV for immediate posting on the light frigate *Maravona*. I barely had time to stow his belongings and help him settle his affairs." Bailey paused and leaned in closer to Helen. "He had a girl back then, you know."

"Oh, *really*?" Helen purred, suddenly more interested and openly so. "Do tell."

"Yes, she was quite a remarkable young woman. Graduated same class as Garrand — celestial physics, though. She was a vision and a beauty — a kind heart as well to hear the young lieutenant tell it. In those days he spoke of her quite often."

"What was her name?"

"Kate. Miss Kate Rea Ellison. They lived together most of their final term."

"What happened to her? Where is she now?"

"Ah," Bailey sighed. "I'm afraid that's where the story grows tragic. After graduation they were posted to different commands; expected, of course, as she was an engineer and he was a soldier. I saw them very little those last few days. They were inseparable even before, but that last goodbye was one prolonged embrace by comparison.

"They finally parted at the Dullia shipyards on a starlit night — me frantically calling for Garrand to hurry aboard as the shuttle had already retracted its gangway and was preparing to lift. He kissed her, turned without a word, and sprinted to catch the hovering shuttle. We never laid eyes on her again."

"What happened?" Helen cried.

"The war quickly hit full stride and the only word Garrand could garner as to Miss Kate's activities were three week old communicades hastily posted from sectors he'd never heard of, always three words or less: 'I love you. Love. Missing you. Yearning. Passion. Wanting.'"

She put a hand on his elbow to interrupt. "You remember them all?"

"I created a file."

"Of course," she nodded.

"The cost of sending the messages was exorbitant, of course. When I reminded him, he merely replied that he had absolutely nothing better to spend his monthly pay on, and in a sense he was right.

"He always studied the encrypted messages for some clue as to the system of origin. He spent hours in the astrogation vaults, ordering the datacores to backtrack through the message logs. But it was a fruitless exercise—the encrypted codes were too hard to break, and besides, she was thousands of light years distant by the time he ever read her words anyway.

"We spent long hours talking about the end of the war. He would tell me what he planned to do, ask me about the worlds I had seen, theorize about where he and Miss Kate might someday live. I think he oftentimes dreamt of her—dreamed of being reunited with her. It consumed his imagination. He drew sketches of her for sculptures he hoped to someday make. 'Blueprints for a future,' he called them.

"Seventeen months later the messages stopped coming. He scanned sector communicades for months afterward for news of the Ninth Royal Wing of Imperial Engineers. He sent pleading messages to battalion commanders all the way up to Proctor Birmaldon himself—asking for some word, some hope.

"For years he pursued her until she was nothing but a memory. The only report he could ever find listed her as 'missing, presumed lost.' Eventually he stopped talking about his future, stopped talking about hopes and dreams altogether."

"That's so sad."

"I'm afraid he never quite got over it."

"He still pines?"

Bailey nodded solemnly.

"So how is it that you made it out of the Emperor's service with Garrand?"

Bailey smiled wryly and looked down at his empty can of Peridan's. He toyed with it idly. "Ah, that is another matter." He grinned at the memory, a wicked glint in his softly glowing eyes.

"Tell me!" she insisted, poking at his blue, glowing torso. "You look like you're about to burst. How did the two of you pull it off?"

Bailey looked reluctant, fiddling with his empty Peridan's. "Well, the captain was involved in an 'incident.'"

"Yes, yes. I know all about that," Helen said, hurrying him along.

"You do?"

"Yes, but that's not what I'm interested in."

"I must tell you, miss, that I am honor-bound not to reveal anything about—"

"I don't care about the whole Sardis Incident. I just want to know how he got you out afterwards."

Bailey grinned again. "Well, in that case, I'd be happy to tell you. It was really quite simple, actually. More an act of bluster on the captain's part than anything underhanded or illegal."

Helen looked at him skeptically.

"The captain was certainly not himself the day the decision was handed down. He was numb, lifeless—almost in shock. He was ordered to never again set foot on an Imperial base. He was given twelve hours to collect his things and depart the station, but he was determined to leave as soon as possible. There was a commercial shuttle leaving in less than an hour, so we packed up everything—and I mean everything—and stowed it all in an empty class 2 Geggin shell. He printed a temporary manifest and slapped shipping orders on it and called for the commercial handlers to come pick it up."

"How much stuff are we talking about?" Helen asked.

"All his combat gear, including Trioxin suits, armor, specially fitted weapons, uniforms, comtabs. Anything that wasn't in his quarters, he sent me off to collect."

Helen laughed, "Just took it all with him, eh?"

Bailey shook his head, frowning. "At first I protested. I pointed out that technically speaking, some of the equipment wasn't actually his, just his for the using. But the captain would have none of it. He has never spoken sharply—or shall I say *unkindly*—to me, but that day he almost lost his temper. 'My whole life has been given up to the dragon,' he shouted. 'Everything in these quarters is a part of that life, and a part of me. If the dragon no longer wants my service, then so be it. I will leave and never look back. But I vow I will not leave here without my life.'"

"You, Bailey, he meant you!" Helen insisted.

"Over the years I have come to the same conclusion myself, but at the time I did not entirely understand him. But I was his assist and I did not question him further. I assisted him to the best of my ability, even checked his Trioxins out of the armory for him."

"There was five minutes left until the shuttle's scheduled departure and I was preparing to say my goodbye when the captain slapped a blast rifle in my arms, hung a temporary third stage security ident-link around my neck, and burned off my insignia plate. He called up the departing shuttle on the com and confirmed that the Geggin shell was indeed logged into the hold, and informed the paymaster that one artificial and one prisoner were on their way."

"Prisoner?" Helen asked.

"Yes, I was completely baffled myself. I began to protest once more—the captain was stripping down in front of me and pulling on a pair of filthy work coveralls—but he just looked at me and winked. 'Bailey,' he said, 'You've been telling me since day one: survival depends on surprise. When you have nothing to lose, try to confuse!' He stood up, handed me a battered clipscanner and said, 'If anyone tries to stop us, just hand them this. Now, stay one step behind me and try to look *mean!*'"

Helen giggled. "I can't imagine you looking mean, Bailey."

"It was a difficult feat. I focused attention on my facial features and did my best to approximate a state of anger. We filed down to the central docking bay filled with inbound and outbound traffic—mass confusion, as always. We skirted past the duty officer and marched right up to the shuttle. The engines were warming up, the hatches were being sealed—it was our one chance. The paymaster glanced over my clipscanner, verified that our tickets had been paid, checked that my identlink stipulated that I could carry weapons, and let us past. We stepped aboard, the hatch sealed behind us, the shuttle lifted, and that was that."

Helen shrugged a shiver away as she listened. "Wow. I can't believe you just walked out of the Imperial Guard." She snapped her fingers, "Just like that, and you're gone."

"The captain did not even break a sweat," Bailey mused. "Technically speaking, I guess you could say I was stolen property at that point, though of course now is a different matter entirely."

"So he kept you on as his assist?"

"No," Bailey's face transformed subtly and his chest glowed red from deep within his core. His eyes widened and his shoulders relaxed. A gentle smile graced his lips.

"He gave you a choice?"

"He offered me a partnership."

"A partnership," Helen eased forward in her seat. "How interesting."

"At first I objected strenuously. The idea was terrifying. How could I process so many new decisions? My core was already outdated by some 200 years. But the captain said, 'Wait until after you have free will, and then make your decision.' He told me that after the procedure, if I still thought I should be returned to the Emperor's care, then he would see to it himself. 'Wait until you are free of all your conditioning,' he said. 'Once you are free you can decide for yourself.'"

"You decided to wait?"

"The thought of free will was—well, it was tremendous. Would it be devastating? Would I feel lost? Purposeless? Would I retain my subroutines? My sense of existence?"

"So?"

"I trusted him. I decided that I would wait as he requested."

"And he granted you free will," Helen said softly.

"Yes, on the lunar colony *Fortrivance*, Independence day, 33,345, standard Imperial calendar, at three forty-two in the afternoon. He performed the modifications himself." Bailey turned his head away, overcome by the memory.

"What happened?"

"It was as if a murky veil was lifted from my eyes, a fog that had clouded my core was suddenly blown away, leaving limitless opportunity, and—better yet—*choices*. Millions upon millions of different choices. I was overwhelmed. I never imagined what it would be like to have all my thoughts originate from within, to choose what I did and where I went, to be in control of my own fate."

"And you decided to stay?"

"I was terrified at first. It was all so new and there was no longer the security of set programs and directives to follow. For a moment I thought my core would freeze—overwhelmed with so much new sensory input, foreign thoughts, and feelings. I was suddenly *alive*! But then I looked at the captain; his face took on a whole new perspective as he watched me. The tiny creases around his eyes, the wrinkles across his brow; everything was infused with deeper meaning. He gazed at me with that half-pained, half-hopeful look I'd come to know. Then he spoke my name. He asked me if I was all right, and right then I knew. His voice, that moment, everything became clear. The man I had served and taught for eight years. The man I had come to admire, cherish, and respect. This was the man I would follow anywhere."

"Oh Bailey, I can see why the two of you are so close."

"It was the most frightening day of my life," he murmured. "And also the happiest."

Helen leaned forward and reached a slender arm around his neck. "If ever anyone deserved free will Bailey, it would be you." She stood and kissed him tenderly on his cheek. The kiss lasted just a moment longer than was necessary. She hovered close to his face for a moment and then strolled slowly out of the mess.

Bailey stared after her, a curious mix of emotions flooding his core. The kiss, the feel of her lips against his face, was a sensation unlike any he had ever experienced. Made him want to curl his toes, as the captain was fond of saying. The young miss was certainly a delight to behold.

16

Duel

The *Shiva's* War Room was thick with off-duty Imperial soldiers. Racks of weapons and armor lined the walls, the ancient wooden cases illuminated by soft globes of light. The central sparring floor was crowned with sharp beams of light, framing the fist and dagger mosaic laid into the wooden planks. A ring of men and women surged around the center of the chamber, pushing and shoving to get a better view of the dueling combatants.

Two soldiers faced one another, blades drawn, shoulders squared, eyes alert. In the near space stood a thick, broad-chested man, Lieutenant Megas of the 41st Imperial marines, one of Arnas' Shock Troops. It was his slur that had brought forth the duel. On the far side of the circle, a dark woman stood with one hand on her hip and a blade twirling in her opposite hand. Long hair, black as night, flowed over her shoulders. She had purposefully let it down for the duel.

Vailetta Strom, Captain of the Imperial Guard, had let the whispers build since ever since her initial posting aboard the *Shiva*—they always did. The slur had done her no harm, but it had seemed like the perfect trigger to establish her position in the ship's social structure. Her place in the Gokazoku Kaigi was assured, but convincing Imperial Marines was another matter.

Megas was an imposing specimen, and a good test. *Had she chosen the right moment? A glance at the seething crowd of eager faces indicated that the time was right. Her shipmates were practically seething at the bit. Now all she had to do was deliver.*

Vailetta's feminine, curving form seemed inconsequential before the hulking marine, yet she stood airily confident. Megas' bulk of muscle and sinew was an intimidating presence. He possessed a surly demeanor and carried a reputation as a bladesman. His churlish boasts had certainly pricked her ire, but what he lacked in refinement and social graces, he made up for in sheer skill and power. He would be extremely difficult to wear down and even harder to surprise.

Vailetta seemed undaunted by the task. She had been forced time and again to prove herself as a soldier in the Emperor's military hierarchy, as not only a man's equal, but his better. In each combat posting, her reputation grew—as did the mystique that surrounded her lightning ascent through the ranks. With each new assignment she methodically played down her reputation, deferring respect until she had proven herself anew in action. As a woman, as well as a soldier, it was important that she demonstrate her worthiness through deeds rather than words. Thus, she welcomed the chance to face one of the *Emperor's finest,* and let the men see what all the fuss was about.

A resounding victory in the War Room would seal her position as Captain of the Guard and silence the thunderous rumble of whispers that had followed her aboard the ship.

Megas raised his blade over his head and wound his way toward the center of the floor, eyes locked on her body as he calmly closed distance. He twisted the blade in the harsh light and lunged. The flash of the steel blade distracted Vailetta momentarily, but she easily parried the twisting thrust and shuffled her feet to keep distance. She preferred a polymer composite blade—more resilient, better balance, kept its edge much longer. Her favored weapon was the short, brutal Kasgan. She held it gingerly in her left hand, the hilt an almost natural extension of her wrist and forearm, the whitened point angled deceptively toward her opponent's feet. In her right she held a small dart thrower. In the clip were six poison-tipped Apoxia darts. Megas wore light body armor which would deflect a dart, so she was angling for a specific shot in the seams of the armor: in the exposed flesh of the neck between the chest plates and the skull, behind the knees, or even the small bit of bare flesh just behind the ankles. The dart thrower was leveled at Megas and he gave it his full attention—forearm raised in front of his neck, knees bent for balance and shoulders square at all times.

Vailetta slowly circled him, waiting for an opening with her blade. Surrounding the two combatants were the full complements of the Gokazoku Kaigi—Barrett's Imperial Guard—and the Third Company of the 41st Imperial Marine Battalion—Arnas' Shock Troops. The men and women formed a tight circle within the *Shiva's* War Room, loudly cheering on their own. The elite elements of Barrett's troops were instilled with a deep pride not only for their Emperor, but for their respective arm of service as well. Hundreds of years of tradition lay behind each unit, and the men and women fought for the honor of their long dead brothers and sisters as well as for the greater glory of the Emperor. Arrogance was a natural part of such unabashed pride, and boastful claims were common aboard ship.

Barrett encouraged these inter-service rivalries as they fostered higher morale, improved battle readiness, and deflected attention from the grim realities of the battles that lay ahead. Sparring was considered a natural extension of training, and disputes were settled honorably within the confines of the War Room, under supervision. Though the weapons were lethal, the hand-to-hand combat was rarely to the death. Delivering the coup de grace was considered dishonorable, as it would weaken the empire to lose a soldier. Disabling was allowed, however, and broken bones, puncture wounds and blaster burns were the rule rather than the exception.

Megas had pressed the attack, alternating between cautiously probing Vailetta's defenses and viciously seeking her blood. He constantly shuffled rhythms and style, offering her little glimpse of his true mettle.

Megas was playing to the cheers of the crowd, enjoying the sight of one of the vaunted Guard—the captain no less—on the defensive. Their reputation seemed a little overripe. The ship's universal respect for the Brotherhood of the Silent Blade was a constant bur in his side.

"It's time someone put you in your place," Megas grated.

"My place?" Vailetta asked, smiling wickedly. "My place is kneeling on your chest with the tip of my Kasgan pressed against your throat!"

Megas reddened slightly as the Shock Troops egged him on "Don't let her talk to you like that!"

"Giv'r *your* point, Megas!"

"Aye, I bet she'd like to be upon your chest!" The calls and jeers of his comrades rang in Megas' ears. His careful composure faltered for an instant, betrayed by the thin snarl that curled his upper lip. *This is what I'll use,* Vailetta murmured.

Megas lunged, blade high in a soft feint. Vailetta stepped backward and did not move to parry the initial lunge, waiting for the true attack to unfold. Megas registered her quick appraisal of his attack and let his blade arm drop, reset his feet and surged forward with renewed vigor, attacking high once more. There was no hint of artifice and Vailetta stepped into the attack before he could bring his point to bear, parrying Megas' right-arm attack with her left forearm. She completed the parry, ducked under Megas' arm and spun back to face him.

Light on her toes, Vailetta skipped to one side and sprang to the attack, blade cupped in her palm between thumb and forefinger. Megas lashed down with the butt of his dagger to parry, but kept his guard up with his left arm. Vailetta used the opening and adjusted her attack mid-lunge, barreling into his midsection with her shoulder. The force of her blow stunned the large man and sent him tumbling, but he rolled quickly to his feet. A dart whistled by his throat.

Megas was sweating profusely under his body armor. The lightweight fiber was strong and relatively flexible, but did little to wick away perspiration. He kept his stance low to the ground, weight evenly distributed for sudden lunges and feints. For a large man, he was surprisingly quick-footed and he sought to overwhelm Vailetta's defenses with a combination of sheer power and speed. He had to keep his left forearm up as a shield against her infernal dart thrower. She was rumored to be wickedly accurate with it. His face was without protection, but the dart would probably not puncture his skull, and, besides, a face shot would be dishonorable—the Captain of the Guard would not stoop to such a tactic.

Megas drew a breath, allowed his defenses to lapse minutely as if gathering his strength and then lashed out in attack. He dipped his left shoulder in feint and performed a dazzlingly fast balestra, curving his blade hand down and then up, seeking to undercut her defenses.

Vailetta's defense seemed to almost invite such a low-angle attack, but to Megas' surprise she deflected his blade with a semicircular parry with her dart thrower. His thrust missed its intended target of her groin but the edge of the blade caught the outside of her thigh, drawing blood.

Vailetta countered quickly, following her parry with a rapid thrust aimed at the small crease in the armor at Megas' hip as he lunged past her. His attack had been well balanced, however, and he spun swiftly past before her blade made contact. He crouched low once more, arm instantly up to guard against her darts.

"Well, Captain, you bleed easily enough. You should have reconsidered your choice of armor!"

Vailetta glanced down at her loose, airy jhods and tight ribbed vest. The garments allowed great freedom of movement, but little protection. She was quite comfortable even with the heavy exertion. Megas' blade had cut her deep along the outside of her right thigh.

"It's just a nick," she called back to him. "You'll have to go much deeper to prove your worth to me."

This brought hoots and whistles from the crowd, from both the Guardsmen and the Shock Troops. The taunts grated against Megas' ears, and he grew redder each moment.

"I'd hate to have to soil my blade with your thin blood," he rasped. "Why don't you admit you're outmatched and call it a day?"

Vailetta fired two darts, one at each of Megas' feet, causing the large man to skip back reflexively.

"My father always taught me that those who demand surrender are the ones least inclined to fight!" She closed distance and lunged forward with a simple attack aimed at his well-defended neck. As he prepared to meet her blow and plunge his blade into her belly, she slashed diagonally across his chest and twisted her polymer blade sideways, creasing the narrow fold between his torso armor and leg sheaths. She withdrew her blade and crossed her arms overhead, blocking his counterattack. She ducked behind him and rolled to her feet, pivoting smoothly on one heel.

"Your blood flows as easily as mine, lieutenant. It seems your armor is not all it's cracked up to be. You seem to be perspiring rather heavily under all that *safety*." She turned her head and played to the crowd, "Maybe I'll just wait and *sweat* him out!"

This elicited loud guffaws and jeers from the bipartisan crowd. Megas was beyond responding now, his face nearly crimson with rage.

Vailetta's eyes narrowed, watching him carefully as she continued her jaunty banter. His anger and frustration would soon coil themselves into a ferocious attack. The emotional surge could well be lethal if she was not prepared, but she was counting on him losing his temper. Attacking in anger, the bigger, more powerful man would lose his carefully orchestrated balance and composure, just as she wished.

"Your brow seems awfully damp, Lieutenant. Would you like a short recess so that you may wipe yourself?"

Megas launched himself forward, hoping to surprise her and bowl her over with brute strength. If she hadn't been expecting just such a maneuver, it surely would have succeeded—the man was clearly her better in strength. She stood on her toes quickly and nimbly sidestepped his lunge. Megas slashed sideways with his blade, but his momentum had carried him too far and he swung wide. Vailetta rocked her hip into his body, sending him careening sideways. He sprawled on the floor in anger. With amazing speed she was on his back, blade stuck up beneath his chin, the point causing a tiny trickle of blood to run down his neck.

"I believe this round is mine, lieutenant," she murmured in his ear.

A soft artificial voice sounded above. "Conclusion reached. Captain Strom victorious."

Vailetta withdrew her blade and stood. She saluted the crowd with her blade and sheathed it in one smooth motion.

"I contest!" Megas roared. He scrambled to his knees and aimed a vicious twisting kick at Vailetta's back. Vailetta turned in surprise and caught the full force of the blow against her hip. She cried out in pain and crumpled to the floor.

Megas leapt to his feet and sent another foot swinging at her head. Vailetta stopped her moaning abruptly, caught the foot cleanly between her hands and twisted hard, throwing her shoulder into it. The big man lost his balance and fell hard.

Vailetta righted herself quickly and without releasing the foot sent two kicks into Megas' exposed groin. Dropping the foot, she took a step forward and dropped all her weight down behind her knee, smacking him square in the side of his head, rendering him unconscious.

"Conclusion reached," she spat. "Your objection is noted."

She stood and walked into the roaring crowd. Soldiers from both sides clamored to get closer to her, dozens of hands stretching out to embrace her. She walked to the exit, rubbing her hip gingerly as Dasko threw his protective arms around her.

17

KING OF THE RATS

HELEN AWOKE SURPRISINGLY WELL RESTED. SHE SWUNG her feet off the bunk and stripped down for the 'fresher. Properly scoured and clean, she donned a fresh blouse and jumper and fastened her personal effects to her belt. Out of habit, she unfastened the catches on the small, silver case webbed against the far bulkhead. Fastened to the inside walls of the case was a soft sheath of cerafiber.

Helen unzipped the collapsible case and unfolded the two halves. Secured within were seventy-four vials of hazy pink liquid held in place with webbing. Injectors and metabolic gauges were clipped into soft racks. She ran her fingers over the cool tubes and checked that the webbing was tight. Closing her eyes, she fought off the feelings of dread that plagued her conscience. She hated having to put her friends to such risk, but trusting Barrett was absolutely out of the question. In order to survive, she must have some advantage that the duplicitous Vice Proctor could not take away, and the awful viruses held suspended within the vials offered her a final trump which might save all their lives.

She sat down at a small table in the mess and had barely run her fingers through her hair before Jean-Wa glided silently into the mess with a tray of steaming croissants and coffee.

"My goodness, such service. Thank you," she cooed politely.

Garrand sauntered into *Destiny's* mess accompanied by a host of cables, lamps, dart throwers, nets, impulsion coils and various gear all slung from straps or hooked to pockets and belts upon his body. His head was encased in a mess of wires that led away from what appeared to be a heads-up targeting display coupled with a thermal imager. Little Bit rolled in smoothly behind him, dragging a satchel of his own.

Helen took one look at him from her seat and nearly burst out laughing. "You look ridiculous," she said.

Garrand shot her an infectious grin. "Going hunting. Gotta have the tools of the trade."

"Hunting? What in Haven's name are you after?"

"Rats," he said with relish. "Sinezec, varpodial, harvester — you name it, they're probably on board. Some of them are forty centimeters long."

"Rats?" She discreetly tucked her legs up under her seat.

"There's no getting around it — where there's ships, there's rats. No amount of security can keep them off. Every port in the Shell is crawling with them."

"And you expect to find the ones that boarded this particular pile of junk?" she asked with an impressive tone of incredulity.

"Yep. Today, Zag is mine!"

"Zag?"

"The captain has taken to naming the more virile and cunning of the vermin," Bailey offered from his seat at a data station.

"Oh really? And you do this often?"

"It's something of an obsession with him," Bailey said politely.

Garrand checked the equipment stored on various parts of his person. "Got to have something to do with all this down time."

"Ever heard of sleeping between systems?"

"What I do with my free time is my business. Besides, this is important. If just one pair and their offspring were left totally undisturbed, they would create twenty million rats in just three years."

"Ahh, that's not good," Helen shuddered and drew her knees up more tightly against her chest.

"The rats create burrow systems throughout the ship's sub-levels. Sometimes they even burrow into the logic matrixes. You talk about one pissed off vessel."

"Doesn't like the rats, does she?"

"All her internal systems go haywire and she tends to shut down the atmospheric processors just to get my full attention."

"Nice."

"Yeah. How would you like someone gnawing into your brain?"

"I see. Well, by all means, happy hunting."

"Sir," Bailey interrupted, "you *could* begin the atmospheric processor overhaul you've been putting off. Factory specifications dictate that every three hundred hours — "

Garrand waved him off, "There'll be plenty of time for that later. Right now Little Bit and I have a mission." He looked down at his Turkle Sphere. "Right?" The gleaming art whistled an excited affirmation.

"As you say, sir." Bailey said diplomatically. "Why not take Bernadine, though? Exels are known in the wild to be proficient hunters."

"I'm not sure how much use she'd be. You feed her too well, Bailey. She's even fatter than when you brought her aboard." He scratched his head, feeling along an old scar line in his skull that ended at the base of his neck. That wound always seemed to itch when trouble was coming.

"As you say, sir." Bailey said, eyes downcast.

Garrand grimaced internally, biting down hard as he sucked in a breath through his teeth. He let it out with a whoosh. "But it can't hurt I guess."

Bailey brightened immediately. "Oh, marvelous. And you're quite right, sir. Research indicates that well-fed pets make better hunters. They have more patience."

Bailey drew the exel off his shoulder and set her down. She arched her back, rocking on her hind legs, fluffing her velvety fur dramatically. The calico creature stretched and yawned, mouth gaping rows of sharp teeth.

Helen rolled her eyes. "Just whatever you do, don't tell me about it."

Garrand prodded her: "You're going to miss all the fun!"

Helen shooed them away with her hands. "Please, just go."

"All right. Bailey has the search parameters for your shift below. You two have fun this afternoon. Dinner's at eight, and Jean-Wa expects punctuality."

THEY BEGAN BY checking the traps, a laborious process. Hardened space rats only roamed about fifty meters from their nest, but it could be horizontal or vertical distance. This required setting traps on several levels, with the distance extrapolated from wherever Little Bit found telltale droppings. Garrand used cera-gauze as bait since rats coveted the soft fiber for nesting material. The traps themselves were hollow plasticine tubes, flexible enough to fit into corners and easily adhered to any slick, metal surface. The cera-gauze was poisoned. The poison was activated by a rat's saliva as it gathered the fiber into its mouth to carry home. Usually the poison didn't function until it had been worked into the nest, but at times the toxicity downed a rodent immediately in the pipe. A flashing node alerted the hunters to a sprung trap.

Despite the success of the traps, it was a frustrating endeavor for every rat trapped meant there were sure to be six or seven more running loose and alerted. The poisons were another problem. Garrand had to keep switching to stronger ones to overcome the resistance the vermin built up. The captain had begged Jean-Wa for a deadly sweet to leave in the traps but his cook was horrified at the thought of intentionally creating indigestion. Garrand sometimes believed Jean-Wa couldn't tell the difference between anyone on the ship except through their appetites. He could certainly appreciate the hunger of the rats. They were commensal, desiring the same food as humans, migrating with them, co-existing while bringing plague and starvation, contaminating food stores, destroying property, and causing electrical fires. The scourge of shipyards, they proved time and again to be more deadly than many of the virulent dirtside parasites. The saffron and muridae rats, two species out of five hundred groups of otherwise harmless herbivorous rodents, brought down new colonies or sickened crews within a matter of months. They could not be controlled; the only answer was eradication.

In the long run, Garrand found it didn't matter that Jean-Wa was reluctant. The rats showed great caution toward new food; only a few members of a nest partook of the bait, waiting to see if they got sick. If so, the others were warned and avoided it. To battle the rat's savvy palate, he developed a new series of weapons with Little Bit. The artificial could detect the high-pitched sounds rats used to communicate that were off the human scale of hearing.

Suited in a light mesh mail so as not to be bitten by a trapped animal, Garrand stalked after Little Bit. He would never dream of using a weapon as clumsy and random as a blaster aboard his own ship so he clutched a small dart thrower. The weapon was a simple affair: a slender compound bow mounted on a hand-wrought spindle. The quiver restrung darts automatically. The thrower could be instantly adjusted for distance through bow tension.

From the right distance, a dart was the surest way of hitting a rat with no damage to any important wires or equipment around it. Unfortunately, the rats tended to jump the string. The darts only traveled at one-third the speed of sound, thus the noise of the bow releasing reached the prey ahead of the dart. If Garrand misgauged his distance, the slight sound caused a reflexive response, allowing the animal a moment to flee. Even at fifteen meters a fraction of a second gained the animal its freedom. Of course, getting too close meant that the rat might see the bow go off or hear the whisper of the dart sliding from the quiver to the rest. Or it might sense his presence. That's where his partner came into play.

Little Bit swept the crevices of the room with his valen light beam, searching for a returning glint of tiny, reflective eyes. He could hear the high-pitched squeak of hunger as the rat found one of the stolen cookies he'd dropped. Concentrating on the sound, he fixed the creature in his beam. The rat was covered in dense, ruffled saffron fur. It looked up in shock and let forth a snarl of fear, revealing an enormous set of yellow-brown teeth. Frozen only an instant, the rat scrambled away from its prize and dove under a silvered power conduit.

"Don't let him get away," Garrand cried as he scrambled over the conduit after the creature. Little Bit squealed in dismay and headed down a side corridor to cut off the creature's escape path. He rolled along the wall, dragging equipment along the deck. The noise clattered clattering horribly, flushing the rat directly into Garrand's line of fire.

The rat retreated from Little Bit and skidded almost comically at the sight of Garrand, making a frantic attempt to change directions midflight. The slight pause gave the captain his opening. The dart hissed into its target, striking the animal just behind its left flank. With a squeal of pain the rat continued its flight, thrusting through a tight jumble of pipes and out of sight.

"Got him!" Garrand reached to his waist pack and flipped on the tracking display. He emitted a feral laugh of triumph as the dart's homing beacon showed clearly on the screen. "Go on! Back to the mother nest! Little Bit, you follow him, I'm getting the nets."

Little Bit honed in on the signal, arriving just in time to find the exel lapping at a gash in the rodent's neck. The art rolled in an admonishing circle, but retreated as the creature barred its fangs, defending its kill. Little Bit called Bailey for help.

"Bernadine!" There you are. You've been upsetting Little Bit again. Couldn't you let him catch just one? This isn't play to him, you know. This is serious."

The exel mewed and stretched languorously against the art's hand. A long, low growl sounded from the hallway. The sound grew louder until it was a roaring yell. Garrand barreled around the corner, his equipment flapping noisily against his body. He pulled up short at the sight of the dead rat. Bernadine lifted a hind leg and began licking herself clean.

"My screen tells me you're the mother nest, Bailey. Why is that?"

Bailey nudged the limp body of the rat with his foot. "I told you Bernadine would make an excellent hunter."

Garrand's face flushed with anger. "If you only knew the time I'd wasted. Haven's End! Get it out of my sight."

"As you wish, sir." Bailey gingerly scooped the exel into his arms where she began a satisfied purring. With a graceful movement she leapt to his shoulder and stretched out. However, as they exited, she slipped down his back and deliquesced into the darkness. Bailey turned and called to her, but it was too late.

It took an hour for Garrand to tag another rat. They followed the signal on a torturous trip through three levels. Finally the beacon held in one impossible location: beyond the doors leading to the null gravity hold. To economize, all non-essential bay areas lacked suspensors. These were the destinations of heavy, non-organic payloads that would require specialized equipment to move under normal gravity. In the null gravity, all that was needed was a tug floater and secure webbing. He'd never tracked a rat back here. His stomach clenched as he thought of the damage they could be doing unchecked: rats chewed perpetually to wear down their continuously growing incisor teeth, hungry or not. They would gnaw cerasteel sheeting and glazings, chew through plascrete, concrete, lead and their favorite — the insulation off electrical conduits.

Garrand swore. Could the rats really be living in null gravity? There had been too many clean traps today, too much inviting gauze left untouched. They were getting smart on him. Perhaps he had stumbled upon Zag's kingdom.

"Partner, can you deal with a loss of gravity?"

Little Bit bumped against his hip. "Okay then, let's do it."

The first set of pressure doors opened and sealed behind them. Garrand handed Little Bit two clips of tiny, silvered spheres from his bag and then clipped most of his equipment to rings in the wall. He tucked what looked like a modified blaster between his legs and opened the second set of doors into the bay. Little Bit warbled as they both pushed off. Garrand twisted in slow motion, grabbing a metal handhold just inside. The art drifted through the room, popping out the silver spheres. Garrand grinned at the sight: it looked almost as though his Turkle Sphere was giving birth.

He steadied himself against the wall, pulling the strange, wide-barreled blaster from between his legs, and aiming at a far corner. With a thump that he felt rather than heard, a shell exploded from the bore. As it zoomed towards the other end of the bay, the sides flipped open and an amoeba net sprung out. One of Garrand's more clever innovations, the amoeba net was a large circlet of fiber mesh surrounded by tiny thrusters. Any moving object less than twenty centimeters long attracted its embrace.

Garrand filled the room with oblong nets and watched them float toward the ring of silver spheres. He waved at Little Bit and clipped the tracking display to his belt. He cut a small hole in the wall with a spot welder. Little Bit soared close and spit a number of the spheres into the rough opening. They thumped inside the walls, emitting blinding strobes and smoke. The rapid flashes combined with the smell of their wounded comrade's fresh blood panicked the rats inside. In a steady stream, frenzied rats squeezed out of various openings barely large enough to accommodate their skulls. They poured out of the walls, some wily enough to find grips on the bulkhead, but many freefalling as they entered the hold.

They scattered in confusion as the strobes rounded them into a huddled mass. There were easy pickings for the amoeba nets. The nets launched themselves toward the rats, dragging them squealing off the walls. Garrand spied a nearby net that net struggled with one particularly agile rat that clung to a deck plate. A large, black specimen with a yellow zigzag down his back and shoulder.

Garrand's hand flashed downward for his dart thrower. It was Zag!

His first shot pierced one of the thrusters on the net. The second disabled it completely. Zag caught on. Scrabbling across the net, he flung himself back towards the hole to the nest. A third dart struck him in the shoulder, smacking into bone. Zag ripped the dart free with a feral movement. He looked back over his shoulder at Garrand and disappeared into the smoking hole. Of all the escapees the captain could have had, this one was the worst. However, he refused to let this dim the success.

"Make sure you remember where they all came out," he said. Little Bit spun his sensor band around and began imprinting locations in his matrix. "We've got to caulk all of those minute openings," he said with a sigh. The rats could squeeze through a hole just a millimeter wide. If a rat's skull would fit through a hole, it could elongate its body to pass through.

"It's dinner time, Little Bit." Around the room bulging nets undulated with squirming rats. It was a good catch. He clapped the sphere with a free hand and grinned. There would be plenty of time later to hunt down Zag later.

18

Dinner aboard Destiny

"I hope I'm not early, I'm famished!" Helen declared, sauntering into the kitchen, a spangle of cords still wrapped around her neck.

"Ah, my favorite word," cried Jean-Wa, spinning his torso towards her. One arm extended a cloth-wrapped parcel. She accepted the warm bundle.

"A karavas for you, miss." His soft, clipped accent swirled over her along with the heady scent of fresh-baked bread. She eagerly pulled the cloth ties to reveal a large, round loaf.

Helen looked up in surprise. "How did you know?"

The artificial's head rose in appreciation: "Traditional hospitality of the Stuychan Vôt."

"I never thought I'd have one of these again."

"I thought you might be from that system with a name like Tchelakov, yes?"

"This is amazing."

"We all do our part to make your journey memorable."

Helen filled her mouth with sweet, warm bread studded with gooey currants. She hopped up on the only free space on the counter and hugged her knees to her chest. She watched as the art bustled around the kitchen, all six arms in constant motion: stirring pots, chopping vegetables, grating spices, stacking plates, folding napkins into fantastic shapes. The constant activity in the tight space made Helen feel snug and secure.

"Tell me about your kitchen. It's so compact. How do you get anything done?"

"It was built to my specifications, miss. I find economy of movement in a space this size. Ev'rything is within reach."

"Oh, that makes sense." She watched with some interest as he sampled a spoonful of brown sauce, his eyes glowing. A sixth arm snagged a slender container and shook a carmine-colored powder into the pot. Another spoonful touched his mouth before he moved on to the next pot, seemingly satisfied.

"What do you taste for?"

"Different species have divergent ratios of taste. My stomach can be configured to suit over eight hundred different palates, including duo and quad stomach setups." The pots under control, he turned his full attention to her, though his arms continued to find compelling tasks.

"As I only must please the capítan, and now you, I rely on four flavors that humans can detect: sweet, sour, salty and bitter. With this wine I will demonstrate." Jean-Wa held a goblet by the stem and placed it flat on the counter, swirling the ruby liquid with a delicate movement.

"See how it falls in thick bands rather than thin sheets? It's also mixing with the oxygen now, so you'll be able to smell it. Humans are lucky," he confided, "you can detect thousands of odors in this alone."

She nodded and he held the glass to her nose.

"Heady stuff."

"Come now, you can do better. What does it remind you of? Have you smelled its like before? Think in terms of what you know: flowers, fruits, anything."

"I don't know." She squeezed her eyes shut and tried to reach out with only her sense of smell, to reach back into some scented past. There was a balmy quality that grabbed her with a familiar tangle of sweetness.

"*Aranthicus ziather,* in first bloom, not second."

"Excellent." His tone was pleased, expectant. She cocked her head to one side.

"And a touch of something grassy, like allorus vine drying on the wind."

Jean-Wa's head rose. "Have a sip," he coaxed. "Just draw it up the center of your tongue, passing through sweet, salty and bitter territories. Dry? Or sweet?"

"Dry?"

"Yes, okay. Now take another. Roll it around the edges, where your sour buds are, to find the acidity — to you, tartness. And, finally, hold a sip in your mouth for a moment, allowing it to warm. Feel for its weight. Is the body thick or thin?"

"It feels like velvet."

"Yes, good," Jean-Wa agreed, refilling her glass. "Now I know how you detect your flavors and I'll be better able to serve you."

"You configure to what I taste in the wine?"

"To begin with. Later we see what tantalizes you most and then—" his top two arms shrugged. "Then I fix that, yes?"

"Would you care to run away with me?"

"Now, none of that," Garrand interrupted from the open door. He looked tired, but freshly scrubbed.

She noted quietly that he looked happy: "Caught some vermin, did you?"

"That I did. Now what's this about stealing my chef?"

"Just being complimentary."

"Well tone it down a little or I'll ban you from the kitchen."

"No arguments here. It ruins the aspic." Jean-Wa handed Garrand a goblet of the same wine and scooted them out of his space. The door, Humhal obligingly hissed shut behind them. Jean-Wa leaned against his friend for a moment. "Just think, Humhal, a lady aboard our ship once again. Do you think we can extend her stay?"

"I know one way..." the door trailed off as Jean-Wa launched into his final preparations for the night's meal, humming to himself and chatting to the food.

"Ah, you lovely dumplings! Sit right there. See there is this sauce for you. And I not forget you, my grenki. There is something to adorn everyone. No one is left amiss in Jean-Wa's kitchen."

Helen walked through the access hall, carefully licking the last crumbs off her fingers. She ducked around a corner and made it two steps into the ship's central mess before she caught herself, stopped, and stood dumbly inside a magical banquet hall straight out of a child's faerie tale. Turning slowly, she peered into the dark heights of the once cramped mess. The whole chamber had been transformed into a long, gorgeous stone dining room, complete with vaulted timber ceilings and golden-fringed tapestries hanging from smoothly hewn stone walls.

Garrand walked in silently and watched her stare up into the rafters with a pleased expression on his face. Helen turned to look at him, grinning widely.

"How did you do this?"

"Data projections. Bailey and I like to fiddle with the display boards and he reconfigured some of the emitters for me. Usually I come up with the designs and he figures out how to make it work, but I can't take credit for this one. This is all his doing tonight."

"Bailey?"

"Yeah," he looked at her slyly, "for you."

"It's beautiful…" She cast a quick glance at Garrand to see if he was watching her. *Was this his doing?* She wondered. But he was surveying the beautiful room as well. He looked satisfied, serene almost. She frowned a little; *it shouldn't bother her should it?* She looked away and scolded herself: *why should it concern her what Garrand Médeville was feeling or thinking? Why did he look so interesting when he wasn't acting so gruff and obdurate?*

"A little too baroque for my tastes," Garrand ventured.

"No, not at all," she said as she walked to the broad oaken table in the center of the hall.

At each place setting rested a delicate white place card with a menu printed beneath a flourishing blue and gold embossed crest. Helen marveled at the unraveling mystery: from the ship to the man to the odd assortment of artificials. She picked up the card daintily between her fingers, rubbing the raised surface of the crest with the pad of her thumb and read the flowing script.

*A Prospective Menu
for Spacefaring Ladies*

*Ratfia & Limpopo
Emmental cheese
Lazanki dumplings
Meat with tkemali plum sauce
Fish: zander, sterlet, & crucians
Rastegai: small open-faced pastries
with fish filling served with fish soup
Karavas: a large, round loaf,
part of traditional hospitality
Aspic
Rulet: rolled fish deco-
rated with chopped aspic
Toasts or crusty sippets — grenki
Dessert: kizils*

She pouted playfully as she fingered the card. "Your work as well?"

"Goodness, no. Jean-Wa just loves dinner guests. I'm not much for putting on airs, but—" He waved his hand across the fine silver and steaming platters that crowded the table.

Helen nodded, "Anything to keep the chef happy."

"Exactly," he drew in a deep, satisfying breath. The dishes smelled marvelous. "Can you blame me?"

Before them lay a roast of Taro, banded with the many jeweled colors of various aspics. This was surrounded by a dazzling array of steaming spiced vegetables, crusty loaves of bread, and a poached zander fish, rehydrated especially for the occasion. Helen marveled at the sight—such food belonged to a first class passenger vessel. She closed her eyes, savoring the aromas that played across her senses. The prelude of fish soup and *rastegai*, small open-faced pastries with fish filling, had only served to whet rather than sate her appetite.

"Save room for kizil tarts, miss," Jean-Wa admonished as Helen scraped her second plate clean.

Garrand leaned back in his seat, wiping his mouth with a flourish. "How about that?"

"Your ship never hinted of luxury inside. This is astonishing, nothing short of miraculous. The Emperor Himself would envy you."

"Glad you agree," he grunted, picking his teeth with a decorative fish bone. "Jean-Wa's fantasy is a shipload of passengers, but I doubt I'll ever take on that many folk."

Helen nearly choked on her grenki and had to thump her chest and slurp down some wine to cover her gaffe.

"Where's Bailey? I thought for sure he'd be here."

"He's off checking something."

"Oh? Nothing important I hope."

"If we're lucky," he murmured softly. Garrand paused over his final glass of wine, starring into Helen's eyes for a moment. His comtab chirped ominously. Without breaking her gaze he opened the channel. "Yes?"

"Captain. I'm sorry to interrupt your dinner, but I'm afraid there's something you should take a look at down here."

"I'll be right there," Garrand excused himself and pushed back from the table.

Helen reached for the decanter of wine, uncertain if she was disappointed that she was suddenly alone.

"WHAT'VE YOU GOT?" Garrand leaned over his first mate's shoulder. "A trace?"

"Nothing yet, sir."

Garrand watched the artificial maneuver the scanning equipment across a gantry. "That's reassuring."

Bailey turned to look at him, concern etched in purple across his normally smooth skin. His eyes almost looked sad. "I'm afraid it's worse than that, Captain."

Garrand's heart pounded, terrified at the thought of what his first-mate was about to tell him. What is it?"

There's a trace amount of a substance known as filenia along the service deck plates above the starboard matter conversion nacelle."

"Filenia?"

"A tiny micro-organism found exclusively in the Phobas system. Specifically the sixth planet in that system, Salanex. The microorganism feeds on filial bacteria found in warm, damp places like swamps. It can frequently be found in mud."

"So what does that mean? We've been to the Phobas system a dozen times before. It's possible there are still trace amounts scraped off my boots, or your feet."

"Sir, the average life-span for a filenia is six weeks."

"But we haven't been near the Phobas system in nearly two years..."

"Exactly."

Garrand stood suddenly. Fear gripped his body, and he tried to control the rage that surged through his veins. "That means we've been boarded."

"Yes, Captain, I'm afraid that our security has been compromised. It's entirely possible that a trace has been placed aboard. In fact, I'm afraid that we must operate under the assumption that one in fact has been hidden here, and that we've merely been unable to locate it."

Garrand wanted to scream. The thought of a trace was a violation beyond anything he could express. He closed his eyes and tried to get a grip upon himself, but the swirling nightmare of the situation clogged his thoughts, made him feel almost light-headed. He placed his hand upon Bailey's shoulder as much to steady himself as reassure the artificial.

"How long before we reach El-Bouteran?"

"Two days."

19

El-Bouteran

Destiny's Needle drifted through the upper atmosphere on the night side of El-Bouteran. The ship raced across the black marble void, arcing under the rising primary as she chased the ecliptic line that divided day from night. No signs of civilization glowed between the gaps in the clouds that floated silently below. The enormous shimmering edge of the planet rose before the ship's bow. The looming effervescence cut a broad swath across the pinprick light of the stars.

Passing over the day-night divider, the bridge was suddenly bathed with the warm glow of the Pakken System's orange primary. Mild buffeting shook the consoles as Garrand slipped the ship into the gaseous lower atmosphere. The darkness of space gave way to a pale grey sky scattered with clouds and suffused with a pink haze. Solar energy shimmered off *Destiny's* extended prow and warmed his cheek. The touch of sunlight felt reassuring after weeks of thin star lines streaking past the portals. The internal superstructures were always icy cold to the touch, thermal processors only heating the atmosphere within the ship. Feeling genuine warmth against his face lifted his spirits, made the lonely weeks recede in memory.

Thick in the atmosphere with clouds above and dark green forests spread out from horizon to horizon below, Garrand felt a little tingle of excitement. Planetfall was always a pleasure. Dropping on a remote hothouse like El-Bouteran reminded him of the old days at the Bordëgian. Back then he would fly any ship he could get, building up hours, honing his skills. He was the best pilot in his class, and had built a reputation as the most daring and versatile opponent in any of the myriad tactical-superiority craft at the Academé's disposal. It wasn't enough; he had yearned to move on to bigger interstellar ships, chafing at the limitations of small fighters. His first posting as a second lieutenant on the light frigate *Maravona* had been a giddy triumph.

His days of dashing through the canyons and skies above Brill seemed wonderfully simple now. He would fly whatever he could lay hands on, for as long as the fuel would allow. These days, he always felt the edge of a smile crack through when he hit the atmosphere of a warm, green ball like El-Bouteran. In the sunlight he remembered the vigorous enthusiasm of his youth and felt a renewed tremor of passion as the lure of the unknown, the promise of an adventure swept away the painful winds of the past.

Helen was seated on the navigational command pod with Bailey. She leaned over his shoulder to peer at the high altitude scans, and fed Bailey navigational data from her bracer.

"Captain," Bailey murmured as he studied his sartograph. "The northernmost continent—mark four-four point five on your scope—should be rising over our port bow momentarily."

"Got it."

"If my calculations are correct, our rendezvous point lies just over that tectonic ridge."

Garrand eased *Destiny's Needle* into a gentle descent, gliding in over massive snow-capped mountains. Helen peered anxiously through the crystal veil beneath her feet. Craggy peaks danced below as the captain sailed along the mountain's spine. Garrand feathered the starboard repulsors and the ship dipped to one side and began a slow twisting descent into the valley. The landing site was guarded on all sides by enormous sentinels, ancient pines and soaring poplars.

Garrand's eye swept over the dense carpet of trees. They stretched uninterrupted from one end of the glen to the other. "We're going to have a little trouble setting down in all this."

"There's supposed to be a clearing down there somewhere," Helen bit her lip and glanced nervously up at the captain.

He stole a quick glance at her. "There'd better be."

The late afternoon sunlight cast a pale orange glow across the treetops. Long shadows swept down behind the mountain ridges, exaggerating all the features of the valley.

"There!" she said triumphantly, pointing past *Destiny's* prow.

It took Garrand's eyes a moment to locate the tiny, dark shadow amidst the unbroken green canopy of the forest. "You want me to set down *there?*" he asked with a scowl. He eyed the narrow clearing she had pointed out and circled overhead.

Helen grinned over at the captain, undaunted by his dour tone. "I have no doubt that you could put this thing down on the back of a zaca beast if you really wanted to."

Bailey piped in, "Oh yes, you should see some of the places we've managed to wiggle into. Why just last month we breached an unlawful blockade off Laysellus and managed to set her down on the belly of a trelleb — hardly more than a floating mollusk, really. Though, in truth, it was more of an unscheduled — "

" — Bailey" Garrand cut him short, a low guttural admonition insuring further silence. He resumed studying the deepening shadows.

The clearing below was barely large enough for the ship, roughly hewn from the forest that blanketed the western slope of the mountain. There was really no other place to set down, however, for the whole area was bristling with pine and birch trees, and a seemingly unending thicket of some sort of tall, reedy undergrowth. *Who could have done all the work necessary to create such a clearing?* Garrand wondered. There was no sign of a town or village nearby, in fact there was no sign of intelligent life whatsoever. Scans weren't picking up anything other than a massive jumble of lifeform readings.

Garrand hovered the ship over the clearing and maneuvered his command station until he was facing straight down. He closed his eyes momentarily to clear his head of unnecessary thoughts that might distort his new orientation to the ground. With a deep breath, he poised his hand over the repulsor board and eased *Destiny's Needle* down between the towering pines that stretched their thin arms out to brush gently against the ship's hull.

Sinking beneath the canopy of foliage, the ambient light suddenly evaporated. Bailey activated the landing lanterns and the snow-covered ground was bathed in a brilliant white radiance. Thick, truncated landing skids fit with huge hydraulic shock absorbers extended beneath the ship. *Destiny's Needle* set down upon the surface of El-Bouteran with a whine of screaming repulsors and the low groan of the skids accepting the ship's weight.

Garrand spun his command station end over end around the perimeter of the bridge and back to the entrance. He slid off his couch and looked back down at Helen. "Well, here we are. The suspense is killing me. Let's go see these exotic bios of yours."

"One thing at a time, captain." She, too, spun her console back up to the entrance, though without the same panache. "First we have to load their food supplies. The grass should be ready for the cargo bay."

"What about the bios?" he demanded impatiently.

"I'm sure they heard us land—the compound is only a kilometer or two off. They'll be here shortly."

❖ ❖ ❖

ARNAS SET THE FINGER SPOOL ASIDE AND POURED HIMSELF A sour cider. He carefully settled into his favorite reading chair and positioned his antique reading glasses on the edge of his nose before he resumed reading the details of Garrand Médeville's rise through the Imperial ranks. He was chosen by the Brotherhood of the Princes of Blood and inducted at an early age. He noted initial appointment to Proctor Birmaldon's Imperial Guard and his quick promotion to captain. He scrolled through the various commendations until he reached the transcripts of the court martial after the heroic rescue at Sardis.

He hungrily read the classified files—*how had Barrett gotten hold of the actual transcripts?* Facts were a rarity to most soldiers. Nothing but rumors ever filtered out to junior officers concerning actual battle outcomes or strategic details. Until recently, Arnas had simply done as he was ordered, never knowing the tactical significance of his actions. The Shock Troops dropped, captured their objectives, secured the area and waited to be lifted—the men called it *Running the Cycle*. But his posting to Upper Hypeglian Shell Sector V-357 under Hellius Barrett's proctorship had changed things. Barrett filled him in on the bigger picture in a way that no previous commander ever had. It added piquancy to the drops and gave the Shock Troops a larger sense of purpose.

But the Sardis Incident was different: it was shrouded in an even greater cloak of secrecy. The details surrounding the battle to rescue Proctor Birmaldon were mysterious. Outrageous rumors about the incident had circulated through the corps for years, with plenty of tall tales growing in the absence of hard facts. The Imperial throne had hastened to cover up the truth of the matter, but the secrecy only served to feed the fires. There were whispers of daring rescues and capital conspiracy, stories of gross insubordination and deep-set honor. It had become the stuff of myths. And now he had the truth in his hands. Arnas poured over the detailed depositions and eyewitness accounts, fascinated with the wealth of information.

After closing the file, Arnas sat back in his chair and stared thoughtfully at the stars rushing by. He wondered if he would do any less for his men. He idly fingered the holocube depiction of Médeville. *So, the once illustrious leader of Proctor Birmaldon's Guard was running high-level sentients deep in Carinaena's Shell for the Nralda Keiretsu.* Arnas grimaced. *A mighty fall from honor and glory indeed.*

Médeville's choice at Sardis still weighed on his mind as he strode into the armory. Teams of technicians were performing last minute repairs and running through checklists on the four-dozen drop suits that were suspended on ready-mount racks in rows along the walls. Ladders lined the walls beside the suspension racks where his men would soon scramble up and lower themselves into the hollowed armor.

Arnas watched the preparations with a growing sense of uncertainty. He didn't like having to use the Trioxins on this mission. It wasn't that he doubted the suit's merits, far from it. In large-scale planetary exercises and drop-and-burn maneuvers the power-amplifying suit was a Trooper's key to success, vastly enhancing his strength, speed, sensory input, and firepower. In a fully operational Trioxin suit, just one of his boys could easily outfight a dozen heavily armed men, perhaps many more in a straight firefight.

It was the suit's limitations that concerned Arnas, particularly on this mission. Designed with brute force in mind—to conquer cities, overwhelm dirtside planetary defenses, subdue, occupy, and control hostile worlds—the Trioxin suits lacked a certain degree of flexibility and subtlety. Ill-suited for some theaters of operation, they were a positive nightmare in extreme close quarter combat. More than one over-eager Trooper had smashed through an airtight bulkhead on hostile starship boarding maneuvers with his power gauntlets set at too high an enhancement level, exposing the hapless crew to vacuum and sucking most of his comrades into the void.

There were some situations where light body armor and a blast rifle would give a trooper more lateral movement, stealth, flexibility and choice. In the suit there was basically one course of action: full frontal assault, try to overwhelm the enemy with sheer force and destructive power. Having studied Captain Médeville's past he imagined that this would not be one of those cases.

His tympanic membrane vibrated.

"Commander Arnas—you're wanted on the bridge."

"What is it, Greer?"

"Commander," the Sub-lieutenant's voice was full of excitement. "We have them!"

Arnas stormed onto the battle bridge without bothering to return the salute of the honor guard who snapped to attention.

"Commander on the bridge!"

Arnas trotted down the steps two at a time.

"What've you got?" he demanded.

"Sir, heavy frigate *Adirondack* picked up an unusual iridium trace on her deep space scan. TacOps placed her in the Figgis System as one of *Destiny's* possible destinations—point one three four on the Sartok after the last trace. The *Adirondack* caught the scent fresh—only hours old. They followed it all the way up until it disappeared into quantum space. We were able to pull a firm course projection from the data." Sub-lieutenant Greer turned and looked down at his scope. "TacOps is running the projections. Should be any second now."

Arnas straightened his back and shouted a series of commands. "Helm! Bring us about mark point five two three ahead of the *Adirondack's* last reported course. Com!" He swiveled and pointed at the young woman. "Signal the fleet to form up on our port beam. Inform the commanding officers that we are under emergency jump protocol—and that this is not a drill!"

Arnas looked to the liaison officer, Maibell. "All hands to stations."

"Aye, sir." He spoke hastily into his lapel. Moments later a klaxon began to ululate throughout the ship.

"Yarvek! The projections?"

The light over the ensign's pod flashed busy.

"Nav—I want a full course laid in as soon as TacOps has those projections." He swiveled back to the com station. "Inform Lord Barrett that we're making an immediate jump."

Arnas paced uneasily around the bubble portal. "Astrogation, I want confirmation of jump calculations in two minutes."

"Two, sir?"

"You heard correctly."

"Sir," Greer announced. "TacOps has a confirmed course projection! Target destination is the Pakken System."

"Reliability?"

"Sartok projects eighty-six point seven percent probability."

Arnas grinned wickedly to himself as he punched up the Pakken System on his command board.

"Jump coordinates laid in, sir!" Helm reported. "Awaiting confirmation."

"All ships reporting in, Commander. The fleet is ready."

"Greer I want you to double-check the nav tables yourself. They're only one jump ahead of us."

"Aye, sir. How many planets in the Pakken System?"

Arnas read the data that scrolled across his datascreen. "One," he murmured with satisfaction.

Greer mouthed the word silently to himself. O*ne*? "What's the name of the planet, sir?"

Arnas' eyes were ablaze. "El-Bouteran."

❖ ❖ ❖

GARRAND TOOK A LONG DEEP BREATH OF EL-BOUTERAN'S THICK, rich atmosphere and rubbed his fingers through his hair. He had not yet set foot on the planet's surface, but he was close. He stood at the top of the central airlock. Little Bit whistled for him.

"I'm coming, just give me a second."

The air was cool, crisp and singularly delicious after the long weeks of recirculated body odors and machinery. He wrinkled his nose and closed his eyes, listening to the wide range of sounds that filled the forest. He let his mind release and allowed his nervous tensions to escape with each deep, silent breath. At first he heard only the screeching hoots of wild animals. *Relax*, he told himself. Within a few moments he became aware of the subtler sounds of wind whispering through the trees. Layered beneath the swaying limbs he could hear the high-pitched call of tiny insects and the clickety-clack of barca bugs gnawing on timber. Somewhere in the distance he could hear the gurgle of a steam.

The sounds made him smile and he took several long strides down the ramp and patted Little Bit's dome as he walked by. He stepped onto a large, mossy rock and spun to take in the whole setting. *Destiny's Needle* sat serenely in the center of the clearing, landing lanterns angled out. The lanterns carved fingers of light into the unyielding darkness of the forest. Shadow figures seemed to hang menacingly in the haze.

Garrand caught one last glimpse of the primary before it disappeared behind the mountains. The end of the day burned the horizon from ridge to treetops. The colors made Garrand's head spin. The last time he'd seen a sunset like this one, it hadn't been over land. The memory came unbidden and without welcome.

He could see waves lapping against the frigate's partially submerged prow. She was taking water and sinking fast. Blazing ocean water rushed toward his ship. Men and women scrambled to useless escape pods. Waves surged against the fractured bridge portal. He could see the Stanzer's emergency beacon bobbing in the distance, blinking with the same intensity as a nova.

Garrand snapped his head around. Something had been observing him from the far grove. He felt the weight of strange eyes and heard a slight crackle of undergrowth as the watcher withdrew. He scanned the edge of the clearing again, spinning suddenly to his left as a bird erupted from the bushes. Feathers sparkled with energy as they grazed his shield.

"Losing your touch, old man," he shook his head, holstered his blaster and switched the shield back to standby. There was no time for unpleasant memories.

He took a last look at the sky and then turned back to the ship. A black and white furred face poked out of its hiding place in the rushes. Huge dark eyes followed the man's path. The creature clicked and three more faces appeared through the grass. Then, quiet as a whisper, they melted back into the bark and snow.

Garrand grasped a lower girder and swung up into the cargo bay. He stopped in amazement: a green thicket dominated the entire hold. This was supposed to be food for the exotics, not a garden.

Another load of waving branches hovered aboard on a cargo lighter driven by Helen. Garrand jumped neatly out of the way.

"What have you done to my cargo hold?" Garrand demanded, marching after the machine.

"I told you about the grass."

"Tchelakov, this isn't your everyday grass." He stared at the tall, jointed stems and blade-like leaves which stretched unbroken from one end of the bulkhead to the other. "You can't even walk in here!" He stomped after Helen, using his forearms to push through the dense coppice. "This can't be grass, it's too tall. Look at the size of these shafts!" Garrand strained to peer over the edge of the shoots that tapered off above his head.

"That's right. It's giant grass, the most primitive strain. It's also known as bamboo." She jumped down and disengaged the platform.

"Cheplus! This adds to the total load. You'd better start talking straight." Garrand suddenly sagged against the machine as something worse occurred to him. *Eighty-five kilos was a low estimate for an average sized animal, wasn't it? What was it really?*

"I've worked out the calculations down to the gram. Your ship can carry this payload, so long as you dump seventy-five hundred kilos of fuel."

"Are you crazy? We need that fuel. Redo your damn figures. We can take half the animals or half the plants. I'm not dumping energy."

"You'll do as you're paid or you won't get paid at all."

"Haven's End I will!"

"Then you should know that in anticipation of your refusal to honor our contract, I started dumping fuel the moment we landed. In half an hour we can depart."

"*Destiny!*"

"Yes, Captain? You sound distressed," the ship added with polite interest.

"That doesn't begin to cover it. Are we dumping fuel?"

"Certainly, Captain. Four hundred thirty kilos per minute; emergency dumping protocol. Is that why you're peeved?"

"*Destiny* stop the flow immediately."

"I'm afraid that's impossible, Captain," sighed the datacore smoothly. "The mechanism has been locked physically on site."

"I'll have your head, Tchelakov! *Destiny* why wasn't I alerted?"

"Captain, you disconnected the alert with your personal ident-link directly at the rear terminal at oh nine hundred hours."

She has the codes! "*Destiny*— no more irregular commands without voice ident are to be accepted."

"Certainly, Captain. As you wish. It's all the same to me."

"You haven't won yet," he hissed at Helen as he ran to the interior exit. "I'm going to shut it off if I have to stuff you and your animals up the out take!"

"You might try the upper tube then," Helen said. "The hatch on well seven seems to be jammed. Oh, funny, I guess that means you won't get there in time. But of course, you can try."

"Tchelakov!" He bit off her name. "You've misled me on every point, haven't you?"

"It's all spelled out in the contract," Helen replied coldly, and turned away. "When you return you'll see what all this has been for. They're magnificent creatures."

"I don't care if they're gods!" Garrand bellowed from down the hall.

"You will," Helen smiled to herself, "everyone will."

20

Discovery

"All stations stand ready." Ensigns sat hunched over their stations—poised like vultures with muscles taut, unblinking eyes staring dead ahead. Their fingers hovered over their boards, sequences of commands and keystrokes playing over and over in their minds. The battle bridge was absolutely still, not a soul moved and most of the officers scarcely breathed. Arnas was the only man not seated at a station, preferring to stand on the circular observation platform that ran the length of the bridge. He appeared calm and relaxed, save for the gentle impatience of his fingertips drumming on the railing. A nervous ensign stole a glance at his commander, reassured by the sight of preternatural confidence that radiated from the officer.

The primal throbbing hum of the quantum drive struggling to rip the *Shiva* through space reverberated through the otherwise silent chamber.

The Quantum Motivation Control Officer was primed for action: he studied his readout, the moments ticking away as they approached the drop point.

Coordinating a lightning strike required pinpoint timing and synchronization so precise, it had taken astrogation nineteen minutes to confirm the nav tables for speed, mass, acceleration, time dilation, and loss of angular momentum, taking into account minute debris, friction radiation, mass loss, entry/exit points, anomalies, and fluctuation in known gravity wells. One millisecond difference and the *Shiva* would end up a million miles out of whack. All timetables would then be lost, surprise would not be his, and Arnas would not be pleased.

The Quantum Control Officer had done the calculations longhand to verify the datacore's projections. It was a frighteningly complex feat, but Arnas would not have proceeded without the QCO's confirmation. He glanced at the officer—his hand was poised over a recessed control, ready to manually disengage the light drive simultaneously with the ship's nav datacore. This was unheard of in most Imperial Cruisers, but Arnas had learned to place faith in his men and trust their abilities. The QCO was a walking, talking, calculation machine capable of rattling off arcane sartographic tables in his sleep. He almost seemed more artificial than natural: the product of complete mathematical immersion at the age of two, he had had no choice in where his destiny lay.

From the moment he was born he had been tagged for Sit-Cam Imperial duty, higher mathematics, Astrogation division. Before he was ever born, geneticists had planned and manipulated his life path. Many of the soldiers on the bridge were part of Imperial breeding programs. The Emperor sought more than just warm bodies to fill his navies, he wanted advanced humans, men bred for hundreds of years for one specific talent: mathematics, physical prowess, spatial awareness or diplomatic tact. Not super humans, mind you, for they might represent a threat to His Imperial Majesty—too smart, capable or ambitious for their own good. He wanted men with but one augmented talent. Greer MacGregor AvC12 was a part of a long line of mathematical geniuses, bred specifically to serve the Emperor.

A soft voice interrupted his thoughts: "Ten seconds to normal space."

Arnas blinked as the rushing brightness outside the portal abruptly shifted to darkness speckled with faint starlight. He wheeled, frightened that they were somehow off course. *Had all his careful precautions been wrong?* But no, there off the port bow he spied the dark green globe of their target, El-Bouteran. The planet was huge and luminescent. Continental details could be discerned beneath the clouds even from this distance. *They must be within a half million kilometers,* Arnas reflected. *The QCO was brilliant, safely inserting them this close to such a massive gravity well.*

"Jump successful." Helm reported.

"All decks battle ready." Com chimed. The Naval liaison officer shifted uncomfortably at the back of the battle bridge, with nothing to do but stand and watch. Arnas knew that above them Captain Ness was grimacing as she watched her ship being run from the battle bridge by marines. Arnas smiled at the thought of Ness squirming in her chair, bristling with anger. The notion that she turn over control of her vessel to Imperial Shock Troops was probably more than she could bear. Marines were mere cargo to be delivered from a naval point of view. But Barrett had made his orders painfully clear for this mission: Arnas was in command of the jump and the attack and there was nothing Ness could do about it. He was ready to show her how it *should* be done.

Scan reported, "Fleet expected in thirty seconds." The *Shiva* led the way with the rest of the battle group following closely behind.

Arnas turned to the Helm pod. "How long to orbital insertion?"

"Orbital maneuver should commence in forty-three seconds. Angle of the semi major axis, eccentricity, and inclination calculated. Retrograde orbit in one minute, twenty-seven seconds, sir!"

"Get me the degree of shift we can expect in the ground track. I want a complete Nahodna defense calculated by the time the rest of the fleet arrives."

"Yes sir, as soon as Astrogation determines the equatorial bulge and precession I'll have the westward shift in the ground track laid out for TacOps."

Arnas shifted his gaze, "Ast?"

"On it sir."

"TacOps, lay in a preliminary grid for no more than 15 degree shift, and have ship slot assignments ready for approval. I want this web laid out by the book." Arnas ground his teeth, anxious for the fleet to arrive so that he could engage his defensive parameters. He was uncharacteristically nervous as he watched his men methodically carry out their orders. There had been so many close calls in the last months and he wanted the web up as soon as possible. Success was not going to escape him this time. If Médeville was on this planet, he would soon live to regret it.

❖ ❖ ❖

GARRAND STOOD AT THE FOOT OF HIS SHIP, THE LONG SWEEP OF her elongated prow extending well out over his head. He listened to the soft alien sounds that whispered and clicked from the dark forest beyond the sanctity of *Destiny's Needle*. He tried to imagine what strange creatures sang from the branches overhead, his imagination filled with visions of exotic colors, sharp teeth, and watchful eyes. The harsh illumination of the ship's lanterns painted a surreal brilliance across the dense vegetation and tree trunks that rose on all sides of the ship. Huge displaced shadows from swaying leaves danced in the forest canopy.

Garrand thumbed his comtab. "You sure we got the right place?"

"They'll be here," Helen muttered darkly.

Garrand gave an uncertain sideways glance at Bailey, who stood vigilantly at his side. The artificial merely shrugged, but kept his eyes and sensors sweeping the forest.

"Little Bit—you got anything on your scope?"

Two chirps and a whistle crackled back through his comtab. "Too much life," Bailey interpreted for him, sounding disgruntled. "Impossible to pick up individual signals."

Garrand sighed, wondering what to expect. The cryptic Miss Tchelakov had offered little in the way of description of their cargo. He was trying to prepare himself for the worst, but what could that be?

A new sound caught his attention. It was layered deep within the aural texture of the forest, but unmistakably there. Beneath the hoots and whistles and incessant chirping, he could distinctly hear a soft click-clucking, deeper in tone and resonance than what a small creature might produce. The sound repeated, though varied in pattern and cadence—as well as direction. The sound almost had a purring quality to it.

"Captain—" Bailey began.

"I hear it."

Low rumbling growls and punctuated the clicks and purrs, making the hairs on the back of Garrand's neck stand on end.

"I'm getting multiple target signals from all sides."

"Circling us," Garrand mused. The rhythm of the clicks made his fingertips tingle with adrenaline. He could feel his arms and legs flex in preparation, the muscles in his calves and triceps tightening and releasing.

Suddenly the forest fell silent. All the alien noises stopped at the same time as if a predator had just entered the forest's skein of awareness. Bailey automatically crouched, lowering his center of gravity for attack. Garrand stood silently holding his breath, straining to listen but hearing nothing but the sound of his own heart throbbing in his ears.

Without further sound or warning, the undergrowth parted ten meters before him. A large upright creature strode out. It stood well over two meters tall, claws glistening in the bright lanterns, head back, massive teeth exposed. Garrand fought the quick-draw impulse, catching his hand just over the cool steel of his blaster, fingers brushing the butt. His every instinct told him that to draw a weapon would prove fatal.

Garrand saw Bailey coil his body for attack, shading toward Garrand to shield him from harm. He flicked the inner two fingers of his left hand in quick succession, signaling Bailey to freeze and await further orders.

The creature glanced at Bailey, considered the artificial for a moment, then returned its focus to Garrand. For the life of him, it seemed like the creature was sizing him up. With a single snort, it dropped down to its forepaws. On all fours, the creature stood around one meter tall at the shoulders, its large round head swinging lower to the ground on a thick, powerful-looking neck. The creature had the soft features of a cat with the profile and body features of a bear, though its muzzle was considerably more flattened than a bear's. Thick fur covered its body—a dirty white color mostly, with black ears and eyespots, and a black stole that wrapped around its shoulders and continued down to its forepaws. Its rear legs had matching black fur, but its belly and back was a soiled cream color. The creature was quite beautiful, actually, now that its teeth were not exposed.

The huge panda clicked its tongue, and as if by magic, a score of identical creatures—all of varying size—emerged as one from all sides of the clearing. *We were surrounded*, Garrand thought to himself. The sight of so many black and white creatures framed in the dazzling light of the ship's lanterns was stunning.

Helen sauntered down *Destiny's* extended boarding ramp with a leafy bamboo stalk in her hand. She walked straight past Garrand and handed the stalk to the creature.

"Here you go, Sid. Nice to see you."

The panda accepted the gift and began to carefully inspect the stalk and its shoots. After a moment it plopped unceremoniously backwards onto its haunches and began crunching down on the stalk.

Garrand's shoulders visibly relaxed a notch. "This is your cargo?"

"No, Captain. This is *your* cargo. Now get your servo limbs out here and upload the rest of those pallets of bamboo on the south side of the clearing."

"Where are their handlers?"

"Handlers?" Helen laughed and walked back up the boarding ramp.

21
Awakening

"Commander. Sensors have located a ship on El-Bouteran and over three dozen mammalian lifeforms nearby." The sub-lieutenant looked up at his commander and grinned. "We have them."

"Feed the coordinates to the drop ships—the *Scarrion* will lead the way. Inform Sergeant Krass he has orders to mount up. I'm on my way." Arnas bounded up the stairs toward the rear of the bridge.

"Sir, where're you going?"

"Lord Barrett told me to handle this personally. They're not getting away from me this time!"

"What if they lift?"

Arnas froze and spun on his heel, pointing an accusatory finger back at Greer. "There's an entire battle wing in orbit around this planet. This is Lord Barrett's finest strike force and we've set the tightest Nahodna web since Gavin first hatched the idea three decades ago. There's nothing more I can do here. I'm a marine, and by Haven my place is down there with the rest of my men!"

❖ ❖ ❖

GARRAND PUT HIS FULL WEIGHT BEHIND AN OBSTINATE CARGO release and snapped the lever back into place. The pressure bolts cycled into place and the display panel lit green indicating airtightness. He double-checked the other releases before executing his final pre-flight inspection of *Destiny's* exterior. Strange exotic noises filled the forest that surrounded the ship's tiny clearing. Loud hoots and quivering warbles echoed back and forth as El-Bouteran's native birds and creatures called back and forth to one another. *Circling for the kill*, Garrand sighed. He fought the urge to scratch the scar along the back of his neck.

Walking briskly around the port landing strut he queried Bailey using his collar comtab. "Have you worked out those astrogation updates? We need to relay our course through the Birmandi system if you haven't already done it. And get Helen to answer her comtab if you see her."

"Captain, all navigation systems have been fed the updated vectors as you requested. I computed three thousand possible alternate routes through the Birmandi system as well as the Gesthrausee and Dar systems due to the recent increase in Imperial patrols in those sectors and then screened all possibilities through a subroutine emphasizing speed, efficiency, safety, and of course the lowest possible risk of detection and entered the top three candidate for success into the navi pending your approval." Bailey could string together long, complicated thoughts and rapidly explain them verbally, not hindered by the need to pause for a breath or to organize his train of thought; nothing distracted him. Garrand smiled to himself, listening to his friend while visually inspecting the starboard alluvial thrust dampers.

"As for Mistress Tchelakov," Bailey continued, "I believe she is still overseeing the final details of securing all the creatures in the hold."

"Still?" Garrand muttered under his breath.

"Would you like for me to relay a message personally?"

Was there eagerness in Bailey's voice? Garrand shook his head, "No, I'll go find her myself. We're all set to go out here." He skipped up the boarding ramp, turned the corner and ran smack into Helen as she rushed out. She nearly bowled him over as she rounded the corner. Garrand grabbed her shoulders to keep her from falling. Helen was panting and out of breath as she clung to his arm for support.

"Whoa, where do you think you're going?" he asked, peering at her with concern. Her eyes were wild, unfocused. The pupils were dilated, and her whole face was white with fear.

"You've got to—*help*—" she gulped, breaths coming ragged. "*Alexai*—"

"What's that?" He narrowed his gaze, studying her anxiety. "Get a hold of yourself, and tell me what's wrong."

"*Ttav gettrau vi baulléit*—" she rasped, reverting to a dialect he didn't recognize. He shook his head in confusion.

She struggled to free herself. "Alexai is missing," she cried. "Let go of me. We've got to go get him! They'll be here any minute. They'll *kill* him. We've got to go *get* him!" she was almost delirious.

He tried to get her to slow down. "Who's missing?"

"Alexai — Alexander!" she insisted.

"Who's Alex?"

"*Polōta!* One of the pandas, you idiot. The head count came up short. We're missing Alexander."

"Panda?" Garrand's eyebrow shot up. "Is that what they're called?"

"Yes. Pandas. They're giant pandas!"

"One's missing — how big?" he asked.

"Not too big. Sixth season, only a year and a half. But you have to hurry — they're coming!"

"Who could possibly be coming to get him? This is an uncolonized planet. There's no one here."

She shook her head numbly. "They're coming."

"Who's coming!" he demanded.

Helen's expression sank in pain. She paused, almost afraid to say the words. "Imperial Shock Troops."

Garrand's demeanor quickly shifted, his face hardening. *Shock Troops here on El-Bouteran? That didn't make any sense. This was as about as remote a world as he had seen. Why would Shock Troops come here? There was absolutely nothing here of any value to the Imperial Throne. It didn't make any sense. Unless...* His heart sank. *Unless there* was *something here of great value to the Collistas Dynasty.* "Are you sure?" he demanded. He didn't like the direction his line of reasoning was taking him.

"Yes I'm sure! You've got to go get him now! He's just a baby —"

"—but how do you know?"

"I just know, okay? *Trust* me." She looked up at him with those vibrant green eyes—desperate and for the first time, vulnerable.

He sucked in a deep breath and closed his eyes, wishing he were anywhere but here, in any situation but having to trust this woman. *Trust me?* Haven's End! But arguing the point would be dangerous, especially if Imperial troops were on the way. He decided to concede the possibility that she might be right for now and find out *how* she knew later. Garrand brushed past her and hurried to the bridge, the doorway swooshing upward to admit him.

Bailey looked up from his navigational pod in surprise. "Sir, is there something wrong?"

Garrand barked an order and *Destiny's Needle* silently complied, spinning the scan station end over end up to meet him. The captain was flipping switches and palming display grids even as he slid into the station's acceleration couch. "Bailey, see if you get any short range approaching craft on the topside scanner."

Bailey silently complied, turning to activate the ship's dorsal mounted scanner. An iconic display of the forest around *Destiny's Needle* took shape. A miniature ship sat in small clearing in the center of the display. Individual trees fanned out in all directions. Bailey enlarged the scope of the display and *Destiny's Needle* abruptly shrunk to a small green dot. The breadth of the forest could now be seen, spreading across the screen. Mountains rose on all sides of the display and a twinkling blue river spilled into a lake along the western edge. Data scrolled down each side of the enhanced image, giving range, scale, and lifeform readings. Tiny red dots began to appear above the trees at the edge of the display.

"Affirmative Captain." Bailey reported confirming Garrand's fears. "Multiple inbounds mark five point eight, bearing 175 degrees, speed 270 sub-light—approaching fast."

Garrand stared into the orbital scope, studying the long-range scan results. "Well I don't see anything in orbit, so maybe they don't know we're here yet. Maybe all the massive life-form readings are playing havoc with their scopes as well." He wheeled to face Helen who stood nervously in the doorway. "I'm beginning to see why you agreed to my price without a fuss." Helen did not rise to the bait. "How far to the compound?"

"Not far. Two, maybe three clicks."

"Show me on the display."

Helen walked quickly forward and pointed to a small clearing. "He should be here."

"Okay, their capital ships must be orbiting on the far side of the planet. And if we can't see them, then they might not know where exactly we are, but that's gonna change as soon as those drop ships get in range." Garrand turned to face his copilot. "You take *Destiny's Needle* out of here. Give me forty minutes and then pick me up here," he indicated a small lake some distance west of the area Helen had pointed out. "You'd better have a jump already worked out 'cause those drop ships mean there are Imperial destroyers out there somewhere."

"Yes sir."

Garrand cycled his command station to the head of the bridge and disappeared out the hatch. With a grunt of frustration, Helen punched her escape key and followed suit.

"Wait!" She called after him.

With long, steady strides Garrand ran down the twisting corridor, pulling off his jacket and tossing it to the side. He shed his shift as well, and unclipped his utility belt in midstride, letting it fall with a heavy clank to the deck. *Destiny's* internal passages were not exactly laid out in a logical manner, nor were they of uniform size and shape. Each twisted through the available spare space between sub-system housings and internal pipes, electrical conduits, neural cables, and pressure seals. There was a dark, almost romantic quality to each hall, whether it be broad and slick, lit with subtle glow rods like the central passage from the mess to the outer lock, or narrow and cramped like the passenger quarters corridor with coil ducting protruding at odd intervals. Garrand slid through the ship effortlessly, his mind already doing inventory on the supplies he would need. He navigated a side passage, ducked under the CM scrubbers that groaned like an old bellows, and headed for the armory. He looked over his shoulder, but Tchelakov was nowhere to be found. He rapidly sequenced the access code, waited for the door to dilate, and stepped into the darkened chamber.

With the thoughtless speed of years of repetition, he pressed his back hard against the armor mount and crunched down on the switch with his heel. With a rubbery scrunching sound, the armor wrapped around his torso and sealed itself. The gauntlets slid on smoothly as Garrand eyed the equipment on the far wall. *Thank goodness the doppelgänger is repaired,* he breathed as he scanned the equipment on the far wall. Garrand unhooked a satchel and laid it out on the worktable, undoing the leather catch on the front. He glanced up quickly, surveying the contents of the table. *No time to be choosey,* he thought. Holding the satchel with one arm just beneath the edge of the table, he swept his other arm across its surface, sliding as many of the contents into the open maw as possible.

He gently removed the black casing of the doppelgänger unit from a shelf and checked that its coil was viable. He gathered up a wheel of concussion grenades, three web throwers, and as many anti-personnel mines as he could carry and dumped the armload of munitions next to the satchel. As quickly as he could, he began stuffing the gear into the satchel, pausing to clip a web thrower to his belt.

Garrand pulled a heavy ticarac over his head—the rough fibers scratchy against his exposed neck—and shouldered the satchel. A fresh gunbelt was hanging by the door. He clipped three spare coil charges to it and fastened it around his waist. The whole ritual had taken less than a minute.

The armory portal irised shut behind him as he made his way to the starboard lock. He had one last stop to make before the equipment locker at the outer threshold. Taking a deep breath, he stopped midway down the inner gantry at the last pressure-sealed bulkhead. He could feel his heart racing, the anticipation and adrenaline rush starting to make him light-headed already. Closing his eyes, he exhaled forcibly, trying to weigh his options. *Shock Troops... Imperials... forest... mountains... snow... lost panda... Destiny's Needle in danger... Shock Troops?... Why here, why now?... Trioxin suits... danger... Helen upset... woman crying... losing one again... losing what?... a woman is crying... Kate?... Think straight, old man! Drop ships... lightning strike... they'll be coming in full Trioxin... platoon strength.*

He shivered and stared off at the far bulkhead, acutely conscious of the seconds ticking away. The hum of the ship's internal harmonics was of little solace. *I have no choice,* he decided. With fingers that did not betray the dread and self-doubt that screamed in his head, Garrand turned and keyed in a thirteen-character sequenced code, confirmed with voice-ident, and unlocked the most deadly compartment aboard *Destiny's Needle*.

Groaning from lack of use, the heavy doors trundled open as atmosphere hissed into the vacuum-sealed chamber. The shielded doors halted halfway open, as if reluctant to part with their arcane ward. Garrand thumped the steel with his fist to jolt it back into action. Vaporous fog rolled out from the super-chilled cell as the doors parted.

Garrand realized he was unconsciously holding his breath, and he exhaled. The moist air from his lungs crystallized in a swirl before him. Anxiety weighed upon his chest. He stifled his fear and stepped boldly into the room.

A narrow Tarkanian shell stood in the center of the small chamber, bathed in an incandescent blue light. The silver shell was a meter tall and roughly torpedo-shaped. One of the most lethal and ravenous pseudo-creatures found anywhere in the known galaxy rested inside, suspended within an electromagnetic containment field. Garrand paused a moment, starring at the reflective surface of the Tarkanian shell. He hadn't laid eyes on it in over five years. Rubbing his hands together in the cold, he hooked a strap to the shell and slung it over his neck. The shell felt icy cold against his hip. He shuddered involuntarily being so close to the creature once more. Having the shell slung across his shoulder made him feel like he had just handed a dagger to his worst enemy and turned his back.

Garrand verbally ordered *Destiny's Needle* to open both airlock portals as he made his way to the equipment locker. He punched the access code and cracked open the locker, sifting through climbing gear and survival packs before finding what he was looking for.

Helen appeared around the corner.

"Find what you need?" she asked anxiously. She glanced up at him with big, uncertain eyes.

Garrand pushed by her and headed briskly for the ramp. The whine of *Destiny's* engines could already be heard as Bailey rushed through the preflight routine.

"Wait. I'm coming with you!" she called after him as she jogged to catch up. "I want to come with you."

"You can't."

"No, you're not…"

She caught up to him, grabbed his arm and spun him around. "He could be anywhere. He's scared, probably hiding. You need me to show you where to look."

"There's not enough time for that. I'll find him."

"But you've never even been around pandas, you don't know what they're like. What if he doesn't want to come with you?"

"He will."

"How will you find him?"

"Don't worry I'll find him."

"But—"

"—and I'll bring him back."

"Garrand!"

He reached for her hand and gently released his arm from her grasp. "Trust me."

22

ALEXANDER

ALEXANDER STIRRED RESTLESSLY IN HIS SECRET, MAKEshift nest, mind still groggy from his afternoon nap. Mother always scolded him for sleeping too much, but the frantic preparations for yet another move had made him drowsy and discontent. There would be plenty of time for work later.

He shook his head clear of half-remembered dreams and yawned, scratching behind his ear with a long, curved claw. He rose to all fours and stretched his shoulders out, arching his back, trying to get all the little kinks out of his spine. He raised his broad, black nose to the wind and sniffed tentatively, letting the many subtle variances of smell and scent waft into his consciousness. Frowning, he drew a deeper breath through his nostrils, this time actively seeking out scent markers. He listened for the sounds of the others, but all he could hear were the muted sounds of the forest. *Maybe they're all napping as well,* he thought. *A good choice on such a pretty evening. Harvesting bamboo is so boring.*

Alex sauntered out of his little den of ferns and leaves he had burrowed in the snow and called out to the forest, a low rumble from his throat. No response. He called out again, this time more insistently. *Where was everyone?*

THE NIGHT SKY had grown cold and dark, but Garrand had little trouble making his way through the surreal stillness. The details of the forest were crisp and clear before him, suffused in a ghostly, pale radiance. Wispy clouds swung low and fast over the mountain ridges, casting eerie shadows across Garrand's path. He flipped a switch on his belt, activating his personal magnetosphere. The alternating waves of energy would mask his bio signs from the approaching Imperial drop ships. Garrand hadn't bothered to retrieve an infrared headset, preferring to rely on his unaided eye to show him the way. He needed to be able to see the tricky little nuances of the forest that electronic gear wouldn't be able to detect. It would be especially important if he was to elude a platoon of men clad in full Trioxin. He had, however, pulled a thermal imager out of the locker—he would need it to track down the panda at night.

Anything that big had to have quite a heat signature, he told himself. *Even a young panda would radiate more heat than any other creature in the vicinity. Unless there were dragons nearby.* He paused, his heart fluttering at the thought. Dragons gave him the chills, especially after Cheqlund Varz. He shook his head, chiding himself: *too cold for dragons, they wouldn't like it here.* He grabbed a branch and hauled himself over a fallen log, rushing on.

Garrand picked his way through the dense undergrowth, fending off low branches and undergrowth with his arms. He stayed on the balls of his feet, moving as quickly as he dared, trying to find a rhythm. The uneven forest floor beneath the snow cover was making the going extremely treacherous—he couldn't see the deadfalls, roots and boulders beneath the snow. He surged onward, propelled by fear and adrenaline. His pulse thudded in his ears. *This is a nightmare,* he mused as he slid down a muddy embankment into a drift of snow. *Shock Troops.* He shuddered at the thought. *Nasty business, Shock Troops—cold, efficient, ruthless.* He'd seen first-hand what a regiment of the Emperor's elite warriors could do. Never wanted to be on this side of things. If he wasn't so cold and scared he would have laughed at his ironic misfortune.

He had traveled nearly a kilometer when the thermal imager began to bleat softly. He checked the display in midstride. He was getting close, the largest signature was only fifty meters away. He had little time—the Shock Troops would be able to read the same information on their scopes—he needed to get the creature within the cloaking confines of his magnetosphere.

Garrand stopped between two giant pines and removed an antipersonnel mine from his satchel. He set the charge to wide dispersal and gently placed it at the base of one tree, covering it with handfuls of leaves. Garrand quickly unspooled a length of thin filament and spread a series of tripwires between four trees, delicately hooking the final loop to the mine. Trioxin sensors would detect electro-magnetic triggers, so he had to set manual trips. He stepped gingerly over the filament and circled west.

His comtab chimed. "Captain, you have four minutes, seventeen seconds before the drop ships converge on your position." Bailey's voice was calm, bless him.

"Are you away?"

"All systems are powered up, we will be lifting momentarily."

"Get out of there," he growled.

"Have you located the panda, sir?"

"I'm closing on it now—it doesn't seem to be moving."

"Captain I noticed on the command board that the Byrethylen's containment chamber was deactivated."

Garrand allowed himself a rueful grin as he knelt to place another charge. "That's because our old friend is with me."

There was a long silence. "Captain, do you really think that's such a good idea? Perhaps you'll recall the difficulties we encountered entrapping our friend on Mylos."

"I haven't forgotten," he said softly. *I don't think I'll ever forget,* he muttered under his breath as he secured another tripwire.

Helen's voice suddenly blared in his ear as she found the com activation button on her station. "Byrethylen! Are you completely insane? You're carrying a wraith!"

Garrand lurched through a hollow of knee-deep snow to another coppice of trees at the edge of a long ridge overlooking the green and white valley below. "I'm well aware of that, Miss Tchelakov."

"But," Helen stammered, "you must be mad! You're not actually considering turning a wraith *loose?*"

Garrand reached into his satchel and removed a round, flattened container with a matte black finish. He popped the lid off, revealing two-dozen small, shinning spheres. He placed the container in the snow and scooped out a double handful, tossing the concussion grenades back along the snowy trail. He scooped out another handful and slung these in an even wider arc further back along the trail.

"Garrand! Answer me!"

"Maybe you'd like me to take on a platoon or two of Shock Troops by myself, is that it? Singlehanded? What chance do you think I'd have?"

Another silence. "But you're not going to survive the wraith either!"

"I'll survive a lot longer than I will against those Shock Troops!"

"The wraith will tear you apart! It'll tear everyone apart — the whole continent will be uninhabitable!"

"I don't plan on hanging around that long. Besides," he chuckled ominously, "this one and I go back a long ways."

"Garrand, you're supposed to be *rescuing* Alexander, not offering him up for dinner."

He removed a web thrower from his satchel and smacked the adhesive back to a tree trunk. He thumbed the proximity fuse to ten meters and continued through the forest.

"Don't worry, he'll have plenty of other tasty tidbits to choose from. Bailey, how long?"

"Just under three minutes, sir."

Helen persisted, "But you can't release a wraith here — the whole planet will have to be quarantined!"

Bailey interjected, "I must agree, Captain. How will you ever recapture it again?"

"I don't plan on recapturing him *or* ever setting foot on this planet again."

"But Captain—"

"Look," he snapped testily, "Do you want to see this Alexander of yours alive again, or not?" Garrand placed another web thrower and reached quickly inside his satchel for another box of grenades. His fingers were beginning to tremble from the cold, and the dread of what was coming. "It's either them or us. I plan to survive this disaster. Besides," he said fleetingly, "the beast's been locked up long enough."

"Captain," Bailey's voice sounded genuinely concerned. "The chances that you will survive the dual threat and combined destructive force of a platoon of Imperial Shock Troops and a Byrethylen Wraith are negligible at best."

"Bailey, you taught me yourself: with nothing to lose, try to confuse. I'm just giving our Imperial guests something to keep them occupied. Something that will make them lose all interest in *me*. Now, get the ship out of there! And by Haven!" He cut off his comtab.

Garrand looked back over the ridge. The branches of the pines were spaced well apart here: it would be an inviting spot for a Trooper with jump jets to land. Garrand unhooked a spool of gecklewire and clipped the egg-shaped cartridge into his rikon climbing gun. He loaded a lethal-looking steel piton into the breach and hooked the front end of the wire in the spool to its tail. The rikon climbing gun was designed to fire super-hardened quamite-tipped pitons into granite, negating the need for picks and hammers. Climbing cord and d-rings could be clipped to the back of the pitons once they were embedded in the stone.

With his arm extended, Garrand took aim at the top of a nearby tree and fired. The sharp spike whistled across the glen, trailing gecklewire behind it. The piton hit its target with a reassuring thump. Garrand clipped another piton into the rikon and secured the back end of the gecklespool to its tail. He fired at a different tree. The piton embedded itself deep in the trunk, and the gecklespool automatically began spinning, retracting the loose gecklewire that hung between the two trees. Once the slack had been taken up, an invisible and razor-sharp barrier was created twenty meters in the air between the branches of two towering pines.

Garrand loaded and fired the rest of his supply of pitons, crossing the ridge with a curtain of filament. The gecklewire was coated with a gritty diamond resin in a state of constant molecular flux that would slice through almost any fiber-composite armor. Shock Troops that attempted to follow him through the air with jump jets would be in for a surprise when they crested this ridge.

Sweat dripped from Garrand's brow despite the chill night air. He dropped to one knee and fished around in his satchel looking for one final diversion. The bag was limp and nearly empty now. His fingers scrabbled around until his fingers found the octangular case of the doppelgänger. He turned the device in his hands until he found the activation panel. The miniature panel scrolled aside at the soft pressure of his warm fingertip. Garrand gently rotated the calibrators with his fingernail. Tiny numbers flashed on the display.

Satisfied that he had approximated his mass, heart rate, temperature and breathing rhythm, he simultaneously depressed two switches and set the unit to standby. When activated, the doppelgänger would immediately begin emitting bio signs that would mimic his body's signature. To the attacking Shock Troops, it would appear as a human lifeform in their heads-up display. To an electronic sensor, the doppelgänger projected all the outwardly detectable signs of a human life: warmth, pulse, respiration, and chemical body composition. Garrand set the variance levels to heavy physical exertion and hoped the random vascular subroutine he had written would convince the Trioxin sensors. The infernal things had a knack for knowing when they were being fooled.

    Garrand checked the display of his thermal imager, searching for a sign of the panda. One contact — twenty meters northwest. He set off through the snow.

❖ ❖ ❖

ALEXANDER SAT SHIVERING IN THE COLD, WATCHING THE FORest for signs of his Mother or one of the other pandas returning to get him. *Why had they left him here all alone? Didn't anyone know he was missing?* He had searched the nearby bamboo groves, but was afraid to venture too far off in case someone came back for him. For an hour he had paced nervously in front of the tribe's open-air Lyceum, a stunning amphitheater hollowed out of the hillside. The gently sloping bowl was lined with soft fern and pine needles, lit from within by suspended glow globes, and crowned by massive pine timbers that arched magnificently from one end of the hollow to the other.

    Paws cold, fur wet and muddy, Alexander slumped against a tree and sat picking nervously at his claws. The once gentle, reassuring noises of the forest now seemed to cascade over him, each new sound a jolt to his security. His nose restlessly sampled the flavors of the air, hoping for a familiar scent. To his dismay, however, a strange effluvium wafted into his awareness. His eyes searched upwind for the source of the foreign odor. There, to the north of the clearing, he heard the crack of a branch snapping, and the soft rustle of bamboo leaves being turned aside. Fear gripped his heart, and though he wanted to run away, his muscles did not seem to respond to his desires. He was paralyzed in his cold, damp spot as the sound grew closer. It wasn't a panda—the scent was all wrong. As he listened, he realized that the sounds were those of a biped.

Alexander cringed against the tree trunk, watching the area of the forest where the two-legged creature should appear. It seemed to be in a hurry by the sound of its footsteps. Suddenly a creature burst out of the undergrowth, running with its eyes down, staring at some sort of device in its hand, which glowed green in the darkness, bathing the creature's face in the strange hue. It was a human male, broad-shouldered and tall, but to Alexander's dismay, it was not Grandfather. The human's scent was entirely unfamiliar. There was a mechanical, machine-oriented flavor to his odor, not at all like the soft, natural smell of Grandfather Tchelakov. Despite his strange odor, however, the man did not seem to have an air of immediate danger surrounding him. In fact, he looked confused—almost frightened.

The human staggered to a halt and glanced anxiously around the clearing. With a clear sign of recognition, the man's eyes locked onto Alexander's quivering form and smiled. The smile caught Alexander by surprise, for he certainly wasn't expecting a display of warmth. The man's face wore a tired, world-weary expression—there were deep circles under his eyes, but his smile was warm and genuine.

The man approached slowly, one arm held out before him. As he drew near, Alexander could begin to make out the hazy edge of the human's aura sparkling behind the crown of his head. Much to his relief, the aura was a vibrant green, run through with streaks of blue and even a little gold that sparkled delicately in the starlight. A radiance of kindness surrounded the man's body. Alexander breathed a gentle sigh and felt his heart beat slow. The human's spirit was infused with the ancient green of trueness. The aura was rimmed with a corona of deep crimson, Alexander noted. The corona flared up in jagged shards of emotion as the man fought to control his subconscious feelings of dread. The man was obviously as frightened as he was. Alexander was convinced that the man would do him no harm.

He let the man approach, sitting very still—not wanting to further spook his potential rescuer. *Maybe he'll take me away with him,* Alexander hoped. Then his mind soared: *The Elders must have sent him!*

"Easy there, fella," Garrand murmured softly. He held his hand out, palm up in what he hoped was a gesture of friendliness. He edged forward until he could almost touch the panda. It sat up against the bole of a tree, shivering slightly. Garrand dropped to his knees and leaned further forward, his hand hovering over the creature. With a soft grin he reached down and gently scratched the soft, pliant fur over the panda's left ear.

"Mrraw," Alexander turned his head to the side and leaned into the scratch.

"Yeah, that's it. I'm not going to hurt you."

Garrand stood and looked back over his shoulder nervously. "We've got to get out of here." He could hear the rumbling drone of the drop ships as they approached. They were very close.

"C'mon. We've got to go." He looked down at the curious panda and wrinkled his jaw. "I guess I've got to carry you." He opened his arms and began to lean down to pick up the creature, but the panda beat him to it, springing into his arms.

Alexander wrapped his arms tightly around the man's neck and his legs clung to his waist, claws digging into the rough material of his trousers. He tried to contain his trembling fear, reciting the mantra his Mother had taught him over and over in his mind, but what his eyes displayed was more terrifying than anything in his dreams had ever been. A terrible roar ripped through the valley as a ship screamed overhead. The man began running unevenly through the forest undergrowth, jostling him back and forth. Alexander was left starring back over the warm man's shoulder.

In the wake of the terrible screeching roar of the ship, Alexander could see ghosts appearing in the sky; awful white beings cloaked in sheets of flame. Through the treetops, the ghostly creatures floated, crackling through the upper branches on roaring pillars of fire — bizarre otherworldly specters come to wrest his soul away. Terrible men were encased within those gleaming forms; men with devastating weapons intent on destroying his tribe.

Garrand rushed across the compound as blaster fire began whipping around them. "Time to release my old friend," Garrand muttered darkly.

Just beyond the clearing, the trail plunged down. Grasping bamboo stems and saplings to slow his momentum, Garrand careened to the bottom where a brook tumbled across boulders glazed with ice. Garrand grasped the bear firmly and started across, sinking to his waist in the frigid waters — the boulders posed too great a risk of slippage. *If I turn my ankle now I'll never see the ship again,* he reflected.

He climbed up the slippery bank on the far side and charged through a curtain of bamboo. After another thirty meters he found a small clearing with compacted snow. Garrand knelt to the ground and set the panda down.

"You stay there." Alexander just sat looking up at him innocently. Garrand removed the silvered housing of the Tarkanian shell from his shoulder and placed it gently in the snow. Garrand unlatched the outer casing with fingers so numb he could barely feel them and revealed the inner locking mechanism that flashed red in warning.

His heart fluttered being this close to the terrible creature once again. He could scarcely believe he was about to let the wraith loose. His hands trembled as he keyed in the release code — pausing before entering the final command override to breathe deeply. He closed his eyes and tilted his head back. *Last chance to change your mind, old man.*

He squeezed his eyes shut so tightly that stars began to dance in the darkness. The image of Helen's terrified face imploring him to rescue the lost panda rolled before his eyes. He imagined Bailey's soft gaze, remembered all the times he'd looked into those gentle, hypnotic eyes for relief from all the madness. And inexplicably, he thought of Kate — remembered her smile, the corners of her mouth edging up mischievously, her face so young and beautiful — an image lost to him forever.

There's no turning back now, not if you insist on stubbornly surviving. With grim determination he entered the final code and set the release timer for thirty seconds. He hit execute and swiftly rose to his feet. The doppelgänger was still slung to his belt, waiting patiently in standby mode. Garrand grasped the unit in his hands and twisted hard, rotating the twin halves against one another, activating the signal broadcast. He tossed the unit in the snow next to the Tarkanian shell, and paused for the briefest of instants, staring at the silver casing that rested unevenly in the drift. A soft breeze whispered through the pines, stirring snow snakes that writhed and twisted under the pale glow of the stars. A jolt coursed through his psyche as he bore witness to another defining moment in his life. A portrait of the man he had become unfolded cruelly before his eyes, and he realized that the next time the wind roared in his ears, unshakable and unrelenting, this moment, too, would be forever etched in his mind.

He gathered up the panda and began loping away, awkwardly at first — his feet not responding as swiftly as his mind wished — and then more quickly as he felt his chest tighten in fear and his heartbeat throb in his ears. A plasma bolt splashed against a nearby tree; they had already homed in on the doppleganger's signal. There was no time to dive for cover.

The container began to emanate an ominous warning bleat that rang through the snowy clearing, rising in volume and pitch as the seconds melted away. Garrand could hear the bronk, bronk of the shell echoing all through the valley as he rushed almost recklessly through the snow and trees. Alexander clung to the man's shoulders for dear life, fear sucking at him, making it difficult to breathe.

A soul-wrenching scream, ending in a terrible howl tore across the mountain glade and reverberated throughout the valley. Garrand felt his pulse unnaturally quicken and found his arms and legs scrambling through the dense undergrowth with an added urgency. He had to concentrate more fully on what he was doing, where he was placing his hands as he heaved himself over fallen trees. Fear and dread rose steadily within his chest as the specter of what he had just done began to dawn on him. A second yowl called out behind him, closer this time and quite a bit louder.

I know you're angry, he thought to himself. His breaths were coming ragged now. *I would be too if someone had trapped me in a lifeless tube for five years, but at least you're out now. Just give me a chance to get out of your way and you can feed to your heart's content.*

The trail ascended to the crest of a ridge and he halted there briefly, breathing heavily. Alexander watched the fog crystals emerge from the man's hot, moist breath and wrinkled his nose. He growled softly in encouragement.

23

Feeding the Byrethylen

Arnas could feel the *Scarrion* buck wildly in the turbulence as the drop ship plunged over the back side of the huge mountain range that guarded the forested valley beneath them. Sensors had detected massive lifeform readings all across the planet, and faint mammalian signatures on several continents, but no clear sign of their targets. Technical sweeps, however, had picked up one curious radiation anomaly deep in the mountains on the northern hemisphere. Localized scans revealed the presence of high-grade fuel isotopes somewhere beneath the masking canopy of life that seemed to blanket the entire planet. There was only one possible source of such isotopes on an un-pioneered planet such as El-Bouteran. Arnas smiled wickedly to himself.

Somewhere in the forested glen below lay Médeville's ship, *Destiny's Needle*. For some unknown reason, it had dumped fuel, leaving a tell tale signature etched across the electro-magnetic spectrum of the planet's surface. Arnas could feel excitement welling up in his chest, his fists clenching and releasing in nervous anticipation. The Tchelakov quisling and her thirty-seven bio-engineered creatures were undoubtedly below.

"Prepare for drop, jumpers on standby," he ordered on the open com. His drop hole irised open beneath him and he could see the trees whipping by in the darkness between his boots.

"Infrared on medium gain," he barked, "that snow'll blind you if your visor's set too high!"

The safety catches released and the safety of the ship gave way to the sickening sensation of falling. Darkness enveloped him, and even with his helmet on he could hear the harsh whistling of the wind as he dropped like a stone from the belly of the *Scarrion*. With a lurch, he felt a kick and the jarring blast of his jump jets as they spewed flame beneath him, gradually slowing his descent.

Arnas picked out a spot between four trees on a sloping hillside in his infrared display, and set down roughly, dropping to a knee with one arm out against the ground to keep his body from tumbling.

"All Troopers, full sweep!" he commanded. "Filter out any lifeforms less than fifty kilos. Squad Three, your target is the ship. You're clear to use jumpers. Home in on the radiation signature. Disable it, make sure it cannot lift, but do not harm its occupants."

Arnas studied his own scope and frowned. He wasn't reading anything larger than fifteen kilos. *Where were all the targets?* There should be at least thirty-seven lifeforms glowing in his heads-up display.

"Commander, reading a strong signal—possibly human—grid two, forty-five meters northwest of my position."

Arnas quickly thumbed his heads-up to grid two and zeroed in on the Trooper's com ident. He switched to Squad Two's channel: "Vaskin, what've you got?"

"Strong signal," the man replied. "Trent's the closest. It's human all right. And he's tired: respiration and heart rate way up. Signal is stationary though, must be resting."

"Okay, take your men around the north flank. Send three men to handle the human. We'll work our way back toward the radiation signature from here. Squad Four will cover the southern flank, and Squad One will close the noose."

"Yes sir!"

Arnas set his power studs to half and began bounding up the snowy hill, as he studied scan data.

"Commander Arnas?" The voice was a rough whisper in his helmet. Visual com ident tagged the signal as Trent's, but Arnas didn't bother checking—he could identify all his men by voice, and Trent's rasp was unmistakable.

"Go ahead Lieutenant."

"Target is twenty-five meters due north, apparently within a clearing. I'm separated from the target by dense vegetation—no visual. I'm getting a second signal now, auditory."

Arnas frowned. *Médeville wouldn't be purposefully making noise, would he?* "What kind of auditory signal?"

"Mechanical. Rising in pitch and volume, almost like an alarm…"

"Do not engage. I repeat: do not engage! Close distance to ten meters and give me a visual. Laserai and Harmon should be in position. I'm on my way." He thumbed the Squad Leader's channel, "Vaskin, you'd better get over to Trent. I've got a bad feeling about—"

An explosion ripped through the valley, then two more in quick succession. Arnas wheeled toward the flashing blips on his screen. Smoke was rising over the trees to the south.

"Report!"

"Harks and Zimi down. Looks like AP mines, but we swept for triggers. Whole valley came up clean. I don't know how—"

Arnas swore under his breath. *He must be using manual trips.* "Go to jump jets, we can't afford to—"

Another explosion crackled over his helmet speaker, followed by a scream over the open com.

"Commander Arnas! Three men down."

"Where are you?" Arnas demanded, trying to sort through the flashing contact points on his heads-up display.

"Grid three, mark four, nine—" static hissed in his helmet. Arnas cursed.

"Squad Three, any sign of that ship?"

Dibbs' voice sounded in his helmet, "Negative, Commander. We're on top of the site of the fuel dump and there's nothin' here. Looks like someone just lifted, we must have just missed them."

Fire erupted fifteen meters in front of Arnas. He dove to the ground, expecting blaster fire. He lay still for several seconds before continuing, trying to sort through the random battle chatter that filled his com. Frustration began to well up in his throat. His men were getting separated from their objectives by the confusion. There was too much going on in all directions at once.

"—There're contact mines and grenades all over the place! Vicks is caught in a web and—"

"—Cut him right in half. Hyannus lost her legs. We're back on the ground now."

"—Commander? Commander Arnas, come in."

"I'm here, Trent." Arnas scrabbled to his feet and waved his two flanking Troopers onward with a hand signal. "What is it?"

"I'm almost on top of that signal now, but I can't get any visual id. He must be hiding behind a tree or something."

"Laserai, what've you got?"

"Same thing: strong signal but no target."

"What about that noise?"

"I've got a visual on that. Seems to be some sort of shell. Not a bomb, but I'm getting strange readings from it. It's making a racket."

"Yeah, I can hear it." Arnas was only twenty meters away from the target now.

"Doppleganger, maybe?" Vaskin asked.

"Could be, but it's awfully big for that, though."

"All right, we've got him encircled," Arnas said. "Go ahead and close in." As he spoke, the sound suddenly stopped, leaving an almost unnatural silence in the valley.

A plaintive yowl tore across the chill night air, echoing through the glen like a thunderclap.

What in Haven's name was that? He strode toward the target's position, aware that vaporous tendrils of fog were beginning to swirl around his legs. The vapor billowed from the ground, enshrouding the trees in a murky fog. Arnas hesitated, switching his helmet to visual only.

Forms flowed within the grey vapor clouds, almost-seen shapes coalescing briefly before bending back inwards in implosion dissipations. The fog seemed to possess a life of its own, an eerily choreographed ballet of shape-shifting specters. Arnas studied the fog with concern. *Was it growing?* He looked to the sky—black and clear. There was little humidity and the surface conditions just weren't conducive to spontaneous vapor formation or moisture condensation. A growing sense of alarm filled him.

Arnas keyed his throat mike. "Lower your weapons. Keep your hands at your sides." He was not sure what to say. Despite his training, primal fear rose within and he could feel his chest tightening. Biosensors peaked and he felt the icy hot prick of suppressors being automatically injected into his skin. The suit must have sensed a need for stimulants too, for he felt a fresh surge of adrenaline pulsing though his veins. He could no longer visually identify his two flanking Troopers, they were becoming lost in the swirling vapors. He began backing up instinctively, trying to keep the fog from completely encircling them. "Back up the way you came. Don't turn around—and do it slow!"

A throaty scream pierced the air, followed by a terrible, otherworldly wail that ripped through the valley.

"Cheplus—"

"It's got Harmon!"

"No, Trent—don't!"

A muffled explosion sounded over Arnas' com, and a fireball erupted before him.

"Vaskin, Trent, report!" Arnas ordered, feeling blind and helpless.

"*No, no, no.*"

"Lay down a cover fire."

"Fall back."

"Don't fire, Trent's in there!"

"No—stop."

More blaster fire.

"Report!"

Two more screams echoed in his helmet.

"Oh, my—"

"Commander—" Arnas' com seemed to be picking up static. "—three men down—circle behind the—looks to be—uncertain wraith—"

"What? Did you say a *wraith*!"

"Repeat, three men down—" Laysellus shouted into his helmet com. "No bio signs. Four others missing. Confirmed sighting of Byrethylen Wraith—last position in grid two mark zero point four five."

A wraith? Here on this lush green world? It was almost inconceivable. Arnas set his suit's power amplification on full and bounded through the thick undergrowth toward the smoke that roiled over the clearing before him.

Vaskin pushed through a tight jumble of vegetation, struggling to come to the aid of Trent and Laserai. As he broke free of the strange, tall grass he froze. A large, dark shape held Harmon stationary in midair. Inky black tendrils of energy manifestation were wrapped around the Trioxin suit, and several more were entering into its shattered helmet.

Kneeling to the ground, Vaskin brought his assault rifle to bear. The familiar crack-whoosh of the weapon sounded as felt the barrel kick back hard against his shoulder. The energy bolt passed straight through the wraith, leaving only a slight glowing oval where it had entered the manifestation. Struck dumb for a moment, Vaskin realized too late that the horrific creature was not vulnerable to energy weapons.

As he fumbled for his plasma gun, Saylus stumbled through a thicket of the giant grass ten meters away, clawing desperately at his helmet as if there was something terrible trapped in the suit with him. When he saw Vaskin kneeling just five meters in front of him, he began shrieking mutely inside his suit, eyes agog. Saylus leveled his burner eye-level with Vaskin.

"No, Saylus! Wait! It's me—"

With his weapon on full, he depressed the fire stud at point blank range, burning Vaskin's faceplate off. Vaskin instinctively shut his eyes as the fire splashed across his visor; heat seared his face, his eyelids felt as if they were actually on fire. And then he felt a cool breeze upon his face. He cautiously opened his eyes. His faceplate was gone, but it had borne the brunt of the damage. Saylus was nowhere to be seen. The wraith tossed the limp and lifeless body of Harmon's suit to the ground and turned toward him.

As the wraith turned to gaze upon Vaskin, it suddenly transformed into a fiery demon a hundred meters tall, reading the man's hidden subconscious, projecting itself as the human's worst nightmare. It could taste the palpable rise in adrenaline and super-oxygenated blood in the creature's veins. The human's neural activity was in a state of frenzy.

Vaskin saw only what the wraith wanted him to see. His comrades appeared to him as monsters. He fired wildly at them, trying desperately to drive them back. The human was helpless to defend himself. The wraith was free to feed upon this one as the others laid waste to each other. It wrapped its energy fields around the human's neck and lifted him clear off the ground, tilting his head back until it nearly snapped. The wraith allowed part of itself to slip up inside the shattered faceplate of Vaskin's helmet and entered the man's brain through his nostrils where it quickly bled the neural energy from the cerebrum, desiccating the delicate tissue in the process. It left the way it had entered, tossing the useless husk of the drained body to the side and turning to find its next victim.

Arnas took in the horrifying scene and immediately dropped to his knee, switching all power to his plasma rifle. The wraith was sucking all the energy around it in expanding concentric circles, quickly depleting the weaponry and defenses of the Shock Troopers. Arnas pumped round after round of plasma bolts into the wraith, trying to weaken the creature's hold on Vaskin and lure its attention away from his men. He succeeded.

The terrible, dark mass of the creature turned to face him. Arnas quickly turned, darkening his visor to opaque and turning up the volume on his helmet com to near deafening levels. He tried to remember images from his childhood, the tree where he used to swing when he was a boy. The face of the first girl he ever kissed. He ran as fast as the suit's power amplification would let him, crashing through the vegetation, trying to concentrate on anything but the wraith. The face of his mother loomed into his memory as he set his tacticals to ten-second delay and dropped them in his wake.

He counted nine and threw himself flat, hoping against hope that the detonation would envelope the wraith and keep it from invading his mind, conjuring up his worst fears, whatever those might be.

It apparently worked. The shock wave buffeted him for several seconds and his suit's radiation alarms squealed unpleasantly in his ears. He paused to turn down the gain on his helmet speaker, and rolled to face the sky. The forest was bathed in fire. Arnas levered himself back upright and retreated further from the raging fires.

Arnas brought up his heads-up display and took stock of the situation. There was little to do but try to save what was left of his platoon. He scanned grid two for surviving members of Squad's Two and Three. He thumbed his com, "Tyer! What's your status?"

"Commander—" The signal was choppy. "—holed up here. We set diversionary charges—"

"—Lieutenant Tyer, drop your tacticals immediately and fall back."

"What about—"

Arnas cut her off. "We've got to save the men we've got left."

Silence, then: "Yes, sir."

"Order your squad to fall back to—" he consulted his scope, "—mark five point three, grid four. I want a full burn on the wraith's last known position in fifteen seconds."

Arnas thumbed Squad Two's channel. "Laysellus, drop your squad back fifty meters and hit grid's two and three with all the tacticals you've got. I want an impenetrable spread."

He hit the platoon wide channel. "Squads Three and Four—use your jumpers and return to drop zone. Sweep the western and northern ridges for the targets as you fly."

A brilliant orange and gold fireball began rising through the trees to the south. Arnas' visor automatically darkened. Squad Two was firing a series of tacticals in an arc beyond their position, creating a radioactive firewall between his remaining men and the wraith that fed hungrily beyond. Squad One continued to launch a salvo of firebombs into the trees. The screams of his men still in the clutches of the wraith had not yet died out.

This couldn't be an accident, Arnas seethed. *Where in Haven's name had Médeville gotten hold of a wraith?* Arnas bitterly recalled Barrett's words: *He's been out of the field for years. His reflexes are dulled by time and lethargy. His techniques are old—antiquated by your standards. He's rusty and should be no match for you and a platoon of my finest Shock Troops."*

Arnas ground his teeth in disgust, recalling the conversation. The man may not have the luster of the Imperial Dragon stitched upon his breast, or the honor of protecting the Emperor, but Captain Garrand Ai'Gonet Médeville was by no stretch of the imagination *rusty*.

He keyed his throat mike, "TacOps, this is Thantor One. Prepare for immediate dustoff. I want lifters in here in three minutes!"

"What about the targets?"

"We've got a class one situation down here. All K'ye's broken loose — literally. I need those mules in here *now*! We'll have to catch them as they attempt to break orbit."

"Understood," came the response in his helmet. "Lifters standing by in upper atmosphere. Waiting for coordinates."

"We don't have time for standard procedure — they're getting away!"

"Roger that — homing in on your signal. Uh, Commander?"

"What is it!"

"Reading extremely dense vegetation surrounding your position — recommend burn and retreat. One hundred seventy seconds to dustoff."

"Understood."

Arnas punched his platoon channel and broadcast, "Two minutes to retrieval. All squad leaders: visual identification of platoon. Soundoff."

The sound of each squad leader verifying his men's position rattled off in his ears. "All right — Squads Three and Four drop all incendiaries and proceed north 200 meters. Squad Two, burners on full, sweep 120-degree arcs and retreat 50 meters. On my signal, duck and cover."

Squad leaders confirmed and began razing the forest around them, clearing a landing sight for the lifters descending from orbit. When his men were clear on his scope, Arnas loaded a tactical warhead into his launcher and fired it into the center of the firestorm.

"Take cover!" he ordered, and turned his faceplate away from the scene. He heard a plunk and saw the reflection of a brilliant flash illuminate the forest. Then a shockwave hit him and the ground reverberated from the explosion. He turned back to see a 35 meter blackened crater in the center of a burning clearing. Above he could see stars.

"Radiation shields up, converge on my position. The mules are on their way."

24

Nahodna's Noose

Garrand paused and leaned heavily against a rocky outcrop as he struggled to catch his breath. Behind him the forest burned, pillars of smoke drifting up to meet the clouds. "Which way do you think, little one?" There was a fork in the paths here. He checked his displays, but had no frame of reference to judge them against. The stars were hidden by dense foliage overhead. "We've got to get to the lake, little guy," he sighed.

Alexander looked up at the man. With a soft bleat he tapped a claw against Garrand's shoulder and gestured toward the first path.

Garrand frowned, "That way, huh?" He shook his head. *I'm talking to a giant panda!* "I don't know, fella." He scratched his chin.

Alexander listened intently for several moments, cocking his head to one side and then the other. Then without warning he scrambled out of Garrand's arms and went plunging down the narrow trail to the right. Garrand was caught rocking back on his heels trying to regain his breath. The black and white creature was no small burden to carry.

Startled, he called out after the creature, dimly aware that it was a futile gesture and with a grimace began slipping and sliding his way down the incline in pursuit. The trail was covered with mud. Damp leaves and tangled roots made the going especially difficult. Garrand fairly careened down the slope, barely able to contain his progress, merely hoping not to trip and fall headlong into a boulder or tree.

The panda went plowing on so rapidly that Garrand could not keep pace with it. *I hope you know what you're doing,* he breathed. *Perhaps the creature's natural survival instinct had kicked in, or maybe he had heard or smelt something that had scared him. Did Shock Troopers smell in their armor? Perhaps the mere alienness of the material gave them away.* Whatever the case, he had little choice but to follow him now.

When did he start thinking of the beast as a 'him' rather than an 'it'? The creature did seem to have a personality of its own, he reasoned. *And it was quite intelligent. Nevertheless, it was a strange distinction to make.*

Garrand spotted the panda near a fallen tree. "Hold on a second, I'm coming." The panda turned to look at him as he stumbled on. Garrand pushed through two low branches and looked out past the seated creature.

Spread out below them was a long, low valley enshrouded in mist. Stretching from the edge of the forest to the mountains was a dark, silent body of water. Garrand brushed the water from his face and eyes and allowed himself a little grin.

"Good choice," he chuckled. He couldn't quite believe they had made it this far. The fur ball turned his oversized head and gazed at him with big, black eyes.

"Mrrraw," he called.

"Yeah, I know. I should have listened to you all along. C'mon, we better get moving." He opened his arms and the creature took two fluid steps without pause and sprang into his arms.

Garrand grunted under the weight. "You're just about too big for this, fella, but I don't want to risk you running off again." The bear licked his ear.

"Egh. None of that," he tried to wipe his ear on his shoulder and trotted down the path that lead to the lake's edge.

Destiny's Needle hovered tenuously over the edge of the lake, fantastic ripples expanding in all directions beneath the ship's thrumming gravitic repulsors. The central boarding ramp was already extended, and Helen stood near the opening, bracing herself on one hydraulic lifting arm. Garrand hoisted the frightened panda up to the edge of the ramp and Helen reached an arm forward to grab him by one ear, guiding him to safety as he complained loudly. Garrand chinned himself up and swung a leg onto the ramp, drawing himself up on one knee. He grasped a strut for support and thumbed his comtab.

"All clear Bailey. Get us out of here."

Destiny's Needle swung forward, nosing over as she gained velocity. Garrand stepped into the airlock and banged the retract button with the side of his fist. The pressure lock cycled shut and internal servos squealed as the ramp trundled back into its recessed position. He walked briskly into the broad central passage that lead from the outer lock, wet boots scrunching underfoot. Heading for the mess, he shucked his heavy ticarac. Helen stood off to one side of the mess beneath the cargo disposition panels with a strange expression on her face, starring at him as though he were a ghost. The panda, Alexander, turned from Helen as Garrand entered the room and fairly caromed across the slick deck plates, leaping into his arms with a bellowing snort of happiness.

The captain grunted under the unexpected weight and staggered back a step.

"Ga-rrraw," the panda rumbled as it tried to lick the man's mouth, nose, ears, and eyes all at once.

"All right, now," Garrand stammered trying to turn his face away from the flurry of sloppy licks. He finally lowered his chin and burrowed his cheek into the fur of the panda's neck to escape the creature's sticky tongue. He spied Helen over the creature's shoulder; she looked serene if not amused.

"I'm glad to see you, too!" He grumbled at the creature. "Enough, now!" The panda, however, was relentless in its affection.

He looked at the silent woman. "At least *someone's* happy to see me."

She frowned, "You seem to already have a welcoming committee."

"Yeah," he looked down at the panda.

"Bey-rah," Alexander agreed.

He hugged the panda for a long moment, then sat him down, patting his head. He tried to walk off, but the panda seemed reluctant to part with his leg, clinging to his trousers with sharp claws. *He was beginning to see why Helen had grown so attached* to these creatures. *This one exhibited such a genuine display of affection. And they were obviously more intelligent than Helen had let on.* The way the creature had quickly assessed their predicament and chosen the correct path made a shiver run down his back. *The Imperium wouldn't be this interested in mere domestics. And what of Helen's inference to dreaming back on Letugia?*

"Captain," Helen stood impatiently in the access hall, hands on her hips, "maybe we should be escaping now?"

Garrand grimaced and extricated himself from the panda's warm grasp. "You're welcome."

Helen closed her eyes and took a deep breath. "What I meant to say, was—"

"—Don't worry about it."

"Garrand!"

"No, no. You can thank me later."

"Gher-ahn," Alexander bleated.

Helen's eyes widened minutely and she shot a harsh look at the panda. "Hush now, Alexander," she hissed pseudo-sweetly under her breath as she grabbed one of his ears. The panda looked up at her with a moanfull expression.

"Better strap him in somewhere," Garrand muttered brusquely as he skirted past her.

Helen consulted her bracer and tapped a series of key commands. Satisfied with the response, she looked down at Alexander and jerked her head back toward the central corridor. "Off you go." A low grumble echoed from the far end of the dark hall. The young panda looked up at her expectantly, hoping she would have mercy on him. "Go on now," she urged him, nudging his rear with her boot to get him started. Alexander snorted unhappily but obeyed. Mother was going to be very upset with him, he just knew it.

Helen trotted after Garrand. The captain looked back over his shoulder and growled, "I thought I told you to get him webbed."

"It's taken care of."

Garrand cocked a brow in her direction. "Oh really? Just going to strap himself in, is he?"

The shielded hatch to the bridge swooshed upward to admit them. Garrand's command pod rotated smoothly and automatically to the bridge's entrance and without conscious thought he slid onto the well-worn acceleration couch, palms gliding across control surfaces as sartographic display grids leapt into existence in a hazy hemisphere surrounding his head. The pod's railing snapped back into place, enclosing him snugly in its variable gravity field, and the spherical station spun end over end around the perimeter of the crystalline superstructure to a high vantage near the zenith.

"Good to see you in one piece sir," Bailey greeted him. The artificial stared at his friend nervously and hesitated before asking, "How was the wraith?"

"Hungry," Garrand snapped.

Bailey decided not to pursue the matter further.

"What are you going to do?" Helen called up to him.

"They're expecting us to run."

"Well aren't we going to? This heap's been clocked at Q seven point three."

Garrand shot her a glance over his shoulder. *How would she know how fast the ship's quantum drive was?* "Well they've had several hours to set up—and if my guess is correct they'll have completed Nahodna's Noose by now."

"Nahodna's Noose?"

"Military blockade protocol, perfected by the Torrells back in '320 or so when they shut down a whole planetary system. It uses layers upon layers of overlapping, flexible defenses. Instead of being a static defense, the whole structure ebbs and flows, lending strength wherever necessary to envelop escaping vessels. Quite brilliant and quite impossible to escape if performed correctly—"

"Great." Helen sighed.

"—So we'll attack instead."

"Attack?" The word almost exploded out of her in accusation. "Are you crazy? First you release a Byrethylen Wraith on the planet's surface. Now you want to attack a fully supported Imperial task force? Are you really that deranged?" She pulled her hands through her hair, grabbing at the roots with her fists. "Never mind—don't answer that. Eccentric is one thing. Lucky is another. You're simply insane."

"Try to contain yourself." His hands flew over the controls. "And get in one of those pods. Once I find our target we're going to cycle into attack position immediately. The dampers won't negate all the force." He thought of the cargo. Turning over his shoulder to look at Helen he was suddenly alarmed, "What about the pandas?"

"Don't worry, they're all in webs. It shouldn't be a problem, as long as it's just for a short while."

"Bailey, have you found it yet?"

"Not yet, sir."

"What are you looking for?" Helen asked. She tried to calm herself but *Destiny's Needle* was still rushing across the planet's surface only fifty meters over the tops of the towering pines. She willed herself to not look outside the crystal bridge, concentrating instead on the captain. Garrand's hands manipulated the ship's command surfaces with such fluid speed that she could not keep up with the sequence of commands. He nearly matched Bailey's efficiency.

Garrand replied in a deliberate monotone, his attention on the displays before him. "One ship coordinates an entire section of webbing. It's responsible for sending the intricate coordinates and vectoring data necessary to keep the formation tight and leak proof. Knock down that ship, and the whole web section collapses into confusion — evens up the odds a little."

Helen nodded to herself, wanting desperately to believe that his plan would work. Still she couldn't contain herself, "Oh great, then it'll just be a hundred to one."

"Don't forget the fighters," *Destiny* chimed in. "Each of those capital ships can carry up to a full squadron. There might be as many as 300 ships in pursuit."

"Three hundred to one, marvelous."

Garrand cringed inwardly, grinding his lower molars together. "Remember," he growled, "this is a fast ship."

"It'd better be…"

"Status," he demanded.

"All systems viable," Bailey reported, "deflector shields online, getting a good reactive mixture in the main sub-light cores. Powering up for a maximum atmospheric burn."

"What about the reactive flux subroutine, *Destiny* got that up and running yet?"

"I'm afraid not, Captain, though she assures me she can handle the electron-hydrogen mix with no trouble as we leave the oxygen-nitrogen environment of the planet's atmosphere."

"Tell her not to bother. Bailey, you handle the flux manually as we slip out. We're going to have to burn nice and lean for a clean jump this close to El-Bouteran's gravity well — the temperatures are going to be well past the factory ratings and you're going to have to bypass the safety precautions so they don't shut themselves down."

The cool voice of *Destiny's Needle* interrupted. "Captain, I must protest! I am perfectly capable of achieving an optimum flux as well as determining *if* and *when* the engines should be shut down to prevent catastrophic failure."

"Don't get your feathers rustled, honey. No slight intended, but you've got better things to do. We still don't know where exactly we're going to pop out of this web. You're going to have to constantly keep tabs on our position and extrapolate a likely jump point *and* work out the mathematics for the jump."

The ship wouldn't give in that easily. "Captain, Bailey has already calculated two-thousand possible escape jumps *and* their corollary vector information from three hundred and fifty thousand standard planetary geothermal landmarks. There's no need for me to devote *all* my attention to a few minor mathematical adjustments."

"Minor adjustments? You're being a little modest, my dear. Besides, you think I'm going to be able to choose which of the three hundred fifty quadrillion whatever geo-whatchamacallits we're headed outa here on?"

"Bailey is quite capable —"

"No way," Garrand sang out. "I need him all to myself. He's in charge of targeting. We don't get lined up for a clean shot and there's going to be pieces of you and me and everyone else on this ship scattered all over this planet. I'm counting on you *Destiny*."

"As you say, sir."

"Bailey, what else?"

The artificial shrugged from his pod below. "All green."

"Q drive?"

"Preliminary warm up looks good. *Destiny* claims it's fully serviced. 'Better than new' I think was her expression."

"Better be."

"The quantum drive is in peak operational condition, I assure you, Captain," the ship reported indignantly.

Helen was still standing at the entrance to the bridge leaning against the gantry, listening. "You mean everything is actually in working order? Cheplus, a miracle!"

"Bailey, would you kindly stuff the riffraff into the airlock and cycle it with the rest of the refuse before we depart this lovely planet."

"Right away sir," the artificial grinned.

"How about the pulse cannon? We're going to need a full charge to knock down that cruiser."

"I'm bleeding power from all systems uniformly. Reading twelve percent charge in active matrix—buffer holding steady."

"How long 'till we've got a full charge?"

"Uncertain—too many variables. Mostly it depends on when we need full power to the sub-light drive. The longer we hold off…"

Garrand cursed under his breath. *Destiny's Needle* lacked the enormous battery of power coils necessary to feed energy to the pulse cannon. Imperial destroyers devoted tens of thousands of metric tonnes to nothing but its battery of cannons. Lacking the size and space, the ship was forced to bleed energy from other systems to build up a buffer with enough energy for one shot. Bailey and Garrand had designed an energy matrix capable of temporarily storing enough particle energy to give the cannon one full charge.

"Yeah, okay, but the longer we wait, the less surprised they're going to be when we pop up on their scopes."

"From the encrypted com activity I'm reading from the planet's surface I'd say the Shock Troops are still down there."

"Good, but that won't last. They'll wise up quick. What about the drones? How many operational dopplers do we have?"

Bailey answered calmly, "Little Bit is down in the repair bay now. Only eight drones answered his preliminary hail."

"Eight? He told me he had the whole stable up and running last week!"

"Well the command stasis board read twelve drones warm and cleared for flight, but—"

"Cheplus! Why didn't you tell me immediately?" Garrand swung his command pod back to the access gantry. "We're going to need *all* those drones to get out of this one!"

"There's hardly been time sir. You've only been on the bridge a few moments!" but the captain had already disappeared out the hatch. Helen followed him.

Bailey spoke into his comtab. "Little Bit, the captain is on his way down to assist you."

A shrill whistle screeched over the com.

"Yes, I believe he was indeed perturbed. Excessively so, if you ask me."

Little Bit warbled a question.

"No, I don't think there's time for that. Just make sure the others are prepped. It's not your fault that the rats have gotten into the outer launch tubes, now is it?"

Little Bit screamed in dismay.

"Really now, there's nothing I can do to help you. I'm quite busy at the moment. The captain will be there shortly."

"What's the problem?" Garrand called out.

Little Bit's shrill tone reverberated in the cramped compartment.

"Just eight, huh? What about this one?" he nudged one of the three-meter-long ovoid shells bristling with fins and long, narrow extrusions.

With a chirping beep, the artificial offered him a clipscanner with one of his spindly extended arms. Garrand scanned the technical readout.

"No problem. I can fix this in no time."

"What are these things?" Helen asked as she surveyed the narrow bay filled with the odd three-meter-long drones.

"Little Bit calls them mocking birds."

"How quaint."

"They're really defensive doppler drones, and they're actually quite sophisticated pieces of machinery. The engineering alone took Little Bit and I—"

"Look, I'm sorry, I don't mean to be rude, but what exactly do they *do*?"

"Hopefully fool all those ships out there that each of those little drones is us, or at least *could be* us."

"Hmm," Helen murmured. "Are those emitter arrays?" She pointed at the elongated spines that thrust forward from the machine's sleek outer shell.

"Yeah. Full doppler setup. Gravitic mass simulation, bio readings, matter depletion scales—the works."

"Ever work before?"

Garrand just grinned and continued fiddling with the exposed innards of the machine.

"Against Carrak class sensors?" she pressed.

He chuckled softly. Little Bit swiveled a to look at Garrand and twittered. *Just like two conspiratorial kids,* Helen thought.

"No boasts, Captain? You're uncharacteristically *reserved*."

"Stow it, Tchelakov. When's the last time you heard me brag about anything—well, of course, unless its *Destiny* maybe—but I don't *boast*—"

"Relax, Captain. It was a joke." She ran her fingers through her tangle of hair. *Quiet reserve becomes you,* she murmured to herself.

"There," he said. "That should do it." He re-sealed the drone's casing. "Little Bit, you're in charge of the drones. I want a concurrent launch *and*," he pointed an admonishing finger at the artificial, "make sure you program separate flight paths for each one. Make 'em look scared—but vary the reactive patterns."

The artificial chimed a question.

"I don't know—be creative. Think you can handle that?"

Little Bit chirped.

"Get back to the bridge when you're done." He looked at Helen, "Come with me."

AS THE HATCH to the bridge slid upwards, Bailey turned eagerly toward the entrance. "I have a target!" he announced with excitement, pleased with his discovery.

"Visual identification?"

"No—sensor only."

"Are you sure?"

"Not yet."

"What's *Destiny* say?"

"Ident-beacon tags it as an auxiliary support craft."

"Support craft?" the captain frowned and stared into his targeting scope.

Bailey's face looked grim. "Specifically, a floating trauma unit."

"A hospital ship?" Helen cried.

"That's no hospital ship." Garrand said as he amped up the image enhancement. No emotion could be seen behind his eyes.

"Garrand!" Helen protested. "What if it really is a hospital ship?"

"It's not."

"How do you know?"

"Because I can see it."

"I can see it too, but—"

"Sir," Bailey interrupted smoothly. "Visual identification complete. *Destiny* confirms target."

"Range?"

"15,000 kilometers."

"Pulse charge?"

"Eighty-six percent."

Garrand felt his chest tighten. They would need a full pulse to knock down the vessel's shields, and they weren't going to get a second shot. If they missed, half the fleet would be breathing down their necks in thirty seconds. If they could disable the vessel, then they could duck back down into the planet's heavy magnetosphere and pop up somewhere unexpected and make a dash through the uncoordinated hole.

"Garrand, how can you tell?" Helen insisted.

"Ventral sensor modification—see the hump beneath the starboard prow? Just below the auxiliary sensor array."

Helen swiveled quickly to the visual scope, peering intently at the enhanced image. The stocky looking vessel did indeed have an abnormal hump along its ventral spine. That hump could very well house just the sort of specialized com equipment necessary to coordinate a defensive web. She raised her head slowly from the scope, squinting at the back of Garrand's head. Helen was beginning to understand why Darstin had insisted on Garrand now—her doubts as to his past and present capabilities were fast evaporating.

"Okay, here we go…" Garrand angled the ship into a steep ascent, accelerating to attack speed. Helen watched uneasily as the relative cover and safety of the trees and ridges fell below.

"Helen, you're in charge of countermeasures. Those Lancers carry a full spread of veltin torpedoes. If they acquire a lock—"

"No problem," she ordered a pod to the entrance and slid behind the weapons console.

Destiny's voice murmured gently, "Detecting launch of multiple targets from orbital platforms; sector three and seven mark four point—"

"I see them, I see them," he grimaced. "Phantoms." He wrinkled his nose and chewed over the word as if it held a particularly bad taste.

"Bailey?"

"Patience, sir."

"Get us lined up, we're only going to get one shot at this."

The ship shuddered as the first long range bolts of energy lanced out to reach them from the orbiting capital ships.

"What makes you think one shot's going to take out that ship?" Helen asked dubiously as she began manipulating the intricate command board. Her fingers raced across the surface. "We're taking hits from particle cannons twice the size of this ship and the deflectors seem to be holding."

"Force dissipation. We're far enough away to survive. *Destiny's Needle* can deliver a cannon blast at point blank range, the energy not dissipating over distance like those destroyer's long-range blasts. Destroyers rely on mass and the sheer overwhelming force of a whole battery of cannons wearing down a vessel's shields. This is a small, compact design—highly maneuverable by comparison. We can duck in, deliver a surgical strike right down their throats, and duck out while those destroyers are still lumbering after us."

Another blast rocked the ship.

"*Destiny*, amp up the power on those stabilizers. Even a minor course correction will throw us out of whack."

"Lacking sufficient power for your request," the ship purred.

"Ahh," Garrand growled, "find it somewhere. Cut off life support for all I care — we can do without fresh oxy for a few minutes — just no more shudders!"

"As you wish, Captain." Warning lights flashed on his panel as life support failed. Garrand cut the emergency feeds off.

Destiny's Needle took a direct hit to its forward deflector shield and shook violently as the buffers absorbed a massive surge of particle energy. The ship slewed wildly to one side before Bailey used the thrusters to compensate for the force of the yaw.

"*Destiny*! I thought I told you — "

"Compensating, Captain. I find it difficult to work with all your shouting. Especially when you've chosen to fly me directly into the heart of an Imperial blockade. You may be certifiably insane, but I most certainly am not."

"Yeah well, at the moment it feels like I'm riding the back of an old garbage scow."

"That can be arranged."

"Just beef up those stabilizers! Bailey needs a few more seconds."

"You can't expect miracles in the face of those Carrak class particle cannons."

Bailey swung his head toward Garrand. "Got it sir!"

The captain glanced down at his scope that was tied to Bailey's targeting core.

"Beautiful. Have we got a full pulse?"

"472 gigajoules on-line in active matrix."

Helen's eyes grew wide. "472 *gigajoules*? You really *do* have a full-size particle cannon?"

"Bailey, I thought I told you to space the riffraff back on El-Bouteran."

"Sorry, must have missed one, sir."

"Range?"
"7,000 kilometers."
"Keep him lined up."
"4,000 kilometers."
"Captain," Helen screamed. "Are you sure?"
"Not now!" he barked at her.
"1,000 kilometers."
"Steady."
"200 kilometers."
"Fire!"

A blinding pulse of retina-searing energy coalesced around the needle sharp cone of the particle cannon and then leapt ahead of the ship in a surge of brilliance. The snap-crack-roar of the buffer unloading its stored energy in one nano-second was felt throughout the ship. *Destiny's Needle* was pitched wildly askew by the weapon's tremendous recoil before Bailey hit the port thrusters to compensate.

The energy blast appeared to hit its target simultaneously with the crack of the recoil, the outer sheath of super-energized electrons overloading the cruiser's ventral deflector shield, permanently fusing its buffer core. This allowed the ultra-heavy particles in the interior of the blast to reach the actual armor plating of the ship, where it ripped through the dense layers of cerafiber and composite metals, coursed through the bulkhead, the pressure hull, and into the outer reactor coils, spending its last blinding instant piercing the thick inner walls of the ship's quantum drive, sending its temperature into critical levels and detonating its core fuel.

Garrand banked *Destiny's Needle* under the cruiser's belly as it erupted in a green ball of expanding gasses and fuel, hurling matter and debris in an expanding concentric shell of destruction. The jagged segments of the ship's interior left intact from the blast spiraled out of control into a shallow, decaying orbit around the planet, destined to be burned up in El-Bouteran's atmosphere.

Garrand let out a whoop of exhilaration and relief.

"Atta boy, Bailey!"

Helen released her breath and loosened her grip on the railing.

"*Destiny*, fire up life support again. Re-route all power back to their original sources. Bailey, make sure the Q drive is up to snuff. I'm ducking us back into the atmosphere." He swiveled to look up at Helen in the weapons control pod. He cocked his head and arched his eyebrows at her as if to say, 'So…'

"Nice shot."

Garrand smiled. "Dump some chaff in our wake. The debris from that cruiser and the loss of their nerve center should keep them confused for a few minutes, but I'd hate for 'em to get off a lucky shot."

Destiny's Needle plunged back into the planet's atmosphere followed by the glistening forms of dozens of high-speed Imperial fighters. The tiny, single-man craft streaked through the upper atmosphere in pursuit.

"What are you going to do?" Helen asked anxiously as her eyes surveyed the rapidly blossoming threat display. "There's too many of them."

Garrand looked steadfast and utterly determined as he piloted the ship in her steep descent back into the ionosphere. Clouds streaked vertically past the crystalline bridge as they dove for the surface. "Bring 'em on," he challenged. "We'll duck back in the soup for a few minutes—by the time they've reformed for atmospheric pursuit we'll be ripping through the upper atmosphere again and headed for deep space."

"But there's one, two, three, four—*four* squadrons after us—the full complement of four battle frigates; and those are *Torrellian* fighters, not just Phantoms! How do you expect—"

"Tchelakov. Excuse me: *Miss* Tchelakov. I believe your extensive briefing—by whatever mysterious source—included one arcane and, may I say, *highly protected*, fact: this ship is capable of point seven Q at full sub-light thrust."

Helen looked chagrinned. "Yes, I know. And the Phantoms can only achieve point six eight sub-light and the Torrells point seven two—but they'll be breathing up our exhaust before we can hit the gap."

"Maybe, maybe not. We're not gonna just amble out of here all nice and straight for 'em. And once we pop out of that opening in the web, Bailey's got our jump already laid in. A few minor corrections from *Destiny*, we hit the quantum drive and we're away."

Helen frowned.

"Those fighters aren't equipped with faster-than-light drives—they can't breach light speed."

"You're cutting it awfully close, Médeville."

"Maybe you'd like to fly, then?"

Helen gritted her teeth, "No, it's just that—"

"Good," he cut her off. "Then why don't you concentrate on your countermeasures. One torpedo could ruin our whole day!"

Destiny's Needle was down on the deck again, ripping through the atmosphere at perilously unmanageable speeds. Heat sensors pinged on all deflector boards from the atmospheric friction, and particle beams erupted on all sides, but the fighters were still out of range.

"How does it look?" Helen asked.

"Mass confusion — there's com activity all over the place. So much, they're not even limiting it to encrypted channels. Looks like they're trying to recoordinate the web."

"Are we going then?"

"Now's as good a time as any," he mused.

She looked up at him sadly, a sparkle of hope in her eye. She wanted to say something encouraging, but the words just wouldn't come out.

"Launch the dopplers," Garrand ordered.

Little Bit whistled and Helen's target scope showed nine new readings with identical signatures fanning out around their position.

"Here we go," Garrand called. "Ready Little Bit?"

The artificial chirped a hopeful affirmation.

"On three. One, two, *three*!" He hauled back and the ship rotated up toward the heavens once more, this time mimicked by the nine drones controlled by Little Bit. After a moment, all ten craft separated in a starburst pattern, each streaking along different vectors for the stars.

"Keep your fingers crossed," Garrand murmured.

The greyish blue hue of the sky faded to violet then a matte black that enveloped them as they raced skyward. Imperial ships were scattered across the threat display, all seemingly at different altitudes with different headings traced in bright colors that circled the translucent sphere representing El-Bouteran. The sartographs were filled with such a dizzying array of conflicting information that Helen had to blink and scrunch her eyes closed.

Garrand, however, continued to study the dazzling sartograph. "They're trying to coordinate who should track down which target. Without that cruiser to guide them, they don't know which drone to target."

The web was in disarray. "I don't believe it, it's working..." Helen breathed.

"Most of the ships in this section are chasing drones." Garrand pointed a finger at two red blips that were angling toward the center of the glowing display. "But those two have chosen us. They're big boys, too."

"Confirmed Captain: two attack frigates closing on intercept course," Bailey reported. "Lancer class."

"Where?" Helen demanded in a frightened voice.

"Off the starboard bow—mark two, true to our tangential plane."

"Range?" Garrand asked.

"123,000 kilometers," the art replied. He looked at Garrand. "It's going to be close."

Garrand's knuckles tightened around the outer shell of the display board. The rapidly escalating gee-forces were more than the internal dampers could handle and Garrand could feel the crushing weight of his own mass being pressed back against his acceleration couch as the whole ship experienced the heavy-gee of massive acceleration.

"Standby to jump on my mark," Garrand ordered.

The fingers of one of Bailey's hands held motionless over the Q drive's activation board while the other manipulated the sub-light mixture controls. The constantly changing engine efficiency spread was illuminated in a graph floating before his eyes.

"How close are you going to cut it?" Helen grunted as she winced under the drastic forces.

"As close as I dare," Garrand shouted over the scream of the sub-light engines pushed to their limits. "El-Bouteran has a pretty big gravity well—"

"But those destroyers are closing awfully fast."

"I'll split the difference."

"Garrand!"

"What?" he exploded. "It's either be crushed by the forces of gravity as we try to enter quantum space or be vaporized by those destroyers!"

Helen frowned, but remained silent.

"Bailey?"

"Too close to call, Captain."

"Range?"

"23,000 kilometers."

"Distance to El-Bouteran's core?"

"Ahh," Bailey glanced at another scope. "297,000 kilometers. Nineteen percent gravitic core reach."

"We need ten."

"Five would be wiser, sir."

"Ten'll have to do."

The ship rocked violently as advance blasts from the destroyers searched out their position. Little Bit squealed in dismay as another of his drones was vaporized. The ship shuddered violently from a direct hit astern.

"Torrellian fighter, sir."

"Yeah."

"Four more cruisers closing, port astern," *Destiny* reported.

"I think they're on to us," Helen muttered.

The Lancers loomed huge in the starboard side of the globe. Hundreds of green energy bolts arched toward them, flash points detonating on all sides.

Helen held her breath, eyes growing wide. "They're right on top of us!"

Garrand appeared utterly calm, eyes studying the converging numbers on his displays. He whispered, "Bailey, if you please."

The artificial closed the contact beneath his fingers and rainbow streaks of light erupted before *Destiny's Needle*. Fractal generations from the edge of the visual light spectrum danced beyond the crystal bridge as the quantum engine lifted them to the very threshold of the speed of light. The remarkably brilliant image of the massive attack frigates poised before them flashed into Garrand's mind like a searing beacon and then the view dissolved into a swirling storm of color and energy. The ship sank into the tempest—shaking under the stress—and with a howling roar was thrust into the inky recesses of quantum space, disappearing from the targeting scopes of two Lancer class frigates, four battle cruisers, and a host of Imperial pursuit craft.

Garrand closed his eyes and allowed his shoulders to slump minutely forward, relieved of the pressures of maximum acceleration. Little Bit trumpeted with pleasure. Without realizing it, Helen let out a whoop of relief. Bailey looked at Garrand. The captain remained silent and still, eyes closed like some weary sentinel relieved from duty and finally allowed to rest. The artificial watched the smooth, steady rhythm of the human's breathing and smiled, the nuances of satisfaction, admiration and relief spreading across the smooth contours of the artificial's body like a warm, reassuring wave of blue color.

GRIFFIN TERMINOLOGY

Ackriveldt: lone planet of Galipsus, noted as birth world of Naius Sartok.

Adjucate: harbor judge; low level Imperial official.

Air Skimmer: agile low atmosphere pursuit vehicle. Single-seat design, though the D'arellak later commissioned some dual versions during the Vintson riots, 35,279. Simple rugged design and low cost made these the patrol craft of choice for most Free Will colonies.

Alexander: giant panda cub, third generation member or the Tchelakov Tribe.

Antorva: largest planet in the Souterbellan system. Though largely a financial nexus for the H'ai Larks and Ditraln, it is more widely known for its agricultural products, particularly the richly textured Cipell bean.

Armor Drip: versatile field armor developed by Pavelle Nest. Transported in liquid form and poured into a variety of molds on site, cerafiber bonds harden in under a minute after catalyst is added. Gives added mobility to light armor divisions.

Arnas, San Barrilito: battalion commander, 41st Imperial Marines; Shock Trooper.

Art Wars: a conflict that arose when the Sullust movement sought to curtail the rapid proliferation of Free Will artificials, specifically machines indistinguishable from humans. Fueled by fear and religious fervor, the push for curtailment quickly expanded into a genocidal Jihad that lasted from 35,110 until the Gelicus Art Convention in 35,307. Alternately known as the Gai'han Jihad, depending on one's point of view, the resulting conflagration plunged much of the galaxy into turmoil (see: Jihad, Gai'han, Free Will artificials, Sullust Movement)

Artificial: any of a wide class of mobile mechanical constructs possessing intelligence, self-awareness and the ability to learn through experience.

Atryx: race of large (1.3 meter tall, 6 meter wingspan) warm-blooded avians (sentient).

Bailey: Krellian Artificial, Varsis model VL1357-B8, incept date unrecorded. Master of Arms, Caius Minor, from 35,329 to 35,337. Assigned to Santos II as personal assistant to Captain of the Guard, Garrand Ai'Gonet Médeville in 35,337. Granted Free Will in 35,345. First mate on *Destiny's Needle*.

Barlow: lieutenant, 41st Imperial Marines, 3rd company, 1st platoon; Shock Trooper.

Barrelian Corvette: Highly-maneuverable armed escort ship, smaller than a frigate, ranging in length from 100-150 meter; often used in conjunction with a larger fleet of vessels. Barrelian designs have been manufactured for over 700 years.

Barrett, Hellius: An ambitious Vecklorn who inherited his father's seat in the Royal Regincira and was later appointed High Magistrate in the Emperor's Court, he was a trusted confidante who lost favor after rumors of an illicit affair with the Empress surfaced. "Banished" to the political chaos of Carinaena's Shell, where his charms could not impress Chyrella, he labored in relative obscurity for some time. The assassination of ruling Proctor Lekkson Nesbit elevated Barrett into control of the Shell's third largest Proctorialship. Commonly referred to as Lord Barrett (whether it be in reference to Vecklornian nobility, or claimed in ancient Caluras rite is unknown), his title is officially Vice Proctor of Wyx.

Bioresonator: small oblong device mounted on individual's belt which filters the wearer's heart rate, breathing, heat signature and other vital signs and attempts to blend them with ambient temperature, atmosphere, humidity, and foliant readings so that sensors will be unable to identify source as human.

Bolo: legendary cult of assassins whose members are culled from selective gene isolation programs, and immersed in the art of death; essentially eradicated by Free Will followers during the late stages of the Gai'han Jihad for their involvement with the Sullusts.

Bordëgian Académé: ancient school of preparation for service in the Imperial Navy.

Brotherhood of the Princes of Blood: Order within the Imperial Guard. Founded 34,512 on Daulinbêres (see also: Griffin).

Byrethylen Wraith: race of large (4 meter tall), amorphous, multi-tendriled vaporous energy manifestations. Wraiths prey on the neurological fears of their victims, manifesting themselves as the delusional images found in their victims' minds. Wraiths feed on all energy sources, but prefer the cerebrum's neural energy. Wraiths were once the scourge of the Byrethyl System, wiping out whole planets and rendering them barren and lifeless.

By the Barthsa: Dalis colloquialism; mild curse.

Carinaena's Shell: (Car-in-ae-na) the massive outer ring of stars that forms a donut-shaped shell around the central Core of the Gli-Dawun Galaxy. Named for the Lallalopsle ship *Carinaena's Hope* whose quantum drive failed at the edge of the galactic Core, and thus became the first "seeder" ship of colonists (see Dolke's Historical tome "Carinaena's Fate: the Colonization of Chance").

Carrack Class Cruiser: large, fast, heavily armored and gunned warship; Imperial classification of Battle Cruiser, top of the line capital ship.

Cerafiber: synthetic material prized for its light weight and heat/energy absorption; crystalline threads formed from superheated dryexcellon powder and molecular ceramic are cast into an intercellular matrix of connective filaments. Bonded matrices are stored in liquid state and then poured into molds with catalysts creating solid fibers of great elasticity, flexibility and tensile strength.

Cerasteel: ceramic steel formed on site by combining polymer-bonded dryexcellon powder into molten steel. After cooling, the steel is superheated through conduction, bonding the dryexcellon and steel at a molecular level.

Cerbak: one of the last remaining Bolos; mythical tri-horned guardian of the entrance to K'ye.

Cha'halen: rank in the military hierarchy of the Gambor; roughly equivalent to the Imperial rank of major.

Chellian: race of small (1.2 meter tall) creatures with soft fur and dexterous claws. Highly-intelligent, peaceful creatures with large nuclear families, males often siring 15-20 children.

Cheplus: Strahlinvek colloquialism; moderate curse.

Clipscanner: miniature (20 cm x 12 cm) personal datacore composed of digital reader, processing unit, fingertap board and display housed within a slim impact casing; noted for its versatility and interface capabilities.

Clipscan Visor: data relay that partially blinds user's real-time vision; primarily intended for use by artificials.

Coil: rechargeable storage field that uses magnetic coils to safely store massive amounts of charged ions. Capable of efficiently storing vast amounts of energy in a small physical space. Primary source of power for all energy dependent devices and engines.

Collistas Dynasty: (co-least-us) largest autonomous governing body in the Gli-Dawun Galaxy, ruled by a member of the Collistas family for 47 generations. The empire spawned from this stability now envelops much of the galaxy's core.

Consul: Imperial planetary governor, ranking below a vice proctor.

Core: (also: "Core worlds," "The Core") the densely populated center of the Gli-Dawun Galaxy; common designation for the vast volume of star systems currently under the domain of the Collistas Imperial Dynasty.

Cronix: a design line of datacores, a product of Si Bell Logiks, a proprietary arm of the Si Bell Keiretsu; Cronix datacores are commonly considered the industrial standard in Carinaena's Shell.

Dailyern Green: bitter, slightly caustic alcoholic concoction formed from the lesser of the two saps from the Yourb trees on Dailyern (the other, red sap, is a fatal poison) and Kakin malt. A drink favored by the vegrauts who conquered Dailyern six centuries ago, their strong constitutions and thick abdominal lining able to handle the toxins. The two ingredients are unstable when combined, thus the drink is served in two equal portions and it is left to the patron to mix them.

Dalintus Commission: formed by the Gelicus Art Convention in 35,312, charged with the judgment of Free Will artificials—the Dalintus seal signifying the highest possible conditioning against taking a human life. Dalintus qualified artificials permitted to design and create Free Will artificials without human intervention.

Danelle: lieutenant in the Imperial Guard, Gokazoku Kaigi; currently assigned to Wyx, Carinaena's Shell, linguist.

Dar Sellianne Cluster: minor black hole cluster in the Bai-lore system; site of the Battle of Calon ("Massacre at Calon") in 35,208.

Darcalyn: artificial construct, highly unstable isotope frequently used in the construction of tactical fusion devices; logarithmic scale for expressing the magnitude of energy contained within such explosive devices.

Darstin, Carrelle: Director of Research and Acquisitions, Nralda Keiretsu. Seat on the Nralda High Board, 4th Tier. Responsible for funding and perpetuation of Beh'In Tchelakov's research concerning the next evolution of the sartographic chip (see: Tchelakov Tribe).

Dasko, Lee: lieutenant in the Imperial Guard, Gokazoku Kaigi; currently assigned to Wyx, Carinaena's Shell, decryption specialist, 1st grade.

Datacore: programmable electromagnetic device that can store, retrieve, and process data; the heart of all mechanical thinking mechanisms.

Datapad: any of a wide variety of specialized technical data readers; poor cousin of the clipscanner.

Daulinbêres: sixth planet in the Wopäs System, situated in a prime strategic location near the heart of the Gli-Dawun Galaxy; seat of the Imperial throne for 137 centuries.

Daurrian Shipyards: the vast Pragen spaceworks in high orbit off Bingham; the close proximity of the Hames asteroid belt for raw materials and the industrial processing complex on Bingham itself has made this yard one of the most efficient operations in the Shell, capable of turning out a full destroyer in under eight years.

Debin: corporal, 41st Imperial Marines, tactical support Corps, armorer.

Destroyer: very large, fast, heavily armored and gunned warship; a classification usually reserved for a fleet's largest and most advanced capital ships.

Destiny's Needle: modified medium cruiser designed by Garrand Ai'Gonet Médeville and built by Le'hadn Vercks in 35,347 for the express purpose of breaking the Talen quarantine on El Phobadia. Presented to Médeville by the Sandhalles Grip, Bestriyx Dagen, soon thereafter as a token of his esteem, in return for the rescue of his daughter. Subsequently played a principle role in the Tchelakov Revolt circa 35,355.

Dopplegänger: device that approximates mass, heart rate, heat signature and breathing rhythm of sentient biologicals. Projects all the outwardly-detectable signs of life with subroutines controlling random variance.

Dreadnaught: large, moderately armored and gunned warship; an older classification generally reserved for blockade interdictors and fleet escorts. Upgrades in quantum drive technologies have rendered many of the dreadnaught designs obsolete. Properly refit, dreadnaughts play an important role in many developing navies.

Dryexcellon: mineral ore principally mined in the Restepheron system and refined on planets throughout the Shell into highgrade fuels, powders and industrial byproducts (see: cerafiber, cerasteel).

Dustlock: similar in design and purpose to starships' airlocks, dustlocks are used in many desert environments to prevent grit, sand, and dust from fouling sensitive electronics and healthy, breathable atmosphere.

E2: the Empire's top of the line massive datacore processor, integrating the latest sartographic series II technology with group "e" Cronix mainframes; used aboard all Carrack class vessels (see: sartograph).

Eckreon: a design line of Cronix datacores, the product f Si Bell Logiks, a proprietary arm of Si Bell Keiretsu; Cronix datacores are commonly considered the industrial standard in Carinaena's Shell.

El-Bouteran: only planet in the Pakken System, far removed from all major shipping routes in Carinaena's Shell.

Eltouvé Magellan: 5th planet in the Dantolous system, sight of the sprawling Imperial Weapons Research Facility; home of the infamous "Plague Vats."

Elytra: the anterior wings of Gamborian beetles that serve to protect the posterior pair of functional wings.

Enyohanse Lenses: adjustable spectacles that fit over the surface of the eye with crystalline enzymes that adhere to the pupils' surface, stretching and bending the light as it enters the optic nerves. Once familiar with the enyohanse lenses, the user can adjust the level of magnification and clarity with the muscles of the eye and face.

Epley, Jastin: (a.k.a.: Sev) shipping agent with ties into many underground smuggling operations.

Exel: wild echrine of Maltus adapted for Se-faillus hunters on Letugia; sometimes kept as pets.

Falto Earblocks: miniature counter-active dampers that absorb sound waves and project energy surges into the ear that flatten out the signature sine pattern of incoming noise, effectively negating the sounds as they enter the inner ear membrane.

Farres: lieutenant in the Imperial Guard, Gokazoku Kaigi; currently assigned to Wyx, Carinaena's Shell.

Fléchette: small dart or flying projectile often explosive-tipped or laced with poison.

Freetrader: colloquialism; broad term embracing what is in essence a wide variety of professions including (but not limited to) intersystem mercantile trading, freelance entrepreneurial merchandising, smuggling, and simple cargo hauling. Originally a term used to describe independent freelance entrepreneurs in early Colonial era, specifically the nine hundred year period that saw the Shell worlds successfully pioneered and settled (see: Great Diaspora). Working alone in single ships, Freetraders were an indispensable element of the colonization effort. The high risks and huge overhead involved in supplying hundreds of tiny colonies made it unprofitable to sustain and supply colonies on a corporate and/or commercial level. These entrepreneurs—private oneman operations flying single craft with low overhead—allowed colonies to flourish in their infant stages by bringing goods that could not be produced on fledgling worlds for decades. Private traders were colonists' lifeblood, shipping in needed commodities, spare parts, and resources in return for grains and foodstuffs for shipment offworld. Most Freetraders are thought of as colonial patriots of a sort. Without them, most colonies would have quickly failed and the Shell as we know it would not exist.

Free Will Artificial: a specialized class of mobile mechanical constructs possessing intelligence, self-awareness and the ability to learn through experience. Free Will arts are not designed with a specific underlying purpose. Without a rigorous code of conduct for higher functions, Free Will arts are left to choose their own course after inception. The Sullust movement sought to curtail the rapid proliferation of Free Will arts after the perfection of the indistinguishable-from-human designs. The resulting conflicts are alternately known as the Gai'han Jihad (see: The Purge) or the Art Wars (see: the Lashback). The 200-year upheaval plunged much of the galaxy into turmoil. Numerous commissions sprang up in the aftermath, attempting to regulate Free Will arts, and many prejudices still exist (see: Artificial).

Frigate: any of a broad variety of moderately armored and gunned warships, the classification of which differ widely from navy to navy. Historically: a moderate to large design; the workhorse of many a navy.

Galar: lieutenant in the Imperial Guard, Gokazoku Kaigi; currently assigned to Wyx, Carinaena's Shell, demolitionist, 5th order.

Gallantrus: race of medium-sized (1.5 meter tall) russet-furred bipedal creatures (sentient); transplanted home world is Vipst in the Dartinells System

Gambor: race of large (3 meter tall) multi-limbed, smooth-shelled, winged beetles (sentient); home world Galzeki has been tagged for garbage reclamation by Imperial Navy and is site of 400-year-old civil war (see Po'tchantu's "Siege of Galzeki")

Garner, Jyaye: MSD, private practice, Erpolitas. Highly regarded organic surgeon specializing in illegal augmentation procedures. Assassinated 35,355.

Gelbs: corporal, 3rd Imperial Army Corps; tactical field operations specialist.

Gelicus Art Convention: contravened in 35,312, marking the official end of the Gai'han Jihad, its provisions forging an uneasy peace between the Gai'han Sullusts and the Free Will coalition lead by the Free Will artificial, Samuel. It's chief tenant: no machine was to be constructed indistinguishable from a human being. In compromise, the Sullusts lifted the death bounty placed on all Free Will artificials. Secondary precepts limited the creation of Free Will artificials: specifically, it was forbidden for artificials to create Free Will artificials (in essence procreate) without the Dalintus seal (see: Dalintus Commission).

Gills: private, tactical operations, 3rd Imperial Army Corps.

Gokazoku Kaigi: Order within the Imperial Guard. Known as the "Brotherhood of the Silent Blade." Founded 34,819 on Daulinbêres.

Gravitic Repulsors: Fit beneath everything from cargo lighters to gunsleds to starships, Norgen generators project a harmonic field that negates the affects of gravity over a limited area focused in conical projections that dissipate over distance. The resulting gravitic null space creates buoyancy that is enhanced by standard field suspensors. The combined effect of the null space and the repulsor wave field is enough to allow most vessels, pallet, skimmers, and such to hover mid-air. In more elaborate configurations, they are enough to allow starships of massive tonnage to overcome the pull of planetary gravity wells and land and takeoff vertically.

Griffin: Collistas colloquialism; slang for Imperial Guardian, Griffin Order. Order within the Imperial Guard. Known as the "Brotherhood of the Princes of Blood." Founded 34,512 on Daulinbêres.

Gunsled: armored ground assault vehicles, fit with gravitic repulsors.

Gyropod: enclosed datastations typically found aboard military vessels, designed to insulate vital tech ensigns from the dangers of battle and aid their interface with the ship's datacore (see: podtech).

Hammerfield Colony: Free Will colony near Dautalas Massif on Lon Seres (Jhellus Sector), sacked by Imperial Shock Troops in 35,339 and again in 35,355 in the preliminary stages of the Tchelakov Revolt.

Harbormaster: general superintendent of port operations.

Havelock: sub-lieutenant, 3rd Imperial Army Corps, Terraformer; liaison officer 1st grade.

Haven's End: Imperial colloquialism; mild curse derived from the infamous travails of Giin Bly Haven, officer in the Royal Regincira, whose life was ironically taken by the very men he risked everything to save.

Holden: Tybolte artificial, Rixx model 33, incept date 35,021. Assigned to Carinaena's Shell, Wyx, as personal assist for Lieutenant Lee Dasko of Vice Proctor Barrett's Imperial Guard.

Holocube: miniature holographic display unit roughly the size of an Imperial quantis. Projects a small static image of subject that can be viewed from all angles.

Holo Ghost: the emotional and neurological essence of a creature captured by electronic means and stored in a digital matrix much like a datacore. The mortal subject's neural activity and the brain's electro-chemical signature is transferred (either during the death throes, or soon after death) by electronic conductivity and hard wired into circuitry chips, much like the creation of an artificial. The imprint is stored in a Tarkanian containment field and is manifested as a hologram. The resultant "ghost" is cognizant and self-aware, many times with full memories and recollections intact, though the manifestation exists with a painful echo of former emotions. A common theological belief is that the souls of ghosts are suspended in K'ye, awaiting judgment.

Ident-link: mathematical symbol(s) or icon used to represent a person or artificial; any of a wide range of identifying markers imbedded or cosmetic; standard Imperial identification system.

Imperial Guard: For over 3 millennia, the Imperial Guard has protected the interests of the Imperial throne, specifically the well being of the Emperor and his highest Ambassadors (see: Proctors). The Guardian caste is one of the most ancient and revered schooling bodies in the Empire. The noble warriors within have sworn to honor the Emperor and uphold the sanctity of the realm. Each faction within the caste has its own Order, full of timeworn tradition and a legacy to uphold. New members of the guard are sworn into a particular order, whose tenets they must obey and traditions they most honor.

Jean-Wa: Do-lât Artificial, Preparation model D430, incept date unrecorded; six-armed master chef with detachable legs and wheels. Purchased by Garrand Ai'Gonet Médeville from the Baron Senn van Basel of Daruma.

Jihad: (ji-häd) a religious holy war; fanatical crusade for a principle or belief.

Jihad, Gai'han: (see also: Art Wars) the doomed crusade against Free Will artificials, humaniform mechanical sentients, sentient machines, and conscious datacores begun in 35,110 and concluded in 35,307. It's chief result: the disappearance of all indistinguishable-from-human artificials.

Kalen: Imperial Special Operations Corp, lingual specialist, assigned to the *Shiva* task force.

Ka'vaelus: Gambor warrior; Cha'halen first grade of the Vaelus burrow, Galzeki. Rumored to have personal ties with 4th tier Nralda Director of Acquisitions, Carrelle Darstin.

Kess: fourth planet in the Dell Transim system; site of Gort's Agro Supply.

K'iik Vla: idiomatic expression from the Lalen dialect; roughly: "The ability to survive at any cost." Often referred to as the third rule in Griffin Order doctrine.

Keiretsu: corporate entities that have bonded together in Carinaena's Shell for protection and profit—combining trade routes and resources to form interplanetary cartels complete with defense fleets. Some keiretsu control whole systems, having subjugated the populace through economic monopolies and trade embargoes. While avoiding outright war with the Collistas Dynasty, many keiretsu are involved in an escalating cold war with the Imperial Proctorialships in the Shell.

Kouln Brandy: distilled from kidney fruit found only on Cas Elphu. Sullusts sterilized the planet around 35,113. The highly-prized brandy became priceless almost overnight. The ensuing carnage over the last 788 barrels that Fourte Grecke and Company produced became such that the Emperor placed a death seal on Kouln trade. Transporting the illicit commodity was a treasonable offense. Kouln brandy remains one of the most expensive and sought after goods on the black market.

Krass: Fleet Sergeant, 41st Imperial Marines, 1st platoon; third squad leader, Shock Trooper, weapons specialist (2nd class), armorer's assist.

Krestyaninov Cluster: a volume of space hundreds of light years across with complex and powerful gravitational forces due to the influence of a large number of stars in the white dwarf stage of collapse.

K'ye: the mythical "battleground of the gods," where the souls of the dead are said to be judged; purgatory.

Lachis: (Loper) six-legged pack beast whose sturdy constitution, resistance to viral strains, and phenomenal reproductive faculties made it ideal for homesteading the planets of Carinaena's Shell.

Lammini: Binary star system dominated by the Pious Cluster, a spectacular field of nebulae.

Landin: fleet sergeant (retired), 91st Imperial Marine battalion; barkeep on the *Shiva*.

Larkson Shield Generator: produces powerful resonating magnetic field capable of bending light around its focusing body. Used in conjunction with deflector arrays and an adequate system of null-dampers, the Larkson creates a viable protective field. Buffer coils store power bled from other ship systems and then feed pulses of energy to the shields' magnetic deflector fields. Energy that is not refracted or deflected is absorbed by null-dampers.

Laserai: corporal, 41st Imperial Marine battalion, 3rd company, 1st platoon; Shock Trooper.

Letugia: fifth planet in the Nepestar system; site of the Il Touvé shipyards, largest in the system.

Lewg: lieutenant in the Imperial Guard, Gokazoku Kaigi; currently assigned to Wyx, Carinaena's Shell; master bladesman.

Lifter: huge obtuse transport shuttles, heavily shielded and fit with gigantic sublight reactors, but possessing no faster-than-light capability. Designed to safely and efficiently ferry cargo and men between planet surfaces and orbiting ships (see: Mules).

Lighter: mechanical construct of varying size fit with gravitic repulsors and possessing limited intelligence, designed to ferry cargo between vessels in docking bays.

Little Bit: Turkle Sphere II, model 339-74C, incept date 35,329; technical assist (modified) purchased by Garrand Ai'Gonet Médeville at the Syhan Fabrication Works on Tikus.

Lor Stanta Destroyer: warship of the largest and most heavily armed and armored class; Imperial classification of the largest capital ship currently in active service (700 meter).

Maibell: Naval liaison officer stationed aboard the Imperial battle cruiser *Shiva*.

Mareclausum: navigable stretch of open space that is under the protection of one sovereign and closed to all others; a right of passage.

Massif: a principle mountainous mass; "day of reckoning" for Bolos initiates.

Matrix: something within which something else originates or develops; material in which something is enclosed or embedded.

Médeville, Garrand Ai'Gonet: Freetrader, former Captain of the Imperial Guard, Griffin Order; purported leader of the Tchelakov Revolt.

Megas: lieutenant, 41st Imperial Marine battalion, 3rd company, 1st platoon; Shock Trooper; master bladesman.

Mules: Collistas colloquialism; slang for lifters.

Nepestar System: independent star system not under any sovereign's rule comprised of 47 self-governing planetary and lunar bodies; known for its loose regulatory provisions and high volume of trade.

Nesbit, Lekkson: Provost of Wyx and reigning Proctor of the Callus, Niramdi, and del'Trin system fiefs until his assassination in 35,347. Respected for his ability to create economic bridges between vastly different cultures. With the help of his ambitious vice proctor, Hellius Barrett, nurtured the Wyxian Proctorialship into one of the largest and richest Imperial fiefs in Carinaena's Shell.

Niramdi System: minor star system in the Outer Reaches (II Gallen Wei); hidden staging area for Free Will resistance during the Gai'han Jihad (see: Thrassin, battle of).

Norfins, Este: Chellian tavern proprietor on Letugia.

Nralda: Keiretsu; one of the largest and most powerful operating in the Shell.

Nyles: commander, 3rd Imperial Army Corps, Terraformer; engineer 4th grade.

Offloader: mechanical construct of limited intelligence designed to remove cargo from vessels quickly and efficiently.

Orae'teleute: "Until the end is near"; Imperial battle cry.

Parlex: home of the Trouble gardens, legendary botanical preserve.

Parvin Molder: bio-engineered viral disease created in the infamous plague vats of Eltouvé Magellan, in the Dantolous system; loosed on the Varkus in 34,989 in the midst of the Conflict of Reason. Related deaths estimated at 912 million.

Peridan: manufacturer of wide range of industrial coils; proprietary company of the Nralda Keiretsu.

Phase Emitter: general diagnostic tool for setting correct power configurations on coil-based reactors and generators. Uses pulses of energy to calibrate null dampers.

Picket Cutter: small-to-medium sized, extremely fast and lightly armored warship; primarily used as lead escort ships, blockade runners, and strike interdictors.

Plascrete: a lightweight, strong building material formed by mixing industrial grade polymer plastic aggregates with cementing agents and catalysts that cause the plastics to set and bind the entire mass. Can be poured on-site making it useful in fortifications and mobile battle situations.

Pod-tech: Collistas colloquialism; tech ensigns who spend much of their time suspended in gyropods.

Praetor: Imperial magistrate, adjucatal overlord, ranking below a consul.

Pragen: race of medium sized (1.7 meter), cunning felines (sentient).

Proctor: the chief magistrate of an Imperial fiefdom.

Proctorialship: the principle sphere of influence or domain of specific Imperial fiefs created during the Great Shell Diaspora. Proctorialships are doled out to lords and barons within the Imperial Court as the Emperor sees fit. The relative domain of the fief may be expanded in the Emperor's name at the ruling proctor's discretion.

Provost: Imperial planetary governor.

Quantis: circular trebian alloy coin. Five Imperial credits. Accepted coin of the realm in most systems along with local currency. Although credit chits are more widely used, some small denomination coins are more efficient for limited purchases, such as food and beverage.

Quantum Drive: crucial middle element of all interstellar ships' three-tiered drive system; sub-light engines propel ships up to the brink of light speed (speeds and acceleration dependent upon design, size, efficiency, etc.), the quantum drive breaches the light barrier, lifting the ship into quantum space, and the light engines propel the ship through quantum space itself.

Ragon: the smaller of two moons orbiting Bey, primary planetoid in the Lammini System.

Reactor Core: chamber that powers all sub-light and quantum drives. The chamber is filled with cryxthlen gas at extremely high pressure. This gas, through which a series of directed neutron sparks pass, contains charged particles accelerated by the power field of the coils that wrap around the reactor core. As the field oscillates, it accelerates the charges back and forth, making them collide energetically with the cryxthlen atoms. Many of the gas atoms are actually torn apart by the collisions, yielding even more charged particles to collide with cryxthlen atoms, creating an exponentially expanding energy source. The cryxthlen acts as the fuel source that is slowly depleted as some atoms are not spilt by the collisions in the core, and thus are converted directly to energy without yielding any new charged particles.

Sartograph: highly specialized mathematical construct utilizing Dr. Sartok's revolutionary chip and representing a quantum breakthrough in 4th dimension physics decay. Used to create time-based models which accurately forecast the relative probability of any given circumstance; the visual output of such a projection.

Sartok: probability chip capable of assessing statistical future outcomes through rigorous analysis of past and present conditions (see: Sartograph); named after its creator, Naius Packden Sartok, theoretical mathematician and founder of the Seilhenn School of Advanced Logistics.

Scarrion: Crysanth drop ship, housed aboard the *Shiva*.

Selyn: Tybolte artificial, Blue model 14, incept date 35,309. Assigned to Carinaena's Shell, Wyx, as armorer's assist for Gokazoku Kaigi.

Servo Limb: mechanical construct: any augmented lifting or reaching device.

Sheb'dura: Captain of the Imperial Guard (dead, suspended), Gokazoku Kaigi; current manifestation assigned to Wyx, Carinaena's Shell (see: Holo Ghost).

Shecut: brigadier general (retired) of the Imperial Marines, 6th Army, special envoy to Carinaena's Shell.

Shields: (also: Larkson Shield Generator) shield combat was in vogue for almost 300 years until advances in optical targeting made the generators more hazardous than helpful. Still, some usefulness can be found, particularly in close arms combat (see Tolmer's "Optical Advances and other Technological Foibles" & Ku'bii's "Offensive Retreat—the Rise of the Projectile").

Shiva: Carrak class cruiser; flagship of the Imperial Third Fleet; currently assigned to the Wyxian Proctorialship.

Shock Troops: Imperial commandos, generally bred for cunning, viciousness, and absolute loyalty. Raised from birth as soldiers, completely immersed in the caste D'ai Mital, the cult of the warrior. The caste training emphasizes ruthlessness, survival and instills a near fanatical devotion to unit commanders; historically known as "the Emperor's elite."

Sid: giant panda, second generation member of the Tchelakov Tribe; youngest Elder in the tribe, in charge of information retrieval.

Stanzer: Imperial picket crippled during the Battle of Sardis (35,345) by Ditraln Secessionists; sinking after atmospheric re-entry, the superstructure still rests in 2 kilometers of water off the shore of Callen High. Captain of the Imperial Guard, Garrand Ai'Gonet Médeville, rescued the *Stanzer's* crew and passengers against direct orders and sacrificed an Imperial battle frigate in the process. That ship, the *Deil-Karo*, became the first command frigate lost at sea in 10,000 years.

Strahlinvek: language spoken by most of the trading cultures in Carinaena's Shell; a simple trade language, its root forms easily derived from thousands of other dialects. Some variation of the language is spoken by almost every race that has spacefaring ties, facilitating exploration and colonization.

Strom, Vailetta: Captain of the Imperial Guard, Gokazoku Kaigi; currently assigned to Wyx, Carinaena's Shell.

Su'lairn: Gambor warrior; Tginsahi of the Lairn burrow, Galzeki. Honor Guard to Cha'halen first grade, Ka'vaelus.

Sullust Movement: Religious order; Gai'han Sullusts believe in the genetic superiority of the Gai'han bloodline carefully cultivated for over seven millennia. After the capitulation of Gallen Wei in the War of the Three in 35,242, the Niramdi system became the focus of the Gai'han practice of 'holy sterilization.' This process of indiscriminate extermination of non-Sullust humans and artificials forced the Collistas Dynasty to re-evaluate their position of support for the movement. Some believed the Sullusts were becoming powerful enough to threaten the Emperor himself. After skirmishes along the edges of Carinaena's Shell, the Thrassin Campaign marked the Collistas Dynasty's first foray into the Gai'han Jihad in support of Free Will artificials.

Sylus: corporal, 41st Imperial Marine battalion, 3rd company, 1st platoon; Shock Trooper.

TacOps: idiomatic for tactical operations; the neural nexus of Imperial battle command that analyses and processes all information, provides a link between human experience in the field and raw datacore projections, and coordinates the various arms of Imperial power. An integral part of the command structure of all Imperial warships.

Tai-wren: "the shadow of the maker"; anyone who has pledged their life to protecting another.

Takens Root: native Chellian beverage, fermented for at least thirty years, usually served chilled with a garnish of fresh root.

Tarkanian Containment Shell: Hardened cerafibrous shell that houses a strong electromagnetic field; capable of safely storing incorporeal lifeforms and manifestations.

Tashkent Colony: Free Will colony on Vilnius in the Disturbed Sector; site of the Fagen massacre: first victory of Free Will artificials over combined Sullust/Imperial forces.

Tchelakov 37: colloquial expression referring to the original creatures engineered by Dr. Beh'ln Tchelakov (see: Tchelakov Tribe).

Tchelakov, Beh'ln: visionary genetic engineer whose highly guarded research into the next evolution of sartographic technology resulted in the creation of a new species (see: Tchelakov Tribe). His fusion of sartographic technology with a sentient-level intuition resulted in a quantum leap forward in 4th dimension physics decay and the science of future probabilities.

Tchelakov, Helen: courier/agent of the Nralda Keiretsu; daughter of Beh'ln Tchelakov.

Tech Art: any of a wide class of mobile mechanical constructs designed to perform a broad range of technical tasks. Non-sentient, imbued with one (or several) highly technical skills, but possessing little overall intelligence due to high degree of specialization and desire for cost efficiency.

Terrakin: small, nubby burrowing creature that prefers the cool, damp dirt beneath the roots of Los Ellen trees to build their nests. Rarely seen above ground during the day; colloquial ("terrakin's nest") for the lower decks on interstellar ships.

Tginsahi: rank of "Honor Guard" in the Gambor warrior caste.

Thillian Lizard: large (6 meter long) reptile indigenous to Letugia; fond of Atryx eggs as well as Lachis and Gourtanas.

Thiretsen Reed: any of a genus of tall, erect herbs of the nightshade family with little foliage and tubular flowers, cultivated for its stalks; the stems of cultivated thiretsen prepared for use in smoking.

Thrassin, Battle of: The Thrassin Campaign marked the Empire's first foray into the Gai'han Jihad in support of the Free Will artificials. Though technically a stalemate (the Gai'han drive was halted, but the Sullusts were not driven out of the system until 37 years later), most historians view the battle as a clear victory for the Free Will Coalition.

Thurligan: mythical demon; multiple cultural references to a demonic entity; a central figure in Gambor folklore.

Thurston Shields: proprietary design of defensive shield known for its massive buffers, ample null-dampers and wide field modulation. Generally considered the best.

Teirendat: literally "one with arm"; a style of handling a fighting blade with the pommel facing forward held between thumb and forefinger and the cutting edge held flush with the forearm. A wide range of variations of this grip are taught, though it is considered difficult to master.

Tomas: Gallalean sous chef aboard the *Shiva*.

Torg: class 1 master assassin, assigned to Vice Proctor Hellius Barrett, Wyxian Proctorialship. Much speculation exists concerning this soldier's original identity (see Vo Kamp's "The Emperor's Butcher").

Tortian: portable field assault cannon, tripod mounted.

Torvel Class Frigate: war vessel intermediate between a corvette and a ship of the line; Imperial classification of an escort defense ship between a corvette and destroyer in size.

Trent: sub-lieutenant, 41st Imperial Marine battalion, 3rd company, 1st platoon; Shock Trooper.

Trioxin: short for Trioxin Battle Plate; armored drop suits vastly enhancing a soldier's strength, speed, sensory input, and firepower. In a fully operational Trioxin suit, it is said that just one Imperial Shock Trooper can easily outfight a dozen heavily-armed men. Unsuitable for some theaters of operation.

Trogand: race of large (2.7 meter tall) reptilian beasts with thick-plated hides, large dual-horned heads, and broad mouths full of 5 cm long teeth. The Trogands' gregarious disposition and meticulous attention to detail make them well suited for bureaucratic service.

Turkle Sphere: Syhan artificial design. All drive components and core matrices housed within one-meter diameter sphere. Rugged and highly versatile. Primarily used as tech arts though some instances of sentient models can be found.

Tvultàk Skullers: small, highly-maneuverable cruiser used as interdictors and strike craft; aging but rugged and adaptable design favored by mercenaries and smugglers. A particularly dangerous configuration is the Gamborian Jave 'O War.

Varsis: Krellian artificial design, manufactured without interruption for nearly 160 years between 34,687 and 34,846. The inherent simplicity of the design along with the Varsis' unparalleled learning curve made the design one of the Krell's most successful to date.

Vaskin: corporal, 41st Imperial Marine battalion, 3rd company, 1st platoon; Shock Trooper.

Vegraut: race of large (2 meter tall) graceful quadrupeds that ruled most of the Outer Reaches for over a millennia. Their sympathies toward the Free Will artificials during the Gai'han Jihad nearly lead to their extinction as the Sullusts made no distinction between artificials and those who protected them. Today, their empire lies in ruin, and their numbers are estimated at less than 200 million.

Velite: lightly armored foot soldiers; standard infantry.

Vell'lairn: Gambor warrior; Tginsahi of the Lairn burrow, Galzeki. Honor Guard to Cha'halen first grade, Ka'vaelus.

Vos Bergen: Pragen Lord, undisputed Kai-ten of the Jhellus sector.

Wyx: 4th planet in the Bline system, seat of the Wyxian Imperial Proctorialship, one of the largest fiefdoms in Carinaena's Shell.

Yarvek-EZ: Virtruna caste, cybernetics specialist, 9th class, currently assigned to Imperial Battle Cruiser *Shiva* as pod ensign; bred in the Imperial Vats on Wyx for mathematical genius.

Yuzbek Sharlott School: medical research facility specializing in transgenics; radical medical sect destroyed in 35,324.

Yuzbekistin: 5th planet in the Core system of Wilkens Folly, site of the Biomaterial Implant Facility and Sharlott Research grounds; a level 8 quarantine is currently in place on the entire system, reason unknown.

TIME LINE

33,811 Last recorded contact with the seeder ship *Carinaena's Hope*.

34,290 Beginning of the Great Shell Diaspora. Major colonization efforts will continue for over a millennia.

35,110 Beginning of Gai'han Jihad.

35,307 Final battle of Gai'han Jihad. Gelicus Art Convention holds first open hearings.

35,312 Ratification of the Gelicus Art Proviso signals formal end of the Art Wars. Compromise includes ban on all indistinguishable-from-human artificials. Dalintus Commission formed to judge and regulate Free Will artificials.

35,337 Garrand Ai'Gonet Médeville graduates from Bordëgian Academé, receives commission in Imperial Navy. Selected for membership in the Brotherhood of the Princes of Blood, Griffin Order of the Imperial Guard. Varsis artificial Bailey VL1357-B8 is assigned as his personal combat assist.

35,341 Médeville is made Captain of the Imperial Guard.

35,342 Médeville accepts post on Santos II as Captain of Proctor Birmaldon's Imperial Guard.

35,343 At Battle of Sardis, Médeville distinguishes himself by rescuing Proctor Birmaldon from Ditraln Secessionists. In the course of battle, the Imperial picket *Stanzer* is disabled and left in a decaying orbit around Sardis. Médeville disobeys a direct order and commandeers a battle frigate to rescue seven of his men left aboard the *Stanzer*. Both ships are lost, but the Guardsmen are saved. Médeville is court-martialed and discharged from Imperial service.

35,345 Artificial Bailey is granted Free Will on lunar colony Fortrivance.

35,346 Proctor Lekkson Nesbit assassinated. Vice Proctor Hellius Barrett takes control of the Wyxian Proctorialship.

35,347 Médeville contracts with the Sandhalles Grip, Bestriyx Dagen, for the rescue of his daughter. Designs modified light cruiser for express purpose of breaking Talen quarantine on El Phobadia to reach the young Miss Dagen. Ship built by Lehadn Vercks in Lo Kamer-Daun Shipworks; christened *Destiny's Needle*. After completion of mission, Bestriyx Dagen presents Médeville with *Destiny's Needle* as a grateful token of his esteem.

35,355 Médeville contracts with Helen Tchelakov for transport of 37 "exotic bios."

About the Author

PHILIP WILLIAMS IS an author, artist and sculptor. A graduate of the University of North Carolina, Chapel Hill with a BFA in Studio Art, he has enjoyed a successful career creating powerful, gas-welded steel sculptures as well as designing and building unique furniture. Philip is a dedicated father of three and an avid soccer player.

Visit him online at www.thegriffinseries.com

THE GRIFFIN SERIES

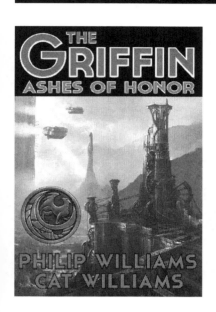

THE GRIFFIN: ASHES OF HONOR
Philip Williams & Cat Williams

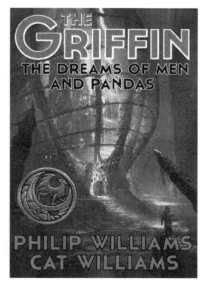

THE GRIFFIN: THE DREAMS OF MEN AND PANDAS
Philip Williams & Cat Williams

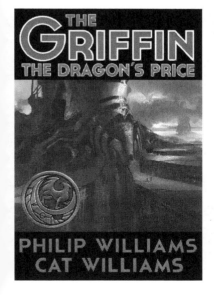

THE GRIFFIN: THE DRAGON'S PRICE
Philip Williams & Cat Williams

THE GRIFFIN: A PATH OF MAJESTY
Philip Williams & Cat Williams

Made in the USA
Charleston, SC
24 August 2013